Praise for *A Da...*

"Enter a world of teeming and ... vitality and amazing detail. Meet characters with tremendous courage and appetite for life and be glad you can return at will to the present."

—Anne Perry, *New York Times* bestselling author

"A captivating tale of mystery, history, and a dash of romance—with an ahead-of-her-time heroine who not only plays the piano with aplomb, but defies Victorian conventions, courts danger, and solves mysteries. Nell Hallam is a heroine to root for."

—Susan Elia MacNeal, author of the *New York Times* bestselling Maggie Hope series

"With a delightful and spirited heroine—and just the right blend of suspense, detection, and romance—*A Dangerous Duet* offers a vivid tapestry of Victorian England, replete with dazzling music halls, intrepid police inspectors, and a menacing underworld."

—Stefanie Pintoff, Edgar Award–winning author

"Historical fiction with a sinister twist and an engaging heroine."

—G. M. Malliet, Agatha Award–winning author of the St. Just and Max Tudor mystery series

"[An] authentically researched and swift-moving tale of a gifted pianist who bravely disregards the specter of inheritable mental illness as she pursues her musical ambitions and plunges herself into a dangerous investigation of gang robbery and murder. With a touch of romance to spice things up!"

—Rosemary Simpson, author of *What the Dead Leave Behind*

A Trace

OF

DECEIT

Also by Karen Odden

A Dangerous Duet
A Lady in the Smoke

A *Trace*

OF

DECEIT

A Novel

KAREN ODDEN

WILLIAM MORROW
An Imprint of HarperCollins*Publishers*

P.S.™ is a trademark of HarperCollins Publishers.

HarperCollins books may be purchased for educational, business, or sales promotional use. For information, please email the Special Markets Department at SPsales@harpercollins.com.

FIRST EDITION

Designed by Diahann Sturge
Title page art © movit / Shutterstock, Inc.
Chapter opener art © Vasya Kobelev / Shutterstock, Inc.

Library of Congress Cataloging-in-Publication Data has been applied for.

ISBN 978-0-06-279662-2

19 20 21 22 23 LSC 10 9 8 7 6 5 4 3 2 1

For George, Julia, and Kyle always
And for Jody Hallam, who is every bit as brave and compassionate
as her namesake

A Trace

OF

DECEIT

Chapter 1

The day I lost Edwin, I think my paintbrush knew before I did.

The studio was silent except for the sounds of bristles stroking against canvas, the rain splattering at the high windows, and the murmur of Mr. Poynter's instructions as he moved among the students. There was nothing to disturb me, and I should have been able to fix my attention perfectly upon the painting on my easel.

But without warning, as if propelled by some contrary part of my brain, my wrist jerked and my brush jittered across the canvas like a live thing, marring my half-finished landscape. It landed on the floor, spattering crimson paint outward in a small, delicate fan of specks, like poppies dotting a field. The room fell silent, paintbrushes paused, and for one frozen moment all I could do was stare.

A gentle cough drew my gaze to Mr. Poynter, who looked over from where he stood beside another student's easel. His gray eyebrows rose into crescents, his mouth parted between his thick mustache and fulsome beard—and then, as I fumbled something between an apology and an explanation, he shrugged and managed an understanding smile before he turned away.

I laid the dirtied paintbrush in the tray and knelt to wipe up the paint with a cloth. Taking a moment to regain my equanimity, I stepped back to survey my progress and felt a pang of disappointment. In my mind was a low stone farmhouse and a weathered barn flanked by a newly plowed field, the dirt a deep, rich umber, and an absinthe-green meadow edged by dusky apple trees—a scene I'd observed as a child from inside a railway carriage. The image appeared to my mind with utter clarity, down to the beveled wooden edge of the window that framed it like a picture. Usually I could transfer that clarity onto the canvas, but today it was going badly. I took a deep breath, inhaling the pungent smells of linseed oil and turpentine. Then I chose a fresh brush and began to repair the damage the errant stroke had done to the meadow.

The mishap betrayed the unease that had been clawing at me all morning. Its source was no mystery: I hadn't heard from Edwin yet this week, and it brought back all too sharply the period in his life when he would vanish for a few days or even a fortnight. My parents and I would have an anxious time of it until eventually he skulked home, thin and shame-faced, every shilling gambled away or spent, his mouth sloppy from opium. Each time, he'd promise to do better, but his resolution never held for long. After my parents died, it was my door he'd skulk toward, usually appearing late in the afternoon, with telltale bits of pigment on his hands and purplish shadows under his eyes, mumbling that he'd been working. I didn't inquire too closely, and it was only later I found out about the forgeries.

Since being released from prison, Edwin swore he was finished with his dissolute habits and would find a way to pursue his artistic career within the law. Indeed, in the last four months, he had exhibited many signs of sincerity; but I had seen him earnestly repentant before. Now it—

"Miss Rowe."

I started and nearly dropped my brush again.

Geoffrey Wright, at the next easel, leaned toward me, his voice low. "Are you all right? You look awfully pale. Perhaps you belong"—a faint pause, as if for delicacy—"at home." The solicitous tone was belied by the half-lowered eyelids and the disdainful set to his mouth. He was one of the men who deeply resented the presence of women at the school, although the founder, Mr. Slade, had made our inclusion a central tenet when he'd established it. More than once, I'd heard Mr. Wright declaiming how the classes on anatomical drawing were all but useless because the model's loins had to be draped when women were present.

"Mr. Wright." Mr. Poynter's voice carried a warning.

Like children chastised for a prank, we turned guiltily to look at our professor. But we saw only his back, his hands clasped behind and his head of tidy gray hair inclined toward Miss Stokes's still life.

Mr. Wright shot me a baleful look before he retreated behind his easel.

I pushed aside my annoyance and worry and summoned my attention back to my canvas.

I knew I was lucky to be here. Unlike Edwin, whose genius for painting had been evident early on, I'd come more slowly and uncertainly to my scrap of talent. I'd been accepted at the

Slade School on the basis of two paintings that I could see now were poorly conceived and, though energetic, not well handled. After many missteps, I'd begun to win some approval from Mr. Poynter for what he called "the small scene," but I'd also begun to understand just how limited my education had been, particularly in comparison with that received by the young men in the class. At times I felt a wretched inadequacy, and though most of the men were kinder than Mr. Wright, often I felt embarrassed at my ignorance. So I spent my evenings reading books on subjects such as geography and history and my days doing my diligent best to accomplish what Mr. Poynter asked.

My work finished for the afternoon, I washed my brushes, set them bristles-end-up in the tin buckets, and hung my smock on one of the wooden hooks on the wall. Fishing in the umbrella rack, I found my own frayed black specimen, still damp from this morning. I opened it as I exited the Slade's airy marble rotunda and braced it against the drizzle as I started up Charing Cross Road toward Edwin's flat.

Since he'd been let out of prison, we had been meeting every other Tuesday, at his request. Typically he sent a message to my rooms on Monday evening, arranging to have dinner in a pub or chophouse somewhere near the Slade, though on one particularly pleasant day, we met for a walk in a nearby park. His manner was often subdued, and our conversation was prone to moments when both of us broke the silence at once, without the ease we'd had as children. Admittedly, I had a part in this: I kept him at some distance, for I was chary of believing wholeheartedly his claims of reform, although his recent steadiness had raised my hopes more than I let him see. But here it was Tuesday afternoon, and I hadn't a word from him. While a part of me was prepared for him to resume his erratic ways, his missive could have been lost, and it wasn't much out of my way to go to his rooms.

I turned off Charing Cross and walked halfway down Judson Place to the building where Edwin rented a room. It was a narrow redbrick house, with two dormer windows like eyes peering out from under a frowning brow. Once a family home, it had been divided into three flats, one on each floor. I went inside the building and started up the thinly carpeted stairs to the top, grasping the wooden banister worn smooth by years of palms and polishing cloths. My own flat, closer to the school, was on an uppermost floor as well. The stairs were a bother, especially when I had items to carry, but like Edwin, I found the light that came through upper windows better for painting. I rounded the landing, already raising my hand to knock.

Oddly, Edwin's door stood wide open. He was nowhere to be seen, but inside his room were two strange men dressed in dark coats. Their backs were to me, and they were bent over, sifting carelessly through Edwin's paintings stacked against the wall. The sight halted me at the threshold, my hand on the doorframe, and I felt a flare of indignation. "What are you doing?" I demanded. "Who are you?"

Even as the words burst from me, I took in the pieces of broken gilt frames on the floor, a chair flipped on its side, a long rent in the curtain that separated this room from the bedroom—and a sudden fear made me shrink back.

The men pivoted and stood upright. I am taller than average for a woman, but both of them were a full head taller than I and broad of shoulder. Their eyes examined me with peculiar acuteness, taking in every detail from my facial features to the damp hem of my dress. Perhaps they saw my alarm, for a quick look passed between them, and the elder of the two stepped forward: "Don't be afraid, miss. I'm Chief Inspector Martin, of Scotland Yard." He jerked his chin toward the other man. "This is Inspector Matthew Hallam."

My heart sank, and my fright gave way to weary disappointment and vexation. It seemed I'd been right to hold my hopes in abeyance. Edwin's resolve to live lawfully was apparently as flimsy as ever. Given the state of his room, there had probably been a dire urgency to his departure.

"Good afternoon, miss." Mr. Hallam was perhaps five-and-twenty, with wavy brown hair and a countenance that would have made a handsome portrait. "Are you a friend of Mr. Rowe's?"

I suppressed a sigh. "I'm his sister."

The chief inspector's head tipped forward. "Is your name Annabel?"

That made me start. "Yes. How did you know?"

"Miss." Inspector Hallam's measured voice drew my gaze back to him. "When did you last see him?"

"Two weeks ago."

"And you haven't heard from him since?"

"No," I replied, wrapping the folds of my umbrella around its ribs. "What has he done?"

Another significant look between them. Clearly they were reluctant to shock me. "It's all right," I assured them. "You can say it."

The inspector's expression softened. "I'm afraid he's gone, miss."

"I've gathered that much," I said resignedly. Edwin had likely taken up gambling again and run off rather than face his debtors.

"Miss?" The inspector seemed to await a response.

I knotted the umbrella's ties to hold it closed. "I assume he owes someone money, and you're here to recover what you can."

The chief inspector spoke up, his voice gruff: "I'm afraid you misunderstand. Your brother is dead."

Dead.

My eyes flicked back to the younger inspector. He saw I hadn't grasped the meaning of his gentler word, and he winced in regret and sympathy.

For a moment, everything was unnaturally silent.

I reached for the nearest chair and sat down, averting my face. All I could feel was my heart thudding in my chest.

Years ago, as a child, I fell out of a tree and landed on my back. I had the sensation of my entire rib cage flattening forcibly to the thickness of a washboard, and as I lay there, staring up at the leafy branches, I remember thinking, *I shall never be able to breathe again. This is how it feels to die.*

I had the same sensation now.

I sat there for some minutes in silence. Neither man broke it. And eventually, unbidden, as my breath returned, came the thought—

Of course Edwin is dead. Of course.

I had anticipated this event so many times. Feared it, longed to prevent it, considered ways to save him, and woken in terror from nightmares of Edwin lying bloody and beaten in improbable places such as vacant museums and the alleys behind railway stations. And now, here it was, and despite all my dread of it, I couldn't take it in, couldn't find the edges of it, like a canvas too large for my reach. My eyes cast about his room, and the very shapes of the world nearby—rectangles, ovals, dark and light lines—seemed to have neither their proper dimensions nor their usual distances from me.

I heard one of the men, as if from far away: "Miss, are you all right?"

"Of course," I managed. My eyes sought something close and dropped to the rip in the forefinger of my glove in my lap. Only a small hole. Not precisely circular and changing shape as I moved my finger. Little more than a fray, really. Easily mended.

The young inspector knelt down beside me, and my eyes met his. They were blue. Almost cerulean. I'd used the color that very day for the sky in my painting. A wonderfully stable pigment, without tinges of green or purple, but not as opaque as cobalt.

"Miss?" The steadiness in his voice dragged me back to the present, and from somewhere inside me rose a violent wave of disbelief and denial.

"Who did you say you were?" I demanded.

"Inspector Hallam."

"You're not wearing a uniform." My voice was truculent to the point of rudeness.

The man's expression told me he understood perfectly well why I didn't want to believe a word he said. But he only replied patiently, "No, miss. We're plainclothesmen. We don't wear them."

"And how do you know for certain he's dead?"

"We found him here, about five hours ago. He's been removed to the morgue."

"But how can you be certain it's Edwin? It could be someone else you found. And my brother has gone missing before, many times. He could have let the room to a friend." Not that I'd ever met any of his friends.

"His landlady confirmed it was Mr. Rowe."

My stomach twisted and my mind scrambled to find an explanation, but hope was fading, and my words came faintly: "She might just have said so, to avoid trouble."

The inspector stood and went to a stack of paintings that rested on their edges beside a box of wooden stretcher bars. He sifted through, removed one, and turned it toward me. "Is this your brother?"

It was a painting I'd made of Edwin years ago, in front of his easel. Father had gone fishing in Scotland for several weeks, and Edwin had returned home temporarily, occupying himself with making a portrait of my mother for her birthday. I'd been at my own easel, trying to catch Edwin at the moment when his brush paused and he looked over at me to smile, one of those crooked grins that began on the right side of his mouth, extended to the left side, and then to his eyes. His hair was a burnished copper that seemed to glow from within and had never darkened to auburn the way mine had. He wore it longer than my father approved, but privately I thought it suited Edwin's lanky frame, as did the loose white shirt, rolled to the elbows. I hadn't finished the painting, for his spaniel was still only a brown blur under the easel, but I'd caught something of Edwin's playfulness, a rarity by then. The day Edwin finished Mother's portrait, he'd put his paints away and scrubbed his hands and nails scrupulously clean of pigment. By the time my father arrived home, just in time for dinner and bearing a tidily wrapped gift for Mother, Edwin was back in the attitude my father despised most, slouched indolently in a chair, glancing over the racing pages in a newspaper.

"Is this your brother?" Inspector Hallam asked again.

Mutely I nodded.

He placed the painting back on the stack, the image of Edwin facing out.

I felt a jab of pain, seeing my brother so vibrantly alive. It had been a true representation, once.

"Can you turn it away," I choked out. "Please."

He did as I asked.

At the moment when the chief inspector told me Edwin was dead, I felt a complete revulsion, an absolute dread of knowing the particulars. So long as I couldn't match his words to any picture I imagined, it couldn't be real. But now, the words slipped from my lips: "How did he die?"

I half expected the inspector to prevaricate, or demur. Instead he ran his hand across the soft area just below his rib cage. "He was stabbed."

"But where?" I gestured to the floor.

His head tipped to the side. "It occurred in the bedroom."

I stared at the bedraggled curtain separating the two rooms—began to rise—

"Miss, you can't go in there," the chief inspector said. "There's no point in you seeing the—the evidence, and it needs to remain undisturbed."

The evidence.

The image of a smear of blood on the floor entered my brain, and sickened, I sank back down. "When did it happen?"

"Yesterday, possibly around this time. Maybe earlier."

I'd slept last night as usual and spent the whole day at the Slade, not knowing.

And yet knowing, too.

"Miss, do you know anyone who might have been angry with him?" the inspector asked.

A sound, something between a laugh and a groan, came involuntarily from between my lips. I could think of plenty of people who might fit that description over the years—because Edwin had beaten them at gambling, or had purchased items on credit and refused to pay, or had forged one of their paintings. Not to mention myself, for I'd once been so angry with him that I had sworn I'd never speak to him again. And then there were those whom he might have injured when he'd been drunk at a pub or drugged in an opium den—people he might not even remember and whom I certainly didn't know.

"Perhaps we should begin with a simpler question," Inspector Hallam said, his voice gentle. "Would you like to tell your parents?"

"They're dead."

As usual, my statement was followed by an uncomfortable, apologetic silence.

"Have you any siblings?"

"No. Only Edwin."

He winced again. "I'm so sorry. I . . ." His voice trailed off, and he drew a wooden chair over so he could sit facing me, elbows on his knees, his hands clasped loosely, his eyes on mine. "Were you twins?"

I shook my head. "He's older, by a few years."

"There's a fair resemblance."

"The hair, I know."

"And the eyes."

Green like pond scum, Edwin had once said, his voice derisive. But how did the inspector know? Had Edwin's eyes been open in death? A vision of my brother's body sprawled, his eyes wide and fixed on the ceiling, a knife handle protruding from his abdomen, appeared in my mind with the clarity of a completed picture. Horror constricted my throat like a drawstring on a reticule.

"Was he expecting you today?" Inspector Hallam asked.

I forced the words out: "Yes—well, no. I mean, we usually see each other on Tuesdays but not here."

"Were you worried about him?"

That was impossible to answer briefly. "Why do you ask?"

"Your expression when you arrived."

I hesitated.

"That happens with siblings sometimes," he said. "They sense when something's amiss."

Amiss was such an inadequate word, for all that had gone badly with Edwin for so long.

The inspector said something, but my thoughts were far away from this room and didn't return in time to draw the words out of the air.

"I beg your pardon?" I asked.

"Er—it's no matter." He shook his head. "How old was he?"

I knew this was a question I should be able to answer. Still, it took a moment. I strained to recall that it was mid-September. His birthday was the ninth of October. "Nearly six-and-twenty."

"The landlady said he lived alone. Was he engaged? Or did he have any special attachments?"

The question struck with the force of a blow. At our last meeting, Edwin had mentioned almost too casually a young woman he'd met—someone's sister—Charlotte or Caroline—

But he would never be engaged or marry now. Never have children—

"Miss?"

I looked up.

"Any special attachments?" he repeated patiently.

"No."

"And what did he do for work?"

"Any number of things." My gaze brushed the stacks of framed canvases around the room. "He's a painter."

"Yes. There are a variety of styles and topics."

Though his voice was mild, I heard the implicit question. "Obviously, most of these are copies, which he's done legally," I said, a note of defensiveness creeping into my voice. "People commission him to reproduce artwork because he's adept at matching techniques and colors. But he also paints originals sometimes, and lately, he's cleaned and restored paintings for several galleries here in London."

He gestured to the space on the wall behind me. "Is that one of his?"

I craned my neck to look. It was a painting I'd done of a young girl and her father at a fruit stall in a market. Goodness knows why Edwin had saved it. The man's hands were choosing the fruit for a well-dressed woman with a pretty wicker basket—but at the time I hadn't been able to properly paint the shape of his curved fingers, or the age spots on his hands, and they came out looking misshapen and diseased. And I hadn't been able to capture his daughter's feelings to my satisfaction, either. Her loyalty to her father, her boredom at the end of a long day, and her shame at observing his need to please this woman had come out a muddle.

I turned back. "No, it's mine. Edwin would have done better."

He let that pass. "Two weeks ago, where did you see him?"

"We met at a pub near the Slade. I'm a student there."

"And how did he seem?"

I wasn't sure how to answer. But he waited silently, and finally I sighed. "He wasn't a lighthearted person. If you don't know already, I imagine you'll find out soon enough. He was caught forging a while back, by one of yours, and put in prison for nearly a year. He was released a few months ago."

A look of sudden comprehension. "I see." He tipped his head sideways toward the broken frames. "Do you have any idea what happened here?"

"None at all," I answered helplessly.

"Hallam."

We both looked up. The chief inspector beckoned, and as the two men vanished behind the torn curtain, I went to the window to look out. Immediately below was a rusty metal gutter filled with the detritus of the city—gray dust and ash, sticks and bits of string, the scraps of what looked like old pigeon nests, now empty.

"Goodbye, Miss Rowe."

I turned. The chief inspector was standing near the door, his hat in hand.

"Goodbye," I echoed uncertainly, for Mr. Hallam showed no signs of departing.

As the door closed behind the chief, I turned to the inspector.

"You're staying?" I asked in some dismay, for I desperately wanted to be alone.

"Yes." He rested a hand lightly on Edwin's desk. "And if you're feeling up to it, I'd like your help."

"With what?"

"Searching this room. We've examined the bedroom, but we'd only just begun in here when you arrived. We want to find anything that might provide a hint about"—the briefest hesitation—"why this happened. It sounds as if you're his closest relation, and you might notice something out of place, or something missing."

I winced. I didn't like the idea of going through Edwin's things. I dreaded what I might find.

"I know this might be difficult, and perhaps it's too much to ask right now." His expression was solicitous, even apologetic. "But the sooner we begin to gather a sense of your brother's life, the more likely it is we'll find who did this. Unfortunately, in these cases, time often matters."

I felt my head bobbing mechanically.

"If you'd rather, I can look while you sit here." He righted the wooden chair. "And if I have questions, I can ask. I'll try to bother you as little as possible."

I swallowed. "No. I'll help you. I'm all right."

He let me see his appreciation. "Thank you."

The inspector and I searched for the next hour or so, looking for anything that might hint at a motive for killing Edwin or anything out of the ordinary. Edwin's furnishings offered little in the way of comfort, but he had dozens of canvases, a trunk, a bookcase with sketchbooks, a desk and worktable laden with notes and papers. Every so often Mr. Hallam would ask me about something he found, or attempt to engage me in some sort of conversation. Perhaps he found the silence awkward, but I had no wish to talk and answered largely in monosyllables. Dutifully I examined Edwin's items of correspondence, sifted through the meager contents of his wardrobe, examined the paintings, and paged through his copy of Osborn's *Handbook* on oil painting and a tattered pattern book of frame styles. I inspected brushes, knives, pots of gesso, bottles of turpentine, the long slender gilder's blade, an agate burnisher, horsehair cloth, and two aprons stained with colors from tawny turmeric yellow to rose madder. But they told me nothing, and my overwhelming feeling was of remorse mingled with grief, a sense of erasing Edwin's presence. With each object I touched, Edwin's hands were no longer the last to hold them.

As daylight faded, I began to tire. My nerves had been taut for too long. Perhaps the inspector sensed my exhaustion, for as he replaced various items in Edwin's trunk, he said, "I don't think there's much else to be done here."

He laid the faintest emphasis on the last word, and in my state of heightened anxiety, I heard a demand. "Where do we have to go next?"

He looked at me rather blankly.

"Do you mean the morgue?" I asked.

"Goodness, no." He shifted a few items about so the lid would close, and he let it down with a soft thump. "There's no need. He's been identified adequately."

"But—but I need to see him," I said with a sudden desperation.

The skin around his eyes tightened in sympathy, and his voice was gentle: "You'll see him at the funeral, properly, won't you? I imagine you've a church?"

I nodded. "Y-yes. St. Barnabas in Wilkes Street."

"Then I suggest you wait until then. Truly, it's for the best."

Numbly, I nodded. "All right."

"May I take you somewhere?" he asked as he reached for his large black overcoat. "To a friend's house, perhaps?"

I'd formed a few casual friendships among the women students, and if I'd shown up on their doorstep, they'd certainly have been kind. But I didn't want their company. I needed to be alone.

I shook my head. "I can manage. I don't live far."

As I donned my coat, a constable arrived, took a seat on the wooden chair, drew a lamp close, and opened a newspaper. Clearly he was there to keep watch over Edwin's room.

I walked home slowly in the lowering dusk. A lamplighter was making his way down the other side of the street, and the sight of the woolly circles of light working against the foggy darkness halted me. If I'd had to paint a scene that suggested the quality of my memories of Edwin, I might not have found a more fitting image than this deepening gray world lit too sparsely by pale gold. I only knew portions of Edwin's life myself, and from those, I had furnished Mr. Hallam with the most cursory sketch of my brother's character and habits. Of course even in a completed portrait, some attributes are put forth—etched onto the countenance or signaled by the presence of a family crest or a musical instrument—while other aspects are merely suggested or left off the canvas altogether. I heard Mr. Poynter's voice in my mind: *No portrait is ever a complete representation of its subject.*

The lamplighter passed me by, and I watched his receding figure. He raised his stick to illuminate one lamp at a time, each one smaller and dimmer than the last, until he vanished from view.

I willed the tears away and kept on for home.

Chapter 2

*I*n my own room, I lit a lamp, laid a fire in the stove, wrapped a blanket around my shoulders, and sank into my comfortable armchair, one that belonged to my mother before she died.

My eyes must have traced the crisscross pattern on the stove's cast-iron door dozens of times, in an attempt to find something familiar, a perception that remained constant rather than shifting from moment to moment. Night had fallen, and the shadows thrown onto the walls by the lamp merged and darkened at the edges as I tried to fix in my mind the fact of Edwin's death. While I'd felt the truth of it when I stood in his rooms, now it eluded me, like something caught out of the corner of my eye, vanishing when I turned to look at it straight on. Perhaps if we had met more regularly, his absence would carry more weight. As it was, it merely felt like another of the many days in the past decade when I hadn't seen him.

But sitting in my mother's chair, my mind turned to her and how, if there was something to be grateful for, it was that she wasn't here for this. She loved Edwin more than she loved anyone, including my father. Spoilt but charming, Edwin was quick with a smile, and when he was a child and had transgressed one of my father's strict rules, a few words of excuse usually won Mother to his side and led her to intercede with my father to reduce his punishment. Mother said once that Edwin could wheedle his way out of a box nailed shut. She'd said it with a sort of amused pride; my father retorted sharply, that was precisely what worried him, for Edwin might go on in this way until he ended up in the sort of nailed box one put underground. Mother's lips had pressed together, and she'd replied shortly, "Albert! That isn't funny in the least!" But I'd seen that Father hadn't been joking.

Edwin wasn't yet seven when his abilities became apparent. Almost immediately, the atmosphere in the house became filled with a peculiar excitement and tension. My father began to demand hours of practice from Edwin, while my mother intervened, pleading for moderation as Edwin began to resent my father's coercion. I was mostly left out of that fraught triangle—beyond the frame, as it were. For years, I watched as my parents grew increasingly bitter toward each other, with my mother's indulgence attempting to compensate for my father's frustration over Edwin wasting his God-given talent. Now all of them were gone, and the irony was this: from what I'd seen in Edwin's room, it seemed he had perhaps begun to devote himself productively and sensibly to his art, in a way both of my parents might have approved—

A knock at the door startled me. The sky outside my window was black, the lamp had gone out, and the only light in the room came from around the edges of the stove's door.

"Who is it?" I called.

"Annabel, it's Felix." His voice was taut, and I knew he'd somehow heard about Edwin.

"Just a moment." I laid aside the blanket and opened the door. Our family friend, Felix Severington, who'd been with my father at Oxford, stood with his right palm against the doorframe, as if in need of its support. His coat was buttoned over his portly figure; his thinning brown hair was windblown; and his fleshy face—he often reminded me of a jowly, sad-eyed bloodhound—was florid from the climb up the stairs. His expression was severely distressed.

"Your landlady—let me up," he said, in two separate breaths.

I nodded. Mrs. Trask knew him by sight. "You heard about Edwin, then."

"Just now. I wasn't sure you were here," he said. "Your windows are dark."

"Yes. I was . . . just sitting."

I drew the door wide so he might enter and lit two lamps while Felix undid the buttons on his coat, shrugged out of it, and hung it and his hat on the rack by the door.

There was a time when I was afraid of Felix—when my memories of him were inextricably tied to my father's irritable bouts of whiskey drinking in the parlor. But Felix had been nothing but decent to me since my parents' death, and from what Edwin said Felix hadn't taken anything stronger than ale in years. I believe Felix felt a special affinity for my brother, for Felix had once revealed that he had been a disappointment to his own father, who had urged him to enter the family business of steel manufacturing. Felix had refused, choosing to study art and history in Paris. Now Felix worked at Bettridge's auction house, where he specialized in European paintings, consigning them for auction and preparing them for sale.

I pulled over a wooden seat, leaving the comfortable arm-chair for him. "Who told you?"

He lowered his bulk, crushing the cushions. "I stopped by his flat on my way home. There's a constable stationed there, keeping watch."

I felt a poke of surprise. "Do you visit Edwin often?"

He shrugged. "Once or twice a week, since he was released. Tonight I wanted to check on the painting he's restoring for us. For Bettridge's, that is. Did he tell you about it?"

Edwin had never mentioned either Felix's visits or his work for the auction house, and the omission gave me a vague feeling of being excluded. "No, he didn't," I replied. "It was kind of you to give him work."

He looked at me oddly. "Well, he's extraordinarily adept, as you know."

"Yes, of course," I said. There was a moment of silence, and then I added, "I'm sure you'll be allowed to retrieve the painting soon."

"I hope so." His broad forehead furrowed with worry. "I hope it isn't gone."

"Was it valuable?"

A snort. "It's the most important lot in our forthcoming auction of eighteenth-century French paintings."

I rewrapped the blanket around me. "What is it?"

"A Boucher."

"A Boucher?" I attempted to reproduce his nuanced French pronunciation, but it came out "boo-shay," and he winced.

"It's a portrait of Madame de Pompadour, done not long after she was made the royal courtesan."

His words made my mouth go dry. At the auctions I'd attended, Bettridge's had offered paintings valued at two or three hundred pounds at most. A portrait of King Louis XV's mistress rendered by François Boucher would be worth at least two or three thousand.

"It's an unusual portrait because although he painted Madame several times, as you know"—he turned a palm toward me—"those canvases were done later. They were also much larger, and they showed her in formal dress. This one is the size of a kit-cat"—his hands sketched a frame approximately three feet high and a little more than two feet wide—"but in the style of a three-quarters, and it includes her hand, here." He touched his collarbone. "You know Boucher does perfect hands. Your brother recognized it immediately, of course. He said it wouldn't take long to clean as the owner had treated it with care. I was supposed to return for it the day after tomorrow. I do hope it's still there."

I gnawed at my lip, dreading telling him. "Felix, I don't think it is."

His eyebrows shot up in alarm. "Why do you say so?"

"I was in his flat all afternoon, looking through his things, and I didn't see a Boucher. And now that I think of it, there was an empty frame of the proper style and size. Gilt on wood, about four inches thick, probably eighteenth century. It was one of several in pieces on the floor."

He rubbed his fingertips over his forehead so hard it went white and then red. "Oh God," he said heavily. "Yes, that could have been it."

"I'm sorry, Felix. I hope I'm wrong, but—"

"No, *I'm* sorry, Annabel," he interrupted. "I don't mean to suggest you should be worrying about a painting when of course Edwin's death is devastating." He pushed himself to standing and paced slowly around the room.

"What is it?"

He turned to face me, the lines of strain cutting deep into the flesh around his mouth. "I'm . . . well, what if the painting was the reason someone killed him?"

I sank backward into my chair as I took in his words.

The thought that Edwin might have been murdered in the process of a theft hadn't even occurred to me. I'd assumed his death had been the result of some more personal dispute. My breath came shallow and fast as I remembered the signs of struggle in Edwin's room. "You think someone might have broken in to steal it? And Edwin found him there—and tried to prevent him—" I didn't finish the thought. A wave of icy horror swept over me, followed by a searing—and wholly unfair—feeling of anger toward Felix for having Edwin clean such a valuable painting in his rooms in the first place.

"Why—" I broke off because my voice sounded accusatory. I took a breath and softened my tone. "Why didn't Edwin do the restoration at Bettridge's?"

"Mostly because he preferred not to. His supplies are in his rooms, and it's peaceful there, so he can concentrate. It's a delicate task, as you know." His eyebrows rose, and I nodded. "But aside from that, we don't have a space on the premises that would be suitable. With the sales season upon us, any room with adequate ventilation and heat is being used for storage. And there's certainly no place quiet." He heaved a sigh that became a groan. "Edwin's cleaned several paintings for us in recent months—less expensive ones—but there's been no trouble at all, and the other specialists have been very pleased at his skill."

Felix lowered himself back into the chair, sank his head into his hands, and I saw the strands of fraying hair strewn over a scalp freckled with brown spots. The sight twisted at my heart, and my anger dropped as quickly as it had risen. Felix had only been trying to help Edwin find work. He hadn't drawn the knife.

"Oh, Felix," I managed. "Would you—would you like some tea?"

"No." A mirthless laugh shook his rounded shoulders. "I'd like something stronger than tea. But make some for yourself. It's a cold night."

I didn't have anything stronger than tea. Mechanically, I put the kettle on top of the stove and knelt down to add some wood from the box. "There's an inspector at Scotland Yard looking into Edwin's death," I said, wanting to say something heartening. "I'll go see him tomorrow."

He raised his head to meet my gaze. "You can't tell him. No one can know it's been taken. Not yet."

I stared in surprise. "But whoever took it is probably the one who killed Edwin. I want to know who it is—as I'm sure you do. And you want to get it back, don't you?"

He shifted uneasily. "I don't want you to think I'm hard-hearted. God knows, Edwin's death is shocking and horrible—I can hardly believe it. But I have to think of Bettridge's—and the owner of the painting as well. This could be ruinous for both of them, if people find out it's missing." He grimaced.

"This was the owner's first consignment with Bettridge's. She changed from Christie's partly out of deference to me."

I lowered myself onto the stool, leaned forward, and clasped my hands. "When is the sale?"

"Less than a week. Monday next, at three o'clock in the afternoon."

"But its disappearance can probably be kept from the public. Surely there's a price at which the consignor would be happy to consider it as good as sold, so you could avoid the publicity. Bettridge's could afford it, couldn't they?"

He looked at me incredulously. "The low estimate is six thousand pounds!"

"*Oh.*" It came out a gasp.

"Bettridge's had to mortgage the building to pay for the renovations. They haven't a shilling to spare." His fingertips scrubbed again at his forehead. "Besides, it isn't only a matter of the seller being kept quiet. The painting is the jewel in the crown of this auction. The catalogs went to print weeks ago, with the Boucher on the cover. They've been distributed to every significant collector of French paintings in London and beyond. It will be the talk of the art world if the piece is withdrawn at this stage." He let out a low moan. "The scandal will taint us for years. People will say we let a masterpiece be stolen from under our noses, and we'll never get another—or that we must have lied about having one in order to puff our sale."

I understood enough about auctions to know what he meant. Advertising the Boucher would both snare additional consignments and attract more affluent buyers to the saleroom.

"And you'd withdraw the forgery at the last minute to prevent the ruse being discovered," I added slowly.

"Precisely. And you know what that will do to Bettridge's—just when they're on the verge of establishing themselves on par with Christie's and Sotheby's. Those two have looked down on us for years, despite their various scandals." He stood and paced the room again. "When Jonas Bettridge finds out it's missing, I'll be struck off immediately."

"But it wasn't your fault it was stolen!"

He pivoted to face me. "But it was I who recommended Edwin."

"Who else might have known Edwin was cleaning it?"

He spread his hands. "Almost anyone at Bettridge's."

"So dozens of people," I said. "The thief could have been any of them. Not to mention an acquaintance of Edwin's, or—"

"I know." He shook his head. "And I'm sure they'll ask me if he was indiscreet. The difficulty is I can't say for certain that he wasn't." His expression changed to one of apology again. "Annabel, I'm sorry. But—"

"I understand," I said. "He might have used the painting as gambling collateral or promised someone a copy."

He looked taken aback by my words. "Well, I didn't mean *that*. I was thinking he might not be able to help showing the painting to a friend who was likely to appreciate it as he did. You should have seen his face when I took it out of its wrappings. He could barely speak for staring." He heaved a sigh and sat back down, his plump hands on his knees, his pale blue eyes troubled. "I know he disappointed you in the past. But his time in prison altered him for the better, Annabel. Truly, it did. From what I could tell, he seemed to want to live his life differently, to make a fresh start. That's why I found him commissions. It was a way for him to earn his living legitimately"—he waved a hand over his shoulder, as if thrusting Edwin's past behind him—"so he wouldn't be tempted to go back to the forgery business or that wretched gallery."

"I'm sure he appreciated your trust in him," I replied. "But, Felix, I have to tell the inspector about the painting."

He scowled so vehemently the skin under his chin trembled. "I've no faith whatsoever in the probity of the police. You remember what happened last year."

I nodded. Five gallery owners had banded together in a ring so they could buy paintings under market value at Christie's, and they'd bribed a Scotland Yard inspector hundreds of pounds to ignore reports of collusion. "I remember. But I don't think Mr. Hallam is that sort. And I could make him promise not to cause trouble for you, or for Bettridge's. He'll want information badly enough to agree to our terms, I imagine, at least until the painting is found."

After a moment, he gave a resigned shrug. "If you can convince him to be discreet . . ." A sudden thought, and a light of hope, came into his eyes. "I wonder if Edwin had already finished with the painting and arranged for it to be transferred back to the auction house. Perhaps he mentioned something about it to Lewis."

"Lewis?"

"Yes. Edwin's friend from school. He lives here in London." He paused. "You've never met him?"

"No." I tried to hide the feeling of loneliness this gave me.

But perhaps he saw something of my feelings in my expression, for his own changed. "I'm sorry, Annabel," he said for the third time; and it occurred to me how each time, he'd been apologizing for a different reason—though so far as I could tell, he was blameless.

He pushed himself up and reached for his hat and coat. "I should be going." His steps were heavy on the way to the door.

I opened it for him. "I'll come to Bettridge's tomorrow after I talk to the inspector. I'll tell him as little as I can."

He stood with his hat in his hands, looking undecided and awkward. But our relationship had never been intimate; it was too much to expect that he'd embrace me or utter anything tender. At last he said, for the fourth time, "I'm sorry, Annabel," and turned away.

I shut the door behind him and in the silence of the empty room, I returned to my armchair, wrapping my blanket close around me, the ends in my fists.

What Felix had told me changed everything. If I was being honest, I shrank from the idea that Edwin's death was a result of some reckless or desperate act of his own.

But Felix seemed certain that Edwin had reformed, and as I reflected on the afternoon, I realized—with something of a jolt—that neither Inspector Hallam nor I had encountered anything that suggested otherwise. We'd found no empty spirit bottles or small brown vials, no angry correspondence, no IOUs or betting tickets. Instead, there were ordinary clothes with nothing hidden in the pockets or seams, painted canvases unambiguously marked with his signature, and tailor's and chandler's bills in keeping with a frugal life. As I tallied up what I'd found—as well as what I hadn't—my sense of fairness revolted at the thought of not doing what I could to discover why Edwin had been killed.

But even as I thought this, I had the disconcerting sense that I was poised at the edge of unfamiliar waters. Mr. Poynter had recently called me "an acute observer of human nature," and indeed, I enjoyed being an onlooker. It was a role I'd adopted young, and of late I had come to realize it stood me in good stead as a painter. By contrast, if I were to undertake a search for the truth, it would no doubt bring me pain, confusion, and discomfort. But how could I not?

The warmth emanating from the stove was fading. I wrapped the doubled edge of the blanket around the hot handle and opened the door. Then I sat back, my hands extended to gather up what heat remained.

My thoughts were as muddied as pond water stirred up with a stick. But one notion began to rise to the surface: in seeking the truth about Edwin, staying close to the inspector would be my best hope. Could we not construct some sort of arrangement in which I would offer him information in exchange for being included in the investigation? Edwin's life had diverged from mine over the last thirteen years, since he'd left for school. But still, he and I had shared a childhood, and I was familiar with at least some of his habits and occupations here in London. Obviously Mr. Hallam couldn't anticipate what information he might need at any given twist or turn, and if I was close at hand, I could provide it as questions arose. Furthermore, from the few questions Mr. Hallam had asked me as we examined Edwin's room, it was fairly clear he did not know much about drawings, paintings, or the art world in which Edwin lived and worked—whereas I did. Yes, I decided, I could be a significant source of information. I only hoped the inspector would see it this way.

The fire had dwindled until all that remained were a few flickering pinpoints of amber light among the ashes. I took up a lamp and carried it to my wardrobe. I sifted through my clothes. I had no black dresses, for I'd outgrown the ones I'd worn in mourning for my parents. My dark gray would have to do until I could have some made.

As I undressed and prepared for bed, a wave of disquiet rose and crested, threatening to engulf me. When it came to Edwin, some of my memories were so vivid they brought me back to the edge of heartbreak, and others made my mouth go dry with remembered fear. As if the scenes were playing out again in front of me, I turned my head away. But my eye caught the motion in the mirror, and I stood still to gaze at my reflection. The face looking back reminded me that I was no longer eight years old, or eleven, or even seventeen. I was a young woman who could tell the inspector truths he needed to know.

Indeed, I had to do it, for there was no one else.

Chapter 3

I'd never been to the Scotland Yard Division before, and it took me some time to find the unremarkable entrance, as it was tucked well out of sight of a main street. With my umbrella up against the blowing rain, I turned off Whitehall Place, passed under a stone archway, and crossed the wet cobbles. As I neared the door, several blue-coated men came out. They passed me with respectful nods, but their gazes were curious and appraising, and I felt the heat rise to my cheeks and had to swallow down an unwarranted feeling of guilt. As I reached the door, I lowered my umbrella and shook the folds to get most of the water off. Just inside was a desk, behind which stood a sergeant with a mustache. I inquired after Mr. Hallam and was told he was occupied.

"He's a busy man this morning, Mr. Hallam is. Several appointments with visitors of int'rest," said the sergeant with a frown. But when I remained silent and stood my ground, he grimaced and nodded resignedly toward a wooden bench along a wall. "Probably won't have time to see you, miss, but wait there, if'n you like. Put your umbrella in the stand. He'll come out when he's finished."

I dropped said item into the metal rack with several others and took a seat, with a tight feeling in the soft place under my ribs. No doubt Mr. Hallam *was* busy, and I could easily imagine him attempting to conceal his dismay at my unscheduled appearance, bestowing a polite smile and, out of kindness, making an effort to listen patiently while simultaneously contemplating how to hurry me away. I began to sketch out the lines of the argument I anticipated having with him. But after rehearsing my logic and justifications for a full half hour, my apprehension had begun to give way to curiosity, and I looked about me.

The weak light of morning filled the three tall narrow windows on the far wall, and through the glass panes I could see the mud-colored brick walls of the building opposite. The room where I sat was large and roughly square, with six doors around the outside, all with brass nameplates. The floor was occupied by a dozen desks spread out in a way that gave only the merest suggestion of having once been in rows. They all had good lamps and one or two plain wooden chairs nearby; most surfaces were piled with papers and files. The inspectors spoke to each other sometimes, always in murmurs, and at first they seemed much alike in their plainclothes. But soon they began to distinguish themselves. At one desk sat a ginger-haired man who twisted the hair on either side of his head as he read the papers in front of him; I imagined him having two bald patches someday. At another desk, a man writing intently had his head down and his left forearm curved partway around the paper, rather in the manner of a dog guarding its dinner. A third man seemed occupied by a report in front of him, but every so often, he raised his head and looked about, his expression uncertain, before returning to his papers. He looked younger than most of the other inspectors; I wondered if he was new to the Yard.

I had been keeping my eye on the six closed doors. But when I finally heard Mr. Hallam's voice, it came from down the corridor to my right. I craned my head around to look. He and another man in plainclothes were standing in a hallway with three more closed doors. They spoke in low tones, and at last Mr. Hallam gestured for the other man to enter one room as he entered the one beside it. I sighed. Perhaps I should have made an appointment instead of waiting until he was free. But just as I was about to give up, Mr. Hallam reappeared, escorting a stout middle-aged man with a pinkish nose and a chin like a ferret. Though Mr. Hallam wore a patient expression, the man's manner was annoyed, and he stalked away, swinging his walking stick so energetically that I drew back and pulled my skirts aside. Perhaps the movement caught Mr. Hallam's eye, for he appeared a moment later, and after a quick blink of surprise he gave me a pleasant, reassuring smile.

"Miss Rowe."

"Could I speak with you?"

"Of course." He gestured for me to precede him down the hallway and opened the last of three doors. I stepped inside and halted. To my surprise, it wasn't a furnished room but a monastic chamber, with a single window to the outdoors, a table, two plain wooden chairs, and a small vent in the middle of one of the white walls.

"Is this where you work?" I blurted out.

"No, I have a desk on the floor. We all share these rooms."

"Oh."

He went to the vent and flicked a lever.

"What is that for?" I asked.

"The rooms connect," he explained. "I closed it so we can speak privately." He drew out a seat for me and went around to the other side of the table.

I stood behind the chair, my hands curved around the top rail. But I found myself unexpectedly feeling as diffident as the young inspector I'd observed in the main room. Mr. Hallam seemed neither annoyed by my presence nor too busy to speak with me, and as a result I wasn't sure how to begin.

"Please," he said and sat down.

Taking a seat, I settled my skirts and drew my coat over my lap.

Yesterday I'd been in such a state of shock that I hadn't studied him properly; now I noticed not only his blue eyes but also more generally his constitution and countenance. Even seated, he appeared a man of greater height and breadth than average. But far from using his size to intimidate me or to assert his authority, he sat back in the chair and even sank into it, as if to minimize himself. He had a jaw that, while not overly heavy, hinted at stubbornness; his dark brows were too level and thick to be strictly handsome, but they suited him; his quiet hands suggested a calm competence; and there was a faint line at the left side of his mouth that deepened as he recognized my scrutiny for what it was. Still, he sat patiently and did not speak. At last, I said, "I was wondering if we might come to an agreement."

His eyebrows rose.

I drew a deep breath and kept the argumentative tone out of my voice. "Edwin's death—"

And there I stopped, for the shape of those words in my own mouth brought me back to the same flattened, breathless feeling as I had yesterday. It took several moments to gather myself, but the inspector waited patiently, and at last I could continue: "It came as a shock, and . . . I need to know what happened."

"Of course." His agreement came readily.

"I have some things I might tell you about him—details which might prove valuable to you in your investigation." The ends of the chair's wooden arms bit into my fingers, and I loosened my grip. "But before I do, I want you to know I don't want to be left behind. I can't merely worry and wait and afterward be given some varnished truth that's deemed suitable for the family."

His expression altered, and I saw the beginning of a frown crease the space between his brows.

"There is so very much about Edwin," I rushed on, "and about his painting and his life that I know. It's impossible to tell you whatever might be relevant, as we've no idea yet what that might be. Yet at any given point in your detection, you may need answers only I can give you."

"That's probably true," he allowed.

I stared, nonplussed. I'd expected him to resist the idea out of hand.

Somewhat warily, I continued, "I'd like you to promise me two things, if you can. That I may accompany you, so far as it is practical, and you will reveal to your chief inspector only what is absolutely necessary from what I tell you."

The frown that had been gathering deepened, and I sensed him weighing my offer. At last he shifted, and his chair creaked underneath him. "In cases of murder, it is not our usual method to enlist the help of civilians, particularly interested parties, largely for their own safety," he said slowly. "But I understand your wishes. I will do what I can to keep you apprised of my discoveries, and I promise to take any information you provide into account." There was a pause, and when I didn't immediately acquiesce, he prodded, "Will that suit?"

It wasn't what I'd hoped for, though I sensed he was trying to accommodate me so far as he was able. Disappointed, I nodded. "I suppose."

"As for discretion, well—I don't think there is anything to be gained by scattering information about like birdseed when it will serve no purpose." His gaze was steady and straight on; but I had seen Edwin fix his gaze in just that way, only to find out later that he had been dissembling or had already broken the promise he was making. Still, I thought I might trust Mr. Hallam with a few small pieces of information and inch my way forward from there.

I sat back until I could feel the wooden slats against my spine and deliberately laid down my first offering:

"I had a visitor last night who has a possible explanation for why Edwin was killed. As you might expect from what you saw in his rooms, it has to do with a painting. But it isn't a copy; it's an original, and a valuable one."

I expected him to look surprised or skeptical, but the only sign of him having heard me was the barely perceptible tightening of the skin around his eyes. He was a man who kept his thoughts private, I realized, and his gestures small. After a moment, he tipped his head and waited for me to continue.

"Mr. Hallam, how much do you know about auction houses?" I asked.

"Not much," he admitted.

Reassured, I drew my coat more securely across my lap as I considered where to begin. "The two principal ones here in London are Christie's and Sotheby's. They're like the Montagues and Capulets. Or perhaps York and Lancaster."

A faint smile appeared. "Feuding houses, you mean."

I nodded. "Rather. Christie's is generally the better regarded, although Sotheby's was founded first. Neither sold paintings in the early years."

"No?"

I shook my head. "Sotheby's first auction was a private library, and Christie's was some Madeira, claret, and a few bales of hay. But Mr. Christie was a friend and neighbor of Thomas Gainsborough—" I broke off. "Do you know who he is?"

"The painter, yes."

"And so first Christie's and then eventually Sotheby's began to sell artwork. The two houses have controlled the European auction world for over a century, but sixteen years ago, Mr. Jacob Bettridge, the father of the current owner, wanted to try his hand at it. And the way the auction world works, the better the items that collectors consign—that is, put up for sale— the better the class of buyers they'll attract to the auction; and when those buyers want to sell, *they'll* consign better pieces, and the house makes more money."

"Because the seller's fee is proportionate?" he asked.

I nodded. "On paintings, the house usually takes a five percent commission from the seller and buyer, both, out of which come the fees for things such as cleaning the work and publicizing the auction. Given that most expenses are fixed, the house naturally prefers to handle more expensive paintings."

"I see."

I shifted, and my chair creaked under me. "There is a collection of important French paintings to be sold next week. It's Bettridge's first successful inroad, as it were, into the upper levels of the market, and Edwin was working on one of the paintings—a portrait by François Boucher."

"I beg your pardon." His voice was still easy, but his blue eyes had gone keen. "Did you say Boucher?"

So he had heard of him. With a feeling of relief that I wouldn't have to explain the rarity and value of the painting, I continued, "Yes. It was a portrait of Madame de Pompadour, King Louis XV's mistress. It's the most important of the lots, with an estimate of something above six thousand pounds, and Edwin had been commissioned to clean it, so it would look its best for the sale."

His body was unnaturally still, as if he were struggling to contain his response, and I wondered at his inordinate surprise. Before I could inquire, he recollected himself and gave a small cough. "So the Boucher was supposed to be in your brother's room."

"Yes. Bettridge's doesn't have a shop for restoration, so they send the work out."

He rose and went to stand at the lone window. I could still see him in profile, and he was tall enough that his gaze slanted downward. He seemed to be following the motion of something on the Thames, perhaps one of the boats. But it also

seemed he was laboring to assimilate what I'd said with information he already knew.

"What is it?" I asked. "Did you find a mention of the Boucher
among Edwin's papers?"

The questions shook him out of his thoughts, and he turned
toward me. "Do you think it was taken out of one of the broken
frames?"

"I couldn't say for certain," I admitted. "But the heavy gilt
one was approximately the proper size and workmanship."

He rubbed his hand across his mouth thoughtfully. "How
long would it take to cut that painting out of the frame without
damaging it?"

"For someone who knows how, a minute or two," I replied.
"Obviously it's easier to carry, rolled up."

"And a good deal less conspicuous."

"Much less," I agreed. "I've been trying to assemble the event
in my mind. What if Edwin came home, surprised the thief,
they struggled"—my breath caught, but I kept on—"and the
thief ran off with the painting."

"It certainly is plausible," he said slowly. He moved so he
could rest his hands on the top rail of his wooden chair. "Who
was your visitor? Someone who works at Bettridge's?"

I nodded. "Yes. And a friend."

"I imagine he's eager to have the painting returned."

"Of course. Not only for the sake of the sale. His reputation,
and Bettridge's, will be in tatters without it."

His expression grew skeptical. "Over one painting?"

"If you owned a valuable painting, would you consign it,
knowing it might go missing before it made it to auction?" I

countered. "Not to mention buyers might think it had been merely a ruse."

Acknowledgment flashed across his face as he grasped the implications. "To lure other collectors," he said. "And then if it's reported stolen, they'd think it's a feint to cover up a lie. Either it's a forgery or was never intended to be sold at all."

"Yes—although I'm sure neither of those things is true," I amended hastily. "My friend would never have taken part in that sort of scheme."

"Well, I see the importance of it. Remind me, when is the auction scheduled?"

"Monday next."

His eyebrows drew down. "Frankly, I care less about the painting than finding a murderer. But it's not lost on me that the thief and the murderer are likely one and the same—and if we find the painting . . ." He sat back down. "Is there anything else you can tell me about the Boucher? Do you know who consigned it?"

I hesitated. "I don't. My friend didn't tell me."

"I need to meet him—your friend, that is."

I had a moment of misgiving at having said so much. It was all well and good for me to tell Mr. Hallam what I knew myself, but Felix had never agreed to speak to anyone. In fact, he'd made clear his attitude toward Yard men. My discomfort mounted as I began to see there was no way forward without introducing the inspector to Felix. I was about to propose certain conditions when he pushed back his chair. "Miss Rowe, will you excuse me for a moment?"

"All right," I said uncertainly.

He left the room and returned a moment later with an envelope that he placed on the desk before he took his seat again.

"I want to share something with you. But first, can you promise you'll be discreet?" he asked.

I managed a wan smile. "I suppose we have to trust each other so far as that goes."

"My thought exactly." He rested his elbows on the arms of the chair and clasped his hands loosely at his waist. "I had a visitor several days ago. A young man named Mr. Pagett. He's the stepson of the late Lord Sibley, who was an influential MP and apparently an avid art collector. Do you know the family?"

I shook my head. "Should I?"

"Mr. Pagett came to report a stolen painting. A Boucher from his stepfather's collection." He paused meaningfully. "A portrait of Madame de Pompadour."

My breath caught. "The same portrait, or a different one?"

"The same, or so he says." He opened the envelope, removed a slender catalog, and handed it to me. BETTRIDGE's was in fine black calligraphy above a rectangular image of the Boucher. Below it were the words: *An Offering of Thirty-Two Important Eighteenth-Century Paintings from France.*

The crisp blue paper was thick and the calligraphy elegant. A quick flip through the pages revealed printed images with descriptions for every painting in the sale. Remembering what Felix had said about the number of catalogs mailed, I realized this must have cost a small fortune. Mr. Bettridge had spared no expense in his bid for respectability and prestige.

Mr. Hallam asked, "Have you seen this?"

"No." I studied the image on the cover. Even in reproduction, the portrait was stunning and sensual. It showed Madame's face and shoulders, with her chin dropped slightly to make the eyes look deeply set and inviting, as if beckoning the viewer. Her right hand was delicately positioned, the fingertips brushing the bare collarbone above her décolletage. I opened the catalog and saw the description on the following page: *A heretofore privately held portrait by François Boucher. Oil on canvas, 1755. 36 × 28 in. Estimate: £6,00–8,000. Proof of provenance upon request.*

I looked up. "Did he have proof of ownership?"

He hesitated. "Well, yes. But it's complicated—not least because as far as Mr. Pagett knew, the painting was burnt to ashes nineteen months ago."

At those words, I laid the catalog in my lap and sat back. He had every speck of my attention now.

"Pagett's stepfather, Lord Sibley, was a viscount with houses in London and Warwickshire," he began. "He traveled abroad frequently and had close friends in France. A few years ago, he bought the Boucher from the original owners. It hung in his house in Brook Street until he placed it in the Pantechnicon for safekeeping."

I sat up straighter. "The Pantechnicon."

"Yes. You know about the fire?"

"Of course," I replied. It was one of the worst fires in London in years, engulfing over an acre in the middle of Belgravia. For three days it threw up clouds of smoke thick as bulwarks, and the sky glowed a lurid orange all through the night. Nearly every fire truck in the city had been called upon to extinguish the flames.

Until it burned to the ground, the Pantechnicon had been a private warehouse, where wealthy West End families stowed their valuables when they left the city for travel abroad or to spend summers at their country estates. The building was ostensibly impervious to water, fire, and thieves—and until the fire broke out, the owners smugly declared that they'd never had so much as a small piece of jewelry go missing. But afterward, the *Spectator* maintained that over two million pounds sterling's worth of fine art, furniture, and valuables were reduced to smoking black piles of ash and rubble. Naturally, many of the families wanted to rebuild their collections, which was why art auctions this past year had been unusually well attended.

"It happened in mid-February of last year," he continued. "Less than two months after Lord Sibley deposited the painting."

"I see."

"A month later, in mid-March, Lord Sibley returned from Europe. The journey had been cold and damp, and he caught the influenza. He died a few weeks later." I made a sound of regret that he acknowledged with a nod. "Mr. Pagett says the only people authorized to enter the Sibleys' room at the Pantechnicon were himself, his stepfather, and their solicitor. So as far as the family knew, the Boucher was burnt to bits, along with other valuable paintings in their collection. They were contacted by the Pantechnicon's owner or manager—I'm not sure which—and offered a settlement for all of them, which Mr. Pagett accepted."

"But then he saw the catalog," I said, beginning to understand.

"Yes. Apparently it arrived in the post while he was away.

Once he saw it, he went straight to Bettridge's. They told him the painting was off premises and unavailable for viewing." He spread his hands. "Obviously it was at Edwin's."

I nodded.

"Not wanting to reveal too much about his interest, he left the auction house and came straight here."

I felt a chill roll over me. "Do you think there's a chance he tried to find Edwin? Do you—"

He shifted in his chair, and it replied with a creak. "No. He's not the type to do that, I don't think. He struck me as proper and law-abiding—and *very* intent on keeping this out of the papers. But he was certainly . . . well . . ." His eyebrows rose. "He was upset and full of theories."

"This would mean the painting Bettridge's is selling is a forgery," I said hesitantly. "That seems impossible."

"Would Edwin have known the difference between a real Boucher and a copy?" he asked.

"If he had them side by side, I think he would. But my friend—" I broke off, but it had become clear that the possibility of secrecy was past. "His name is Felix Severington. He's their specialist for European paintings, and he could distinguish a forgery, even without the original for comparison. He knew Boucher's work intimately, and he would never jeopardize his reputation by accepting a questionable painting for sale, no matter how much it might bring at auction."

"Hm." He frowned, not in disbelief, but as if he were putting these bits of information with others. "How long has he worked for Bettridge's?"

"Five years or so. Prior to that he was at Christie's and one of the galleries here in London. Before that, Paris."

"And he handled all types of European paintings?"

I nodded, and a thought occurred to me. "Did Mr. Pagett find any of his family's other paintings in the catalog—any others that were in the Pantechnicon at the time?"

"No. He looked because there *were* a few other French paintings stored in the Pantechnicon. Most of the collection was Dutch or Flemish, though."

"So they wouldn't have been included in this sale," I said.

Mr. Hallam leaned forward, clasped his hands, and rested his forearms against the table's edge. "Mr. Pagett proposed another alternative to forgery. In fact, he leans toward believing it was stolen out of the building before the fire."

I was silent for a moment, adjusting my thoughts to this new idea. "If that were true, I suppose he could hold the Pantechnicon owners responsible. But does he have any legal standing for bringing a case? The family's been compensated for the loss."

"Well, yes. But the painting is worth more than six times what he was given in the settlement. Like many people who trusted the Pantechnicon's reputation, Lord Sibley insured the paintings for only a portion of their value. So Mr. Pagett believes he has a right to at least a portion of the proceeds from the sale." He touched the empty envelope absently, squaring it with the edge of the table. "He also made all sorts of noises about prosecuting the person who stole it, how he must be found and punished. He even raised the question of a greater crime—that if the thief stole the Boucher, other paintings might have been stolen as well. Maybe the fire was merely a cover."

I stared. "Is he suggesting that someone set fire to that whole building merely to conceal the theft of some paintings? That would be madness!"

Mr. Hallam shrugged. "The cause of the Pantechnicon fire was never discovered, and plenty of us here at the Yard have devoted time trying."

I sat back, thinking hard. "Who else knew the Boucher was in the Pantechnicon? Surely there must have been others. Perhaps Lord Sibley's wife? Or members of the household?"

"Lord Sibley's wife—that is, Mr. Pagett's mother—passed away some time ago, and I've no idea what was known by anyone else. I plan to visit Mr. Pagett shortly to inquire about that—and other things."

"Might I come with you?" I shifted my coat.

"Just a moment." Mr. Hallam leaned back. "Your friend . . . Felix, was it?"

"Felix Severington."

"He won't be pleased to discover he might have been selling a stolen painting."

"No, of course not."

"Might we go visit him first?" he asked. "I had planned to spend the morning putting the word out to some fences we know, but I can ask someone else to do that. Time matters, particularly in cases like this."

"Why in particular?"

He rose and held out his hand for my coat, to help me with the sleeves. "The longer we take, the more likely it is the papers will notice. A scandal involving an auction house and an expensive painting is the stuff they thrive on." He paused with his hand on the doorknob as I fastened the buttons. "The problem is, they muck around with the facts, put ideas into the mind of the public, and make our task more difficult." He peered down at my shoes. "Do you mind a walk?"

"Not at all," I assured him.

He opened the door and we exited into the main room, where a dozen or so coats hung from pegs on a wall. He lifted an immense black overcoat from one of them, did up the buttons, then plucked his hat from a shelf and a large umbrella from a tall bucket. As we approached the entrance, I drew my own umbrella from the stand and walked through the door he held open.

I crossed the cobbles, and as we passed under the arch to the street, I took a deep breath in.

I hadn't realized what a relief it would be to do something.

Chapter 4

*O*ur umbrellas held aloft against a light rain, we crossed the cobbled yard and walked together to Winters Street, just off New Bond, stopping before a door with an elegant brass *B* above it.

Bettridge's occupied a building assembled out of three separate houses. Some years ago, in number fourteen, Jacob Bettridge held his first auction, featuring hardwood molds of flowers, leaves, and the like, used for making ornaments for walls and ceilings. A decade later, when number twelve became available, his son Jonas bought it, biding his time for number thirteen—which fortuitously came on the market two years ago. Bettridge immediately tore down the internal walls for all three houses and renovated the space to include a main auction room reported to be grander and more elegant than either Christie's or Sotheby's.

Although I'd attended auctions here in years past, I hadn't seen the building since the improvements, and they were obvious immediately. In the foyer, a new electrified chandelier caught the gloss of dark wood wainscoting. An elaborate arrangement of flowers stood atop a square brass-inlaid Regency table. To the side was a Louis XIV desk of ebony, brass, and tortoiseshell from the workshop of André-Charles Boulle, unless it was an excellent reproduction. Behind it sat a young man who looked at us expectantly. I gave my name and asked for Mr. Severington. The young man vanished, and after a moment, a door opened and he reappeared with Felix immediately behind him. When my friend saw I wasn't alone, his eyes darted a question.

I approached his side and murmured so only Felix could hear: "Mr. Hallam of Scotland Yard."

His eyebrows drew down, and his lips pursed so tightly they vanished. "Annabel." Only one word, but the tone underlined his annoyance.

"Please, Felix," I said, my voice soft. "We need to talk privately. There's something you need to know."

He sighed and led us to a private sitting room, where a few Queen Anne chairs were gathered around a marble-topped table. I couldn't help but contrast this with the room at the Yard. Perhaps Mr. Hallam was thinking something similar for after a quick glance around, the right side of his mouth curved briefly.

We each took a seat, and the inspector offered his card. Felix barely glanced at it before sliding it into his pocketbook and turning to me. "What is it, Annabel?"

"I'd like Mr. Hallam to tell you. The information is his," I said.

Felix was silent for the inspector's recital, but his face lost most of its color. As Mr. Hallam concluded, Felix leaned back, rested his elbow on the chair arm, and pinched fiercely at the flesh of his forehead. The faint web of red blood vessels around his nose seemed to darken. "Stolen or—or forged and exchanged. For God's sake."

"I know," I said softly.

"And from Lord Sibley," Felix muttered.

"You knew him?" Mr. Hallam asked.

"I knew of him, certainly, though we had no personal dealings. His collection is significant. His stepson oversees it now." Felix groaned aloud. "If this story gets out, people will twist it every which way. Christie's and Sotheby's—not to mention the galleries!—will be only too happy to spread the worst sort of rumors." He dropped his head into his hands. "I'll appear either a humbug or a complete fool, not knowing Lord Sibley was the proper owner of the painting. I cannot believe this has happened!"

"Is there any possibility the painting you saw was a forgery?" Mr. Hallam asked.

He looked up, his expression disdainful. "No, of course not." His gaze shifted to me. "Not even your brother could copy a painting so well."

Mr. Hallam frowned. I took it to mean he was puzzling something out; Felix took it as a sign of disbelief, and he glared at the inspector. "If I had the painting, I could bloody well prove it to you. But obviously I can't!" He threw up his hands. "This is an impossible situation."

"Were there any documents?" I interjected.

"To prove its authenticity? Of course." He started for the door. "I keep all that here. Edwin would have no use for them. Just a moment." He left and returned with a small sheaf of papers that he did not offer at first. He held it close to his shirt-front and frowned down at Mr. Hallam. "Look here. Are you certain Mr. Pagett isn't mistaken? Had he actually *seen* the painting his father purchased? Often verbal descriptions can be very misleading. And how can you be sure he remembered it accurately, all these months later? Boucher painted several portraits of Madame, and—"

"He *had* seen the painting before it went to the Pantechnicon," Mr. Hallam interrupted. "And his father had ordered a tintype of the work. The Sibley family has kept visual records of all the pieces in their collection since the 1830s, beginning with daguerreotypes." He paused. "Did the consignor show you a receipt for purchase?"

"No, it was a gift from her husband. But the family is beyond reproach. They've bought and sold paintings at auction for years." Felix handed him pages deliberately and in succession: "Here is a letter from Boucher to the first owner, Philippe LeMarc, in which the painting is described in some detail, including the unusual size." He pointed toward the bottom of the page. "It's dated from Boucher's home in the Rue Vernet." He handed the next page, and then the last, to Mr. Hallam. "This is a copy of an entry from Monsieur LeMarc's original catalog, with a description, including measurements. And here is a record of insurance, verified by his solicitor. So you see, this was *not* a forgery."

The inspector took his time with the pages, reading each closely, and then passing it to me in turn. It was simple, really: three documents, all of which seemed straightforward, confirming the identity and authenticity of the Boucher. Finally I tucked them together neatly and returned them to Felix, who put them in the inner pocket of his coat.

"There is no receipt of sale from Boucher to LeMarc?" Mr. Hallam asked.

"No," Felix said flatly. "Between members of a certain class, there would not be."

"Really?" Mr. Hallam darted a glance at me, and I gave a small nod.

"How would a receipt prove authenticity?" Felix retorted. "Paintings are passed down from generation to generation through marriages or among family members, and there are rarely if ever receipts."

"I notice there is no note of guaranty, either," Mr. Hallam said. "I understand that is common practice when a painting is removed from premises, for cleaning or examination by an interested buyer."

At his words, Felix froze. His gaze latched onto mine, and he turned haltingly to face me. "Annabel . . ." He dragged his breath in through his mouth and let it out. "Our solicitor insists on it whenever a painting is taken out . . ."

"Of course," I said understandingly. "Although I don't think you'll be able to recover anything like six thousand pounds from Edwin's belongings, unless he has some treasure hidden away somewhere. I'm sorry, Felix." I felt sincerely regretful; Felix's eyes were becoming dark with something like horror—as if he believed he might be held liable.

"You didn't attach *your* name to it, did you?" I asked anxiously.

His hand rubbed hard at his mouth for a moment, as if he wished he could hold back the words. "No . . . but, Annabel . . . your family's house. It wouldn't cover the value of the painting, but . . ."

My breath caught, and the margins of the room seemed to blur and darken.

My father's will bequeathed the title to Edwin, as was customary, but any income it generated was mine until I married. Shortly after my parents died, I vacated the house, having no need of a residence that size and no means to maintain it. Edwin's situation was similar, so our solicitor made arrangements to let it to a family by the name of Weathers, and the profits after expenses were my sole source of support.

Abruptly I stood and paced about on the plush carpet. "Felix." It came out in a ragged breath. "For goodness' sake."

"I *know*, Annabel." He rubbed unhappily at his knees. "It's—it *was*—it was merely a formality . . . but now—"

"So the house could be seized?" I felt a shiver of heat run down my arms to my hands.

"Do you have an interest in it?" Mr. Hallam asked.

I turned; I'd almost forgotten he was there. "The rental monies come to me. It's not much, but it's enough to pay my fees at the Slade and my expenses, if I'm frugal."

"Does your brother have a will?"

"I've no idea," Felix said. "I don't imagine so."

Shakily, I lowered myself into the chair. The news struck me with the force of a blow, and it was several moments before I could return my attention to the present.

Mr. Hallam had asked something and Felix was glowering as he replied. "The guaranties are drawn up by our solicitor. I'll have to retrieve a copy to see the terms. Naturally, the portrait would need to be returned in time for the auction, but I assume the guaranty gave Edwin the standard thirty days." His lips pursed. "Not that I hold out much hope for its recovery."

"The painting has to be somewhere," Mr. Hallam replied. "No one would go to such lengths to steal it merely to destroy it."

"Unless he's some sort of savage," Felix retorted.

"I doubt that's the case," said Mr. Hallam matter-of-factly. "My hope is your consignor can point us toward someone who would want it badly enough to steal it—or want money badly enough to sell it."

His intent was clear, and Felix scowled resentfully. At last, however, he muttered, "Her name is Mrs. Jesper, and she's a gentlewoman, beyond reproach. She's going to be horrified by all of this."

"We'll all have to be sensitive to her feelings," I said.

Felix closed his eyes, spanned his forehead with his thumb and forefinger, and rubbed. "Of course she must be informed immediately. I'll send a note round, asking if I might call on her. She's in the final stages of preparing her house for the removers, so I'm fairly sure she'll be home this afternoon."

"I'm sorry, but I need to be the one who calls on her," Mr. Hallam said.

Felix's head jerked up and his expression was incredulous. "Mr. Hallam," he said, his voice clipped. "She is still in full mourning and as such is only receiving her sister and a few close friends, including myself. Frankly, I doubt she'd speak to you willingly or openly." His tone became derisive. "Her husband died last year in a carriage accident, and you Yard men behaved as if she were to blame. For God's sake, she was a passenger, sitting beside him! And I've never seen two people more genuinely attached. It was appalling."

"I won't treat her as a suspect," Mr. Hallam replied evenly. "There is nothing to be gained by that."

Felix grunted his disbelief.

"You said she was preparing for the removers," I interposed. "Is she selling her house?"

Felix shook his head. "The house belongs to his family, but yes—she has to move and retrench. It distresses her to sell this Boucher because it was her last gift from Stephen. But it will provide an income for the rest of her life. Or rather, it would have." He gave Mr. Hallam a hard look. "I don't imagine your sort takes into account her difficulties."

"I have no wish to give her additional pain," Mr. Hallam replied calmly. "Indeed, I am even willing to have you present, if you think it would put her at ease, so long as you don't mention anything about Edwin's death or that the Boucher belonged to Lord Sibley—at least not at first. We will simply tell her the painting was being restored off premises and was stolen. That alone will no doubt be something of a shock."

"So you intend to give her part of the truth and see what she says." A resentful look came over Felix's face. "Bah! I despise this sort of duplicity. In fact, I don't like any of this."

"None of us do, Felix," I said quietly. "This situation is painful for all of us."

That brought him up short, as I knew it would, and his annoyance gave way to contrition. "I'm sorry, Annabel. And I'll speak to our solicitor immediately. I'll try to find out something for you by this afternoon."

"Where shall we find Mrs. Jesper?" Mr. Hallam asked.

With a deliberation that made his displeasure clear, Felix drew out his pocketbook, took out a loose page, and wrote out the address. "I'll see you at four o'clock. Please wait until I arrive."

Mr. Hallam's hand was outstretched, but Felix handed the paper to me.

Chapter 5

The rain had stopped while we were inside Bettridge's. As we stepped onto the pavement, we left our umbrellas closed, and Mr. Hallam said, "We have some time. Have you eaten?"

I shook my head. Indeed, I hadn't taken anything substantial since yesterday morning, but the news about the note of guaranty had shaken me. Even as the thought of it returned, the knot beneath my rib cage twisted.

Mr. Hallam directed us to a tea shop at the far end of Winters Street, found a table near the back of the crowded room, and ordered one tray of sandwiches and another of scones, with tea for me and coffee for him.

Once all the items were placed meticulously on our table, with every plate and saucer hanging just over the edge, he leaned forward. "Miss Rowe, it's very possible we'll recover the painting. There are fences for stolen artwork, and we've a network of people who let us know when items of interest appear."

"But—"

"And it probably seems like searching for a needle in

a haystack," he continued. "But consider how large a painting is. Last week, I found a ruby-and-diamond brooch no bigger than one of those." He gestured toward a plate with three pats of butter in the shape of miniature flowers. "So it can be done."

He was trying to reassure me, and I nodded my thanks. "Well, I hope it's found, of course. But—well, I think Felix is right. I rather doubt that Edwin made a will. However, if Edwin did, and he bequeathed the house to me, does it mean I'm liable for the painting?"

He nodded reluctantly. "The guaranty will follow the house. But it would take the solicitors a while to sort through your brother's affairs. It'll give us some time." He gave an encouraging smile. "I know it's difficult, but try not to worry yet."

I attempted a smile.

"You should eat something." He rearranged the dishes to put the sandwiches closer to me.

I picked one up and took a bite. I would have sworn I felt too fraught with anxiety to choke it down, but the bread helped settle my stomach, and after a few more bites and some tea, I began to feel better. He must have been hungry himself, for our conversation was minimal until a good portion of the items on the trays had disappeared.

At last I sat back with a sigh. "Thank you for that. It's kind of you to take the time, when I'm sure you're very busy."

"Well, I hadn't eaten today myself." He gave a wry smile. "And frankly, your case is my most pressing concern at the moment."

I looked at him dubiously.

"At the direction of my chief inspector," he added. "Because of its link to Lord Sibley."

I blinked. "Truly?"

He poured himself more coffee, and though I'd never liked to drink it, the aroma was rich and velvety.

"Last week, when Mr. Pagett came in, he saw Chief Inspector Martin first—demanded it, actually. The Sibley family has powerful friends." He gave me a look. "As a result, I was asked to hand off most of my other cases for the time being and focus on his."

I began to see.

"It was only a coincidence I was called initially for your brother's case. But thank God I was. Who knows how long it would've taken to make the connection to the painting otherwise."

I made a sound of agreement. "These cases are two sides of the same coin, aren't they?"

"So to speak." He sat back and took up his cup. In his large hand, it looked undersized. "May I ask you something?"

I tensed but nodded.

"Why did you say that the painting on your brother's wall wasn't very good?" he asked. "I thought it was well done— not that I'm any judge. What's the matter with it?"

It wasn't a question I'd been expecting. As I poured my second cup of tea, it occurred to me he was making a benign effort to put me at ease or disarm me. Either way, I had a ready response. I set down the pot. "The hands aren't well done; the man's skin isn't the proper color or texture; and the expression on the girl's face isn't what I intended. I know I said Edwin would do it better, but I would do it better myself now. That was from years ago." I paused. "Do you know many painters, Mr. Hallam?"

He shook his head. "None but you."

I swallowed my tea and grimaced. I'd forgotten the sugar. Mr. Hallam watched as I put a spoonful in the cup and stirred.

"Was it always your passion to attend the Slade?" he asked.

I couldn't help a short laugh. "Hardly. It wasn't even in existence until four years ago."

His eyebrows rose. "I didn't realize."

"Mr. Slade opened it within University College so men and women could study together. It's one of the few such art schools of its kind, and so far as I know the only one in London to allow women."

He looked thoughtful. "Hm. I suppose the Royal Academy of Music was ahead of its time. It's admitted women for decades. My sister is there for piano."

"What's her name?"

"Nell. It's just the two of us. We lost our mother when we were young, and our father several years ago."

So he is without parents, too, I realized with a jab of sympathy. "I'm sorry."

He gave a quick smile of acknowledgment. "When did you know you wanted to paint?"

I shrugged. "I don't remember, honestly. I took it up mostly because Edwin did."

"Are you happy at the Slade?"

"Now I am."

He gave me a curious look.

"It was difficult when I started. I wasn't sure I belonged."

"Did you ask to attend?"

"Not at all." I took a sip of tea, and the mild warmth slid over my tongue. "One day, my father informed me that he'd set aside money for Edwin to attend art school. But it seemed Edwin would likely end up—"

In an early grave was what my father had said, but the words caught in my throat.

"Not going," Mr. Hallam supplied tactfully.

I nodded. "My father paid the fees less as a kindness to me than as a spiteful gesture toward Edwin. But still, it was tuition, and I took it."

"Did he not see your talent, then?"

"Not really," I replied and set down the cup. My father had never shown more than a cursory interest in my painting. Later, when I was at the Slade, I was grateful for it. Unlike Edwin, I had the freedom to fumble my way forward without having to report every comment Mr. Poynter made about my work the first term.

"Well, clearly someone recognized your ability. They admitted you."

I smiled. "I've a feeling there weren't many women applying for positions. Plenty of the male students feel we've taken spots that might have been given to other men—and they make it abundantly clear." I sighed. "In a way, I can understand their point. I certainly wasn't as well prepared as most of them, and I was too tentative at first. But being with the other students has helped."

He took a moment to absorb that. "When did your brother begin to paint?"

This was more the sort of question I was expecting.

Yet I remained silent because I knew my answer would be only the beginning of a story that I wasn't eager to retrace.

After a moment, he set down his cup and eased back in his

chair. "It isn't always a comfortable thing, asking these questions," he admitted. "It's awkward, on both sides. But I've found when trying to understand how something like this happens, often the best place to begin is a man's habits, including his earliest tendencies and the sorts of incidents that shaped his mature character."

Character.

That word flew like an arrow to the part of my brain that held memories of my father. I could hear his voice in my head as clearly as if he were beside me, speaking in my ear.

Something must have shown in my expression, for Mr. Hallam leaned forward with a questioning look. "What is it?"

I shook my head. "My father used to talk about character. He told Edwin that his was weak and unfixed."

He frowned. "That's rather severe. How old was Edwin?"

"Ten or eleven, I suppose."

He gave a snort and poured more coffee from the pot. "I'm glad character isn't fixed by then. I was sullen and selfish at that age." He took up his cup. "People change."

"Edwin certainly did." And—though I didn't say so to Mr. Hallam—therein lay the problem. The different versions of Edwin's character were like a palimpsest, paintings laid one over the other, with vestiges showing through. I had a few early memories of Edwin laughing and impish and bright-eyed. Later when he and my father were in regular rows, Edwin was often resentful or despondent. And then came the day Edwin left for school, his despair etched upon his face, starkly white against his coppery curls. In the background hovered my mother in tears, my father with his mouth curled in disdain—

Mr. Hallam's spoon clinked against the cup as he stirred in milk. His countenance was composed and patient, but I reminded myself he was looking for usable information, not this murk of memories and feelings, and I fought down the sadness that lodged like a stone in my throat.

"What was he like as a child?" he asked quietly. "Sometimes it's easier to begin there."

Yes, those early memories were set in purer, bolder colors, not muddled by all that came later. I folded the napkin into a tidy rectangle and smoothed it in my lap.

"My mother always said we were opposites," I began. "Even as an infant, I was docile while Edwin was restless and colicky. He outgrew that, of course. I don't remember much of our time in Gloucester, but Edwin was already beginning to draw. One of the earliest memories I have is of him when he was six years old. It was spring, and Mother, Edwin, and I had been outside in the garden." I paused, recollecting the sight of my small hands against the dark brown dirt, the box of delicate pale green seedlings, and the feeling of being terribly pleased because Mother had praised me for digging holes that were just the right size.

Mr. Hallam set his cup down in its saucer; the sound recalled me to the present and nudged me to continue.

"We'd spent most of the afternoon out of doors. Mother had removed her hat, and Edwin had sketched her kneeling at the edge of the garden, her sleeves rolled to her elbows, her hair in wisps across her face." I paused as I realized I didn't remember my mother that day so much as Edwin's drawing, which I saw later. "At last we came in for tea. Mother and I were upstairs, for we hadn't realized my father had come home. And then we heard Edwin crying out."

Mr. Hallam looked a question.

"My father had seen the sketch," I continued, "and he asked

Edwin who'd been to visit. Edwin told him no one, and that he'd sketched it himself. My father didn't believe him and punished him for his lies and conceit." I swallowed, remembering Edwin's cries of pain, audible through my bedroom door. Peculiarly, I remembered the moment as if I were the object of someone else's view: I was sitting motionless on the floor, my hands frozen in place over the buttons on my doll's dress, with those delicate pearl buttons the only bit of brightness in the scene. My lips were parted in surprise and fear, my round cheeks were soft and childish, and my eyes were wide open in silent alarm. Then the memory shifted: I was back inside myself as I heard my mother's door opening, her footsteps racing down the stairs, and her voice crying my father's name.

"But he wasn't lying." Mr. Hallam's voice broke into my thoughts.

"No," I said. "To be fair, there was no reason to think Edwin could do such a thing. So far as my father knew, Edwin had never drawn anything before."

"Clearly he had."

"Yes. I found his first sketchbook among my mother's things after she died." I poured another cup of tea and dropped in some sugar. "To this day, I don't know why my father was so angry at the thought of someone visiting while he was away. But he stormed out of the house, and when he returned that night, Mother insisted that Edwin *had* drawn it, and as proof asked him to sketch my face, which he promptly did, in front of my father, so he could see for himself." I still remember being called to the parlor to sit for it and my fear at my father's scowling, skeptical face—until Edwin finished, and I was allowed to slide off the chair.

Mr. Hallam's expression was watchful. "Did your father admit his mistake?"

I still felt the sting of his injustice. "No," I said shortly. "My father wasn't that sort. But afterward he told Edwin things would be different."

"Why was that?"

"My father believed if a boy was given such a talent by God it was a sin to squander it."

"He was a religious man?"

"Yes, although not by profession. He was a clerk at National Provincial Bank. But sometimes he'd use religion to bolster his point." A note of anger edged into my voice. "Father told Edwin it was his responsibility to fulfill whatever role God had planned for him—and by extension, it was my father's responsibility to make sure Edwin did so."

A look of understanding crossed his face.

I chose a scone and broke off a piece. "Edwin's first tutor was Mr. Worley, who came to our house in Gloucester, but it wasn't long before he told Father that Edwin was unusually talented, and he should hire someone better suited. At about this time, a new position with the bank in Bishopsgate became available for my father, so we moved to London, and he hired Mr. Black to tutor Edwin in the usual subjects and Mr. Devlin for painting and drawing."

Mr. Hallam handed over the butter plate. "How old was Edwin at the time?"

"Thank you," I said. "Seven or eight."

"Did he like these new tutors?"

I paused in my buttering to remember. "Yes, I think so. Especially Mr. Devlin. He was a kind man, and patient, so long as he believed we were attending to him and doing our best to follow instructions. But like any teacher, he became annoyed when Edwin was inattentive or stubborn or sulky, or made excuses for why he hadn't finished his work."

"You said *we*," he interjected. "'So long as he believed *we* were attending.'"

"I was allowed to sit with them during the lessons. We didn't have a governess, and I think my parents thought it no harm for me to learn."

"I see." He, too, chose a scone and spread a piece with butter. "And did Edwin develop his talent?"

"Tremendously, but as Edwin improved, Father became more demanding, wanting him to spend hours every day working. He'd obtain commissions for Edwin to execute and insisted that he spend his leisure time in museums, copying the masters. But Edwin hated museums, and being dragged about, and being directed all the time. Eventually he began to resist my father's demands."

"When was this?"

"He was eleven. Mr. Devlin's wife took ill, and he took her abroad, so my father decided Edwin should go away to a school with a proper art teacher."

I remembered that day vividly. Father had taken Edwin into the parlor to tell him that he would leave the following month. Edwin emerged with a white, set face and his shoulders rounded in dejection. He ran along half a dozen streets to a small green, and I followed, eventually finding him with his back to one of the elms. His hands, so steady with a paintbrush, were trembling as they plucked apart one leaf after another, down to its veins. He didn't say a word, and I sat beside him and rested my head against his upper arm, not knowing how to comfort him. At last he stopped rending the leaves, sighed, and put his arm around my shoulders. We sat together for some time, the breeze stirring the branches overhead into a gentle sibilance, until we heard the church bells tolling the hour for dinner. I felt Edwin tense beside me, like a deer preparing to run, and my heart plummeted as I realized what Edwin's absence from our house would mean for me. "I don't want you to go," I whispered, and he made a sound of accord. Then he stood, brushed off his pants, and put out his hand to pull me up.

"What was the name of the school?" Mr. Hallam asked.

"Tennersley," I replied. "It's a few hours north toward Birmingham. The art teacher was well known and admired. But Edwin didn't like it much, and he began to play truant. Once he jumped on a train and made it all the way home. Of course Father was furious and took Edwin straight back the next morning."

"Was Edwin homesick?"

I poured more tea. "I don't know. He came home at the breaks, but he didn't seem particularly happy to be back. And each time, he seemed less his usual self, less interested in the things we once did together. I suppose some of that's natural," I said deprecatingly. "He was older and having such different experiences. A boy that age doesn't want to play games with his sister. But he just seemed so . . . withdrawn. He'd vanish for hours or lock himself away in his room with his books, though I sensed he wasn't studying."

"How long was he at school?"

I added sugar and stirred. "Until he was almost sixteen. That's when he ran away for the last time. He returned to London and for a while he stayed with a friend whose mother took in boarders—"

"Do you remember the friend's name?"

I frowned, trying to recall. "I'm sure I heard it. It was something common, I think. White or Waters, perhaps. Felix might know." I paused, hoping the memory would become clear, but it didn't, and I shook my head. "Eventually Edwin ran out of money and returned home. But by then he was profoundly . . . altered." I heard my voice change, and I took a few sips of tea before I continued, "He would barely speak to me, or to my father. The only person he seemed to listen to was my mother, and even she had very little influence. Father still gave him a small allowance and tried to help him find commissions, but Edwin stayed away longer and longer, sometimes disappearing for weeks at a time. I know he found occasional work as a copyist, and he apprenticed at a gallery for a while where he learned the finer points of restoration. But he was gambling and—and visiting opium dens, and eventually he fell into debt that he couldn't pay off. He began borrowing money in my father's name and then couldn't come home to face him. So he found rooms here or there, wherever he could. Every few months, he'd come back, full of apologies, promising to change—but then, he'd vanish, and . . . well, after a few years of this, my father was ready to abandon Edwin to his fate, though my mother always held out hope."

His expression changed, as if he'd fit a piece of a puzzle into place. "Is that why when we told you that he was gone . . ."

I nodded. "I expected he'd simply run off again."

"I see."

"And then he became involved in the forgery scheme, and

went to prison—and when he came out, he said he was re-formed for good."

"Did you believe him?"

I dropped my gaze to my half-empty cup. The tea was a diluted ochre, and the cup was cold. "I don't know. Felix says the change was sincere. I . . . well, I was reluctant to trust him."

"Understandably."

I set the cup back in its saucer. "Tell me, Mr. Hallam, how does this sort of thing help you learn why Edwin was killed?"

His shoulders shifted. "I don't know, exactly. Sometimes the old details fit together with new ones and . . ." His voice faded, and he shrugged apologetically. "I don't mean to be evasive. Every investigation is different. But usually putting events in sequence—with names, dates, and so forth—helps us construct the truth. It's simple, but then again"—a quick smile—"Nell teases me that I work better in straight lines."

It wasn't how I thought of truth, but I could see what he meant.

Slowly, I turned the cup clockwise in its saucer so the handle disappeared and appeared again. "Assuming Felix is right, what is your guess about how the painting was taken out of the Pantechnicon?"

"I've no idea," he said frankly. "Believe me, I've been assembling a list of potential scenarios, as well as questions for Mrs. Jesper." He finished his coffee and pushed the cup aside. "One possibility is the painting destroyed in the Pantechnicon was a forgery."

I started. "You mean the real painting and a forgery had been exchanged before it was deposited? Perhaps at Lord Sibley's house?"

"Or someone could have switched them afterward, inside the Sibleys' room at the Pantechnicon."

"That's possible," I allowed. "Although the forgery would have to be very good for the exchange not to be detected. But why would someone bring in a painting only to remove it again? Wouldn't that raise the guard's suspicion?"

"I don't think so. Someone could have changed his mind," he replied. "Mr. Pagett told me he often spent hours in the Sibleys' room, sorting the paintings, placing them side by side as he determined what to hang on his walls and where."

I could imagine that.

"And while an inventory is maintained for each room," he continued, "the description would likely be brief—something less specific than the one in the auction catalog. So if the inventory listed merely 'French portrait of a woman,' one painting might plausibly be mistaken for another. Of course, all those written records were lost in the fire." He spread his hands. "I know Felix is certain it's the original, but if Mrs. Jesper's painting *were* a forgery, how could you tell?"

I smoothed my napkin again and laced my fingers on top of it. "The difference can be something as minute as a variation in the shape of the signature or the placement of it. Merely a quarter of an inch to the right or left can give it away. But Edwin would say the signature is easy to mimic. It's more difficult to reproduce the precise way a painter wraps the canvas around the bars, and the length or weight or roundness of the brushstrokes, or the tone of the painting."

He looked dubious. "That sounds rather intangible."

"I suppose, but even a layman can usually detect the difference when the two are side by side."

"Hm." He shifted in a way that suggested he was growing uncomfortable in his chair. "I don't imagine that situation arises very often, unless it's someplace like your brother's studio."

His words sparked a memory. "Actually, I know where we could find something of the sort."

His eyebrows rose. "Available for public view?"

"Oh, yes. It's in the open." I placed my napkin beside my plate. "Would you like to see it?"

He glanced at the clock on the mantel, rose from the table with evident relief, and deposited some coins by his saucer. "Please."

I led him to Trafalgar Square, past the lions and Lord Nelson's Column, up the steps, and between the Grecian pillars of the National Gallery.

This was one of my favorite places in all of London. It became my daily refuge, particularly after Edwin was back in London but no longer living with us. His conspicuous absence from our home brought out the worst in my parents and swamped us all in a muddy silence. It shaped the resentful pinch around my mother's mouth, the way she stirred the sugar into her tea with painstaking attention so she never had to meet my father's gaze at the breakfast table. It provoked my father's clenched hand around the neck of the whiskey bottle as he sat alone in the parlor with his Bible, his pencil jabbing at the margins beside certain lines.

There was none of that fierce misery here at the Gallery. Instead, the spacious foyer was redolent with roses, for a wealthy benefactress had donated the funds to maintain a welcoming bouquet on the ceramic pedestal in the center of the room. We climbed a flight of marble stairs, elegant as a tiered cake with royal icing. At the top, I led Mr. Hallam down the central hallway with its white, bearded busts stationed at regular intervals and then through two rooms of paintings. He began to trail behind me, slowing in front of a vivid pair of sixth-century Byzantine icons painted on wood and pausing at a Dutch interior by Vermeer that happened to be one of my favorites. He stood for several minutes before a dramatic seascape by Turner. I'd never liked being rushed past paintings myself, so I waited silently in the doorway. Finally he stepped away and followed me into the next room. There, one wall was occupied by a quartet of portraits, each of a different member of the House of Lords, originally painted in oils by Sir Edward Bleckle.

I kept my voice low, so as not to be overheard by a small party of ladies nearby. "Look carefully at these four, Inspector. Do you see how one of these is different from the rest?"

Hands behind his back, he approached each in turn, bending close to look intently at various parts of the canvas before he returned to where I stood. "I confess I don't. The signature seems the same, both in shape and placement, as you say. Making allowances for differences in their features, the attitudes of the four men are almost exactly alike. I can't see how the canvas is wrapped, of course, but the frames are similar, and they're all the same size. What am I missing?"

I stepped close to the wall, between the third and fourth paintings, so I could point. "Look here," I said softly, gesturing to the background of the third. "Do you see how there is a subtle weight to the left side of the stroke? It's easiest to see with the dark gray. And here, the paint is thickened at the fold of the red cloth on his arm?"

He nodded.

"Now, look here."

He turned to the fourth painting and examined the bit of

canvas near the end of my finger. After looking back and forth between the two, he turned to me in some surprise. "I see it, now that you mention it. The brushstroke seems more even, and the paint isn't piled on so much. But how did you—"

"Now take a look at the other two and tell me which of these two isn't original."

He examined the first two paintings, leaning toward them, his hands clasped behind his back. "These have brushstrokes that are weighted, as you say, to the left." He came close to the fourth painting. "So you would say this is a forgery."

"It's a very good reproduction," I corrected him.

"And the museum doesn't know."

"They do, actually."

He looked at me, startled.

"Lord Bridgewater commissioned it," I said in an undertone, still mindful of the ladies hovering around a landscape on the next wall. "The original hangs in his house above a sideboard, I'm told. In the room where he takes breakfast."

"How do you know this?"

"Because Edwin made the copy," I explained. "He signed it on the back, and Lord Bridgewater provided a letter to the effect that he'd authorized this reproduction."

His lips parted, and for once he seemed to be jolted out of his composure. "Well." He turned back to the paintings and shook his head in disbelief. "He's remarkably skilled."

"Yes." I paused, and my voice flattened. "He was."

His glance carried an apology. After a moment, he murmured, "Why does the museum have the copy?"

"The museum retains ownership of the original, though it is on loan to Lord Bridgewater for the duration of his life." I felt a shadow of a smile cross my lips. "The museum was persuaded to accept the terms by a gift of five hundred pounds—for which no receipt was issued."

A look of understanding crossed his face. "An agreement among members of a certain class," he said softly and turned back to the painting. "Well, if the man wants to gaze upon a complimentary likeness of his face every morning and is willing to pay for the pleasure"—he shrugged—"so be it." He stepped back to survey the quartet and added wryly, "I must say they are all handsome men, gathered together like this. If you roamed London you might not find a group of four such men anywhere but here."

I stifled a laugh. "Perhaps Sir Bleckle took some liberties."

We left the museum, and as we reached the street, he said, "Now I can see why your brother was so successful as a copy-ist." I sensed where this was leading, and when I didn't reply, he added, "I should tell you, I read the notes from your brother's case."

I felt myself squirm internally. I knew the gist of what they contained. Based on the testimony of the two Needham brothers and another witness, the judge found Edwin guilty of painting forgeries and providing them to Mr. Needham for sale in his gallery. Following his release from jail, Edwin told me his version of what had happened, which departed from the Needhams' accounts in several salient ways. I hadn't been sure how much of it to believe. And what did it matter, practically speaking? He had served his sentence, and now he was free.

But he's not. He's gone.

I heard the words as if someone had shouted them, and they drowned out whatever Mr. Hallam was saying. The pain they brought stopped my feet so abruptly that he was several yards ahead before he realized that I was no longer with him. Once again, I had the flattened, breathless feeling, and I stood stock-still on the pavement, gasping for air.

A warm hand took my elbow, and I looked up to see Mr. Hallam's eyes full of sympathy. "I'm sorry." The breeze blew his hair across his forehead and he shook it back.

"I'm all right," I managed. "It's just . . . I forget he's gone, and then I remember, but . . ."

"It's as if you'd never known it before." His tone told me he was speaking from his own experience.

I nodded, and after a moment we continued on, rounding the corner. The air here was thick with the yeasty smell of a pub.

"I'm sorry. What were you saying?" I asked.

"That the report seemed incomplete to me," Mr. Hallam said.

"Why?"

We separated to allow two men carrying boxes to pass.

"Because the notes were very sparse," he said. "And your brother bore all the fault for the forgeries, while the gallery bore none. That isn't the way things usually happen." A sideways glance. "It just made me wonder."

It was clearly an invitation.

My steps halted again, and this time he stopped with me, turning so I could see his face. I searched those blue eyes for some sign of deception, a glimmer that betrayed he was saying this only to win my confidence. But I saw only a thoughtful curiosity.

I walked on, and he fell into step. "According to Edwin, it began when he did some restoration work for Mr. Needham—cleaning paintings and repairing frames and so forth. Several times he made copies that he'd been told were legitimately commissioned by the owners. But some time after that, Mr. Needham let it slip that a few of them weren't, and he made out that Edwin had known all along. Edwin understood he'd been lured in, and at first he refused to do any more work for them. But the Needhams threatened they'd tell the police what he'd done, and Edwin needed money because . . . well, by then my father wasn't giving him anything. So sometimes, when a painting was sold to someone who seemed not to know much about art, Mr. Needham would ask the customer to leave the painting at the gallery, so it might be cleaned and boxed for travel. Then, he'd have Edwin make a copy, which Needham would pass off as the original. Edwin could finish a painting in three days, if he had to."

"Needham assumed the customer wouldn't know the difference," he supplied. "But someone did?"

"No." I dodged a man wheeling a sack barrow stacked with crates. "Mr. Needham couldn't hang the same painting back on his wall, of course, so he'd send the original to his brother's gallery up north."

"So in effect they sold the same painting twice," Mr. Hallam said.

"Yes. But someone who'd bought a painting from the London gallery happened to be up in Oxford and saw the original. That's how they were caught."

"Hm." He sank his hands in the pockets of his coat and paused at the corner to let a carriage pass. "In the trial transcript, the Needhams claim that having gained their trust, Edwin illegally copied paintings after hours and then took the originals to the Oxford gallery on his own, collecting a fee for 'finding' the work. It sounds implausible to me that the brothers never compared their records."

"I know. Edwin says he tried to explain how they tricked him into making unlawful copies at first. But the judge only cared that he'd made others with full knowledge."

He frowned. "Surely Edwin knew he was taking a significant risk."

"Yes." I sighed. "He was never very good at weighing risks."

We started across the street, avoiding a fresh pile of horse droppings that made me cover my nose and mouth until we were past.

"Why didn't he pursue his craft legitimately?" he asked. "Surely there was a way he could earn a living without—well, without skirting the law."

I shook my head. "I don't know. The only thing I can say is perhaps he thought he *was* pursuing it legitimately. It was only later he realized he wasn't, and by then . . ."

He opened his mouth to ask yet another question, but I decided it was time to ask one of my own. "What about you, Mr. Hallam? Why did you become interested in people skirting the law?"

He drew himself up and a grin curved his mouth. "Turnabout is fair play?"

I returned his smile. "Was your father a policeman?"

"Lord, no. He was a navy man. He probably would've liked to see me there, but I don't like boats."

I thought of how he'd stood in front of the Turner painting. "You don't?"

"I get seasick and turn an ugly shade of green," he said. "Nell says I look like an unhappy toad." I couldn't help my laugh.

"But Father had a friend who was an inspector," he continued, "and when I was young, I admired him a good deal.

Rather the way a mere mortal might look upon Hercules." He pulled a face, as if he were making a private joke with a younger version of himself. "His name was Michael Rafferty, and he used to come once a week or so for a nip of scotch with my father. He'd talk about his work, ask Father's advice sometimes. Not in any official capacity, you understand. Just as you'd ask a friend you respected because he's seen something of the world."

"Of course."

"When I was younger, I'd sit outside the door to listen, and when I was older, I was allowed to join them—though not for the scotch." We sidestepped a boy on a bicycle. "Do you ever read the penny-dreadfuls, Miss Rowe?"

I shook my head. "No."

"Well, some of Mr. Rafferty's accounts were even more sensational than those. Danger, deception, and the most peculiar people. His mother had been a storyteller, and he inherited the gift." He directed me around a right-handed corner. "And then, one day—I couldn't have been more than thirteen—he was working on an investigation that involved some documents in German. Both Nell and I had been tutored in it, so between us, we helped him translate the passages. Made me feel terribly important."

I smiled. "Naturally it would."

"From time to time, he brought other puzzling things we could help with." He shrugged self-deprecatingly. "It may not sound like much, but it was enough to intrigue me."

"So you became a policeman because you like puzzles," I said, as we stopped at a corner and waited for two hansom cabs to roll by.

He didn't answer at first; and when I looked up, I saw the humor had faded from his face.

"Well," he said. We crossed the street before he added, "Partly. But it was also because some of his stories showed me the injustice of things. It made me want to . . . to try to . . . well, to right the ship, as my father would say."

I was struck by the genuine feeling in his voice. "Do you believe that everything can be resolved like a puzzle, through the courts of law?"

"I used to," he said honestly. "But the truth is, not everything can. Not least because we—we policemen, I mean—fail sometimes. We're not quick enough, or we come to the wrong conclusions. And sometimes the case is so peculiar that the law doesn't address it yet. Watch yourself there." He pointed to a gap in the pavement.

I stepped over it. "Did you start at the Yard?"

He shook his head. "No one does. I was in uniform in Lambeth first. Barely nineteen, overly serious, determined to prove myself—and I had no idea how little I knew." His tone was wryly amused. "I'm sure people found me ridiculous."

Perhaps they had, I thought. *But I doubt they would now.*

Indeed, despite his self-deprecation, it was becoming clear to me that the inspector felt things deeply and carried a good deal of responsibility on his shoulders. But I wasn't about to share such an observation. Instead I looked up at the clock on a nearby church. "It's nearly half past three. We don't want to be late."

Chapter 6

*J*ust before four o'clock, Mr. Hallam and I found the address Felix had provided on a lovely street north of St. James's Park. It was a three-story house, with five pale gray stone steps leading up to a painted black door upon which hung a shining brass knocker in the shape of an anchor.

We waited on the pavement, and after a few moments a cab drew up and Felix dismounted. He nodded to us, climbed the steps, and tapped the knocker twice. A maid opened the door and ushered us inside. The foyer was painted tastefully, but the house was clearly in a state of upheaval. In the front hall were carpets, rolled, labeled, and ready for removal. Through an open door, I saw a room full of furniture draped in crisp white holland. Several flat wooden crates suitable for transporting paintings lay on the floor amid boxes the proper size for lamps and other valuables. Two men were arranging boards into place to make another crate, and a third stood by with a hammer.

Only one painting still hung in the hallway. It showed

a garden with a low fountain, painted in an unusual style, but one I'd seen recently, though I couldn't remember where. The work looked vaguely unfinished, with the flowers suggested by bits of color rather than depicted as in life, and yet the sunlight seemed to glint as if a breeze were blowing across the scene. My curiosity drew me, and I examined the signature in the corner. *P. Cézanne,* with the letters all separated and the *z* an upright squiggle. My breath caught, for now I remembered where I'd seen his work. This artist was one of the group that had arranged an independent exhibit after being ostracized from the French Salon last spring. Mr. Poynter had shown us a few printed reproductions of their paintings along with the reviews that appeared in the papers. Some of the criticism had made me wince in sympathy for the artists. I remembered one phrase in particular: "This school will sicken or disgust every viewer." But this painting had neither effect on me, and though Felix seemed wholly uninterested, I examined it until the maid returned. She strained to make herself heard over the intermittent banging of the carpenter's hammer and led us through a pair of wooden doors.

Here in the parlor, the furniture was still in place and uncovered. I imagined that aside from Mrs. Jesper's bedroom, this was perhaps the sole refuge of the lady of the house. The tables were nearly empty of decorative objects, with only a few silver frames and a book or two. But the lamps shed a good light, and paintings still hung on the wall. There were four: two Dutch Old Masters, a still life, and a landscape. I moved closer to the Old Masters, so I could see them clearly; one was superior to the other. A Van Eyck? I peered at the signature and saw it was his, probably from his later period: an exquisite study of a young woman, her head half turned away, her hand curved around an apple in a way to suggest both innocence and absentmindedness. The light brushing her cap and her cheek was painted so skillfully I felt a stab of envy.

Felix materialized beside me. "It's very fine, isn't it? Perhaps one of the best in the collection. Her father acquired it years ago, before Celia was born."

We heard footsteps, and all three of us turned toward the door. A woman of about thirty years of age came through the door and closed it behind her to mute the noise of the workmen. She was slender and fine-boned, with plain features; her brown hair was drawn back from her forehead and fixed in a low chignon, and I thought I saw in her face the marks of sorrow and strain. She was still dressed in mourning, with her only ornament a pair of silver-and-jet earrings. Her hand on the knob, she paused to study Mr. Hallam and me. She held herself with an air of quiet dignity, competence, and intelligence. This was a woman who wouldn't be easily ruffled, or surprised into betraying information she wished to keep to herself. As she came toward us, I saw she walked with a limp.

"Hello, Felix," she said, her voice low and musical. She extended her hand, and he inclined toward her, taking her hand in one of his and patting it with the other. "I received your note. Is something the matter?"

"I'm afraid so, Celia," he said heavily. But he turned and gestured toward us. "This is Miss Annabel Rowe. She is an artist herself, studying at the Slade."

"An artist," she echoed warmly and turned toward me. I saw that although her other features might be plain, her eyes—hazel and fringed with dark lashes—were beautiful, wide and expressive. "It's a pleasure," she said with a gentle smile. "I wish *I* could paint, but I merely collect—or, rather, tend to my family's collection."

"This is a brilliant Van Eyck," I said, gesturing to it.

A spark of pleasure and approval came into her eyes, and her smile deepened enough to put a faint dimple in her cheek. "Thank you. It is one of my favorites."

"And this is Inspector Matthew Hallam of Scotland Yard," Felix added. She stiffened, and her smile slipped away, but she nodded civilly and gestured to the cluster of furniture in the middle of the room. I took a seat slightly apart, so I might observe the three of them. Felix hunched in an imposing leather chair, his shoulders rounded protectively toward Mrs. Jesper. Mr. Hallam sat in its match, with his spine straight and his demeanor subdued. Mrs. Jesper perched on the edge of an upholstered sofa that was supported by impossibly spindly legs, her quiet hands delicate as carved ivory against the deep black bombazine of her skirt. She turned to face Felix expectantly.

He leaned forward. "My dear Celia, I am so very sorry to tell you this. But the painting you consigned—the Boucher—has been stolen."

Her beautiful eyes blinked twice, and her cheeks blanched. "Stolen," she said under her breath, and her gaze flicked over her shoulder to Mr. Hallam and me before returning to Felix. "By whom? How?"

"We don't know yet," Felix answered. "The Yard is looking into it. And I feel myself largely to blame. As I told you we would, I sent the painting to be cleaned prior to the sale, so the colors would show up to best advantage. It was taken from the restorer's studio."

Her lips parted, but she made no reply.

Felix leaned forward. "Naturally, we'll do all we can to re-solve the matter. But this is why the inspector is with me today. He has some questions for you."

She shifted backward, as if to put a shred more distance between Mr. Hallam and herself. "Of course." Her expression was composed but I heard the constraint in her voice.

I sensed Mr. Hallam did as well. When he spoke, his tone was perfectly courteous and respectful. "Mrs. Jesper, how did the painting come to be in your possession?"

"It was intended as a gift from my late husband. However, he passed away before he could give it to me. Until I began to make arrangements to move from this house, I had no idea it was even in the cabinet. When I found it, I was surprised; but my husband had done this sort of thing before." She gave a graceful wave of her hand. "Bought things and tucked them away there, to give me later."

"I understand. Could you show us the cabinet?"

She rose, and we all followed her into a library. A trio of tall windows at the far end admitted plenty of light for us to see. This room, like the parlor, had been partially packed. The upper-most bookshelves had been emptied, and some of their contents were in sealed boxes on the floor next to a rolling wooden lad-der. A marble-topped table and a semicircular wood table were stacked with books. My eyes scanned the spines and found titles in French, German, English, Latin, and a language whose let-ters I didn't recognize.

Mrs. Jesper led us to the center of a paneled wall, pressed on a small tile in the inlay, and a panel shifted outward. She laid her fingertips along its wooden edge and swung it open to reveal a recess approximately a foot deep, three feet wide, and six feet high. Within it were two shelves, both empty.

She pointed to the larger, upper compartment. "It was there."

"Was it wrapped?"

"It was enclosed in a bespoke wooden case. I opened it, of course, and recognized it for what it was." She gave a small, sad smile. "My husband's last extravagance."

I didn't dare look at Felix or Mr. Hallam. "You've seen Boucher's work before?" I asked.

She closed the panel. "Yes. And I recognized Madame de Pompadour from a traveling exhibition at the National Gallery two years ago."

I'd seen the same exhibition.

"Was there anything else in this cabinet, with the painting?" Mr. Hallam asked.

"Yes. A necklace, in a box. Our jeweler confirmed Stephen purchased it, intending it for my birthday."

"When is that?"

"The ninth of March. Our anniversary is the following week."

We walked back into the parlor and took our places again. I was almost holding my breath, waiting to see what the inspector would say next.

"May I ask why you chose to sell it?" he asked.

A spark flashed to her eye. "I assume you mean, why, given my apparent resources"—her right hand gestured in a way that encompassed the house—"would I sell my husband's final gift. It doesn't please me to do so. But I have no stake in the Jesper Shipping Company and no claim upon any of its profits from the day that Stephen died." Her spine straightened, as if to show that she hadn't made this admission to elicit our sympathy. "You see, his grandfather began the company, and he stipulated that it be passed on only to the male heirs."

"It's not a joint-stock company?" Mr. Hallam interjected in surprise.

"No, it's still privately held. Naturally, Stephen made provisions for me out of his own fortune in case of his death, but our income came from the company. His portion immediately passed to his cousins Arnold and Francis."

"When did your husband's grandfather begin the company?" Mr. Hallam asked. The question may have come across as idle, but I'd begun to recognize the tone his voice took when he had a particular purpose in asking.

"In 1816, just after the wars. He was a captain in the navy, and he began with a single sailing ship. He imported wine from France, port from Portugal, lace from Belgium, that sort of thing. And he'd carry woolens and manufactured goods back. Now they use mostly steamships, of course, and I believe there are twenty-four of them."

"Do the ships ever carry paintings?"

"Not that Stephen mentioned in particular," she said coolly. Clearly she imagined he was halfway toward accusing her husband of wrongdoing.

"Mrs. Jesper, I'm afraid that your husband may not, in fact, have intended the painting as a gift for you." Mr. Hallam's voice was gentle. "He did not own the painting. We believe he may have been merely holding it—keeping it safe for someone else."

She recoiled, and over her face came shock, disbelief, and then—finally—horror, as she realized the implications. At last she spoke, her voice barely above a whisper: "What do you mean?"

"It's our understanding this painting was owned by the late Lord Sibley."

Her eyes widened. "Lord Sibley? The MP? Why on earth would you think so?"

"His stepson saw the painting on the cover of the auction catalog and came to the Yard immediately. He provided written proof—including a notarized photographic record from his solicitor—that his father purchased this painting from the Le-Marc family early in 1872."

She gave a wretched little moan, and for a moment I was afraid she was going to faint. Perhaps Felix thought the same, for he shifted to sit beside her on the couch, but she seemed not to notice. Her fingers clutched at the fabric on the upholstered arm and she stared at Mr. Hallam. "How on earth was it in our library cabinet? Are you saying my husband stole it?"

"Not at all. As I said, he may have been holding the painting for Lord Sibley, and in fact that is my suspicion," he said hurriedly. "But do you have any idea when the painting might have been brought into the house?"

She shook her head in bewilderment. "I've no idea—none at all. We were always in and out of the house, so he could have brought it any day, any night . . ." Her eyes sought Felix's. "What does this mean?"

"I'm very sorry," he said unhappily. "I'm sure Bettridge's will make restitution in every possible way we can, to all the injured parties." But even in her shock Mrs. Jesper seemed to hear the tentative note in his voice, and I watched her expression change as she realized the truth: if the painting wasn't hers, Bettridge's would bear no responsibility to her.

"Oh dear God," she murmured under her breath. Her slender neck bowed, and her gaze dropped to her lap. Suddenly, her head jerked up and she turned toward Felix: "Surely you know I had no idea—"

He rested his hand on her arm. "Celia, of course. Don't even think it. No one would."

She gave a ragged gasp, but his words seemed to give her a measure of comfort.

"Mrs. Jesper, how well was your husband acquainted with Lord Sibley?" Mr. Hallam asked.

Her eyebrows rose in delicate arcs. "He *wasn't,* so far as I know. Of course we knew who he was—but to my knowledge, my husband and he never met. We're not in those social circles."

There was a long moment, and then she flinched, her expression suggesting that a deeply painful possibility had occurred to her.

Her right hand, slender and slack and ringless, went to her chest. "I'm sorry, I'm not feeling well. I need to lie down."

Felix immediately rose and pulled the silken cord for the bell. A maid appeared in the doorway.

One glance at her mistress's drawn face, and she leapt forward. "Mrs. Jesper," she cried.

"Please, Betsy, I'd like to go to my room."

"Yes, mum." Betsy bent to put a hand on Mrs. Jesper's elbow and another at her waist. She gave the three of us a disapproving glance and helped her mistress out of the room. Sitting in silence, we followed their progress by the sounds of their shoes on the bare stairs.

As the footsteps faded, Felix turned to Mr. Hallam. "Are you satisfied?"

I flinched at the coldness in his voice. "Felix! That's not fair. None of us wants to cause her distress—"

"It's all right," Mr. Hallam interrupted, and though there was a flash of resentment in his eyes, his voice was even. "Clearly she believed the painting was purchased for her, like the necklace, as a gift."

"I told you as much," Felix muttered.

Mr. Hallam's jaw tightened, but he only turned wordlessly and started out of the room. Both of us followed, and Felix headed toward the back of the house, leaving Mr. Hallam and me in the hallway with the Cézanne.

"I'm sorry," I said quietly. "Felix is upset. He didn't mean it."

He turned over his palm in a deprecating gesture. "I understand. I feel sorry for her myself—this, on top of losing her husband and her home."

As I made a sound of agreement, Felix reappeared, his face heavy with disapproval and frustration. He stalked past us and opened the door, and the three of us left. As I walked down the steps to the street, into my mind came the image of Mrs. Jesper, upstairs in a chair, her face buried in her hands as she sobbed. I felt a pang of regret, for I wished I could offer her something in the way of encouragement or comfort. On the contrary: I could only provide details about the theft that she would find still more disturbing.

Without another word to either Mr. Hallam or me, Felix climbed into a cab, and we watched as it rolled away. Only then did I realize, with a quickening of fear, that Felix had said not a word about the guaranty. I attempted to reassure myself with the thought that most likely the solicitor hadn't answered his query yet. I'd see Felix tomorrow, at the funeral. Perhaps he would have news for me then.

Chapter 7

The morning of Edwin's funeral, the air in the church was cold and damp and smelled of burnt wax. Behind the main altar, the wall of the apse held an intricate stained glass window, but with the sky full of clouds, the window's colors were dull.

I'd been allowed a quiet moment with Edwin in a side chapel before the pallbearers brought his casket in for the service. With his eyes closed and his face blandly expressionless, Edwin appeared wholly unlike he'd ever been in life. Perhaps that is why my sorrow felt blunted and unreal. By contrast, there was a sharp quality to my memory of the last time I stood before a coffin like this. It was Mother's. Edwin was beside me, and we'd both been sobbing. I sighed. The quality of my heartbreak was different—and so much more complicated—now.

The bells tolled eleven, and I left the chapel and entered the nave. As I expected, most of the pews were empty; there were perhaps thirty mourners present altogether. Most of them sat silently, looking straight ahead or with their heads dropped over the prayer book. To my surprise and gratification, Mr. Poynter and some students from the Slade had come, and several gave me nods of sympathy. Aside from Felix and my aunt Caroline, I was wholly unacquainted with most of the others present, and once again I had the sensation of having been left out of a significant part of Edwin's life. Faces young, old, round, reddened by the wind, sturdy, delicate, with brown eyes heavily lashed, with reddish spots on the pale cheeks—

Who were all these people to him?

I took my place in the front pew beside my aunt. She barely acknowledged my greeting. My subdued demeanor was met with disapproval rather than sympathy, and whether she was my closest blood relative or not, I fervently wished she had stayed in Leeds. My aunt stared straight ahead, her wide bosom stretching the black silk across her chest, her chin high, as if to keep the flesh underneath from wobbling.

Behind me, there were a few tears and clearings of throats, the rustle of bombazine skirts, the creak of a wooden pew as people took their places. The rector, Mr. Martin, had told me he'd been asked by the police not to allude to the manner of Edwin's death, so as he began the service he only spoke somberly about the unexpectedness of Edwin's passing.

I couldn't concentrate on the words of the service or the sermon and found myself again thinking of my mother's funeral and also of my father's. His had occurred first; his father, a dour and deeply religious man, took charge of it, and it was a grim affair. My mother was too ill to attend, so Edwin and I attended alone, half of our hearts back at the house with her. When she died four days afterward, a superstitious neighbor said it was because my father had mistakenly been carried out of the house headfirst. Had the undertakers done it properly, my father wouldn't have been able to beckon to my mother to follow him, and she'd still be alive. Edwin had cursed the old biddy and stormed off, not reappearing until the morning of Mother's funeral.

By then, most family members had heard that Edwin had brought the disease into the house and refused to acknowledge him at all. Aunt Caroline, religious and self-righteous, had swept up the aisle in her heavy black weeds and ignored both Edwin and me. After we returned from Mother's grave, she had the servants drape the mirrors of our house. It wasn't from any foolish superstition that Mother's likeness would have been trapped in the glass, she insisted; it was out of a need to instill a proper degree of shame and contrition in Edwin. Surely, she said, Edwin shouldn't be examining his visage but rather considering the state of his soul. She needn't have bothered; Edwin never came inside the house again after my mother was gone.

And now here was Aunt Caroline again. Throughout the entire service, her eyes remained dry. She was making a point, I knew: Edwin wasn't worthy of her tears.

My mother's eyes wouldn't have been dry. She would have wept for Edwin, for his wasted life, for the pain he must have suffered in death. She had loved him and kept her faith in him despite everything he'd done. I felt a lump as rough and unyielding as a lump of quartz in my throat. How desperately I wished she were here now.

MY AUNT PLANTED herself beside me as I accepted the condolences of people leaving the church. I'd rather have done this alone, but she was one of those who took profound satisfaction in demonstrating to herself and everyone else that she was performing her duty.

"Miss Rowe." I turned to find Mr. Poynter extending his hand jerkily toward me to take mine. "I am so very sorry."

"Thank you."

"We . . . that is—" He halted and two pink spots appeared at his cheeks. "Please do not feel as though you need to rush back to your studies. We will hold your place, of course."

"Thank you," I said again—and again, and again, as students from my school approached, expressed their condolences, and moved on. Out of the corner of my eye, I saw Mr. Poynter speaking with Mr. Hallam and then Felix. He stayed until the last student from the Slade approached: Geoffrey Wright, looking shamefaced. But he drew near, and no matter what resentment he held about my presence at the Slade, there was a light of honest sympathy in his face, and I was sincere in my thanks for his coming. And then Mr. Poynter, like a benevolent caretaker, shepherded them all away.

I was grateful as well when people I didn't know slipped by without greeting me. There was an elderly woman with a cane who leaned on the arm of a younger woman whose face showed signs of tears. A young man shot a bitter look in my direction that at any other time might have unsettled me, or at least made me curious, but I had no time to consider him. With a sense of relief I greeted the second-to-last mourner—a man who was tall and attractive with brown curly hair, broad shoulders, and a confident way of moving. He introduced himself: "Will Giffen, miss," he said. "Edwin and I were at Tennersley together."

"Oh."

He tipped his head forward with an ingratiating smile. "Don't suppose he ever mentioned me?"

"I'm . . . I'm afraid not," I fumbled, not wanting to hurt his feelings. "He . . . well, he didn't talk much about his time at school."

A peculiar expression flashed across his face, so quickly I couldn't read it. Was it regret or relief?

"Well," he said. "I'm sorry for your loss."

"Thank you." By this point the words came mechanically from my lips, and he moved on.

The last to approach was a middle-aged cleric who came toward me with an uneven gait, favoring his right leg. He was short for a man, for he was barely my height, but sturdily built. He had brown hair, graying at the temples but still thick and wavy. Above his white collar, his face was ruddy, as if he spent a good bit of time outdoors, and his nose was bulbous. But his brown eyes were kind, and the smile he gave me was mild and amiable. I sensed he'd held back so that he might speak to me at some length, and he extended his hand to take mine. "You must be Annabel."

I nodded.

"I'm Mr. Pascoe, and I serve as vicar at St. Pancras Old Church, in Camden."

He gazed at me expectantly, but I must have looked nonplussed, for I couldn't imagine how he knew Edwin. My brother had never been to church voluntarily that I knew of. "Edwin attended your services?" I asked politely.

"No. I never won him over so far as that." He gave a slight, rueful smile. "I visited him when he was in prison."

"Oh," I said in surprise. "I was told he wasn't allowed visitors."

He brushed one hand against his vestments. "They make exceptions for us."

I bit my lip. "Of course."

"I attended him twice a week when he was there, and we saw each other less regularly afterward—but still, once a fortnight or so." He hesitated and glanced toward my aunt, who was talking with Mr. Martin. Instinctively I took a few steps away from her. He inclined his head toward me, his voice lowered. "The rector said it was sudden. May I ask, was it an accident?"

A tremor ran over me. "No."

His face crumpled with sorrow and frustration. "What a terrible waste. His life before prison . . . I know it was . . ." He spread his hands wordlessly, then let them fall to his sides. "But he was a brilliant and sensitive man."

"He was neither brilliant nor sensitive," came my aunt's voice over my shoulder. "He was selfish and calculating and never, not a day in his life, did he consider the feelings of anyone else! He killed my brother and your mother, and he never repented of it. He only got what he deserved, and we all know it!"

I whirled to find her gray eyes blazing in her round pasty face. "Aunt Caroline, stop it! You don't know what you're saying."

Mr. Martin was at her side. "Mrs. Hastings, please." He put his hand on her elbow and drew her away.

My heart was beating furiously in my chest, and my breath was coming in gasps.

Mr. Pascoe's brown eyes were full of sympathy. "I'm very sorry," he said. "For what it's worth, I don't hold with your aunt's opinions." A pause. "He spoke of you often, you know."

It was, of course, the sort of thing one said to a surviving sister, but I sensed he meant it kindly, and a conventional response rose to my lips: "Did he?"

He drew me toward a pew, and we sat down. "He felt a terrible weight of grief and guilt for what he'd done to you and to your parents—the truancy, the opium, the forgeries, all of it."

I started in surprise. *So the vicar knew.*

"A terrible weight," he repeated soberly. "He had discovered a different path, you know, during his time in prison." His expression was full of regret. "I just wish . . ."

Haltingly, I said, "Our friend Felix said so as well."

"Edwin understood your skepticism. He told me how many times he promised that he would change, only to relapse into his old habits." I felt my throat tighten, and I remained silent. His head tipped. "Did you know he made a will?"

I started again. "What?"

He nodded. "He made it the week after he was released from prison, and I witnessed it. With the exception of a few sentimental bequests, you're his sole heir."

I felt the blood drain from my face, and he peered at me anxiously.

"I'm so sorry," he said. "I didn't intend to add to your distress. I thought it might be some comfort to you."

I stared at the back of the pew in front of us. There was a knot in the wood, and the grain ran around it, like a stream would run around a boulder.

"Miss Rowe, I . . ."

"There are so *many* things he didn't tell me," I blurted. "About Felix's visits and the painting he was cleaning and—

and you. But a will that leaves me our parents' house? Why wouldn't he tell me *that*?"

"I think—" The vicar averted his eyes for a moment. Then he sighed and met my gaze. "I think he didn't want you to feel obligated to forgive him."

It took me a moment to understand, and then I did.

Of course. Edwin wanted me to forgive him from my heart, not because he filled my purse.

I couldn't think of a word of reply. I just sat stunned and silent, staring at the knot and the grain in the wood, until the vicar shifted and gave an exhale that I felt near my left ear. "The will is with a solicitor. Mr. Jamison, on Yarrow Street. I'll send a note round to him about what has happened and tell him he can expect you. Will that do?"

Mutely I nodded.

"Our church door is always open. If you ever wish to speak with me, you'll find us on Pancras Road, just north of the railway station."

I swallowed and said for what must have been the hundredth time, "Thank you."

He rose and stepped out of the pew, but before he left he put a gentle hand on my shoulder and said tenderly, as if to a child, "God bless you, my dear."

And for the first time since I'd heard the news that Edwin died, when tears pricked at the corners of my eyes, I let them come.

ONLY HALF A dozen of us made the walk from the church to the gravesite for the burial, which Felix had arranged. A recent storm had stripped the branches of the elms, and I felt as though I were looking upon the scene from above, through the bare limbs of the trees.

The rector shepherded me through the remainder of the service. Felix stood at my side; Mr. Hallam remained at a distance, watching to the end, I believe, for any unexpected faces at the gravesite. The moment the casket was lowered into the ground, my aunt turned away with a resolute sniff. Felix stepped aside with a sigh, and the last to leave was Mr. Martin. He stood beside me and spoke a few priestly words of comfort that I barely heard.

And then, at last, I was alone by the grave. I looked down into the hole and saw the coffin, several shades paler than the nut-brown earth around it. The white flowers I placed on top had rolled off, or been blown to the side, dropping into the crevasse between the wood and the dirt, leaving only the oblong box, devoid of ornament and polished to a dull sheen.

God, what a fool I'd been.

The feeling of self-loathing struck me as fiercely as a bitter wind on naked skin. There was no getting away from the consequences of my stubbornness and my stupidity, keeping myself at a distance from him. Of course I knew that people could die swiftly. My parents had taken ill and were gone in a matter of days. But Edwin was only twenty-five! I had counted on there being *time*—time enough for me to be angry with him; to hold myself aloof so that he might learn what it had felt like to be abandoned; to inscribe indelibly my uncertainty and fear upon his heart, so that he would never, *ever* do it to me again. And then, at last, I would let him see I'd forgiven him. That, really, I'd forgive him anything, so long as he came back for good.

I thought there would be time for all of that.

Now there wasn't time for any of it.

And while I had been tending my resentment and distrust, Edwin had made sure I'd be taken care of, if anything happened to him.

The wind stirred the trees, shifting the shadows of the limbs across the ground and tumbling detritus into the grave. The dampness of the late-afternoon air knifed its way into my insides, and I shivered. Yet again, Edwin's death took on a fresh, startling clarity. Perhaps it was because everything seemed to be moving, while the coffin remained so still.

Mr. Hallam came to my side and took my elbow, nudging me gently away from the grave, through the trees, and onto the gravel path, the small stones rough through the thin soles of my shoes. He asked if he should come and fetch me the next day, prior to going to the Sibleys' house to speak with Mr. Pagett. I told him there was no need. I would come to the Yard.

Felix appeared beside us and muttered something to the effect that whatever Mr. Hallam had to say could wait until tomorrow. I heard the coldness in his voice, and I sensed Mr. Hallam's resentment, but I was in no state to conciliate either of them.

I let Felix lead me away. He helped me into a cab, settled me in my flat with a cup of hot tea, and asked several times if there was anything else he might do. Each time I replied in the negative, and at last he left me. I held the cup until the tea had gone cold and then I set it aside undrunk and fell into bed, feeling as weary and worn as if I'd been marched from one side of London to the other.

Chapter 8

If I hadn't promised Mr. Hallam, I might not have risen from bed the next morning. I had a sense of profound aimlessness, a hollowness at my core, and a heaviness in my hands and feet that made me clumsy. Apathetically I got up, donned my dark gray dress, and made my way down to the street. The milky fog kept me from seeing more than a few paces ahead, and I was only steps from the entrance to the Yard when I saw Mr. Hallam waiting for me under the arch. As we got into a cab, he said again how sorry he was about Edwin. Perhaps I should have told him about the will, but for some reason I wanted to keep it to myself. So I merely thanked him and kept my eyes on the street outside, watching the crowds of people appearing and vanishing like apparitions in the swirling haze.

Before we reached the Sibleys' house, Mr. Hallam let drop into the silence something to the effect that he was glad to have me with him, as Mr. Pagett might be more amenable to conversation with someone who was knowledgeable about art.

I turned. "Was he unpleasant when he came to the Yard?"

"He took it upon himself to educate me about Boucher." He rocked with the motion of the cab. "So now I know that Boucher was one of the most celebrated practitioners of rococo style, both in painting and the decorative arts, and a personification and embodiment of eighteenth-century French sophistication."

The phrasing was so different from Mr. Hallam's usual naturalness that I winced. "He said that?"

"Mm-hm." He shrugged philosophically. "Clearly paintings are his passion. He considers himself responsible for his stepfather's legacy. He's compiling some sort of book about the family collection."

"A catalogue raisonné?"

"I think that's the term he used." The carriage took a corner sharply, and he grabbed at the leather strap on the wall. "I gather it's a listing with descriptions of all the items."

I nodded. "Well, I don't promise to know everything Mr. Pagett does, especially as he sounds like the sort who will be determined to prove that I don't."

"He's a prickly one, and a bit peculiar." He paused. "As he left, he made a comment—in German, under his breath—about how I'd be at home in Antwerp. What did he mean by that?"

"Oh . . . er . . ." I stammered and then abandoned the attempt to soften the insult. "In the sixteenth century, paintings were often valued by weight, particularly in the Antwerp market."

"Ah." A faint smile flickered.

We lapsed again into silence, and a few minutes later the carriage drew up to an elegant house with a black wrought-iron fence at the front. Mr. Hallam helped me out of the cab and paid the driver. "To be fair," he said, "the day I met him, the news of the painting coming to auction was fresh. He's had some time to regain his composure. I think you'll be able to hold your own."

"I hope so," I said. He lifted the latch and swung open the gate, and as we started toward the cascade of marble steps I said hurriedly, "Mr. Hallam, please don't tell him I'm a student at the Slade."

He halted. "Why not? I imagine that's the very thing that might cause him to trust you."

I shook my head. "I don't think it will impress him. He'll probably take it to mean I'm . . . a dilettante or . . . or some sort of present-day bluestocking. You might just tell him I know something about art." I hesitated. "And perhaps . . . well, please don't tell him about me being Edwin's sister. I'd prefer not to have to accept the sympathy of a stranger." I'd had enough of that yesterday.

He gave an understanding nod.

"I assume you're planning to tell him that the painting was stolen," I ventured.

He raised the brass knocker. "Eventually, yes. Not least because I want to see whether he knows anything about its disappearance."

The thought that I might be facing a man who'd had something to do with Edwin's murder gave me a chill.

But just then the door opened, and a footman looked at us expectantly.

"Mr. Hallam from Scotland Yard, and Miss Rowe," the inspector said. "For Mr. Pagett."

"I shall see if Mr. Pagett is at home."

"We have an appointment," Mr. Hallam added.

The man stiffened, and he forced an emphasis upon nearly every other syllable: "Mr. Pagett returned from travel abroad late last night. I shall see if he is available for visitors."

He held the door for us to enter the foyer, a lovely oval room with square marble tiles on the floor. Against the beige walls, fine white moldings that framed pairs of brass sconces hung at regular intervals.

"Please wait here." The footman turned away, and the inspector and I exchanged glances.

Given that the walls were curved, there was only one flat enough for a painting; upon it hung a formal portrait. We approached, and I read the engraved brass plate secured to the dark wood frame. "'Lord Anthony Sibley, MP.'"

"His stepfather," Mr. Hallam observed.

The man appeared to have been about twenty-five when the portrait was made. The lighting was well done, illuminating the subject's honey-colored hair. He had a nose that might have become beakish later in life, but attractive blue eyes, a firm chin, and a pleasing smile that brought out a dimple in his left cheek. Lord Sibley's right hand rested tranquilly on top of a wooden desk with an emerald-green leather inset. Beside his hand was a book that bore the Oxford coat of arms with its distinctive azure background.

"Handsome fellow" was Mr. Hallam's comment. "So is this a three-quarters?"

I stepped back to take the measure of the painting. With surprise, I realized what it was. "No. It's similar in style, but it's a kit-cat."

"Kit-cat? Like the club?"

I nodded. "All the members of the Kit-Cat Club had their portraits done. The walls of the club were quite low, so they could only accommodate portraits of a certain height, if the member was painted true to life. So *kit-cat* came to refer to both the style—the subject painted life-size—and to the size of the canvas—three feet by roughly two and a half." I paused. "Like the Boucher."

Understanding lit his eyes. "Thirty-six by twenty-eight. I remember from the catalog."

"That's part of what's so unusual about the portrait. I've never heard of a kit-cat of a woman." I smiled. "I wonder if Boucher meant it as a tribute to her originality."

The footman returned, and I fell silent. The expression on his face reflected how much he disapproved of us having moved from our original marble squares. "Mr. Pagett requests that you wait in the front parlor."

He led us down the hallway to the third door, motioned us in with a stiff hand, and closed the door behind us, as if to prevent us from wandering about the house.

"At least he'll see us," Mr. Hallam muttered.

I wasn't sorry to be left alone to admire the room, which to my eye was tastefully masculine. The walls were painted an impractical pale blue-gray, a shade incapable of hiding the stains from oil lamps or pipe smoke but which set off the gilt frames to perfection. The walls were crowned with moldings painted a pearly white. Long maroon draperies were drawn back with plain ties to reveal a meticulously groomed court-yard garden beyond. The furniture was of dark wood and leather, with brass fittings; among the two sofas and several leather chairs were square tables that held lamps and books in picturesque stacks.

The ten paintings in the room were hung properly, at eye level, rather than up too high, the way some people placed them in order to make a room appear larger, or to hide the art's flaws. As I surveyed the first few works, I realized that we'd likely been put here so that the superiority of the family's collection of French paintings might be thrust in our faces. But regardless of the heavy-handedness of Mr. Pagett's maneuver, someone in the family had a very good eye.

Side by side on one of the walls hung a pair of portraits in the style of La Tour. The first showed a sober-looking young man seated on a bench, with his interests and his membership in the leisure class represented by a book, a globe, and two slim gray pointers, their noses pointed in opposite directions; the second was of a young woman, also seated, but at a desk, with her quill and paper and some books. The composition and lighting were similar, but the artist's attitude toward his subjects couldn't have been more different. Whereas the young man's skin was sallow, hers was pink; while his expression was mirthless with a hint of resentment, hers betrayed warmth and humor verging on impishness.

"These are neither kit-cats nor three-quarters," Mr. Hallam murmured, as if we were in a museum. "You see, I'm learning."

I nodded approvingly. "Yes, these are full-length."

The next group, three paintings on a longer wall, included a scene from a garden party in the style of Watteau, with ladies and gentlemen in formal dress conducting their amorous affairs; and two landscapes in unsaturated greens and browns that were well done but, to my mind, conventional, and I moved on.

Mr. Hallam had followed me in silence as I continued my tour around the room, and he nearly bumped into me as I halted abruptly before the sixth painting, which hung on a wall by itself. It was an oversize canvas depicting a scene in an elegant parlor, and as I studied it, I felt my pulse quicken. The light dropped beautifully from the window into the room, shaping shadows that might have done credit to Rembrandt himself. Precisely at the center of the canvas was a pale porcelain teacup being handed from maid to mistress, but the dispersal of colors and the gazes of the subjects drew my eye in widening arcs. I drew closer to see the textures of the piano, the carpet, the silk of the girls' dresses; they were expertly rendered, without any thickening of paint that sometimes marks the work of an amateur. The gentleman's hands—the bane of many artists' existence—were done well, down to the fingernails and a ring with a red stone—

"You like this?" Mr. Hallam asked.

I let out my breath. "I think it's brilliant."

"Brilliant?" His expression was perplexed. "I was about to say the scene was ordinary, and I wondered why you were staring. What have I missed?"

There was something about his manner, at once humble and openly curious, that made me feel pleased to explain. "First, why don't you tell me what you see?"

He studied the painting, and after a moment he said, "A wealthy family at home. The light feels more like afternoon than morning. The mother looks proud but irritable, and is taking a cup of tea from the maid. Her daughters are at the piano, and they're both flirting with the young man. He's a bit of a dandy." He turned to me. "And you?"

I pointed at the upper left quadrant of the canvas. "Do you see the man's formal portrait, by the fireplace? I would guess he's the father who is missing from this scene. If he is dead, the mother knows she needs to settle her daughters before she dies; if she doesn't, and the estate is entailed, they'll be left penniless." My fingertip shifted to the lower left corner. "You see the fray on the carpet?"

"Yes." His voice held a note of surprise.

"So the mother is irritable and anxious, hoping the young man will marry one of the daughters. But look at him. He rests his hand on the piano, and the red stone in his ring is the same color as the curtains and the roses in the carpet, as if he already belongs. But though the man stands near the daughters, his face is turned toward the maid."

I watched as his eyes retraced the painting. "So behind this seemingly benign scene is a tragedy waiting to happen," he concluded. He turned to me, his expression uncertain, even troubled. "Is that what you call brilliant?"

"There's nothing brilliant about infidelity or privation," I corrected him gently. "But do you remember what you said the other day about truth coming from putting events in order?" I tipped my head toward the painting. "This is *my* kind of truth, capturing a moment when faces and gestures betray feelings and motives. This is what I want to do—to show people as they truly are, with all their weakness and fear and longing."

Immediately after I said it, I realized how earnest and didactic—perhaps even officious—I sounded. But to my relief, he didn't laugh. Instead his expression cleared. "I remember the painting in Edwin's room, of the young girl and her father at the market," he said. "You caught the moment of the girl's resentment and the father's fatigue."

I was surprised he remembered so clearly. "I was trying to, yes."

"That's another kind of truth, and just as valid," he admitted. "Although we're not so far apart in our methods. I study people's faces and actions, too, in order to understand their motivations—and to know when they're lying to me."

"Yes, I suppose you would."

He tipped his chin in the direction of the two portraits. "You don't care for those."

"Oh." I shrugged apologetically. "They have merit, surely, but often the subject becomes no more than a conventional symbol, a representative of the politics and the mores of the time. Usually the painter includes a heap of iconographic objects to reflect aspects of character or occupation." I looked up at the parlor scene again, and my eye caught on another detail. "But in a work like this, what's absent is sometimes just as significant as what's present. It suggests what people have lost, or what they've never had. Do you see the dark spot on the wallpaper, just there? It shows they've had to sell a painting." I pointed to an almost invisible rectangle.

"Please don't touch that," came a clipped voice behind us.

Not for worlds would I have touched another artist's painted canvas, but I didn't quibble. My hand dropped into the folds of my skirt as I turned.

At last, Mr. Pagett had made his appearance. He was a tall man of about thirty, with wavy brown hair swept back from a broad forehead, a smallish nose, and a mouth that suggested meticulousness. He was dressed with care, down to his smartly tailored hems that brushed his polished boots. When Mr. Hallam introduced me as an art scholar, his annoyance gave way to a sort of weary tolerance, and my heart sank as I realized that my being here might only make Mr. Pagett less amiable.

"And what do you think of our paintings, Miss Rowe?" Mr. Pagett asked.

I'd had plenty of experience the past two years in giving my opinions on artwork. I knew to take my time, to be deliberate, and to speak only about what I knew.

I turned to take in the four paintings on the opposite wall. Again, French, eighteenth-century; perhaps the works of Fragonard, who had been a pupil of Boucher's. But the two pairs didn't properly occupy the space, the way the paintings on the other walls did, as if a work had been removed. Further, I noticed the similarity of all the frames and understood what it might reveal about Mr. Pagett's ambitions; however, I would keep that observation to myself.

At last I turned to him. "I can say without reservation that you have fine representatives of all the eighteenth-century French schools." I gestured to each in turn. "The portraits, the fête galante, the landscapes, the allegorical paintings, and this genre painting. I couldn't attribute these with any certainty. But given that those"—I pointed toward the set of four—"are possibly by Fragonard, and those"—I indicated the portraits—"might be by La Tour, who also painted Madame de Pompadour, I can appreciate that the Boucher would be central to your collection."

His expression lost some of its condescension. "Do you know Boucher's work?"

"Somewhat," I answered modestly.

He gave a nod of satisfaction, and I felt my breath ease; I'd passed, at least provisionally.

I turned to the painting of the parlor scene. "This one . . . I think it's remarkable. Who is the artist?"

Despite himself, he looked gratified. "A young man named Jacques Delaurme. He passed away last year of consumption, poor fellow. He was only twenty-nine."

Mr. Hallam had discreetly stepped away, leaving Mr. Pagett and me together in front of the painting. Mr. Pagett's arms were crossed over his chest, his head oddly askew on his neck, as if he needed an extra inch or two to properly examine the painting, but I heard the note of true admiration and enthusiasm for this work. "Delaurme remains underappreciated because he only left behind thirteen finished paintings, all interiors like this. Each has its merits, and this one is the best."

I couldn't help but imagine how Mr. Poynter would respond to a student who expressed himself with such absolute certainty in his own judgment. Out of tact, I concealed my wonder, but I could sincerely voice my appreciation for the painting: "Well, I think it is brilliant, both in terms of technique and the story it tells. The lighting, the hands, the gazes, the fabrics and textures. The delicate balance of the three, or even four different triangles among the six characters."

"Six?" Mr. Pagett said, turning in surprise.

"The father's portrait, beside the mantel," I said. "Surely he's as much a part of this painting as anyone. It's his absence that structures all the other triangles—the fear, the giddiness, the longing."

He snorted. "You make it sound like a romance novel. But I'm delighted you appreciate its quality." A pause, and his voice altered. "It was my first purchase after my father's death." I murmured some conventional words of sympathy, which he dismissed with a wave of his left hand. "This room represents only part of our collection. The paintings from the Dutch Golden Age are in the dining room, and the Venetian school is in the library. We've always had an eye for improving our holdings."

The door opened and a maid appeared, her cleaning brushes clanking against the metal pail. At the sight of us, she halted, openmouthed.

He spun around. "Mary!"

"Beg pardon, sir. I didn't know—"

"Never mind," he growled. "Let us alone, and be quiet about it."

He pivoted back to us, so he missed the resentful look she gave him before she turned away, closing the door behind her with a scrupulously obedient click.

His arms once again folded across his chest, his eyes flicked to Mr. Hallam and then back to me. "I understand that the theft of a French painting might not rise to the importance of a murder or a railway disaster. But the Boucher is—as I told Mr. Hallam—extremely valuable and important to the world."

"I do understand," I said. "Especially after being allowed to see this part of your collection."

Either he didn't understand that I'd detected his stratagem or he refused to be embarrassed by it.

"As I told the inspector, it was one of my father's most astute purchases—truly the piece around which all of this"—he gestured with his arm—"should be arranged."

"Then why did your father place it in the Pantechnicon?" I asked.

There was a moment when the gray eyes went cold, and I had a vague feeling of discomfort, as if I'd rubbed the nap of velvet the wrong way.

"I believe he considered taking it to our country house. I couldn't say for certain." He shrugged and brushed his fingertips lightly along the edge of a table, as if to remove a speck of dust. "He didn't always share his plans with me, or with Franks."

"Franks?" Mr. Hallam interposed.

He looked up. "Mr. Wilbur Franks. He cleans and hangs all of our paintings. He has for years."

"And—I beg your pardon," Mr. Hallam said, "but I've forgotten. When did your father purchase the painting?"

I felt a small jolt of surprise. Mr. Hallam knew the answer to that, and I realized he had used the question to steer the conversation.

"In January of 1872. After the Franco-Prussian War, members of the LeMarc family left Paris and lived with us until they could find a suitable residence to rent in London. Naturally, they brought some of their prized paintings, and my father purchased the Boucher, partly to provide them with funds."

"The LeMarc family were close friends, then?" Mr. Hallam asked.

"Yes, for years." His tone was neutral—but something in his expression seemed amiss.

"Is it a large family?"

Mr. Pagett's lip curled faintly. "I've no idea the size of the family. I imagine it's enormous, in the usual way of most Catholics. But only Monsieur LeMarc and his daughter Heloise stayed here."

"Was that uncomfortable?" Mr. Hallam asked. "You don't seem pleased about it."

"I don't particularly enjoy houseguests for long periods."

In a house this size? I wondered. There might be half a dozen guests and no need to see them ever.

"Ah." Mr. Hallam shifted his weight from one foot to the other, as if to set that line of conversation visibly aside. "So—your father sent the Boucher to the Pantechnicon for storage. When was that?"

"Toward the end of December in 1873. He was planning to travel back to Paris with the LeMarc family after the New Year. The capital was deemed safe, as the Germans were departing and the government seemed to have recovered stability."

"How many other paintings did you store in the Pantechnicon?" Mr. Hallam asked.

"Forty-four in all."

"Any as valuable as the Boucher?"

"A few. A Rembrandt and a Titian." He glanced at me to be sure I recognized the names. "Most of them were lesser works, though, ones that we held onto for sentimental reasons, or because my father anticipated selling or trading them later on."

"Hm." Mr. Hallam paused. "I imagine your father was devastated by the loss of so much of his collection in the fire."

Mr. Pagett merely looked at him as if he'd said something unworthy of a response.

"How did your father die?" I asked.

Mr. Pagett's voice flattened, as if reciting facts that he had provided many times in the past. "My father remained in Paris for nearly two months, and when he returned, he caught some strain of the influenza—probably from a chill he'd taken on the crossing. The doctors came, of course, and did their best. But a few weeks later, he was gone."

I heard a tremor as he spoke the last words. Perhaps he heard it as well, for he gave a hoarse cough before he resumed. "His greatest legacy is this collection, so I don't want a forgery paraded about as if he were a fool—or to have some sort of scandal arise that would call into question any aspect of his discretion and judgment. He was a brilliant man."

"I understand," I said, and indeed I felt some sympathy—except I also sensed he was hedging. "And is there no possibility the painting was removed from the Pantechnicon before it burned?"

Mr. Pagett shook his head. "The only person besides my father and myself who ever took works in or out was our family solicitor, Ambrose Leigh. And he didn't remove it. Not only has he denied it, he was in Edinburgh in the weeks prior to the fire." He frowned. "The only reasonable explanation is that the painting is a forgery and Mr. Severington has been duped."

"You know him?" I asked.

"Solely by reputation, until the day I received the auction catalog. Mr. Bettridge wasn't available, so I saw Mr. Severington, who tried to convince me that the Boucher was authentic." He spread his hands in a gesture that suggested his frustration. "He had papers, but as we all know, those can be forged and fabricated. When I asked to see the work itself, he said that it was out being cleaned, but he wouldn't tell me who was doing it, or where it was being held. That's why I went to Scotland Yard." At this, he seemed to remember Mr. Hallam. "I assume that you haven't any further news?"

"Well, we do, some of which I can share with you," Mr. Hallam replied. "However, I have a few more questions."

Mr. Pagett made a show of patience. "Very well."

"Who would have known whether the original was here in the house or in the Pantechnicon?"

Mr. Pagett frowned. "I couldn't say with certainty. Heloise and her father, I imagine. My sister Jane. Members of our housekeeping staff. Mr. Franks, of course. Perhaps there were others."

"And your father went only to Paris on that last trip?"

Mr. Pagett bristled. "What are you insinuating? That he was doing something secretive or illicit?"

"Not at all. I am only asking as a matter of course."

"If he went elsewhere, he didn't mention it to me."

"Did he travel elsewhere in Europe, besides France, in the year or two before he died?"

"Yes, of course."

Mr. Hallam's eyebrows rose, and he waited.

Mr. Pagett huffed. "Amsterdam, I'm sure. Antwerp, probably."

"And when he traveled, did he take anyone with him—a servant or a friend?"

"Usually he took his valet. But he didn't that time," Mr. Pagett replied.

"I'd like to see your father's travel log and any journals he might have kept from the time he purchased the painting until his death."

"He didn't keep a journal. His valet, Mr. Dowling, kept a log."

"Could we speak with him?"

"He's taken another position." Mr. Pagett looked both dubious and annoyed. "Look here, I have to say, I don't see the point in nosing about my father's travel or his private affairs or whether he took his valet or not. The painting was either forged or stolen out of the Pantechnicon. My father's travel plans can hardly be relevant." He glared pointedly at Mr. Hallam. "My father's loyal friends are hardly going to appreciate you digging about in search of some sort of sordid story."

"That is not my—"

"And now some unwitting fellow is going to be sold a forgery or a painting to which he has no legal right. *That* is what you should be considering." Mr. Pagett's voice hardened. "I told you that first day, you need to take a sharp look at Bettridge's. Whatever you may say about Christie's and Sotheby's, they have a proper appreciation for art. But Bettridge's is a joint-stock company, concerned with the profits of their stockholders, so naturally they will run their business like it's a newspaper or a sawmill or—or a slaughterhouse!" His eyes were ablaze with feeling, and his cheeks were flushed. "But pieces of art are not discrete commodities! They cannot be bought and sold like—like a plank of wood or a pig." He spread his hands palms up, the long fingers splayed wide. "They belong to traditions—collections! They transcend mere individuals!"

I began to see why Mr. Hallam had characterized Mr. Pagett as peculiar. He certainly possessed strong opinions.

Mr. Hallam clasped his hands behind his back. "I understand how deeply you feel about art." He took a few steps to the left and then the right. "I am going to tell you something as a courtesy, but I ask that you don't reveal it to anyone."

"All right."

"The painting will not appear in the auction."

Even as Mr. Hallam said it, I fixed my eyes on Mr. Pagett, so I might see his reaction.

He drew back, and his eyes were wide and unblinking, his lips parted, and his face paled. "So it *is* a forgery." It came out as little more than a whisper, and after a moment, his shock gave way to gratification that his surmise had been correct and then to chagrin that the original truly was lost. His entire body slumped as if with disappointment, and I would have sworn his feelings were genuine. Whatever information he was keeping from us, he hadn't stolen the painting and most likely had nothing to do with my brother's death.

He paced to the window that overlooked the garden and stared out. "This is . . . not . . ." His exhale was resigned. "I didn't realize how much I was hoping she had escaped the fire."

We gave him a minute to regain his equanimity.

At last Mr. Hallam broke the silence: "Can you think of anyone else who felt the way you do about the painting?"

He spoke half over his shoulder. "No," he said glumly. "There are plenty of people who'd want a Boucher but . . ." He was shaking his head and staring out the window.

Mr. Hallam caught my eye and nodded, then picked up his coat. "Please send your father's travel records to the Yard as soon as possible."

"Yes," he mumbled distractedly.

"We'll bid you good morning."

The words roused Mr. Pagett, and he turned toward us. "I beg your pardon. This news has been something of a shock." He heaved a sigh. "I suppose it's absurd. Until two weeks ago, I thought she was gone—so to have her gone again shouldn't matter, but it does." His eyebrows drew together. "I'd like to view the forgery for myself."

"I'm sorry. It isn't possible at this time."

His scowl deepened.

"I hope someday to be able to allow you to see it," Mr. Hallam said. "I just ask you to be patient."

His mouth tightened, but he managed to reply civilly, "Very well."

"And please send over your father's travel records," Mr. Hallam reminded him.

He blinked. "Yes. Yes, of course."

Mr. Pagett walked to the parlor door and opened it for us. The footman was waiting to show us out to the street, and I left the house feeling relieved to have the interview behind us. We were only half a dozen steps away from the house before Mr. Hallam asked for my impressions.

"You're certainly right about him being odd," I replied. "But what was the phrase you used? 'Proper and law-abiding'? I have to agree. I don't think he had anything to do with the theft, or my brother's death. Do you?"

"No. I think he's aloof and eccentric, but his shock when he heard the Boucher wouldn't appear at auction seemed genuine." He gave a curious glance. "What about his collection? I sensed you could have said more."

"Well, yes," I admitted. "Nothing he needed to hear, but I noticed a few things in particular. The first is that those four allegorical paintings weren't spaced with the same proportions as others in the room. They were farther apart."

"What do you make of that?"

"My guess is that another painting hung between the two pairs. If it was the Boucher, it was considered part of the collection at some point. And Mr. Pagett hasn't found something to replace it."

"Hm."

"The second thing is, someone has spent a good deal of money on the backdrop for the collection."

"You mean the walls?" Mr. Hallam asked.

"Yes. Decorative painting is expensive," I said. "And when you put different colors in the rooms, and in those delicate shades, each color has to be made here, at the house, by an artisan."

The pavement was crowded, and Mr. Hallam kept his hands clasped behind him as he paced beside me. "The paint looked fairly new. No stains around the fireplace."

I nodded. "His father died over a year ago, so my guess is Mr. Pagett may have ordered it."

"Hm."

"And did you notice the frames, how similar they all were?"

"I saw they were all gilt and heavy." His hand came out from behind his back to bracket the air, his thumb and forefinger spanning four or five inches.

"It's a particular style called a Régence frame," I said. "A style dating from the early 1700s. But it wasn't the *only* kind of frame used for French paintings. Yet all of them were framed alike—"

"Including the large one that he bought after his father's death," he interrupted.

"Yes." I could almost see him slotting this event into order.

"So he had them reframed, and recently," Mr. Hallam said. "That sounds costly. Why would he bother?"

We stepped around a broadsheet boy who was bawling so loudly his face was red as a beet.

I replied, "People do it sometimes to create stylistic continuity in a collection. It suggests to me that the son is trying to put his own stamp on it."

Mr. Hallam's eyes narrowed. "Perhaps the father wasn't as passionate about the collection as the son obviously is. After all, he didn't return until over a month after the Pantechnicon fire."

My steps slowed as I took this in. "You're right. Mr. Pagett would have come home, wouldn't he?"

"I imagine he'd have swum across the Channel if he had to."

The image of Mr. Pagett flailing through the waves made me smile. "I think you're right." We walked on in silence, and I found myself trying to recall other moments in the conversation. "Is it true Bettridge's is a joint-stock company? I've always assumed Mr. Bettridge was the owner."

"The family still owns forty percent of the stock, but yes, they offered shares two years ago to raise funds."

"For the renovation, probably," I realized.

"Mm." He paused at a corner. "Say, are you all right from here, going home? I have some things I need to look into."

"Of course," I said readily. It wasn't even noon, but I was tired; I wanted to be home and to sit quietly, to find some solace if I could. With relief, I bid him good day and turned away, although to my surprise, when I reached the opposite side of the street and looked back, Mr. Hallam was still watching me with what looked like concern. Surprised and touched, I gave a wave of reassurance, and he smiled and tipped his hat before he turned his back and went on his way.

I walked on, feeling a mix of uncertainty and gratification. Indeed, as I reached the door and took the key from my reticule, I had the peculiar fancy that a strand of twine had been unrolled between us, and it remained in place, tied off securely at the corners of that street.

Chapter 9

Later that day, for the first time since Edwin's death, I approached my easel, though I was unsure of my intention. With the certainty of habit, my hand reached for the nail where I kept my old apron. It was skimpier than my smock at the Slade but covered my dress well enough. I ran my hands over the front. Bits of dried paint felt smoother than the coarse drabbet. I chose my paints and brushes, and those simple acts, familiar as sipping tea or brushing my hair, began to soothe the turmoil and sorrow of the past few days. I stood in front of the canvas for some time before I loaded my brush with sepia and began to block out the two figures taking shape in my mind.

After several hours, the image had become clear: Mr. Pagett and Lord Sibley, vis-à-vis. The living man stood with his back angled toward the viewer, his head turned for a partial profile, and his hands clasped behind his back; the father sat just as in the kit-cat, with his gaze focused on some distant point beyond his son. Though it was merely the underpainting, I felt satisfied that I'd captured something in the son's stance—something verging on frustration mixed with longing and grief. It wasn't until I removed my apron that I realized I had put the son's hands behind his back, as if he were concealing a secret, instead of crossed over his chest, as they'd been when Mr. Pagett stared at Delaurme's interior.

Slowly I began preparing for bed; I was braiding my hair when a knock sounded at my door, startling me. I crossed the room and spoke against the closed door, "Who is it?"

"It's Felix, Annabel. Open the door, for God's sake."

Hastily I drew my dressing gown tighter around me, twisted the key, and opened the door. He stood there hatless, his wisps of hair going every which way, his pink forehead damp with perspiration, breathing as though he'd run the entire mile from his flat. He had a rolled newspaper clasped in his right hand like a policeman's truncheon, and he smelled vaguely of spirits.

"What's the matter, Felix? Are you all right?"

"No." He scowled heavily. "It's a bloody mess. And now the papers have got hold of it."

I caught a glimpse of the masthead. The *Beacon*.

I beckoned him inside and closed the door. "Felix, honestly. Everyone knows that paper is hardly reputable."

"It doesn't matter. It's there in black and white for everyone to read." He thrust the roll toward me. "And they slander Edwin. I didn't want you to hear about it from someone else."

Mechanically, I took the paper and began to unfurl it. "They mention Edwin by name?"

He waved a hand, as if dispelling a bad odor. "They've twisted everything. Look for yourself."

He shrugged out of his coat, wiped his perspiring forehead

with his handkerchief, and went over to the window, where he stood with his face turned toward the outside, as if he couldn't bear to watch me read. His shirt was strained across the shoulders, and his plump hands were in fists. Whatever the paper said, I couldn't help but think he was taking it too much to heart.

I turned up the lamp, smoothed the paper on the table, and felt my heart sink. The headline declared in large letters BETTRIDGE'S GRAND SWINDLE! and the article took up the entire lower half of the front page. It began:

> Auction houses have long been haunts of deception, avarice, and exploitation. Despite their claims to a genteel sensibility, Christie's and Sotheby's have both been caught puffing the objects they sell, and they have shown no compunction at earning their handsome commissions off the misfortunes of others. Now, a third auction house has provided us with such a brazen display of fraudulence that we can only stand agape and assume that it shall ascend to the apex of the auction world before long . . .

I skimmed the rest of the article. It was full of suppositions and inquiries intended to inflame the worst suspicions: that Bettridge knew the painting was a forgery and planned to sell it anyway; that Mr. Edwin Rowe, a convicted forger, had not only cleaned the painting but made a copy and was murdered to conceal the crime; that the plainclothesmen of Scotland Yard, as usual, were accepting bribes to delay solving the crime until after the auction; that Felix was either a poor, unwitting dupe or a conspirator; that the Sibley family, whose late patriarch prized the Boucher beyond price, had been irreparably injured by Bettridge's duplicity. I felt the bile rising in my throat as I read to the conclusion:

> Chicanery such as this raises a family's hopes only to dash them! According to one expert, it is likely, in fact, that the original painting remains in existence and is available for discreet purchase. Meanwhile, the forged painting has achieved its purpose, serving as a large magnet to draw, like small shards of metal, other French paintings out of private collections, the owners being wise to the fact that in the frenzy culti-vated by the auction house, collectors will eagerly pur-chase anything, if only to feel triumphant. To those who attend the auction, we say to you only: *Caveat emptor!*

Felix still stared broodingly out the window.

"It's terrible, Felix," I admitted. "But aside from a few bare facts, it's full of inaccuracies."

"You know that doesn't matter." He turned and made his way to the armchair, sinking his bulk into it. "There's just enough truth here to make it credible."

I ran my eyes over the article again, with a growing sense of puzzlement. "Felix, who would have told a newspaperman about Edwin cleaning the painting—or his murder?" I looked up from the page. "Surely not someone at Bettridge's. I imagine they want to keep the whole affair as quiet as possible."

"I've no idea. No doubt Bettridge will blame me for this, too," he said bitterly. "Disgruntled servant and all that."

"What do you mean, 'for this, too'?"

He hunched forward, his elbows resting on his knees, his hands clasped. His pale blue eyes met mine. "Edwin never signed the guaranty."

My breath caught in the back of my throat. "What?"

"The solicitor was supposed to have him sign it. He forgot." He sighed. "I only found out this afternoon."

The wave of relief on my account made me feel weak in the knees, and I groped for the chair beside me and sat down. "So the solicitor is liable for the loss, isn't he?"

He grimaced. "He *says* he gave the letter to me for Edwin's signature. He's lying to cover his mistake, but he's Bettridge's bloody nephew, so no. I'm to blame."

The newspaper slid to the floor. "Oh, Felix. That's not fair."

"I was asked to leave the premises today, at least temporarily. As I expected I would be. It was only a matter of time."

I groaned and retrieved the paper, folding it in my lap. "I'm so sorry."

He dropped his head into his hands, pressing their heels into his forehead. "The truth is, I understand it. They need a scapegoat if they're to keep any sort of respectability." The words came out muffled. "They can hardly have me stay on, with the auction in three days and still no sign of the painting." He looked up, a spark of hope in his eyes. "Unless the inspector has discovered any clue to its whereabouts."

"Nothing definite yet," I said reluctantly. "But he seems clever and capable. I'm sure something will happen soon." I hesitated.

"I should tell you, Felix. Edwin did make a will, leaving me the house."

His eyebrows rose faintly.

"It's with a solicitor. A friend of his—a vicar—told me at the funeral."

"Mr. Pascoe?" he asked.

I nodded and leaned forward. "There may be something for you."

He shrugged despondently. "It wouldn't be enough." He sighed. "But I'm glad for your sake."

I didn't know what to say, so I kept silent, and after a moment, he heaved himself out of the chair. The lamplight was gentle, but even so, he looked much older than his forty-five years. He fumbled with the buttons on his coat, then paused and reached into his inner pocket. "Here," he said and handed me a copy of the auction catalog. "I thought you might want this. It may be all you ever see of her."

I walked with him to the door and wished I had some reason for hope, or words of comfort.

THE *BEACON* IN hand, I went to Scotland Yard early enough the next morning that most of the desks were empty. However, Mr. Hallam was at his, and he looked up with astonishment. "I only just sent one of the boys with a message for you."

"I didn't receive it. I must have left home before he arrived." I held out the paper with its oversize headline. "Have you seen this? Felix brought it to me last night."

"No." He took it from me and began to read, his scowl deepening. Somewhere around the middle of the piece, he blew out his breath in disgust. His eyes still on the paper, he muttered, "Damn him."

I bristled. "It's hardly *his* fault! The solicitor—"

"Not Felix," he interrupted, looking up. "John Fishel. The one who wrote this inflammatory piece of trash."

I started, for out of keeping with his usual composure, Mr. Hallam's eyes sparked with anger, and he slapped the paper onto his desk. I took it up and looked in vain for the author's name. "How do you know?"

"I recognize the vitriol—and the cleverness of the wording."

"Cleverness," I echoed.

"Yes. He's not *saying* anything." He took the paper back from me and read: "'Who is to say the "cleaning" isn't being performed by Mr. Rowe merely to keep someone from discovering the painting is a forgery?' You see? It's merely a question, so he can't be accused of slander." He stood up and took his coat from the back of his chair. "Have you time to pay a visit?"

"To Mr. Fishel?" I asked warily. I had no desire to partake in a heated confrontation.

"Lord, no. To a friend of mine. A different sort of newspaperman."

"Oh . . . all right."

He held the door for me, and we crossed the yard and turned north onto Whitehall. It was early enough that we could walk side by side. There were no loud noises to prevent our speaking, only the boat whistles rising from the river and wheels rolling over the cobbles. Still, he was silent and preoccupied, and his scowl suggested his thoughts weren't pleasant. But as we encountered a rough patch of macadam, he took my elbow, and I felt a quiet flare of pleasure that he did so as if it were the most natural thing in the world.

"At this hour, we won't find a cab until we reach the Strand," he said.

"I don't mind the walk," I assured him.

We walked another half block, and at last he broke the silence: "There aren't many people I wholeheartedly despise, but Fishel is one of them." We veered away from two men carrying lumber, and he resumed: "I don't know how he does it, but he obtains police information that is supposed to be secret, and he causes no end of trouble for us. Last year, I was assigned to a case in which four people in Bethnal Green had been murdered. I knew who'd done it, and I had him under surveillance. I didn't move for two days. But Fishel saw me sitting there, surmised what I was doing, and published his guesses in his paper under the guise of providing a service, letting the public know about a potential danger." His stride had lengthened, so I had to take three steps to two of his. "Of course the man took the warning and stole a carriage to get away. He killed a driver to do it."

I gasped. "So his death is Fishel's fault, isn't it?"

"Not under existing jurisprudence."

"But—"

"Fishel knows the limits of the law precisely, and he knows how to sell papers. He's an unethical, soulless excuse for a man. The problem is he's shrewd and intuitive. He preys upon public fears of being exploited or cheated and includes just enough facts to make his story credible and whip people into a frenzy." By this point I was half a step behind, and he turned. "Sorry, I'm walking too fast." He gave a hard little laugh. "I'll admit I hate him, especially because he loves a chance to discredit the police. Last year he devoted a series of three articles to showing how our plainclothes could allow us to extort money from hardworking shopkeepers."

"Well, I can understand why you hate him." We paused at a corner to let a cart pass. "He sounds almost dangerous. Not in the same way as a criminal with a weapon, but—"

"He *is* dangerous," he interrupted, and we started across the street. "He's just a different sort of public menace. The situation is especially difficult because Chief Inspector Martin doesn't take Fishel seriously. He says it's merely words on paper, and it shouldn't affect our work." He shook his head. "But a witness who believes that we're out to swindle the public won't talk to any of us freely."

We rounded a corner, and I said, "What I don't understand is where Fishel obtained the accurate information he had, particularly about Edwin. He must have spoken to someone who had special knowledge about the painting itself. I can't imagine it's Mr. Pagett—he'd hate the idea of a scandal, and I gathered he didn't much like newspapers."

"No, they were lumped in with slaughterhouses," he agreed.

"Celia would never have spoken to him. So I think it must have been someone inside Bettridge's, don't you?"

"You're sure it wasn't Felix?" Mr. Hallam asked.

"I'm positive. He was distraught when I saw him last night." I sidestepped a boy shouldering a crate of potatoes. "Felix told me that Edwin had cleaned other paintings for Bettridge's in the past few months, so perhaps Fishel spoke to a different specialist."

"Or he talked to someone from the other auction houses—or

one of the galleries. They'd certainly have a motive to make Bettridge's look fraudulent, and Fishel could either bribe someone for information or blackmail him." Mr. Hallam had produced the illicit possibilities so easily it made me stare. Well, I reminded myself, this was the world he lived in.

"There's something else," I said. "Felix says Edwin never signed the guaranty."

His eyes widened, and he mulled this for a moment. "So they have no legal lien against your parents' house."

"No. And it's mine now, assuming the papers are in order."

He halted. "So Edwin made a will?"

"Yes. It's with a solicitor. Mr. Pascoe, the vicar who came to the funeral, told me so."

He wore a look of satisfaction. "Good." And we walked on.

"It doesn't help Felix, though," I said unhappily. "According to him, the solicitor claims he gave Felix the guaranty for Edwin to sign, but Felix insists he didn't. Officially, it's the solicitor's responsibility, but apparently he's a relation of Mr. Bettridge."

"Hm." He grimaced. "It's unlikely Bettridge's will have any legal recourse against Felix. They can't seize his property any more than they can seize yours—but I imagine they'll not keep him on."

"I'm afraid you're right," I replied. "He was put on leave yesterday."

"That's a shame," he said and directed me across the street. "Well, it may come right in the end."

"I hope so." We reached a long black line of available hansom cabs, and I reminded him, "You still haven't told me where we are going."

"To see my friend Tom Flynn. He writes for the *Falcon*, but he's not like Fishel. In fact, most of the newspapermen I know are good men and well informed. I've often received helpful information from one or another of them."

"Why are we seeing Mr. Flynn in particular?"

"He regularly covers Parliamentary matters. I thought he might provide some insight into the late Lord Sibley, give us an idea of anything that he and Stephen Jesper might have in common. Quicker than trying to find it ourselves."

"Oh," I said. "Do you think he might help Felix?"

"You mean by putting out the proper story?" He swung open the cab door and held it for me. "He might, at some point."

We climbed in, and when we were settled and Mr. Hallam had given the address, I asked, "Is it true, what Fishel wrote in the article about the police? Do people try to bribe you?"

"Yes."

I stared. "How often?"

"Plenty." He grimaced. "Despite what Fishel says, most of us don't take them." He shook his head. "You start down that path, and—well, it doesn't last long. No one trusts you once they know you can be bought. And it always comes to light, sooner or later."

THE *FALCON* WAS housed in a building not far from the Thames. As our cab drew up and stopped, I could smell the river, the rancid stink of the slaughterhouses, and the tang of the spice and tea warehouses coming up through the alleys. The three-story building was made of gray brick, with a sculpted figure of a malevolent-looking black iron bird up top and half a dozen wrought-iron lanterns, unlit at this hour of the morning, across the front.

Mr. Hallam pushed the door open and led me up several sets of worn wooden stairs. I held my skirts well out of the way and watched where I put my feet, for the treads were worn, and one was missing altogether. I heard the thumping of a machine—the press, I assumed—like a great heart, and, as we passed the first-floor landing, I heard a group of men talking and laughing behind a door. Mr. Hallam kept on, and when we reached the uppermost floor, he led me down a dim, dusty hallway until he paused at an open door.

The first thing I saw of Mr. Flynn was his head, mostly bald, with a shock of wavy brown hair in the middle.

"Tom."

He looked up and I noticed his eyes: bright, curious, and an unusual olive green. He was in his mid-thirties, with a round face, a small nose, and a pugnacious chin. He was missing the tip of his first finger on his left hand, and I couldn't help but wonder how he'd lost it. He stood up and extended his right to Mr. Hallam. "There you are. Hullo. Was expecting you earlier."

It came to me that we were late because I'd delayed us at the Yard. Mr. Hallam said, "Sorry. This is Miss Annabel Rowe. She's a painter at the Slade."

Mr. Flynn grunted and waved us into two wooden chairs. "What do you need? Don't mean to be abrupt. I've a deadline."

"How well did you know the late Lord Sibley?"

"Lord Sibley?" Mr. Flynn's eyebrows rose up into points. "What—"

Mr. Hallam gave him a look, and Mr. Flynn raised his hands in a quick gesture of surrender, then leaned back, tapping his fingertips in a staccato on the edge of the desk as he spoke. "I knew him well. He was one of the first who'd speak to me, back when I began reporting. What are you looking for?"

"What sort of man was he?"

"Imposing. Outspoken, even to rudeness, if he thought you were a fool." A swift shrug. "Persuasive, to be sure, and he was established enough that people tended to listen. Married, two children, a stepson and daughter; no hints of scandal that I know of. A respected art collector . . ." A pause, a quick glance at me, and I saw he'd made the connection to the Slade.

"What about his politics?" Mr. Hallam asked.

Mr. Flynn wrinkled his small nose so it swerved sideways and sniffed. "Oh." He cocked his head as he thought. "Mixed. In a way that was unusual for someone of his age and position. With his wealth and title, you'd think he'd be a staunch Tory—but he was sympathetic to several of Gladstone's measures."

"Which ones?"

"Smaller government, lower taxation, balanced budgets. Believed in the class system, the landed gentry, the House of Lords, and all that." He waved a hand back and forth. "But Sibley also believed in some class equality—which is why he helped draft a bill to eliminate purchased commissions in the army. That first one was shouted down by Cantrell and his lot, but the later one was ratified." He paused. "In the year before he died, he became downright strident about England's position with respect to mainland Europe. And that view was unpopular with plenty of MPs in his party, as well as the Whigs."

"Was he hawkish?" Mr. Hallam asked.

"No-o-o." Mr. Flynn sat back, rubbing his thumb absently over the stub of his truncated finger. "He was worried about the Germans. Even before they invaded France, Lord Sibley said we should be forging stronger economic and political alliances in Europe, particularly with France and Turkey and Russia, or we'd be edged out. And history's proved him partly right. The Franco-Prussian War changed everything." He scratched at the top of his head, which sent some of his hair up into a tuft. "Afterward, Lord Sibley got up on his legs in the House and called the Germans 'a coarse, violent, and acquisitive race.' Said von Bismarck would use the three years that he'd be occupying France to lay the groundwork for invading our shores. He even proposed helping France to pay back their war reparations faster, so they could send the Germans home." He snorted. "I was up in the balcony that day, and the place was in an uproar. Germany has its admirers, you know, and our new prime minister has praised von Bismarck."

"So Sibley had his enemies."

"Oh, yes." His gaze was speculative. "You're not thinking his death was—"

"No. Not that." Mr. Hallam hesitated and his voice dropped. "Keep this quiet for now, but there's some confusion about a painting he owned."

Mr. Flynn took a deep inhale and blew it out in a puff. "Are you talking about the piece Fishel wrote?"

I blinked in astonishment at his intuition, but Mr. Hallam nodded as if he'd expected the question and bent over his pocketbook to scribble a note. "What can you tell me about Mr. Pagett?"

The newspaperman shrugged again, but his expression registered disapproval. "He's an odd one. I've only met him once or twice but both times he blathered on about the importance of funding proper museums for posterity, and the need to fix entrance fees in order to discourage ignorant people who didn't appreciate art properly. He was bloody earnest—but at least in the circle where I was standing, it was met with dead air."

Mr. Hallam closed his pocketbook. "Thank you, Tom."

"Anything else?"

"No, that's all."

"Then good luck." A quick smile, and his head bent over his pages again.

We were several steps down the hall when a shout of "Wait!" drew us back to the threshold. Mr. Flynn was frowning. "Fishel said the painting was supposed to have burnt in the Pantechnicon. D'you need to talk to someone about the fire?"

Mr. Hallam nodded. "Do you know someone?"

"Hmph. You could talk to—God's sake, what was his bloody name? John? No, George—George Radermacher." He shoved his chair back, making the legs screech across the floor, and strode to a cabinet. I realized then that he was shorter than I had imagined—perhaps only an inch or two taller than I. There was a meaningful disparity between his size and his vitality.

"Managed the place," Mr. Flynn said. On a shelf were dozens of small pocketbooks and some loose papers, and he riffled briskly through them. "Wouldn't say a word to me at the time. But it's been over a year, so maybe he'll talk to you, considering why you want to know. Seemed a good bloke." He took out one pocketbook from a stack, thumbed through it, put it back, and plucked another, turned several pages, then scribbled an address on a slip of paper and handed it to Mr. Hallam.

I was in awe. All those notebooks and he knew where to find that piece of information on a single page.

Mr. Hallam held up the bit of paper. "Thanks for this. I owe you."

"Speaking of that." Mr. Flynn squinted up at him. "You don't happen to have an extra pair of tickets for the concert next month, do you? There's not a single one left for love or money."

Mr. Hallam grinned. "I'll ask Nell to leave them at the window for you."

He pulled at an imaginary cap. "Thanks. Much obliged." Then he dropped back into his chair and we left.

"Tickets for what?" I asked as we walked down those treacherous stairs.

"My sister is performing. It's one of Chopin's scherzos, and the original performer has canceled his appearance, so she's stepping in."

I stared. Even I knew that a Chopin scherzo wasn't a piece one merely stepped into. "Where is the performance?"

He glanced sideways. "At St. James's."

"Oh." It came out as the start of a laugh. He'd given me the impression that Nell was merely a student. I was beginning to recognize his tendency toward understatement.

"Will the auction begin on time, do you think?" he asked as he opened the front door for me. The cab was on the other side of the street, waiting for us.

"I assume so. They usually do," I replied. "Have you ever attended one before?"

"Not an art auction."

"I was just thinking that I should come." I had my arguments ready. "I've been to several at Bettridge's, and I know what to expect. Not only that, I would recognize most people who were at Edwin's funeral. I can help you find anyone who was at both."

He nodded. "I'd be grateful if you would."

I met his gaze. "I thought I'd have to convince you."

"Not at all. It's a public event." He held out his hand to help me into the cab. "You go ahead. I have to go down to the docks." I climbed inside and expected him to close the door, but he held it open as if there were more he wanted to say. "Tomorrow's Sunday," he said finally. "There's nothing to be done until after the auction. Why don't you get some rest?"

I nodded. "I will."

"Good." He looked relieved. "I'll see you on Monday."

I smiled. "I'll be there early."

"I will, too." He handed the driver a coin, and bid me goodbye. I watched curiously as he walked away and vanished into an alley that led down to the Thames.

Chapter 10

I took Mr. Hallam's advice to heart and spent most of Sunday morning idling at home, reading a novel—something I hadn't done in months. In the afternoon, I worked for a few hours at my easel, and then took a long walk through Hyde Park along the Serpentine. At last, I had a hearty tea, came home, and fell fast asleep, slumbering straight through until the sun was bright in the sky. For the first time in days, I woke feeling refreshed and ready for whatever the day would bring.

As I drew near Bettridge's, I saw a crowd clustering near the front door, and I felt a flutter of anticipation under my rib cage. At the threshold of the auction hall, I paused in wonder, for Bettridge's had transformed the room since I'd seen it two years ago. Where there had once been dim gas lighting, now six electrified crystal chandeliers blazed and sparkled overhead, so that any artwork hung on the walls or placed upon the stage would be easily visible. Instead of ordinary paint, the walls were covered in a fresh sage-green silk down to a rich mahogany wainscoting, and in lieu of plain wooden

seats and benches there stood perfect rows of chairs upholstered in black velvet, shirred at the corners. An elevated stage,
with gilt at the edge and a carved pillar on either side, held an
auctioneer's podium adorned with a shining brass *B*; and beside
it stood a wrought-iron easel, where the paintings would be
placed in sequence.

The room was filling rapidly with a steady stream of gap-
ers and gawkers and potential buyers, though only a fraction
of the attendees carried a catalog. The crowd was comprised
mostly of men, but some women—mostly wives, I assumed—
attended as well. There was an air of affluence about everyone
seated.

Along the side of the room stood half a dozen men and one
woman. The woman appeared vaguely ill at ease but resolute.
She held a pocketbook and a pen, and while several of the men
around her conducted quiet conversations, she scribbled notes.
They were writers for the newspapers, I realized. Well—why
could I not fall in with them? They had an excellent vantage
point. I drew out a small sketchbook I always carried and took
my place at the end of the line. It put me about halfway back in
the room, which suited me. I didn't want to be up front, where
people might take notice.

I stood with my left shoulder to the wall, my heart thudding
unevenly. As I watched for Mr. Hallam at the entrance, my
eyes also darted through the audience, down one row, up the
next, looking for anyone familiar. And with each individual I
examined, I couldn't help but wonder: *Was this who killed Edwin? Was he here to gloat over having undermined the auction?* I
searched diligently, but the only face I recognized was Felix's.
Poor Felix. I dared not approach him where he sat in the back

row. His face was so pale and stricken, I wondered if Mr. Bettridge had already cast him off permanently.

At last I saw Mr. Hallam enter at the back. He scanned the room, and his eyes seemed to brush over me. Anxiously, I wondered if I should raise my sketchbook to catch his attention. But he began sauntering in my direction, and I felt an easing inside my chest. I bent over and began a sketch of the stage on a blank page. To my relief, the journalists were speaking intently among themselves, so my conversation with Mr. Hallam would likely go unnoticed. The grandfather clock on the opposite wall showed there were only ten minutes until the auction would begin.

Mr. Hallam took his place close behind me. I cast a quick glance upward. His gaze was fixed upon the gathering crowd, and his lips barely moved. "Hullo."

Taking my cue from him, I surveyed the audience and murmured, "There are a good many people here. Just as Felix said."

"Yes." His voice was pleasant. "Don't show any surprise at my question, all right? But by chance did you visit your brother's rooms last night?"

I bent my head over my sketch again. "No. Why?"

"They were searched again."

It took all my self-possession to keep my head down. "How? I thought they were being watched."

"We kept the constable there until yesterday afternoon. He returned the key to the landlady around half past four."

"How did they get in?"

"The doorjamb was splintered by the lock."

I felt a sharp spike of anger at the thought of the thief rummaging through Edwin's belongings again. But what was he looking for this time?

"Was anything taken?" I asked.

"Doesn't appear so. We might not even have known someone broke in except that about an hour after the constable left, the landlady heard footsteps on the stairs, and when she went to check Edwin's room, she saw the broken wood. She sent a message to the Yard right away." He slipped a key into my hand. "A copy for you. She asked the constable when you would be fetching Edwin's things. Apparently the rent is paid up for several more weeks, so you have time."

I'd planned to sort through Edwin's belongings at some point, of course, but I'd been putting it off. Perhaps Mr. Hallam sensed my reluctance, for he said in an undertone, "I understand that's not going to be easy. If you like, I can help you. And there is a storeroom at the Yard with some space you can use temporarily, though I'm not sure you'd want to leave any of his paintings in it for long. It's damp."

I felt his kindness like warmth down to my bones. "Thank you," I said gratefully and slid the key into my pocket. "I will want a few of Edwin's things, of course, for sentimental reasons." A pause. "But why would the thief come back? It's not as if any of the other paintings were of any particular value."

"My thought is it might not have been the same person."

My breath caught in my throat, and I stared up at him. "You mean, someone may have thought the Boucher was still there?"

He raised an eyebrow and shrugged. "Maybe."

"For goodness' sake," I whispered.

"I know." His eyes left mine to scan the room again, and I

folded my sketchbook and leaned against the wall. We might have been strangers, uttering empty pleasantries.

"And just so you know," he added, "Lord Sibley did travel to France in January, with the LeMarcs and without his valet. His son sent his journals over with a manservant, first thing this morning."

"What were the dates?"

"Lord Sibley landed in Calais on the ninth of January. His ship home departed from the port of Ostend on the twenty-second of March."

"Belgium?" I said in surprise.

All at once there was a general rustle from the crowd, and like everyone else, we turned our attention to the front of the room. A slender, elegantly dressed man approximately thirty years of age emerged from behind a curtain and crossed the stage. This was Mr. Jonas Bettridge, son of the man who'd started the house. He stood with his two hands resting deliberately on the auctioneer's podium and waited for the room to settle. Gradually the members of the audience dropped into their seats and quieted. An air of expectancy and tension pervaded the room, and I felt my throat constrict as I tried to swallow.

When would he announce that the Boucher would not be sold that day? From other auctions I'd attended, I knew paintings could be withdrawn or added at the last minute, and usually an announcement was made at the beginning of the sale. But if Bettridge made the announcement about the Boucher now, would he lose a good part of his audience before the sale even began?

From where I stood at the side of the room, I could observe the faces, and here and there I saw watchfulness or uncertainty.

The *Beacon* wasn't an esteemed paper. Probably most of the people in this room had never read an issue. Still, Fishel's article likely had been seen by some, and in the art world, word circulated rapidly. Perhaps Mr. Bettridge had anticipated this, for he wore an expression of decisiveness and authority.

"Good afternoon, ladies and gentlemen," he began, his voice deep and dignified and resonant, essential for an auctioneer. "Welcome to this auction of important French paintings. We appreciate your attendance and your patience and apologize for the delay. We have an important announcement before we begin. We regret to inform you the painting of Madame de Pompadour by François Boucher will not be offered at this time."

Gasps and murmurs, and then one angry voice was followed by others:

"I knew it!"

"You've lured us here under false pretenses!"

"This is a scandal!"

"This would never happen at Christie's!"

"What do you think you're playing at?"

"Blackguards!"

The cries crested to a roar. Several men were waving the catalog—or their fists—and dozens of people had risen from their chairs and begun to make their way to the end of the rows to depart.

Mr. Bettridge put up his hands and raised his own voice to be heard above the furor.

"However," he said loudly. "We are pleased to offer a heretofore privately held portrait by Jacques-Louis David."

At the artist's name, there was a break in the shouting followed by noises of disbelief. People's eyebrows drew down and their mouths screwed up into knots of skepticism and derision. But a name such as David was too much of a lure to resist. As Mr. Bettridge intended, those who had started toward the door made their way back to their seats, where they perched like skittish birds ready to fly at the first sign of trickery.

Bettridge turned to his left and raised his arm slowly, a theatrical gesture that might have suggested the entrance of a deus ex machina in a Greek play. Two assistants carried out a large painting in a heavy gilt frame and placed it precisely on the easel near the front of the stage.

I felt a wave of admiration for Bettridge, who had pulled an ace out of his sleeve. Where on earth had he found a painting of this quality at the last minute? And he had been shrewd in his selection of replacement—for it was a portrait of a woman, and those who liked Boucher's painting might well like this one, which featured a woman younger than Madame but no less lovely and engaging. Like Madame she met the gaze of the viewer straight on, as if accustomed to being an object of admiration, and her hand, gently cupping her cheek, suggested both ease and sophistication. The smile hovering at her mouth was less worldly than Madame's, but it was full of delight and charm. Even from where I stood, it was clear the eyes were painted brilliantly, and the soft ringlets of hair and the folds of her rose-colored dress were exquisite.

The room went silent as people took in the masterpiece before them.

Mr. Bettridge gave a gentle cough and began to speak, sure of their attention now. "This is a portrait of the young Henriette, sister of the painter Eugène Delacroix. She was later known as Madame de Verninac and was David's subject on more than one occasion, but this is the first portrait. Signed and dated 1796 by the artist in the lower left corner as usual, the portrait is oil on canvas and measures approximately sixty by forty-four inches." A pause. "This painting has been held privately for eighty-five years and has not been on public view anywhere until today. It would be an extraordinary addition to any collection." His lips pressed into a pained smile. "Note the loveliness of the hands, the delicacy of the features."

His voice broke over the last words, and although his face was resolutely expressionless, I thought I understood. This David was a portrait from his private collection. He had forfeited it to save the reputation of the auction house. Publicly held or not, it bore his name.

I cast a glance at Felix and saw his thoughts were probably close to mine. He looked positively ill, his complexion gone gray.

Mr. Hallam nudged me, looked a question, and bent his head close so I might answer.

"Probably even more desirable than the Boucher," I murmured. "He's offering it first to keep the crowd."

He nodded, and his eyes narrowed as he scanned the room again.

I turned to look. Expressions ran the gamut now: awe, excitement, resentment, greed, delight, shock, disgust, and skepticism.

Mr. Bettridge withdrew a tidy sheaf of papers from his breast pocket and held it aloft. "We have proof of the provenance here, and as a gesture of good faith, and to mitigate any inconvenience that might ensue from its late introduction into our sale, Bettridge's will pay for its installation at any location here in London or within reasonable reach of the city."

With his words, the prevailing emotion in the room shifted toward excitement verging on delirium, and I marveled at how swiftly it had occurred.

As I scanned the room, my eye was caught by a man standing just inside the entrance. He wore his hat pulled low enough that I could only see his chin, but there was something familiar about him that caught my attention. He began to make his way in our direction, and at last he came close enough that I could see who it was.

Mr. Pagett.

He positioned himself beside me and eyed us warily. "Inspector Hallam, Miss Rowe."

Mr. Hallam stiffened at hearing his title, but no one nearby seemed to have overheard; everyone's attention was focused on the painting at the front of the room.

Both Mr. Hallam and I kept our eyes on the auctioneer. Mr. Pagett leaned close and hissed, "Was it you who leaked the information to the *Beacon*?"

I gasped and glanced out of the corner of my eye. Mr. Hallam's jaw was clenched, and his words came through gritted teeth: "Of course not. That paper has derailed more police investigations than I can count."

"Very well." He seemed to accept that, and I let my breath out in relief.

Mr. Bettridge had begun the standard announcement of the auction procedures, and Mr. Pagett leaned in again. "I was wondering how Bettridge might handle the withdrawal of the Boucher. This was a clever solution, although I've no doubt it's killing him."

I turned my head, so I could ask softly, "It's from his private collection?"

He made a sound of acquiescence. "There are people who'd pay dearly for it, but they aren't here. He won't get what it's worth. I wonder what he'll ask to start."

If Mr. Bettridge hated having to sell the David, he wasn't going to let it go for a modest price.

The room was full of the noises of people shifting about, turning the pages of the program, and murmuring excitedly. Mr. Pagett added in an undertone: "I assume you are talking with Mrs. Jesper."

My breath rasped against the back of my throat, and after a moment I glanced at Mr. Hallam, who seemed to have turned to stone.

"She needs to explain how that painting came into her possession," Mr. Pagett growled. "If you do not ask her, I will."

"Do not jeopardize this investigation." Mr. Hallam spoke quietly but his eyes were intent. "I told you from the first, we don't want to tip our hand. You need to be patient."

"I will. But I'm not letting this go." And with that he left us.

"Damn everything," Mr. Hallam muttered. "How did he learn her name?"

"You think he spoke with Fishel?"

"No. Fishel would have included her name in the article if he knew it." He shook his head, and his eyes flicked around the room. "He must know someone here at Bettridge's."

A faint cough came from Mr. Bettridge at the podium. He surveyed the room coolly. "We open the bidding at two thousand pounds."

The entire room cried out at his audacity.

It would have been a high opening bid for a painting offered at Christie's. Here, it was outrageous. I turned to look at the audience, half expecting them to laugh in derision or to start for the exit in disgust.

But three hands shot up in the air.

And then a fourth: Mr. Pagett's.

The bidding proceeded rapidly—almost dizzyingly—and I am not sure I breathed normally as the price rose. At last the auctioneer's hammer rang out:

"Sold! To Sir Joshua Lorry, for nine thousand five hundred pounds!"

A shout broke out, followed by applause. The room was buzzing with shock, excitement, giddiness—

The desire to buy raced through it like a runaway train.

Mr. Bettridge wisely wasted no time in having the next painting brought out.

"Our next lot is a fine *tableau de mode* by Jean François de Troy, dated 1732. It is signed on the verso . . ."

MR. HALLAM AND I waited through the auction's conclusion but witnessed nothing that roused our suspicion or curiosity. Every one of the paintings sold, with only a small painting by Lemoyne bringing less than its estimate. There was a second fervent bidding war, over a lovely Watteau, that ended with a man and a woman glaring at each other across the room, the man putting up his hand to raise the price by five hundred pounds at one go. The room gasped in amazement, and the lady gathered her umbrella and stalked out of the room, swinging it fiercely fore and aft. Mr. Hallam raised his eyebrow at me, and I shrugged. At last the sale ended, the room emptied, and finally we left Bettridge's and walked out to the street.

"I didn't notice anything or anyone out of the ordinary," he said. "What did you think?"

"The prices were higher than I'd have thought."

"Well, feelings seemed to be running high, too."

I made a sound of agreement. "Did you see Mr. Pagett's face when he lost the David?"

He nodded.

"I feel as though it's only going to make him more upset about the Boucher," I said. "What are you going to do about Mrs. Jesper? You can't let Mr. Pagett talk to her."

He drew me over to the side, under a shop awning. The edge rippled above us in the stiff breeze. "No. And in fact I think you should speak with her. Alone. Today. Now, in fact."

I stared. "What? Why?" I felt uneasy, as though I were being thrust into a room where I didn't belong.

"Well, first off, as Severington said, she doesn't care for policemen. She was much warmer toward you when we met."

"But—"

"And remember, she isn't a suspect," he interrupted. "As such, you can converse with her as a—a friend might. But I believe there is a connection between her husband and the late Lord Sibley that may shed light on why that painting was hidden in her house. It may have nothing to do with Edwin's death—but it may have something to do with Mr. Pagett, and I'm feeling uneasy about him. He's just so terribly invested in these paintings."

I nodded. "All right. But if I'm going to ask her questions,

I'd like to tell her that it was Edwin who was cleaning the Boucher."

He was silent for a moment, considering.

"What harm would it do?" I pleaded. "She's bound to discover it sooner or later. Rowe isn't such a common name, and given the article in the *Beacon*, the report will soon be in other papers, if it isn't already. Shouldn't I tell her, in case she hasn't seen it? And answer questions, if she has them?"

There was a glint of approval in his eyes. "I think you're right."

I felt a sense of relief, and in return for his concession, I asked, "Is there anything in particular you'd like me to say to her?"

He shook his head. "Use your judgment. But see if you can learn more about Mr. Jesper—his background, his education, his family. Any political activity, or his leanings or opinions on Europe. You heard what Tom said about Lord Sibley." He smiled briefly. "I imagine that you'll be able to discern for yourself the direction the conversation should go, once you're there. Just inquire, as you would of a friend. Of course, to quote you, what's missing might be significant, so pay attention to any point where Mrs. Jesper veers away from answering. And keep in mind the connection might have something to do with Mrs. Jesper herself, so perhaps find out what you can about her family."

"And what will you be doing?" It came out rather sharply.

He gave me a look. "Something I need to do without you." But his tone was good-natured, and I was relieved to see a glint of humor in his eye.

We walked on in silence for several blocks, for the pavement was crowded, and most people were moving in the opposite direction.

Abruptly he halted, and his head swiveled. Something had caught his eye and fixed his attention. I craned my neck to see between heads and hats, but I saw only some ordinary stores: a milliner, a haberdasher, a tobacconist.

"Is something the matter?" I asked.

"No." We stood together, but his gaze was still turned away, observing the retreating backs of the pedestrians.

"What did you see?" I asked urgently. When he didn't reply, I stepped around him so I could look up into his face.

He wore an expression of stunned disbelief. But even as I watched his face altered, and after a moment, he shook his head pragmatically. "A woman who looked like my mother."

Something inside my chest softened. "I remember how that felt. After Mother died, I'd see someone out of the corner of my eye and think it was her, before I remembered."

"My mother isn't dead."

I stared. "What? I thought you said—"

"I said I lost her," he interrupted. Then he corrected himself: "*We* lost her. She left us."

"Why? Where did she go?" My mind jumped to the possible reasons a woman would leave her family—

"To Paris," he replied. "She had a brain disease that caused her to slide between mania and melancholy. During one of her episodes, she decided her temperament and her musical talent were too elevated for London." He shrugged. "So she sold her mother's silver and bought a ticket for passage on a boat. She was gone two days later."

I winced, imagining such a betrayal.

"She never came back, and we never heard from her." He paused, his eyes averted. "My sister wasn't even a year old."

And you were still very young, I thought with a pang.

"Did you look for her?" I asked.

He nodded. "After my father died, I went through his desk and found an old clipping from a Paris newspaper. It showed my mother performing in a concert hall under her mother's name. I went to find her, but it had been years, and there was no trace of her. So she might still be alive." His eyebrows rose and fell. "Or not."

"Oh, Matthew. I'm sorry." His given name had slipped out on the wave of sympathy I felt. "That sort of uncertainty, it's . . ." I didn't have words for it, but I could imagine how each time he saw a woman who resembled his mother, the pain would return, cutting him anew. As my mother said once, a knife lying inside a dark drawer stays sharp.

"I probably should have given up finding her by now, but I don't know if I ever really can." He gave a small, bleak smile. "Obviously, I did to some extent. I didn't stay in France. But disappearing is a rotten thing to do to people who love you."

I swallowed hard. "I know."

A gust of damp wind flapped the collar of both our coats, and he glanced up at the sky. "It looks like rain." He touched my arm, and we walked in silence to the corner, where he gestured in the direction opposite from Mrs. Jesper's. "I've something to do this way. I'll leave you here."

"All right."

He drew a pair of gloves out of his pocket and put them

on. "Mrs. Jesper needs an ally, Annabel, much more than she needs a policeman. You may not realize how well suited you are for that, but your sincerity and compassion will help her."

I'd been surprised at his taking me into his confidence. Now I was surprised again. I felt my cheeks warm, but I managed to reply calmly, "I'll do my best."

And we parted, each of us heading our own way.

Chapter 11

The Jesper home was less than a half hour's walk from the auction house, but it was long enough for me to turn over Matthew's words in my head, and to consider the situation from Mrs. Jesper's point of view.

I climbed the steps and rang the bell. Betsy the maid opened the door and frowned.

"Please, may I come in?" I asked. "I'm not here to distress her, I promise."

She pursed her lips, her mistrust of me deep enough to form dimples in the soft areas at the sides of her mouth. But I couldn't take offense. I liked her all the better for being loyal. She drew back from the door and motioned me in. "I'll see if she's at home," she said and left me standing in the foyer. When she returned, her expression still held disapproval, but she said, "She'll see you, but she hasn't much time."

I was shown to the parlor, where Felix, the inspector, and I had met Mrs. Jesper the first time. She was already present, standing behind the couch when I entered, and her face was composed but her spine belied her tension. She was braced for a blow, and my heart went out to her.

"Good afternoon, Miss Rowe."

"Thank you for seeing me," I said.

"Where is your inspector?" she asked, her voice measured.

"He . . . well, we attended the auction, and I just left him," I admitted honestly. "He said he had something he needed to do alone."

Her delicate brows lifted.

Impulsively, I dared to speak part of the truth: "He also suggested you could use an ally, more than you need a policeman."

Her eyes dropped to her hands where they rested on the back of the couch, and when she looked up, her flush suggested a mix of rue and embarrassment. "So you have been coerced into taking the role."

"Not coerced," I said and stepped forward. "Not at all. The other day when we left, I felt nothing but sympathy—and a deep regret for the shock we'd given you."

Her expression softened at my words. She came around the front of the couch, then gestured toward a chair close by, and we sat. A ray of afternoon sun streamed in from the window behind me, and her silver-and-jet earrings caught the light. Her hazel eyes were fixed on me, and I began, "Two interesting things happened at the auction. May I tell you?"

"Of course."

"The first is that Mr. Pagett, Lord Sibley's stepson, has somehow discovered your name."

She frowned slightly. "Is that a problem?"

"No. But he"—I fumbled—"he wants to know how you came by the painting."

She grimaced. "Well, that's understandable. So do I. What is the second thing?"

"Mr. Bettridge announced at the start that the Boucher had been withdrawn. But he also announced that a rare David portrait from a private collection would be offered in its place."

Her head tipped slightly as she considered this. "It's a reasonable substitution."

"Yes, most of the audience seemed placated—and intrigued. He may have managed to save his house's reputation, even if some people wonder if it was just a sleight of hand."

"I expect so." She plucked absently at her skirt. "I wonder where he found such a work so quickly."

"Mr. Pagett suggested it might be from his private collection."

"Mm. Perhaps."

I was silent for a moment, considering where to begin, but before I could speak, she said abruptly, "Do you know, the day you were here, I took at face value your friendship with Felix, and your being a painter. I was so stunned by what Felix told me that it was only later I wondered where precisely you figured in all this." Her wide eyes met mine intently, as if she longed to penetrate to the truth of the matter. "Now here you are again, this time alone. I assume Felix shared why I'm not at ease with policemen, and no doubt your inspector sent you because he has further questions for me. But before I say anything else, I'd like you to clarify your interest in my affairs."

Her tone was direct but reasonable, and I felt a wave of relief at the civility of her words. "Mrs. Jesper, I am happy to do that. In fact, it's partly why I'm here. I asked Mr. Hallam if I might confide in you, and he agreed."

Her chest rose and fell, and the tension in her frame eased.

"The truth is," I said, "my brother, Edwin, was the person commissioned to clean the painting for the auction. On Tuesday last, I went to his room to see him. But I found the inspector there because Edwin"—my breath caught—"had been murdered."

Her eyes widened, and her lips formed into a small O.

"It wasn't until later that night, when Felix came to see me and told me about the Boucher, that we began to guess why. I'd spent some time in Edwin's room that day, searching through his things with the inspector, and I knew there was no portrait of Madame de Pompadour."

"Oh dear God." Her eyes closed for a moment, and when they opened, they were full of sorrow and growing horror. "So he was killed for that painting?"

"Well, the room was in shambles, and some frames were broken and empty, so it seems likely. The inspector believes Edwin may have"—I swallowed down the tightness in my throat, so I could continue—"interrupted the thief in his search."

A faint groan, and her hands came up to cover her face for a moment before they dropped back into her lap. "Your brother should have just let him leave with it. No painting is worth a man's life."

"Honestly, I think Edwin would have let him go, given the choice. But if the thief was seen, then he . . ."

"Of course. He was caught." She gave a ragged sigh. "I had no idea. I'm so very sorry for your loss—and here I was feeling indignant and suspicious of your motives in coming here. I'm sorry."

"Please don't be," I said, leaning forward. "There is no

possibility that you could have intuited any of this. And I suppose I could have told you when we met, but it seemed hearing about the painting's disappearance was quite enough of a shock for one afternoon."

She gave a wan smile. "It *was*." She looked down at the hands clasped in her lap, and when she raised her chin, there were pink spots in her cheeks. "It was painful and terribly mortifying. I felt like such a fool. Not even knowing the painting wasn't mine when I tried to sell it. And having no idea when or how Stephen had brought it here . . . You must have thought me oblivious and—and benighted and *idiotic*, for goodness' sake."

"Mrs. Jesper—"

"Call me Celia, please." A wince. "We're speaking rather candidly, don't you think, not to be calling each other by our Christian names?"

"Annabel, then."

She nodded.

I spoke earnestly. "We didn't think any of those things. I—well, I can't speak for anyone else, but I sensed you would never dream of selling what didn't rightfully belong to you. You had the papers, after all. And of course I understand your distress at discovering that the painting belonged to a man you thought your husband barely knew."

Her face went still.

I shifted in my chair. "Forgive me, but I sense what pained you most is the idea of him keeping a secret from you. And I can imagine how upsetting that would be. But perhaps if your husband kept something concealed, it was because the secret belonged to Lord Sibley and not to him."

"I could understand if that were the case." Her brow furrowed, and she sighed. "You can't imagine how I've tortured myself since your visit—wondering if everything I knew about my husband was in error. Oh, I know we only ever discern people's characters in part. Even our most intimate friends aren't transparent to us. But I spent hours that night staring at his photograph, wondering if I'd misread his countenance all along . . . or if he'd changed, somehow."

Her words made a lump rise in my throat. "I know."

She might have dismissed my reply as mere politeness, but instead she caught me up. "You do?"

I nodded. "My brother was . . . erratic. I often wondered what to expect from him."

Her eyebrows rose and she leaned forward. "That's what's so difficult! Five days ago, I thought I knew Stephen as fully as it is possible to know anyone! I'd have sworn he had no secrets from me. But now? I seem to be uncovering them at every turn."

"Oh?"

She made a restless movement, as if she couldn't contain her inner discomfort. "After you left, I dug out his journals and read them. I hadn't done so before because—well, they're just daily records, really, nothing personal. Mostly a log of his travels and expenses. But I discovered that about six months after we were married, he . . ." The flush returned to her cheeks. "He began to travel regularly to Birmingham. Trips he never told me about."

I understood the reason for her embarrassment. "Did he perhaps have shipping concerns there?"

"I doubt it. The company's ships are all based in Liverpool and here in London."

I couldn't think of a word to say.

"I know what it looks like," she burst out. "And my heart tells me he was incapable of being unfaithful. But is that merely what I want to believe?" Her expression was strained. "It doesn't seem at all like him; he was so kind and affectionate, for our whole marriage, and he shared his concerns with me, his feelings about . . . oh, everything." She turned up her right palm. "But perhaps it was merely to mitigate his guilt. I feel completely . . ." Her voice faded, and she shook her head.

"How long did the visits go on?"

"They were frequent for about six months, and then they tapered off. The last one was fourteen months after they started." Tears came to her eyes, and she blinked rapidly to keep them at bay. After a moment, she rose and went to a long table piled with books and other items. She retrieved a silver picture frame, returned to her seat, and silently handed it to me.

The image looked like one of Mr. Hughes's renowned society photographs, but the man who looked out from the frame had nothing of the stiff dandy or the portly gentleman about him. While he wasn't strictly handsome—his hairline was receding and his nose was slightly snubbed—his eyes were clear and intelligent, and the lines around his mouth suggested a fine sense of humor.

"He has an attractive face," I said truthfully.

"Yes." She held the frame between her two hands, her eyes fixed on it with such love and longing that I had to look away.

At last she set the photograph on the table in front of us, at an angle where we could both see it, and her voice was calm again when she asked, "Did Felix tell you much about him, and our marriage?"

I shook my head.

"I was already twenty-six when Stephen and I met, six years ago. He was thirty-four. We were married in April of the following year." Pensively she touched her fingertips to her mouth. "I had been engaged before then, to a man who . . . you see, I lost my mother very young, and then my father passed away. So at first Leonard's protectiveness made me feel cared for. But later, it felt—" She grimaced. "Well, it doesn't matter. The point is, he broke the engagement, although he represented to the world that *I* had broken it off. He said he offered that story to protect me from the humiliation. But I'd have rather he told the truth. I felt as though it made me look changeful and inconstant."

"I understand."

"When I met Stephen, he was kind, but he didn't make me feel like a child who needed to be coddled and protected from the world. He'd say things under his breath to make me laugh." Her expression softened, and she smiled so a deep dimple formed in her cheek. "One of the things I liked about him was he was forthright and—and open."

"Was he very occupied with his business?" I ventured.

She shifted her position to perch her elbow on the arm of the couch and leaned her head on her hand. "Yes, I'd say he was, but only when he was working. Oh, he spoke with me sometimes about the shipping business, and there were days when I could tell there were difficulties and problems, but it didn't preoccupy him." Her smile grew wistful. "When he came home, he said he wanted to enjoy his dinner in peace and hear about my day. And in the evenings, he wanted to sit by the fire with me and play chess or have me read aloud."

"You play chess?" I asked.

She nodded. "My father taught me. He was a barrister—a brilliant one—so he was terribly in demand and away a good deal. But sometimes he'd be home in the evening, and he'd ask for a game to soothe his nerves. He didn't have any sons, just daughters, and my sister Gwendolyn didn't like the game. She'd invent stories about the pieces instead of playing with them."

"Stories?"

A small laugh escaped. "About how the bishop was secretly in love with the queen, who'd tried to murder her husband, the king. She always liked to tell stories, while I preferred to read them. As a child, I spent so much time alone that I came to think of other people's stories as gifts."

"Does your sister live here in London?"

"Yes, though she's been in Edinburgh the last few weeks. She writes novels." One eyebrow rose, and she gave a wry smile.

I smiled with her. "That sounds fitting."

Her smile faded, and her fingers absently pleated the fabric of her skirt. "Why do *you* think the Boucher was here? Do you think it was something connected with Stephen's business?"

"I don't know," I admitted. "Mr. Hallam believes the painting isn't the only connection between Lord Sibley and your husband. Do you have any idea what another connection might be? A club, or a business dealing, or even a mutual friend?"

"Believe me," she said, "I've been turning the possibilities over in my mind since your last visit, and I'm at a loss. We didn't meet socially, and Stephen never mentioned him that I can remember. Even the painting . . ." She shook her head. "If Lord Sibley purchased that painting, he was a serious collector. Stephen wasn't. So even the painting isn't the connection it might be."

"I see what you mean." I took a breath. "I want to share some things that we—Mr. Hallam and I—have discovered, in the hopes that maybe they'll make more sense to you, or perhaps you can add to them." With that, I plunged in, telling her the most important pieces of information the inspector and I had learned thus far.

As I concluded she sat motionless for a long minute. At last, she stood and went to the nearby window. Her slender figure was silhouetted against the light. Her fingertips touched the sill; I saw they were trembling.

"Are you all right?" I asked.

She turned. "Aren't you frightened by all of this?"

"Frightened?" I echoed.

"Don't you realize the most obvious connection between Lord Sibley and Stephen—not to mention your brother?" Her eyes were blazing dark in her pale face. "They've all died." My expression must have revealed my thoughts for she waved impatiently. "I don't believe the painting is cursed or any such nonsense. But it makes me think whatever the connection was between Lord Sibley and my husband—and perhaps your brother as well—it led to their deaths. Don't you wonder the same?"

"Well, not really," I said honestly. "Edwin's death was so long after the others'. Lord Sibley's death was from the influenza, and your husband's death was an accident."

"Felix told you?"

"About the carriage? Yes."

"But . . . what if it wasn't an accident?" Her voice was tight with tension. "Even at the time, I wondered. Stephen was always scrupulous about keeping our carriages in good repair and the horses well cared for."

"I see." I felt a prickling along the back of my neck and down my arms, and my voice was faint: "Felix didn't give me the particulars."

"We were together in our open trap, and Stephen was driving." She began to pace back and forth, her hands fidgeting at her waist. "It was an unusually mild day for the end of February, after a spell of terrible cold. We were on Trenton Street—do you know it?"

I shook my head.

"It slopes downhill, and we were rolling forward, when suddenly I felt an odd jolt—more than usual on cobblestones— followed by a loud noise, and our poor horse spooked and reared." She halted, staring into the middle distance, as if she were watching the scene in the street all over again. Her voice had become curiously monotone. "The trap continued to roll forward, but it lurched, as if it had gone over a curb, and it was clear the axle was damaged. Stephen all but threw me out of the carriage before it picked up more speed. But he stayed in it." There was a catch in her voice. "I know what he was doing. He was trying to keep from hitting anyone else. By the time I'd recovered myself and turned to watch, Stephen had lost control of the horse, and the trap was careening toward a building at the corner. He was thrown from his seat—" She halted mid-step. "And then the trap flipped and came down on top of him."

She had put a vivid picture into my mind.

"You saw it?" I asked.

She shook her head. "The carriage blocked my view. My leg was broken"—she tapped her leg—"that's why I have this limp now. I couldn't get up. I couldn't go to him." The pain of her helplessness was etched starkly on her face. "The doctor said the weight of the trap broke his ribs, making them sharp as knives inside his chest. They punctured his left lung, and it filled with blood." She blinked several times, as if in disbelief. "He drowned in it, you see, right there in a street that was dry as a bone, and I couldn't go to him."

"I'm so sorry," I said gently. "Your husband sounds wonderfully brave and selfless."

"So far as I've known him, he was both of those things. That's partly why I don't think his trips to Birmingham were for—for what they might have been." She gave a sad smile. "He truly believed that a good person participates in the events of the world—intervenes when needed, steps in rather than turning away, speaks the truth even when it is unpopular. It's something I always admired about him." She looked faintly ashamed. "I tend to hold myself back."

You and I are alike in that, I thought.

"He was always curious about people, especially if they came from other parts of the world." She shrugged. "It's not surprising, I suppose, given all the traveling as a child."

"He didn't grow up here in London?"

"Well, nominally. But he spent most of the year with his father on the ships. He took his books with him and had a tutor sometimes. He read voraciously." Her eyes wandered to the shelves in this room, all of which were empty. "He always knew he'd join his father's company, but he wanted to go to university first."

"I saw the books in the library when we were here last time. Is that where he learned his languages, traveling?"

She came back to the couch and sat. "He had a good ear for them. The crewmen all spoke different languages, of course—German, Dutch, French, Spanish, Portuguese, even Arabic—and when they'd arrive in port, they'd sometimes spend days or even weeks on land. Stephen would linger about the warehouses or shipyards or shops, just listening until he picked up a few phrases. He was never shy about talking to strangers." Her expression betrayed admiration and pride. "He was open to new things—new languages, new people, new ideas. It was Stephen who convinced his partners to change over to tramper steamers."

"Tramper steamers?"

"Yes. The company now belongs to the Baltic Exchange, so their ships bring any goods to any port, at any time, rather than working on a set schedule. As a result, the company ships fewer consumable goods and more machinery and tools, steelwork for bridges and pipes, and such. There is a large demand in Europe now for these things, and while timing is more critical, the profits are better." She paused. "Was the Sibley family connected in any way with shipping or the building of bridges and roads—or perhaps some other industry with goods that require shipping?"

"Not that anyone's mentioned. I assume most of their wealth comes from the funds and rents, in the way of most of the landed class." I paused. "What about the LeMarc family? The ones who owned the painting originally. Did your husband know them?"

"I don't recall the name." She stood and paced again, her brow creased in concentration. "I'm trying to assemble all of this in my head, and I can't help but wonder at the coincidences. The painting could only have been in the Pantechnicon for a matter of—what—six or eight weeks, at most? And during those few weeks, the man who owns the painting departs for France; the Pantechnicon goes up in flames, after having stood perfectly intact for forty years; the man who was holding the painting for the owner dies; and then the owner dies. Doesn't it seem peculiar?"

I acknowledged it did.

"So did someone remove the painting for Lord Sibley," she continued, "knowing there would be a fire? If someone did, was it Stephen? And if not, why give it to Stephen to hold? The questions keep accumulating."

"I know," I agreed. "And why is this painting so important? There were others in the Sibleys' storage room that were even more valuable, including a Rembrandt, which would probably be valued at nearly twice the amount. Why wouldn't a thief take that one instead?"

Our silent musing was interrupted by the door opening. Betsy entered carrying a tray of tea things tinkling against each other. I glanced up at the clock. "I'm sorry. I didn't realize it was so late."

"I brought enough for two, mum," Betsy said to her mistress as she set the tray on the table.

"Thank you, Betsy." Celia sat down to pour.

Betsy left, and I took a sip of the tea; it was hot and strong and tasted vaguely of lavender. "Would you call yourself a serious collector, like the Sibleys?"

A diffident look. "Not really. I haven't the money they do, for one thing. But it is my special interest, and my family has collected for years." She glanced at the portrait above the fireplace.

"That's a Gainsborough, isn't it?"

"Yes. Of my father." She smiled ruefully. "It would probably fetch a good amount at auction, but of course I won't part with it at any price. We have a fine Watteau and a good Renoir, and a few Dutch Masters as well. I'd show them to you, but they've already been packed in crates, I'm afraid."

"I saw the Cézanne in the hallway."

Her eyebrows rose. "You're familiar with his work?"

"Not really. I saw the signature." I smiled. "I did view some prints at school, and I recall what the papers said about him."

"Stephen bought that for me last year, not long before he died."

It was the first opening I had to voice what had been in the back of my mind since my first visit. "It's very different from the Boucher," I said tentatively.

She gave me a keen look. "You mean to ask whether I doubted that Stephen would have bought the Boucher for me as a gift."

"Well, yes," I admitted.

"Now the thought occurs to me, of course, but before last week it didn't." She set the teacup onto her saucer soundlessly. "He's purchased five paintings for me over the years. Only one other was from a previous century."

"Really?" I reached to pour myself more tea.

"He liked to support emerging artists. I think often he was charmed not by the artwork itself but by the idea that a young man or woman was ambitious, trying to make their way." She shrugged. "Each time, he concealed the painting in the special closet until a special occasion came around."

"That's a lovely tradition," I said.

Her smile flickered and faded. "Yes," she said, averting her gaze. "It was."

I hadn't meant to steer her thoughts toward her loss, and I produced the first practical question that occurred to me. "You said he had planned to go to university," I said. "Did he?"

She nodded. "He studied politics, economics, and the history of Europe at the Katholieke Universiteit Leuven, near Brussels. His special interest was France." Her eyes widened as a thought occurred to her. "Do you know where Lord Sibley attended? Perhaps—"

"Oxford," I interrupted, but her words sparked a notion of my own. "Tell me, how—precisely—did your husband feel about France? And the Germans, after the war?"

"Oh." She winced and propped her elbow back on the chair arm. "He was very sympathetic to France's plight. You see, his family had dear friends in Paris and Alsace, and several of them died fighting the Prussians. Others died in the siege. But even before the war, Stephen was concerned that England and France were trapped in ways of regarding each other that were terribly outdated—and dangerous for our foreign policy."

"What do you mean?"

"Well, France and England have been at war with each other on and off since Normandy was part of England," she said.

I didn't know it had been, I thought with a twinge of embarrassment.

"According to Stephen," she continued, "for most of those six hundred years, England considered itself vis-à-vis France. She was perpetually our strongest adversary, and we were hers." Her expression was earnest; clearly she had been convinced of

her late husband's ideas. "But Europe is changing, and countries such as Russia and Germany are developing their econo-
mies, building alliances, and strengthening their positions.
That's why, even before the war, Stephen was worried about
how the balance of power in Europe was shifting, and how
England would fit in."

My heart tripped. Her report of Stephen's concerns reminded
me of what Mr. Flynn had said of Lord Sibley. A thrumming
started in the back of my brain.

"When did the Franco-Prussian War begin?" I asked. "Was
it 1871?"

She shifted against the cushion. "No, 1870, in July. Germany had secretly gathered three-quarters of a million soldiers
and dozens of trainloads of munitions at the border, with Bismarck waiting until just the right moment to provoke France
into declaring war. That would make the southern states beg
protection from Prussia, and Bismarck would have his united
Germany, which was his purpose all along."

I stared. "That's rather Machiavellian."

She nodded. "German troops reached Paris in September,
and the city was under siege for four long, dreadful months. It
was terribly chaotic, and people in the countryside were starving.
I know that Stephen's company was shipping more supplies than
usual." Her delicate features were drawn with regret. "Germany
was permitted to occupy France for three years, until the reparations were paid off. By then the balance of power had shifted in
Europe, perhaps forever. It troubled Stephen very much."

I rested the teacup in my palm. "I wonder if that might be
where he and Lord Sibley have some common ground."

"Did Lord Sibley have sympathies in that direction?"

"Well, he hated Germany," I said. "And he invited the Le-Marc family into his home when they fled Paris."

"Oh!" She blinked in surprise.

"From what I gather, Lord Sibley was against England isolating itself from Europe. He even proposed legislation that would forge a stronger economic tie with France."

She went still, and when she leaned forward to set down her cup and saucer, they jittered softly against the table. "Well, that's something Stephen and he could have agreed on, certainly."

"Celia, did Mr. Jesper keep records of his travels? I'm just wondering if he and Lord Sibley might have crossed paths abroad. Lord Sibley was in France for several months last year before he died, visiting the LeMarc family—but he traveled to Europe often."

She nibbled delicately at her lower lip. "I know Stephen went to France shortly after the war ended, but most of his foreign trips were to Holland and Belgium, where his company has divisions."

Surely those countries were common destinations for a wealthy traveler. Still, my heart skipped a beat. "Mr. Pagett mentioned his stepfather traveled to Amsterdam and Antwerp." I paused. "I assumed it was to buy paintings. The art markets there are so robust. But perhaps he had another reason."

She looked disconcerted. "Is there any way to ascertain his exact travel dates? I can provide you with at least most of Stephen's itineraries."

"Would it be too much trouble?"

"Not at all. He wasn't gone so very often, and I haven't packed my diaries yet, thank goodness."

She went to her desk and set about the task of paging

through some small leather-bound books and compiling the list. Not wanting to hover, I took a turn around the room and went to the window to look out. Hansom cabs rolled along the street; a young woman tucked her hand inside the arm of an older gentleman; a crossing-sweep rested his weight against his broom. The entire scene could be painted in shades of gray and green, with the exception of a few bits of color for the flowers on the woman's hat.

"Annabel?"

I turned.

She held out a piece of paper, with each of Stephen's trips and dates entered separately. Her expression held some consternation. "There's one odd thing I should mention about the last one, in December 1873. He told me he went to Belgium, but he may have made an ancillary trip to France. He brought me some special lace from Paris."

"How do you know?"

"The packaging showed the address. It was a present, for Christmas."

"I'm sure he didn't omit it to deceive you," I said hesitantly.

"Oh, I don't think so, either," she agreed. "Or he would've redone the wrapping on the lace." She frowned. "But now I wonder if he *didn't* go to Paris. Perhaps Lord Sibley was in Paris and brought the lace to Belgium."

"He might have," I said, folding the paper into quarters. "I'll give this to Mr. Hallam. He may find similarities with Lord Sibley's travel."

She rested her forearm along the chair's wooden back, her hand curved around the corner, her dark silk sleeve falling as gracefully as if she were sitting for her portrait. "We certainly can't base anything on the packaging of some lace. But you'll tell me, won't you, if Mr. Hallam finds that he and Lord Sibley were meeting?"

I nodded. "You said your husband went to school in Leuven. Did he correspond with anyone there? Any old friends or professors?"

She shook her head. "He mentioned them to me in passing, but I'm afraid I don't remember the names."

"What about his books?" I asked. "Perhaps one of them was written by a professor of his."

"We could look." She led the way into the library and pointed. "These three tables have his books from university."

We each began with a stack, paging through the volumes, and I tried to conceal my astonishment at the breadth of topics. There were books on European history, the Orient, Africa, religion, botany, architecture, astronomy, shipbuilding, the oceans, mapmaking, war, politics, trade, geography, and philosophy. Many were in English, though others were in Dutch, German, and French; however, we found none by a professor at the university.

And then I found an inscription, in a heavy, masculine hand, on the first page of a bound volume of Plato's *Works*. I might have missed it except the ink ran close to the edge of the page. "Here," I said and handed it to her. "Can you translate this?"

Celia glanced over the first few words. "It's German." Then she read aloud: "'To my dear Stephen, with my best wishes for continued success in your studies. May you . . .'" She shook her head. "I beg your pardon. The man's writing is atrocious.

It says, 'May you always sustain your profound faith in humanity. J. Mertens. Leuven, 1857.'" She looked up. "Now I remember. Stephen mentioned him."

"Perhaps *he* knows if your husband met Lord Sibley there, and why."

She closed the book and drew it to her chest. "It's possible," she said slowly.

"Where is Leuven?" I asked.

She bit her lip. "Perhaps twenty-five miles south of Antwerp. On a train, it would be no more than an hour or two."

I felt a beat of encouragement at discovering this connection, however loose, between the two men. But Celia's entire frame had gone tense.

"Is something the matter?" I asked.

She managed a smile. "No. I just . . ."

I kept silent, waiting.

When at last she spoke, there was a tremor in her voice. "I hate the idea that he had a secret from me. But I very much want to know the truth, no matter what it is."

"Of course."

We started back to the parlor, her arms still clasping the book to her chest. "I'll never be easy in my mind until I know what he was doing, and what Lord Sibley was to him. I'll find a moment this evening to write to the professor." She glanced around. "I still have a good deal of packing up, and the removers are coming for the last bit on Saturday."

I took the hint, went to the couch, and picked up my gloves and my wrap. "I have some things to do this afternoon myself."

"Oh, I didn't mean to—wait, please." She laid the book on a table and came close, looking up to meet my gaze. I noticed again how beautiful her eyes were, with the mix of brown and gold and green. "If the professor conveys something upsetting," she said steadily, "I don't want you to feel sorry about it. This is my choice. I dislike the idea of being a coward about the truth."

I felt a wave of sympathy. "I do hope you find that there is an explanation for your husband's actions that accords with what you know of him." I swallowed. "From what you've told me, I cannot believe that he would do anything unethical or—or disloyal."

A faint, grateful tuck appeared at the corner of her mouth.

We walked into the hallway, and she noticed my glance at the sparkling Cézanne. She paused to give me the opportunity to look. "Do you paint landscapes?"

"Not often, and not well."

"You know what they said of his work. That it was inane. Terrible." She brushed her fingertips across the gold frame, as if to remove a speck of dust. "But it gives me a peculiar feeling, the same sort of openness or . . . expansiveness around my heart that I used to feel with Stephen."

My own heart ached for her. "I understand."

We continued toward the door, and she waited to open it until I finished buttoning my coat.

"Celia, there's one last thing," I said. "Last night the *Beacon* published a rotten article on their front page. It contained all sorts of spurious ideas and innuendoes, including that the Boucher was a forgery and the auction house knew it all along." I hesitated. "They called it 'Bettridge's Grand Swindle.'"

Her mouth pressed into a thin line.

"I know." I took a deep breath. "In the next few days, you

may see more unpleasant publicity in the press. The inspector asked me to advise you to not take much notice."

"Thank you for warning me. It's not likely I'd have seen it—I don't read that paper, and honestly, I haven't had much time to read anything the past fortnight—but it's better to know."

I nodded and tentatively put out my hand to bid her good-bye. To my surprise, she clasped mine warmly, with both of hers. "Thank you for being kind," she said. "For breaking the news gently, and for understanding."

Her appreciativeness felt larger than I deserved. Feeling gratified but awkward, I merely squeezed her hands in return.

When I reached my flat, I made myself some bread and butter and took up my sketchbook and pencil, for I had a picture forming in my mind of Celia that I longed to capture. I fed myself with my left hand and sketched thumbnails with my right. Though the moment when she turned and rested her arm along the back of the chair had the grace befitting a portrait, the moment that drew me with its complexity was Celia sitting on the couch, her hands holding the framed photograph of her husband.

It only took three sketches before the picture's composition began to take shape. The light entered from a window on the left side of the canvas. The couch I placed straight on, with Celia seated, holding her husband's photograph in its silver frame. I swallowed down the last of the bread as I went to my easel, my left hand reaching to take the apron off the nail.

I slipped the apron's loop over my head, wrapped the ties to the back, and knotted them. I brought my three best lamps close, chose a canvas of my usual size, two feet by three, and placed it horizontally on the easel.

I began to block out the elements with Celia at the center. Though I worked with purpose, after an hour, I felt dissatisfied with the result. Celia and the frame needed a third element, something more substantial than the window light to balance the image. Tentatively I moved her over to the right and sketched in myself on the left. I was little more than a gray blur, but it was enough.

The fire in the stove had gone out entirely by the time I laid aside the brush and stepped back to look.

It was the first picture in which I'd ever included myself—though I envisioned only part of myself, in profile, silhouetted against the light coming in at the window. But it felt fitting, for my presence completed the central triangle: as I looked at Celia, she gazed upon her husband's picture, and the top of the silver picture frame became a line that pointed straight back to my face. I'd dropped in her diaries on the couch beside her, tidy little leather-bound books, suggestive in the way the pages were thicker at the outer edges than their bindings, as if stories could burst out of them. And I'd captured the similarity in our positions to my satisfaction, at least for now.

I took two steps to the right and looked again. This new angle revealed another possible triangle, in the way the folds of our skirts—her black ones and my dark gray ones—fell together below our knees, under the table. I would have to move the figure of myself closer to the center of the canvas for it to look the way I wanted, but there was something wonderfully evocative about the fabric of our skirts blurring together.

It hinted not just at our similarity but at the dark possibility we both faced, of finding out an unexpected truth about someone we loved.

As I removed my apron and hung it on its nail, the thought struck me: Had Matthew sent me to Celia because we had this in common, and he saw she might be an ally for me as well? Thinking about how much he seemed to notice, it didn't seem out of the question. I felt a welling of warmth and gratitude toward him, and the weight that lurked in my chest these days seemed to lighten.

I resolved that tomorrow morning, after I went to the Yard, I would go to Edwin's and look at his sketchbooks. I knew Edwin's habit of drawing whatever was in front of him on a given day. Those sketchbooks would reveal the truth about who Edwin was when he was away from me, all those years. If Celia could bear to face unpleasant secrets, so could I.

Chapter 12

I headed for the Yard early enough the next morning that the street sweepers were out and the costermongers were just setting up their carts.

When I reached the cobbled yard, it was deserted. I opened the door to find the division nearly empty as well, and quiet. The desk sergeant was one of only three men in the open room. The other two were looking over papers at their desks. When I asked for Mr. Hallam, the desk sergeant glanced around and responded by pointing over his shoulder. "He should be 'ere in a while. You can sit there, if'n you like."

I sat on the bench I'd occupied before. As I settled myself to wait, I saw Inspector Martin cross the room. His eyes drifted over me, seemingly without recognition, but abruptly he halted and came toward me with swift steps. A few feet away, he stared down from his height. In his eyes was an expression of amazement and displeasure.

"Miss Rowe."

"Hello, Inspector."

His voice was accusing. "What on earth are you doing here?"

A note of warning sounded in the back of my mind. "I'm waiting to speak with M—Mr. Hallam."

His eyes narrowed. "What is this regarding?"

The warning bell was chiming loud and clear, and in that moment I understood Matthew had kept my involvement, and all the small ways I had been helping with the investigation, a secret from the chief inspector. I glanced over and saw a young man at his desk, staring with frank curiosity. His face dropped instantly over the papers on his desk.

Let the chief think what he would of me; I only wanted to depart without giving anything away. But I could think of nothing to say, and I felt the blood rising to my cheeks.

Apparently my silence flummoxed him, but after a moment, he recovered his aplomb. He drew himself up, pursed his lips, and shook his head firmly. "Miss Rowe, I must ask you to leave. Mr. Hallam is not here in any event; but even if he were, we don't encourage the loitering of civilians. I'm very sorry about your brother, but we are still investigating. When we have any news, we will impart it to you. Until then, please return to your usual daily routines." He reached a hand down to pry me up off the bench, then steered me toward the door. "And if Mr. Hallam wishes to speak with you regarding your brother's case, he will find you."

He closed the door firmly behind me, and as I crossed the courtyard, I felt both a profound relief at my escape and a growing sense of bewilderment. If it was so improper for me to help Matthew, why hadn't he told me so?

I'd ask him when I saw him next. Surely someone would mention that I'd been in, and he'd send a message or come to find me at my rooms. Meanwhile, I could go to Edwin's earlier than I'd planned.

As I APPROACHED the flat, I opened my reticule to take out Edwin's key.

It had been a week since his death, and with no one opening the doors and windows, the odor of linseed oil and turpentine had suffused the room, as if to compensate for his absence. Although the flat had been entered illicitly, I saw no obvious signs of disturbance. Then again, last week I hadn't been in a state to take particular notice of where we'd left items after looking at them.

I approached Edwin's worktable and ran my hands over the wooden edge, feeling several nicks that time had worn smooth. There were two tin cups, one for his bristle brushes, the other for his sables, with perhaps a dozen in each, all stored properly with the bristles up. I brushed my fingertips across the sables to feel their silky softness.

Through the closed window, I heard church bells strike three-quarters of an hour and fade, and in the silence that followed, I moved slowly toward the shelf with his sketchbooks. I shifted them about so I could read the dates, written in his sharp, angular script in the upper left-hand corner of the cover. The books were all out of order. I took them down—there were at least two dozen, some with covers warped by rain or stained by food or drink—and laid them in sequence on his worktable.

The first began a month prior to him leaving home for school and ran through November of that year, and I chose it together with the subsequent one to examine first. I dragged Edwin's one comfortable chair toward the window, so I wouldn't require a lamp. The sky was a clear azure blue, and the September sun dropped a butter-yellow oblong onto the wood floor.

I began to page through. Even if there had been no date on the cover, I knew enough of Edwin's life that I could have guessed at the time period, just by his skill level and the subject matter. The early sketches in this book included the front of our London house, a hansom cab, a tree from our yard, my mother in her tiny garden—

And—to my surprise—myself at an easel.

In the drawing, the back of my canvas was merely suggested by a few lines on the left side of the page. He'd drawn me in a position closer to portrait than profile, with my hair pulled back, so my features were clearly visible. My cheeks were round, and my nose and chin were still unformed in the way of children's, but my eyes were fixed purposefully on my canvas, my mouth was pouted in concentration, and though my hand looked small, it held the paintbrush properly. Edwin had taken care over the drawing, and despite my youth and apparent earnestness, the entire tone suggested warm approval rather than condescension.

My chest tightened, and I laid the sketchbook in my lap.

All at once I remembered a row I'd had with Edwin not long after he'd been released from prison, when he was staying with me. I didn't recall how our quarrel began, but at one point he'd burst out, "Of course you were important to me!"

"Important?" I echoed in amazement. "I hardly heard from you after you left! Two letters the entire time you were at school, and—"

"I didn't *leave*," he snapped back, his green eyes—mirrors of mine—flashing. "Father sent me away, remember?"

"Yes, but I don't just mean when you left for school," I retorted. "What about afterward, when you came back to London? You were gone. *Always* gone!"

"Because being home was bloody hellish! You know that!"

"Yes, I know it," I snapped. "Because I was *there*. You could get away!"

He looked incredulous. "You got away, too! You're at the Slade!"

I thought I heard a note of envy. "You can't begrudge me—"

"I don't!" With a groan he spun away and then turned back, his arms outstretched as if his frustration were too large to contain. "I don't begrudge you the Slade. Not at all! You belong there! I've always hoped for your success—always!"

"How would I know?" My voice didn't even sound like my own. "You've certainly never said so to me!"

His chin jerked to the left and back again, as if he had to take a swift second look at something that surprised him. Slowly he put a hand to the wall, as if needing the support to take in what I'd said. There was a bruised, bewildered look about his eyes. "I've always cared more about you than anyone, Annabel." His voice broke. "For God's sake, I thought you knew."

I hadn't replied, but I let him see my skepticism.

He blew out a breath. "Well," he said finally. His shoulders rounded and his gaze fell to the floor. "Well," he said again. Then he gathered his coat and left.

I had half expected him not to return, but he did, though it wasn't until hours later. I was in bed, but awake. When I heard the key in the lock, I stiffened, listening for the sounds of drunken fumbling or quiet curses over having to prepare for bed in the dark. There was neither, only the squeak of the sofa as he lay down and eventually the faint sound of his whistling snore. The next morning, his manner was tentative. He said he was sorry we'd quarreled, and he'd found rooms to let that would be available the following afternoon.

I stared at Edwin's sketch of me.

Yes, I had reasons for my distrust of him. But it had been ugly spite that caused me to show Edwin my disbelief that day.

Dear God, what I'd give to take those few seconds back.

There was a long silence in which I felt an uneven beat in my chest, as if the irregular rumble of cab wheels over the cobbles below had by some sorcery been transmitted up through the walls and floors to my susceptible heart.

Tears filled my eyes, and it was a long time before I could turn to the next page.

In the second half of this sketchbook, Tennersley emerged in bits and pieces. Edwin never sketched the entire building, but as I paged through, I began to assemble the school in my mind: two stone wings flanking a central hall with a bell tower on top; a chapel with an altar attended by acolytes; a waterfall and a river nearby; a hill where sheep grazed on gorse; a spinney where a solitary young man sat under one of the trees; an empty classroom with a blackboard, half covered in writing; a bowl of stew with bread on a plate beside; and dozens of boys in profiles and portraits.

I paused at one page in particular because the sketched face brought someone to mind. After a moment, I realized it might be the boyish version of the man from the funeral—the one who had given me a peculiarly resentful look and slipped away without a word. After that, I examined the faces more closely, wondering if I might come across the other man at the funeral, the one who said he was a school friend of Edwin's. What was his name? I closed my eyes and strained to remember him speaking it.

Will Giffen. That was it.

And near the end of the book, I found him. He and a dark-haired boy were bundled into warm coats and standing together on the far bank of a river. Edwin depicted them at the moment of a shared laugh—but something about the scene felt unpleasant, even sinister. The dark slashes in the water, the rocks, the bare branches on the trees—indeed, the entire landscape felt bleak, brutal, and unyielding.

I flipped back to an earlier page to see the river as Edwin had drawn it first, lilting with light and shadows.

With a growing unease, I picked up the next sketchbook.

A few pages in, I found the boy who had become the young, silent man from the funeral again—looking a bit older and warier. This time, the word *Witty* was scrawled underneath. Will Giffen appeared as well, and numerous other boys, including the one whose dark hair flopped over his forehead. There were some excellent sketches of a bearded man, smiling or laughing, who was presumably Edwin's art teacher. My favorite was one in which he stood beside a student, before an easel, his hand pointing as if to instruct. There was nothing sweet or sentimental about the teacher and student; the drawing was oddly austere, but Edwin had captured something of the intensity of the moment.

I went to the table to gather a stack of the sketchbooks and returned to my chair. Edwin was sketching more prolifically now, filling a sketchbook every six weeks or so, and expanding his subjects beyond the school grounds: a street in a market town, carriages, storefronts, a uniformed railway servant, door knockers, teacups, women in hats and dresses, locomotives, brickwork, barns, furniture, flowers, fences. To someone else it might have looked mindlessly indiscriminate, but as I paged through, I understood Edwin's method. He was honing his skills, more interested in shapes and textures and shadows than the objects themselves.

By the time I finished examining these books, the sunny oblong had vanished. The late-afternoon light was dim, and my eyes were fatigued, but I lit two lamps, hung them from hooks in the ceiling, and gathered the next few sketchbooks. It wasn't until I studied the dates that I realized two months were unaccounted for. I knew Edwin wouldn't simply stop drawing for that long. I rose and sifted through the remaining sketchbooks, then went to the shelf to be sure I hadn't missed one. But there was no sign of it.

Why would the sketchbook be gone? Had Edwin hidden it? Surely he wouldn't discard it. And if someone had searched the flat looking for Edwin's impressions of the school, why not take all the Tennersley books?

Had this been what the thief had been after the second time?

I began to search: the desk, a trunk, some boxes. I looked between the stacked paintings and even underneath the carpet. Finally I paused at the torn curtain that partitioned off Edwin's bedroom and hesitantly drew it aside.

To my relief the room had been stripped bare, aside from a metal bed with a mattress covered in a plain white sheet. There was no sign of blood on the floor. Nothing hung on the walls, and the shelves were empty. With a feeling of gratitude for whoever had erased the physical signs of Edwin's death, I let the curtain fall, gathered up a wool blanket I'd found in the trunk, wrapped it around my shoulders, and sank down on the floor, taking up the next book.

These sketches were of London. His drawings were now more mature, deft and sharp in their lines, as if his experiences demanded a different degree of pressure from his pencil upon the page. The images of the Thames in particular conveyed a fierce energy, with the boat masts piercing the sky and the water roiling below ships, their sides stained with the marks of their labor. There were street scenes as well as portraits—a child on a bicycle, a woman carrying a caged bird, a man shifting a sack of grain. Nowhere did I find even the most cursory sketch of my father, but halfway through the book I found an excellent drawing of my mother. I've no idea where she was; it wasn't anywhere I recognized. She sat on a wooden bench, underneath a tree, a book in her lap. She smiled up at Edwin, squinting against the sun because her hat lay on the bench beside her. I could see the wind in the folds of her skirt. Edwin had taken his time over this; there was a delicacy that suggested his affection and ease with her, feelings utterly absent from the Tennersley drawings.

Suddenly there was a creak of a door opening.

I looked up, my heart in my throat, my hands instinctively clutching the book flat against my chest.

Matthew stood at the threshold, his expression relieved. "I'm very glad it's you up here and not someone else."

I let go of a jagged exhale. "You scared me half to death!"

"Sorry." He tipped his head toward the window. "I saw the light from the street."

I twisted around to look at the dark panes, rendered mirror-like by the glow of the two lamps. They would have appeared like beacons from below.

I drew a deep breath to slow my racing heart.

He set his truncheon on the table and went to the window, checking the hasps to be sure they were completely closed. "Quite a chill in here. Aren't you cold?"

Now that he mentioned it I noticed. "It was warmer earlier, with the sun."

"May I?" He gestured toward the stove.

I nodded. "Of course."

He removed his coat and laid it over a table, crouched down to shift some wood from the pile into the stove, crumpled some paper, and lit it. Standing before the opening, he rubbed his hands as if they were numb, although he didn't look cold and the fire was already toasting the air. Matthew remained silent, and I sensed he had some news he was reluctant to impart.

"Where were you this morning?" I asked, thinking it might help him begin. "I went to the Yard to find you. Your chief inspector all but pushed me out the door. I gathered he didn't know I've been helping."

He flexed his hands gently once or twice as if the knuckles were sore; then he closed the stove door and dropped his hands to his sides. "I've something I need to tell you."

"All right." I picked myself up off the floor and settled myself in the chair, one of Edwin's sketchbooks in my lap.

He drew a wooden chair opposite and sat facing me. "You remember coming in and finding us here."

"Of course."

The snap and tiny fizzes of the fire, muted by the iron door of the stove, filled the silence.

"Matthew?"

His manner was that of someone feeling his way forward over precarious ground. "Both the chief inspector and I felt rather puzzled by you at first, for there were a few pieces of circumstantial evidence that, if viewed in a certain light, suggested you might have something to do with Edwin's death."

Even before I took in the full import of this, I felt the blood drain from my face. Had I truly been a suspect? What motive could I possibly have for killing Edwin?

"What do you mean?" It came out barely above a whisper. "What evidence?"

His voice was restrained. "First, there were reddish bits on the hem of your dress."

I felt my eyes widen. "But it was *paint*. I'd dropped my brush that day."

"You also didn't seem surprised by his death." His eyebrows rose, and he paused to allow me to acknowledge that truth, if only to myself. "I don't know if you recall, but you simply sat down, and your expression was very calm. Typically people respond with surprise or tears when we tell them a relation has died. And then, when I asked if someone might want to hurt him, you almost laughed. Not as if it were humorous, but . . ."

I couldn't even reply.

"Last—and most important—was your letter to Edwin."

My mind darted back to that afternoon in search of a missive we'd found but came up with nothing. Bewildered, I said, "I don't remember any—"

"It was in the desk drawer." His voice was somber. "We searched it before you arrived."

"Very well. What did it say?"

"That you hated him for what he did to your parents, and you wished that he'd died instead of either of them." His eyes, watchful, never left mine. "It had no date, but it was signed—clearly—with your name."

A blaze of shame raced from my crown to my feet. Overcome, I stood and went to the window. The chill from outside penetrated the diamond panes and I drew in my breath so the air could cool the heat in my lungs. My hands found the pair of hasps and clung to their metal edges until they bit into my fingers.

I couldn't recall everything I'd said in that letter, but what little Matthew had quoted brought back the hateful, bitter state I'd been in when I wrote it, and a groan escaped my lips. The thought of Edwin reading that letter—and perhaps rereading it over the years—made something inside me shrivel with a combination of anguish and remorse.

"I shouldn't have written those things," I said shakily. "Or at least I should never have sent it—it was after my mother died . . ." My voice dwindled, and I stared out at the street, at the shops across the way, their interiors dark, and the gas lamps casting a glare on the plate-glass windows. "He never mentioned the letter to me. I didn't even know it reached him." My throat was thick with tears. "I wish to God it hadn't."

Behind me the chair creaked and his steps came close—close enough that he could touch my shoulder. "Annabel."

His voice was full of kindness, and I choked out, "Why

have you been so decent to me? You must have thought I was a monster."

"Not a monster," he corrected and turned me toward him. The faintest smile came and went, but his eyes were somber. "But it did make me wonder what he'd done to make you so angry. Because a letter like that—well, clearly it was written under extreme duress."

I winced and forced out the question: "So you thought I might have had something to do with his death?"

"Instinctively, no." He shook his head. "The chief and I both saw how indignant you were when you found us in your brother's room. He thought you might be concerned about the paintings. But it didn't seem that way to me. Your every instinct was to defend your brother."

I managed a nod.

"Yet I couldn't acquit you merely because . . . well, because my instincts said to. So I took the opportunity to observe you rather closely that afternoon."

That took me aback. "You did?"

"Yes." He paused. "You handled Edwin's things gently, with tenderness. Slowly your face took on a look of grief as you absorbed what had happened. And when I asked you questions, your answers suggested a relationship that had been difficult—but it appeared you felt more regret than anger about it."

"That's true," I said softly. A distant church bell chimed the half hour; a closer one echoed it more clearly. "Is that why you let me come along, why you accepted my offer of help?" And then, as another thought occurred to me: "Or was it because your chief inspector still suspected me?"

"He asked me to arrange for surveillance, at least for a few days, and he ordered me to follow you home," he admitted. "Although I would have done it anyway. I surmised you wouldn't be thinking about your own safety, and it was late."

I nodded. Aside from the lamplighter, I recalled nothing of that walk to my flat.

"We set a constable to watch you the next morning." A smile tugged at his mouth. "You can imagine his surprise when you came straight to the Yard."

I couldn't help but smile by way of reply.

"I'd been told that Mr. Pagett's case was a priority," he continued, "so I had passed your case on to another inspector. However, once I realized that your concerns were intertwined with Mr. Pagett's . . . well, accepting your offer to help seemed to be the most practical course. Eventually my chief was convinced you had nothing to do with Edwin's death, and he told me to keep you at a distance." He looked apologetic. "When we're building a case, there can be no possibility that any personal considerations have tarnished the evidence. He has to follow procedures *very* properly right now. We all do."

"Why especially now?"

"Because the political situation has changed," he replied. "When Disraeli became prime minister last year, some of his cabinet pushed to dispense with plainclothesmen altogether. In the end, it was decided to keep us, but then several months ago, our superintendent was found to be colluding in a thieving ring."

I felt my eyes widen.

"Naturally, when it came to replacing him, the police commissioner found the straightest arrow he could. Chief Inspector

Martin is meticulous and exacting, and he expects his orders to be followed to the letter. That's why he was"—he paused briefly—"surprised when you showed up at the Yard this morning."

Now I realized the awkward situation I'd created for him. Alarmed, I asked, "Will you be disciplined for it? I didn't say a word—"

He shook his head. "No. I think he assumed you were naturally concerned. He just abhors any hint of interference or oversight from a civilian." He grinned, and I saw he was trying to cheer me. "I assured him you were uncommonly inquisitive but could be reasoned with."

A soft laugh escaped. "I wish you'd told me. I never meant to put you in a difficult position."

"I know. I chose to take it."

"Why?"

He took my hand gently in his own, turned it over, and drew his thumb over my palm in a way that sent heat along my every nerve. "Because you deserve an ally in this." His eyes were dark with sympathy. "The day of the funeral, when I saw you standing by Edwin's grave, you looked so full of uncertainty and despair that . . . well, I knew you had questions about Edwin, and you'd have no peace until you understood what had happened to the brother you loved and lost." His voice dropped. "I'm familiar enough with the feeling myself to recognize it in someone else."

Suddenly I understood. He longed to help people find the truth and peace he hadn't yet found for himself. "That's why you became a policeman," I said, and when he made no reply, I added quietly, "Am I right?"

He gave a single nod. "That's a good part of it, yes."

In that moment, the two of us stood facing each other, my hand still in his, close enough that I could feel the warmth coming off him, and I felt suddenly, acutely aware that we were alone. I could have reached out my other hand and touched his cheek, traced his mouth with my thumb—

He swallowed, and I perceived him pulling back as if from a precipice. He released my hand, shifted his weight to step away, and took up one of Edwin's sketchbooks.

"What have you found?" he asked, his voice pragmatic.

The moment had vanished like a trace of smoke in the wind. But at least I understood why.

In an attempt to match his practical demeanor, I picked up the first sketchbook of Tennersley, paged through, and turned the book so he could see it right side up. "Here's the school he attended—the river—and here are some of the boys. His friends, I suppose. But look at this." I opened to the page with the young man from the funeral. "He was at the funeral and introduced himself. Will Giffen." I turned a few pages. "And so was this man. He left without speaking to me, although he gave me a strange look, almost as if something I'd done had made him angry." I took up the next journal and paged through. "There's another sketch of him back here—"

"Wait."

I stopped turning and flipped back one page and then another.

"There." He pointed.

It was a sketch of a young man, with dark hair and eyes, cheekbones that brought attractive angles and planes to his face, and a finely cut mouth. But the dark eyes were flat and cold. Edwin didn't like this young man; I could tell.

"Who's that?" Matthew's voice had sharpened.

"I don't know. Most of them aren't labeled. It must be one of the other boys at the school. He doesn't look very friendly, does he?"

"He was at the auction."

I stared. "He was? You're sure?"

He nodded, his eyes fixed on the page. "If Edwin's sketch is accurate, I think so. Are there any more of him?"

I flipped through the last few pages of the sketchbook until I found one on which several boys' faces were drawn more meticulously than in the earlier versions. Whoever this dark-haired boy was, Edwin had caught him in a moment of callousness and arrogance.

Matthew blew out his breath. "I'd swear that's him. We entered the room at the same time. He sat on the opposite side."

A cold feeling began at the top of my scalp and crawled its way down my spine. "Matthew, this means . . ."

He nodded. "Edwin's death might have been personal—not a result of the theft, but—"

"Somehow connected to Tennersley." I felt a beat of alarm. "And if this man was an art student with Edwin, that could explain why he took the Boucher."

Matthew's expression changed to understanding. "Because he would recognize its value."

I nodded.

"Oh Lord." Matthew scrubbed hard at his scalp with a hand, as if to energize the organ inside it. "This upends the way I've been thinking about everything, and . . . sorry, I'm just trying to put things in order." He gestured toward the sketchbooks. "Was he unhappy there?"

"I think so. Not at first—but later, yes. His sketches become sharper and bleaker in tone."

"What year did he leave?"

I calculated backward. "He wasn't yet sixteen, so it must have been the spring of 1865."

"He came home?"

"He returned to London," I corrected him. "But he didn't come home, not at first. I told you he went to live with a friend—mostly to avoid my father. Father didn't want to see Edwin, said he was a disgrace."

"Did you see him at all?"

I shook my head. "Father wouldn't allow it. I didn't even know where he was staying. Mother saw him, I think, but only when my father was away, and she never told me where he was."

"In your letter you said something about Edwin's habit of going to dangerous places, how it led to your parents' deaths."

I nodded unhappily. "At the time, the doctor said their deaths were caused by the miasmas down by the river near the . . . the opium dens. He believed my father brought some of it home on his clothes, which is why my mother died as well."

"Edwin was in an opium den, then?"

I noted gratefully the lack of horror in his voice. He might have been asking about the weather.

"My father had to go and fetch him out."

"How did he know where Edwin was?"

A cold draft from the window brushed the back of my neck, making me shiver. I wrapped the blanket more securely around me, and tried to turn the memories of that horrible night into words. "A boy came to our door, very late, to say Edwin was in an opium den and unconscious. He would die if he wasn't taken to a doctor. So my father went to find him."

"He had some fatherly feeling still."

"No," I said quietly. "My mother got down on her knees and begged him."

He drew in his breath. "I see."

The scene was as clear in my mind as when I first watched it. "He was disgusted with Edwin—and disgusted with himself for giving in to my mother. I remember as he left, he said to her, 'I'm doing this for you, Louisa, not for him. And it is the last favor you may ever ask of me.'" I paused and my voice sounded far away, even to myself. "Little did he know that his prediction would come to pass. They were both dead within a fortnight."

Matthew remained silent.

I sighed. "So Father brought Edwin home, and the doctor came each day to bleed him and dose him with tonics. Mother slept on a pallet in his room every night. As Edwin began to recover, my father and mother both fell ill. My father died first, my mother a few days later. By then Edwin had run off again. Weak as he was, he said he couldn't bear to be there, watching her suffer." Into my mind came the image of my mother in her bed, sweating and shivering at once. "She begged me to help Edwin, to keep him from going back to opium, and not to abandon him. I told her I would try. But in those weeks after she died, I was very angry with him, and that's when I wrote that letter." A pause. "Later the doctor admitted he might have been wrong about Edwin causing their deaths."

"Oh?"

"I think he said what he did because he was upset." I remembered Dr. Walker, full of bitterness toward my absent brother as he and I stood at my mother's deathbed. His hand shook as he laid aside his stethoscope. "But later, Felix told me the doctor mentioned several similar cases of fever in houses near ours. So it wasn't necessarily Edwin's fault."

"Hm." A pause. "When did you next see Edwin?"

"Not for a long time," I said. "He was arrested for forgery, and he was in jail for a year, not allowed visitors—with the exception of the vicar. I wasn't told when he would be released. But one day I came out of the Slade and found him waiting for me. He looked thin and desperately unhappy. He apologized profusely, said he despised himself, and understood why I would hate him, but he had nowhere else to go." I sighed. "So I brought him home. He only stayed for a few days." I looked down at my fingers where they held the blanket. "We had a row, and the next day he told me he'd found a place to live. He gave me this address and left." Matthew remained silent, and I wrapped the blanket more closely around me. "I told you I knew Edwin better than anyone, and it's true that we were close as children. But when it comes to the last few years, before jail, I hardly knew him at all. The places he went, the people he met . . ." My voice faded. "I didn't know half the people at his funeral." I gave a brittle laugh. "What a rotten little family history."

A long minute passed, and then he reached into his pocket.

"Yours was one of two letters we found in Edwin's desk the day he died." He held the letter out to me. "The other was this, from your father."

I remembered watching my father compose his letters to Edwin at the desk in his study. The bald spot at the top of his head shone in the lamplight as he bent over the pages, and the nub made a furious scratching sound on the paper. One night the ink bottle flew off the desk as he jerked the pen out of it. The black stain on the carpet never came out.

Matthew was still holding Father's letter for me to take, but I hesitated. "I can only imagine what it says," I said.

He grimaced. "Yes. I wouldn't want to receive such a letter as this."

That decided me. "I don't want to read it. At least, not now."

His hand dropped. "Very well. Although there is a passage in here that pertains to you."

"There is?"

He opened it and turned the paper over, so he could read from the back. "'Your sister,'" he read, "'is everything you are not. Whereas you are lazy and embittered, she is industrious and devoted; whereas you have squandered your talents, she has embraced and developed hers; whereas you have devolved to a mere copyist, she has gained originality. All that you could have been, she is, and I have no regrets as to the provisions in my will.'" He looked up. "Does he mean giving you the income from the house?"

I nodded. "Probably. When was it written?"

"November of 1872." He folded the pages back into their original shape. "Would you like to have this, for what he wrote about you?"

"No, thank you."

He looked at me curiously, but I understood all too well the reason for my father's ardent praise in a letter I was never meant to see.

"I'll keep it for now." Matthew slid the letter back inside his coat pocket and withdrew his pocketbook together with a different piece of paper, folded in quarters. "I've something else to show you. The layout of the Pantechnicon. I went to see George Radermacher today."

"Oh?"

"He's a garrulous fellow, quite lonely, I think." He paused. "He had a famous visitor last week, the novelist George Eliot."

My eyebrows rose. "The author of *Middlemarch*?"

He nodded. "Apparently, she had come by to inquire if he'd catalog her books. He was pleased as punch, had to tell me all about it before I got a word in edgewise." A wry look. "Finally, about half an hour along, I managed to steer him toward talking about the Pantechnicon. He opened up readily enough, and told me all about how he'd have made a good policeman himself because he was an expert at detecting when people were trying to cheat them."

"Cheat them," I echoed.

He nodded. "Some depositors would go so far as to have special headboards built with secret compartments, to avoid paying high insurance rates."

"I don't understand."

"Well, say it cost twenty pounds to insure a headboard for a year. It was seventy to insure some very expensive jewelry. So people would hide the jewelry inside the headboard."

"Oh, I see."

He set aside the pocketbook and unfolded the paper, revealing a rough sketch. "Here's the street and the building. It was five stories high, covered almost two acres of land." He pointed. "These are the hallways and square rooms. Most of the building was stone. There were steel doors at intervals that could be shut to contain a fire, and the roof was girded so it wouldn't collapse if it was doused with water. The second, fourth, and fifth floors were all rooms for individual collectors, and they could be locked. There were approximately twenty-five hundred depositors, including everyone from landed gentry to railway board members and MPs"—he glanced up—"many of whom had substantial art collections. Sir Richard Wallace had two entire rooms for himself. He lost a good portion of his painting collection, valued at something upward of one hundred and fifty thousand pounds."

"I remember reading about that," I replied.

One eyebrow rose. "It's astounding, isn't it?"

"Did Mr. Radermacher remember anything about the Sibley collection?"

"The Sibleys had a room for themselves." A gleam came into his eye. "But when I asked about the Boucher, he said the arrangement for that particular painting might have been a shared dock. He couldn't remember at first, and then after a bit, he seemed more certain."

"A shared dock?"

"It's when a person or family rents a space for a specific item in their collection that another, unrelated person can remove at any time. Shared docks were housed in a separate room, so the Boucher wasn't with the rest of the collection."

My mouth fell open. "So the painting could have been placed by Lord Sibley—"

"And withdrawn by Mr. Jesper. Yes." He paused. "Legally."

"Were shared docks common?" I asked.

He shrugged. "It wasn't out of the ordinary. Most often it was a solicitor who was authorized, but it could be any two individuals." He flipped through his pocketbook to refer to some notes and then returned to the sketch. "This"—he pointed to a corner—"is the northwest corner, where the paintings were held. And it's where the fire began. It spread this way, along the corridors to the south and east. So it's very likely that if someone did start the fire in that particular section of the building, it was because they were targeting a painting."

"It may not be only a painting that was targeted," I said slowly, and I relayed to him the substance of my conversation with Celia, including her husband's trips to Birmingham and what she had suggested about Stephen's and Lord Sibley's deaths.

He was quiet for several minutes after I finished. At last he said, "There's one additional piece of news. Someone is trying to sell the painting."

I sat bolt upright. "What? You've found it?"

A ghost of a smile. "I didn't say that. I found someone who heard from someone else that it's available for sale."

"And you've no idea who is selling it?"

"No, but I'm—"

A sharp rap at the door startled us both.

I froze in place, but Matthew instantly reached one hand for his truncheon and the other for me, pulled me to standing, and jerked his head in the direction of the bedroom. Silently, I stepped over Edwin's journals and slipped behind the torn curtain.

Chapter 13

"Who is it?" Matthew asked.

"My name is Mr. Pascoe. I was a friend of Edwin's."

"It's all right, Matthew. It's the vicar from the funeral," I whispered.

"Stay there a moment," he said.

Obediently, I remained where I was as Matthew opened the door.

"I beg your pardon." The man's voice was strained but low, as if he was trying to conceal his agitation. "I'm looking for Miss Annabel Rowe. I hoped someone here might tell me where I could find her—and then I saw the light."

I came out from the back room and walked toward the door. The vicar wore a black coat and a weather-beaten hat, and he carried a newspaper in his left hand. I caught a glimpse of the masthead of the *Beacon* and guessed what brought him here at half past eight in the evening. "Please come in, Mr. Pascoe," I said.

Silently Matthew stepped aside, and the vicar entered, looking from Matthew to me, his expression discomfited.

I felt myself flush; of course he'd wonder what we were doing alone in Edwin's rooms at this hour.

"This is Inspector Hallam, from the Yard," I said as matter-of-factly as I could manage. "He's looking into Edwin's murder. We were just going through Edwin's sketchbooks." I gestured toward the one comfortable chair. "Please, sit down. Would you like tea?"

"No, thank you." He laid the newspaper on the worktable and removed his coat with a deliberateness that suggested he was accustomed to maintaining his equanimity in trying circumstances, although I noticed his cleric's collar was askew, and he'd left a middle button undone on his shirt.

He sat down and rubbed fiercely at his hair so it spiked in several directions. "Miss Rowe, I beg your pardon for disturbing you, but I only just read this paper, and I had to come straightaway."

"How did you know Edwin's address?" Matthew asked idly.

"I'd been here to visit him once or twice." He turned back to me to add, "Generally he came to see me at the church."

I drew one of Edwin's stools close to the vicar, perched on it, and waited to hear what he'd say.

He steepled his hands as if in prayer and touched the fingertips of his forefingers gently to his chin, his expression grave. "At the funeral, the priest gave out that Edwin's death was sudden, of course, and naturally most of us assumed it was the result of an accident, though it wasn't made explicit. Afterward, when you told me it wasn't . . . well, I thought . . . that is, I assumed he had taken his own life."

My shock at the idea silenced me, but Matthew leaned toward the vicar. "Why would you think so?"

"When he was in prison, he spoke of it several times."

My mouth went dry. "Was he in earnest?"

The vicar's eyes met mine, and his expression was full of regret. "It wasn't uttered impetuously, if that's what you mean. I've seen men speak of committing that desperate act, and I know when someone is considering it with some purpose. And then, less than a week before Edwin died, he returned some books I'd lent him." He spread his hands. "At the time I thought nothing of it. He seemed tranquil and cheerful. He even teased me a bit about some notes I'd made in the margin. So I assumed he was merely returning books he'd finished reading. Then, after he died, I wondered if he returned them because . . ."

"Because he wanted to put his affairs in order," Matthew supplied.

"Yes." He pointed to the newspaper. "But tonight I saw this. Is it true? Was Edwin murdered? Are you certain?"

"He was killed in such a way that he couldn't have done it himself," Matthew said quietly.

At Matthew's words, the vicar's head dropped into his hands. "That poor boy," he muttered. We sat in silence, and when the vicar raised his head, his eyes were wet. But a heavy burden seemed to have slipped away, and I thought I understood.

"You were afraid you hadn't helped him enough," I said softly.

He looked ashamed. "My own concerns are nothing compared with your grief. But I'll admit, since the funeral, I've raked through my memories, trying to see a sign of . . . of his desire to destroy himself, and I couldn't find one. The last few months, he seemed increasingly at peace, as if he were settling into his new life." He leaned forward, his expression earnest. "When he came to drop off those books, I saw no signs of the dark thoughts he had when I first met him."

"What was he like then? In prison?" I asked.

"Oh . . . the first few visits were very difficult," he admitted. "He was distrustful and sullen and angry, unwilling to accept any sort of comfort from me. He wasn't even much interested in the food I brought—indeed, he hardly ate at all." He sighed. "Several times I left feeling quite discouraged, and it wasn't until I brought him books that he began to respond. At first I tried the Bible, of course. But he absolutely refused to hear it."

Recalling how my father would recite scriptures about ungrateful sons, I imagined I understood why.

Mr. Pascoe spread his hands. "He said he didn't believe in a benevolent God."

"Yet you didn't give up on him," Matthew said.

"Of course not." A smile flickered. "Plenty of my conversations with prisoners begin that way."

Matthew made a sound of acknowledgment.

"What books did you give him instead?" I asked.

"The volumes of my favorite philosophers. He seemed to take a modicum of comfort in the works of David Hume."

"The Scottish skeptic?" Matthew asked.

"Yes. Edwin's intellect was lively—and at times so quick and so shrewd that I found the intricacies of his thoughts difficult to follow. More than once after I left, I'd spend my walk back to Camden mulling over some point he'd made." He shrugged. "He may have left school prematurely, but not before he'd absorbed patterns of logic and argument. Truly, he might have made an extraordinary philosopher." His right hand scratched at his temple. "Eventually he came to trust and confide in me. Over time, I attempted to persuade him that a certain kind of contemplation—I didn't call it prayer—might help him grapple with his sorrow. Sometimes there were moments when light was forgotten and despair took over. But those moments were fewer and farther between." He leaned toward me. "Forgive me—but I think he began to escape the shadow of your father's expectations and disappointment. He didn't have to quarrel with him anymore. Do you see?"

I nodded. Edwin had made a few comments along those lines in the weeks before his death.

"And as his time in prison drew to an end, he was determined to avoid his old ways and make amends. I know he spoke of this with you."

"Yes, he did," I said slowly. "I must admit, Vicar, at first I wasn't sure how sincere he was. I'd seen him apologetic before—so many times." I shook my head. "Eventually Father gave up on him and told him never to come back. I think it broke my mother's heart."

"And yours?" Mr. Pascoe asked gently.

My throat tightened. "Mine, too."

He reached over to pat my hand and gave me a smile. "He'd always thought of the two of you as allies, even after he was sent away to school. And—" He broke off. "Well, I think it took him time to understand how his reckless years affected you."

I couldn't trust myself to speak.

"I counseled him to be patient," he said. "It would take more than a few months to win back your trust. But I assured him that time often heals even the deepest wounds. And from what he'd told me of you, I believed you were generous enough to forgive him."

I'd been the beneficiary of this man's compassion, and I hadn't even known it. I felt tears prick at the corners of my eyes. "Thank you for that. I'm—I'm so grateful that Edwin had you," I said. "I never knew it was you who'd helped him. And he *was* changed when he came out of prison, certainly for the better."

"Knowing that makes me feel a bit easier, I suppose." He laid his open hand over his shirtfront and rubbed absently. After a moment, he gave a sigh and shifted toward the front of the chair. "I suppose I should go."

"Before you do," Matthew said, "would you mind if I asked you a few questions?"

"Of course." The vicar settled back against the cushion.

"When did you last see Edwin?"

He tipped his head to the side as he thought back. "He came to see me on Wednesdays. So I suppose it was about a week before he died."

"You said he was cheerful," Matthew said. "But did he say anything about his work?"

"He mentioned he'd received two commissions that he thought would be remunerative. One was for a copy of a landscape and the other for cleaning a painting. I assume it's the one mentioned in the newspaper, the French portrait."

"Did Edwin ever talk to you about the painting itself?" Matthew asked.

"No."

"And did he mention anything peculiar—or say anything about disagreements with anyone the last time you saw him?"

"Not at all." He frowned as he considered. "Mostly we discussed John Locke."

Matthew nodded. "Thank you."

"Of course." He stood and put on his coat. As he walked toward the door, I noticed his limp had diminished.

I retrieved the newspaper he'd brought and handed it to him. "Did you injure your leg?"

He paused at the threshold and grimaced. "Yes, a few weeks ago. Stupid of me. I stepped in a hole in the garden and twisted my ankle. It's better now, although it might be worse tomorrow. I ran in search of a cab tonight. I was so stunned by this"—he waved the paper—"all I could think of was getting here as quickly as I could."

"There's one other thing," I said. "In Edwin's sketchbooks, certain drawings suggest Edwin was unhappy at Tennersley. Did he ever say anything to you about it?"

I saw the flinch around his eyes, as if he'd dodged a physical blow. Then his face smoothed. "Miss Rowe, I'm sorry. Anything confided in me as a priest is sacred, between Edwin and God."

It was as good as an admission that Edwin had told the vicar something, and I felt a sudden heat along the back of my spine. "I can appreciate you honoring that confidence for as long as Edwin was alive, Vicar. But it's possible it has something to do with his death."

"With his death my promise to him becomes all the more important to honor," he said. He lowered his chin and looked at me from under his brows. "I'm sorry."

He turned and stepped onto the landing, but I was desperate to keep him for another minute.

"One of his sketchbooks is missing. Do you know anything about it?"

He started down the stairs and answered over his shoulder, "If it is missing, I imagine it is because your brother no longer had any use for it."

I hurried out to the landing and leaned over the banister. "One of his fellow students came to the funeral. A man named Will Giffen. Do you know him?"

He continued down the stairs. "I do not."

"Mr. Pascoe, please," I begged. "Do you think we should visit Tennersley? Will we find anything there?"

He stiffened, and paused on the step, turning to look up at me. By the light of the sconce on the landing below I saw a flash of resentment in his eyes. I felt a pang of regret at having persisted. But after a moment, his expression softened. "Good night, and God bless you both."

I listened to his footsteps until they faded and the door thudded behind him.

"That was unexpected," Matthew said. "And informative."

I grimaced. "I shouldn't have kept on. I made him angry."

"I imagine upon reflection, he'll understand."

"I hope so."

He took up his coat. "It's late. Shall we go?"

I donned my own coat and gloves, stacked Edwin's sketchbooks on the table, and locked the door. At the street, we turned in the direction of my flat, our steps taking us from one gaslight to the next. The night air was cold, and Matthew had no gloves. He thrust his hands into the pockets of his coat.

Finally, when we'd walked most of the way, he broke the silence: "What the vicar said about Edwin considering you his ally surprised me. I guess I hadn't had that impression from you, and your father's letter suggests you were more rivals than allies."

I gave a short laugh. "Well, my father certainly did what he could to cultivate it."

"He did?"

"When I was a child, I was allowed to sit in on Edwin's lessons—not because they would help me in any way but because my father believed that it might spur Edwin on." My voice flattened. "He'd praise me as a way of rousing Edwin."

"Ah," Matthew said. "As he did in the letter."

"Yes. Edwin always saw it for what it was, of course."

"Hm."

My thoughts were taking a different turn. "For years, I regarded Edwin's behavior as a rebellious response to my father's constant haranguing. But clearly something happened at that school. Just the way the vicar said—"

"Yes, I noticed that, too," Matthew said. "And the look on his face when you asked."

We had arrived at my door, and I turned to him. "I need to go to Tennersley," I said. His expression was wary—and as he opened his mouth, I added, "Please don't make a fuss."

"Of course you should go. And I'll join you." He frowned. "If your brother's murder has something to do with what happened there—if someone will kill to keep it a secret—then you're not going alone."

Chapter 14

Matthew couldn't leave until midmorning, and we met in front of the Doric pillars of Euston station for a railway train going north. "I've already purchased the tickets," he said and led me inside to the Great Hall, where the windows just below a lofty coffered ceiling admitted a grayish light. Most of the tracks were occupied by trains, their engines belching steam, their carriages the sites of rapid loading and unloading of passengers and freight. The air was warmer than the outdoors, and the stink of coal and the bitter tang of hot metal stung the back of my throat.

"London and Nawf Western down train for Live'pool!" bawled one of the railway servants. His left hand was clenched around his watch, which hung on a chain from his waistcoat. "Twe-e-n'y minutes! Twe-e-n'y minutes to depa'ture! Stops at Watford Junction! Connections at Bletchley for Oxford 'nd Cambridge! Transfers at Roade for a' points nawf! Transfer at Rugby fo' Nuneaton and Lichfield! Stops at Birmingham, Wolverhampton, and

Stafford. Transfers at Crewe for Holyhead. Nineteen minutes to depa'ture! The down train! Nineteen minutes—"

His voice receded as we passed him. Most people on the platform continued to move as fitfully as fish in a barrel, but Matthew maneuvered us toward the doorway of the first-class carriage halfway back in the train, reached a hand to help me mount a set of wooden blocks, and found us seats facing each other. The carriage smelled musty, and the brown velvet was faded around the tarnished brass tacks.

"I can't ride backward," he said apologetically. "Do you mind?"

"Not at all."

The locomotive pulled us slowly out from under the roof of the station and through the cramped, crowded streets of the city. At last the buildings thinned, and with London behind us, the distinct sounds of the pistons working up and down converged into a steady hum, and the train settled into a pace that sent the telegraph poles receding with increasing speed. As we reached the countryside, my eye fixed on a road spinning away into a stand of trees, a dusky purple tide of heather in the middle distance, a huddle of houses on a remote hill.

How seldom I left London, and how circumscribed my life is by my flat and the Slade, I thought. Not that I would have it otherwise, but now that I was away, it came to me with a pinch of longing how much I missed the varied colors of the countryside's landscape, the ability to see long distances, and the limpid quality of the light.

The last time I had ridden a train through scenery like this had been with my father and Edwin. Mother had stayed home, but Edwin was on holiday from school. We took a rare journey to visit my father's ailing mother in Eastbourne, a seaside town on the southeast coast. I must have been eight or nine because my toes barely brushed the carriage floor while Edwin, sitting beside me, could plant his heels on the boards. Across from us, Father had fallen fast asleep, his jaw slack in a way that I never saw when he was awake. It left his mouth slightly open, and Edwin had leaned over close to my ear to whisper, "What would happen if a fly flew in?"

With the suddenness of a needle poking through cloth came another memory of Edwin from that fortnight: the two of us alone on a crescent of wheat-colored beach with speckled gray rocks at the margin. Edwin's trousers were rolled up to the knee, revealing his legs, thin and white. His feet were bare, and laughing, he raced toward the rocks, then turned back to shout encouragement: "Come on, Bel!" I'd trotted after him as quickly as I could in my skirts, and we'd spent hours prowling among the rocks and pools, inspecting crabs and hunting for shells. Our search had produced three large speckled ones that we brought back for Mother to put in her garden. Over the years, two of them had been smashed somehow, but one of them remained whole until after my parents died. The morning my mother's casket was removed from the house, one of the pallbearers accidentally stepped on it. I came out the door and saw it crushed into jagged pieces. And—absurdly—that was the moment when I felt as if the whole world were broken.

As the train slowed momentarily, my tears rose, faster than I could blink them back. I felt a soft handkerchief pushed into my hand, and I pressed it to my eyes, holding my breath to keep from sobbing out loud.

But now that I'd remembered the moment at the beach, I couldn't get the picture of Edwin out of my mind, and my grief rose like a tempest. I found myself crying fiercely, partly out of regret because until now I hadn't remembered that lovely moment at the shore. It worked like a wedge in a crack, letting light into a darkened place, throwing into sharp relief what might have been. While there weren't many happy memories of Edwin after he left for school, this one showed Edwin in his best light, and it belonged only to the two of us. I only hoped Edwin had remembered it better than I had all this time. Now it was mine alone—and if I hadn't taken this train ride, would it have been lost to me?

I felt a rising agitation. What else was I not remembering, if I'd forgotten something like that?

And then doubt crept in like a smudge.

Had that day at the beach indeed happened this way, or was I only wishing it had been so? Had Edwin in fact called to me, or was that merely what I would have wanted?

My tears slowed, and I recovered myself enough to realize Matthew had watched me in silence the entire time. I felt a rising embarrassment and muttered something by way of apology.

"For months after my father died, my grief came and went," Matthew said quietly. "Often it was a smell that brought it on. The Macassar oil he used, or his favorite tea, or his scotch. Did something just remind you of Edwin?"

I sniffed and nodded. "This railway trip. My father and Edwin and I went to the seashore once, and Edwin was . . . he was still happy." I paused and added, chokingly, "Ever since I looked at those sketchbooks, images come to mind of things I've pushed aside for years. Except the memory of the day at the beach is so beautiful that I don't even know if what I remember is entirely true."

"I think all our memories have a trace of deceit in them," Matthew said, his expression sympathetic. "Our recollection is a flawed, imperfect thing, unstable and prone to suggestion. I see it all the time when we ask people for evidence. Despite their best intentions, they report things that can't possibly be true—such as a train arriving at a particular time when official records show it was two hours delayed. Or they'll say something happened at a particular intersection of streets—when those streets don't ever meet. Or they change their stories because they wish the truth were different, or because they remember new things, or because they read an account in the newspaper." He shrugged. "Memory is the exact opposite of a painting or a photograph, I suppose. It's just the nature of it."

I smiled wanly. As we were pulled into Watford Junction, I watched as a scene very like the one at Euston replayed itself: the railway servants, the people mounting and dismounting the train, the hawkers with their pasties and broadsheets and newspapers. And then the train started up again, we rounded a curve, and it all vanished.

"I lost a friend several months ago," Matthew said. "An inspector. We'd come up from Lambeth together."

I turned away from the window. "I'm sorry. What was his name?"

Matthew was sitting forward, his elbows on his knees, his body shifting with the movement of the train. "William. William Crewe. He was murdered. Stabbed. Same as Edwin."

I drew in my breath. "Do you mean to say they're connected somehow?"

His eyes widened and he said hastily, "No! Lord, no. That's not—I'm sorry. I'm not explaining this properly. I'm telling you this because"—he took a deep breath—"because I know it's difficult, when we lose someone, to confront the amount of grief we feel." His blue eyes were dark with feeling. "It's like a bloody mountain. And when William died—well, the details don't matter, but I was partly to blame. I didn't go looking for him when I should've. I waited too long." His face tightened with pain, and he averted his eyes for a moment before meeting my gaze again. "My point is, after it happened, I threw myself into the investigation. Three weeks it took me to find the man who did it, arrest him, and make sure he paid with his life." A pause, and his words came more slowly. "You'd think seeing him punished would help. But it didn't. At the end of it, my guilt and my grief were still there and all the larger for having been neglected." His voice was uneven, as if something were rubbing his throat raw. "What I mean is we may find out who did this to your brother—and even punish him for it—but it's not likely to make your grief any less. When William died, someone told me the only things that help are tears and time. So don't apologize for weeping." He leaned forward, close, and his hand came up to tuck a curl away from my face, and for a second his palm lay flush and warm against my cheek. "I think I've made a muddle of this. I only mean to help."

Our eyes met and held for a long moment.

"Not a muddle at all. Thank you," I whispered.

The train gave a jolt. The side of his mouth curved up briefly in a smile, his hand dropped away, and he leaned back. We sat quietly for a dozen miles or so, but it was a comfortable silence. I gazed out the window, letting my eyes rest on the rolling hills, the trees feathered with orange and gold, the old walls of rough stone outlining the fields, a herd of cows placidly chewing their cud—and I felt a measure of peace, a slight lifting of the heaviness in my chest.

At last we reached Bletchley, and as the train left the station he broke the silence: "The next stop is ours."

We neared Milton Keynes, and the train slowed to a halt. It was half past two by the clock at the station, and as we stepped away from the platform, we could see a grass-covered knoll not far away. On top of it stood Tennersley, reared against a blue sky with clouds scudding westward.

Chapter 15

The school was enclosed by a black wrought-iron fence tipped with points in the shape of arrowheads. As we drew close, it was as if the pencil sketches from Edwin's books were colored in, for he'd represented the place truly. I saw the two wings of the main building, an elegant three-story edifice, with a square tower made of hewn caramel-colored stone. But though the style dated from a previous century, the stone appeared freshly scrubbed. The trees and shrubs placed at precise intervals softened the starkness of its walls, but they seemed to have been recently planted, lacking the robustness of mature plants.

The gate was open, and we followed the curved drive to the front door, an ostentatious oak affair. It opened easily, however, and we found ourselves in a square entrance hall with electric lamps and two mirror-image sets of wooden stairs leading to the upper floors. The smell struck me immediately—a mix of cooked food and wood polish. A door to the left stood open, and I saw a young man looking over what seemed to be accounts at a wooden desk.

"I beg your pardon," Matthew said, leaning into the room. "Might I have a word with the headmaster?"

The young man looked up, his brown eyes blinking behind his spectacles. "Oh! Beg pardon, I didn't hear you." He pushed himself to standing. "I'm Marcus, one of the prefects here. May I tell him who's calling?"

"Matthew Hallam, of Scotland Yard, just come from London."

He froze and his face blanched. I wondered if the look of guilt he wore was indicative or merely reflexive at hearing the words *Scotland Yard*.

"Yes, of course," he stammered. "I'll fetch him."

He took the stairs two at a time, and a few moments later he returned, followed by a man of about thirty-five with a tidy brown beard. His fingers curled around his lapels, and he came forward with a pleasant, open smile.

"How do you do? I'm headmaster here. Albert Donnelly." He reached a hand toward Matthew and nodded to me. "Please, come upstairs."

We followed him to the floor above and entered his office.

The large room occupied the back corner of the central tower. It had windows on two sides, with an expansive view, elegant paneling, and a Turkish carpet. Below I heard the sounds of boys playing what sounded like rugby, their cries and shouts penetrating the diamond-shaped panes. The desk sat at an odd angle, but as Mr. Donnelly sat down in his chair and we took seats across from him, I realized the wisdom of the arrangement: he could merely turn his head to keep an eye on the fields below.

Matthew sat back against the wooden slats. "We have some

questions about a young man who was once a student here. His name was Edwin Rowe, and he attended from the fall of 1861 through the spring of 1865. Did you know him?"

He shook his head ruefully. "Before my time, I'm afraid. I've only recently taken the position as head beginning last December."

"Is there anyone here who might remember him?" I asked. "He was my brother."

"Ah, I see." He fiddled with a button on his waistcoat. "I doubt it. You see, we had a fire here, in 1869, and the school was closed as a result. It took us some time to rebuild. Naturally, we couldn't ask the teachers to remain indefinitely without a position or a salary, so they moved on."

A fire would explain the scrubbed appearance of the stonework and the immaturity of the trees outside.

"Was the entire building burnt down?" Matthew asked.

"The stone was salvageable, of course. I'm afraid the interiors of the central tower and the west wing, including the chapel"—he waved toward the wing on his right—"were utterly destroyed. The east wing was the only part that remained intact."

"Do you have any records of the school? Any pictures of the students?" I wanted to know.

He was already shaking his head. "We have some of our previous teachers' portraits that survived because they were hung in the gathering room in the east wing. But photographs and rosters and all of those sorts of things are gone. Such a tragedy, really." He made a loose fist around his beard and stroked it. "Perhaps you'd like to visit the man who was headmaster. He might have some memorabilia from that time."

"Do you have his name?"

"Mr. Rawlings. Charles Rawlings. He lives in retirement on the Isle of Wight, I believe. We still send him a circular. Let me see . . ." He opened a desk drawer and drew out a folder, consulted a page, and wrote a note on a piece of paper that he pushed toward us. "Here's his address."

"Would you mind if we looked at the east wing?" I asked. "I'd like to see someplace where Edwin spent time."

"Of course." He rose, and we took his cue. "And if there's anything else I can do, please let me know."

He led us back downstairs and gave directions to Marcus.

"Yes, sir." The prefect hopped up anxiously and chose a brass key from one of a dozen that were hanging from metal hooks in a wooden cabinet. "It's this way . . . er, please, sir . . . and miss."

His evident discomfort made me long to put him at ease, but I had a feeling anything I said would only make things worse. I glanced at Matthew; he wore an understanding smile.

We followed Marcus across the entrance to a door; it opened with less ease than the door we'd come through, and the hallway felt small and shabby compared with the entranceway. Marcus was lanky the way young men are sometimes, as if his bones hadn't properly knit together yet, and as he walked ahead, some of the straight brown hairs at the crown of his head bounced.

He turned to glance back at us. "Mr. Donnelly told you about the fire, then?"

"Yes," Matthew replied. "Does anyone know how it started?"

"The fire chief said it was probably a lamp in one of the rooms," he offered. "But no way to be certain."

We reached the end of the corridor, and he used the key to open a door that squeaked shrilly. I felt a rush of air that was at once chilly and stale, and we stepped inside a rectangular room hung with framed portraits, most of which could have used a good cleaning. At one end stood an enormous hearth, swept bare but stained dark from old fires. The only light came from diamond-paned windows above; some of them rattled in their casements, and the cool air found its way down to us.

"Is this room not used anymore?" Matthew asked.

"Oh, we use it sometimes," Marcus said. "For events and presentations, that sort of thing. There's a special dinner next week."

"How long have you attended the school?"

"Five years. I've one more left."

"How would you describe it? Are most of the boys happy here?"

"Of course!" he said smartly. "It's a very good place."

My eye was caught by an engraved plaque on the wall, and I walked toward it. "What's this?"

"It's the honor roll." He pointed to a plaque on the opposite wall. "It starts there, with the very first forms."

Matthew studied the newer panel. "Are you Theodore Marcus?"

He flushed a bit. "Yes."

"I see your name there for mathematics and Latin," Matthew noted. "Congratulations."

His flush deepened. "Thank you, sir. Bit of friendly competition for those. Top boys get privileges, you see. We're allowed to go into town and that sort of thing."

My eye sought the dates near the top of the plaque. And there was Edwin's name for art, three years running.

"I . . . er, I should get back to my work," Marcus said nervously.

"All right," Matthew replied. "Do you mind if we stay here for a bit?"

He looked relieved. "Not at all. Stop by the office before you leave, so I know to lock up."

I smiled to thank him, and a moment after he left Matthew sneezed loudly.

"It's dusty, isn't it?" I commented, running a finger along the upper edge of the wainscoting. "Did you see Edwin's name?"

"For art, yes." He gazed up at the portraits hanging between the square moldings above the oak panels. "Look at all these," he said. The first showed a sober-looking man in a heavy white wig, his left hand resting on a globe. We walked from portrait to portrait, passing by the ones with names and dates before Edwin's time.

At last we reached several with dates that corresponded with Edwin's tenure here:

Lionel McAdams
Geoffrey Conlin
Michael Sterns Sacks
Robert Louis Melford

The styles of the portraits varied little. Most of the men were seated at desks. None wore wigs. Their dress was modest and even severe, but none of the men looked unsympathetic, and most were comely. I half expected Matthew to make a comment about how much the artists had flattered their subjects.

Instead he was pacing along the entire section of the wall, staring intently at each nameplate. "Where is the art master?" he demanded.

"What?"

"Up until now, there are teachers in five subjects—you see the books?" He strode back to the earlier group of paintings and pointed as he came toward me. "See on their desks? Books in Latin. Mathematics, obviously, with the Euclid and compass. This one has history books and a globe. This one has Plato and Shakespeare. And here is the art teacher, with the easel in the background. But where is the art teacher in this group?"

"Maybe someone was here for a long time," I said.

He peered at the last art master's portrait. "William Maxwell Waters served from 1852 to 1858." He strode along the wall until he reached the next painting whose background featured an easel. "The next is 1866 to 1869, when the fire happened." He turned to me, and his blue eyes were bright. "1859 to 1865 is six full years. You're the one who told me to look for what's missing."

Uneasily, I backed away from the wall and took in the portraits. Matthew was right, and I knew my father had sent Edwin here in large part for the respected art master.

"It's odd," I admitted.

Matthew grunted agreement.

We completed our parade down the other side of the hall, paying particular attention to the dates, for masters in all the subjects. Aside from the fire, nothing seemed to interrupt the presence of a teacher in a particular subject.

We paused in front of the awards plaque with Edwin's name.

"I wonder how jealous the other boys were of that," I said. "Do you think this is why he was unhappy here? Because the bit of friendly competition wasn't so friendly?"

"Perhaps," Matthew allowed.

We stopped in to say goodbye to Marcus and let him know he might lock up.

"Do you happen to know who Edwin's art teacher might have been in, say, 1865? I notice there's a portrait missing," Matthew said.

He looked blank. "I'm sorry, couldn't say. I never noticed."

"Another question for Mr. Rawlings," I murmured, and he nodded.

We said goodbye and exited the way we'd entered, by the enormous front door. Matthew was silent on the walk back to the station, but as we reached the platform, he uttered a groan. "Good Lord. The Isle of Wight, of all places."

I looked at him in surprise. "I can go by myself if you've other things to do. This visit probably won't reveal anything about Edwin's murder or the painting. But I still want to know what happened to Edwin here."

He grimaced. "It's not that I've other things to do. It's the boat ride."

"Oh!" I remembered what he'd said about his seasickness and winced in sympathy. "I really can go by myself, you know."

He waved a hand dismissively.

The locomotive rounded the corner, and there was a general stirring of the people on the platform. The brakes dragged the train to a stop, and we mounted and settled into a carriage. Outside the window three dogs gamboled close by, and I hoped they knew to stay at a safe distance once the train started to move.

The whistle blew, and the dogs settled side by side on their haunches to watch the train depart. I found myself laughing softly, for they seemed almost human in their grasp of the situation, their mouths forming a series of smiling farewell barks I couldn't hear over the noise of the engine.

TWILIGHT FELL OVER the countryside. The fields lay long and low, shadows stretching across them. The lights of houses in the distance twinkled, delicate as moths among the trees. Eventually, we drew near London, with its hundreds of yellow lights wallowing in a fog that obscured all signs of stars. We disembarked at Euston station, and Matthew put me in a cab, remaining at the curb until the wheels began to turn.

Fatigued, I rested my head against the cushion and closed my eyes, not opening them again until the driver stopped and announced we'd arrived at my flat. I dismounted, opened the front door, and began climbing the stairs. As I reached the landing below mine, I fumbled my key out of my reticule, wanting nothing more than a cup of hot tea and to shed my dusty clothes. I heard a scraping sound and a grunt above me, and I stared up into the shadows.

There was a bulky dark figure looming next to my door that began to sway.

I let out a cry, and the figure spoke immediately. "Annabel, it's me. Felix." His voice sounded peculiar.

I peered at him in the dim light coming from a lamp on the landing below. "Felix! What are you doing here? What's the matter?"

As I stepped onto the landing beside him, he tried to stand, pushing off the floor with his hands. But he swayed as he reached his full height, and as I grasped him by the shoulders, thinking he was ill, I smelled whiskey thick on his breath.

"Felix," I said in surprise. "Why . . . you're drunk."

"I'm so sorry, Annabel. I'm s' sorry." His words slurred, rising and falling in waves. "Edwin . . ."

I sighed. The poor man. I understood his guilt, but Edwin would never have wanted him to feel so tormented that he turned to whiskey for consolation. When Felix was sober again, I'd talk to him, try to help him if I could.

"Felix, you should go home," I said gently.

His voice was mumbling and incoherent, and his head fell forward. "Should never've ashked him to . . ."

"Come along, Felix," I said as I took hold of his arm to guide him toward the stairs. "Can you manage?"

With my right hand firmly on the banister and my left arm around his prodigious waist, I guided him downstairs. Several times he teetered, and I feared we'd both go tumbling, but at last we reached the pavement outside.

"I'm so sorry," he mumbled. "So 'shamed. Should've helped him find shun . . . something to do." He emitted a heavy, whiskey-infused exhale. "Shouldn't ha' gone to jail . . ."

I craned my head, looking for a cab. Over my shoulder, I reassured him: "Please don't, Felix. You were only ever kind to him."

A cab turned onto the street, and the driver raised his whip in response to my wave. As the cab halted at the curb, the driver assessed the situation and climbed down from his box with a sigh to open the door. With his help, I got Felix inside. "A friend of his died. He's very upset," I said, by way of explanation. I gave Felix's address and handed the driver some extra coins on top of the usual fare.

His smile was wry but not unkind. "I'll see to him. Don't worry, lass."

I thanked him, returned upstairs, unlocked my door, and undid the fastenings of my cloak. As I hung it on its usual hook, Felix's words came back to me, together with Matthew's question about why Edwin hadn't pursued his craft legitimately. Had Felix been unwilling or unable to help Edwin years ago and now felt sorry about it?

I'd been weary before, but Felix's presence on my landing had startled me, and in the aftermath, my nerves were still jangling. With jerky fingers, I lit the lamp, stoked the stove, and put the kettle on for tea. As I waited for the water to boil, I caught up the auction catalog Felix had left during his last visit. From the cover smiled Madame de Pompadour, secure in her position as the king's mistress. I moved close to the lamp, so I could study the picture more thoroughly. She seemed to welcome the scrutiny, to meet the gaze of her viewer with an expression that held both bold assurance and the promise of intimacy. Her eyes were wide and alight with laughter and intrigue, though her lips were demurely closed. If I were a man, I'd have found her extraordinarily attractive, perhaps irresistible, especially if I believed all that warmth was for me. My eyes shifted from her to the background. On the wall hung a painting of a boy fishing in a river. Something about the droop of his pole caught my eye, and when I realized what it was, I couldn't help but laugh inwardly at the joke. Madame had been born Jeanne Antoinette Poisson—*poisson* meaning "fish" in French—and his fishing pole was pointing almost directly at her right ear. Behind her stood a marble-topped table with three leather-bound books—probably an allusion to her patronage of Voltaire and Smith—and a pure white basin, possibly a piece of porcelain brought from the factory at Sèvres that she'd built. There was no indication anywhere of the tuberculosis her body harbored, and which eventually killed her.

Involuntarily, my thoughts veered toward Felix and the danger I sensed for him. I understood how the strain of the last few days might have driven him back to taking spirits. But what if he hadn't come here to my flat? What if he'd spent the night stumbling around the streets? He might have been robbed or beaten or worse. I wished I could somehow keep him out of the pubs, but the best thing I could do for him was to find the painting, for that could possibly reinstate him with Bettridge's.

"Where did you go, Madame?" I asked softly. "And what else could I possibly do to find you?"

But her eyes, beautiful and enigmatic, gave me no sign.

Chapter 16

On the railway train that took us to Portsmouth, I was of two minds whether to tell Matthew about Felix's visit. In the end, I decided not to, at least for the time being. The two men were already wary of each other, and I felt protective of Felix. Besides, nothing would be gained by Matthew learning about Felix floundering at my door in the dark.

As we stood on the dock at Portsmouth, Matthew drew out a paper map to show me that the Isle of Wight was roughly diamond-shaped. The River Medina was like the blade of a carving knife that plunged from the northernmost corner straight down into the heart of the island, with its tip at the town of Newport, where the headmaster lived. Matthew's plan was for us to take the shortest possible boat trip to the harbor at Ryde and then the railway train inland.

I soon realized this route was best, for even before we left the dock Matthew's complexion turned greenish and a sheen of sweat appeared above his brow. I knew the journey should take only an hour, and Spithead, the strait between England and the island, was the most sheltered section of the English Channel. Still, there was a stiff breeze, the waves rose high enough that the rail was slick, and occasionally a mist of spray reached my face. I found the journey went easier if I bent my knees and rode with the waves, expecting no rhythm, instead of fighting the capricious bounce and roll of the ship.

"Are you feeling all right?" Matthew asked, raising his voice to be heard in the wind. "Best to stay above if you can and keep your eyes on the horizon. The fresh air may help you."

I felt perfectly fine, but I kept that to myself. "Will anything help *you*?"

"No."

"I've never been out on a boat like this. The most I've done is row about in a quiet cove." I wondered if talking might take his mind off his sickness or exacerbate it. Somewhat cautiously, I asked, "When is the last time you were on a boat?"

"A few years ago."

"For your police work?"

He took his eyes off the horizon to shoot me a sideways glance. "It was when I went looking for my mother. It's a good thing Nell was back here, otherwise I'd never've set foot on the boat home. I'd still be in France. Never mind that I can't speak a word except *bonjour* and *verre de vin*."

I chuckled and observed a cluster of four fishing boats, two of which had men hauling in dark nets full of shining silvery fish. The solidity of the boats and the men balanced the erratic play of light on the waves.

"What are you looking at?" Matthew asked.

"Do you remember the painting in the Jespers' front hall?" I nodded toward the water. "This makes me think of it."

He grunted. "I thought the painting was a garden."

"It was," I confirmed. "I just mean the way it's broken up in pieces, with our eyes drawn to bits of color and light. Mr. Poynter showed us some prints last year of Cézanne's work, and it's all like the garden. He doesn't particularly admire the French painters, but he gives them high marks for originality of purpose. He believes they're trying to show us how we *look* at a garden, rather than showing us the garden itself."

Matthew appeared dubious, so I put it another way. "Let's say you come upon two men, one of them attacking the other. Is your eye more focused on the piece of silver pipe in his hand or the brown wall behind them?"

He made a face to show he thought I was being absurd, but he answered. "The pipe."

"Why?"

"Because it's dangerous."

"Precisely. And also because it is shining and moving and in the foreground. Our eyes tend to choose light over dark, to perceive what's moving over what's still, and to notice what calls up fear, or any strong feeling, over something mundane." A wave struck the boat, and I clung to the rail as I rocked back on my heels. "Mr. Poynter says he thinks these French painters are trying to make us aware of how our eyes assemble pictures for us, in parts." I paused. "And if you think about it, as we move around the world, we *don't* look at everything with equal attention. Some things we don't bother with at all."

"Hm."

We both watched as a large sailing ship moved past, its white sails swelling to fullness, wrinkling in the wind, and billowing again, as smooth as a fresh case drawn over a pillow.

"So, there." He gestured with his chin toward the receding ship. "Just now, I asked myself, what do I notice? As you said, it's what moves—the sails, and the two sailors climbing the rigging, not the closed portholes. And I see the waves but I ignore the flat sea in the background." He paused. "At least first off."

"We'll make a painter of you yet."

He chortled. "Even I know there's a difference between noticing and wielding a brush." His smile faded, and he looked pensive. "Perhaps you're right. I probably don't pay enough attention to what doesn't capture my eye straightaway."

"Well, as a detective, your task is to find what's out of the ordinary," I demurred. "You needn't concern yourself with all the average pedestrians on their way home from the shops. It's your task to catch the boy who's stolen the loaf of bread." He pulled a face, and I added hastily, "Not that you're simply catching petty thieves—but metaphorically speaking."

"I know. But sometimes, precisely because I am working on cases that are more complicated than stealing a loaf of bread, it might be a person walking home who warrants a second look."

Something about his tone made me ask, "Are you thinking of anyone in particular?"

He didn't reply, and I thought I understood why.

"You're suspicious of Felix, aren't you?" I asked.

"How long have you known him?"

The boat rocked sideways with a wave and I tightened my hands on the rail. "As far back as I can remember. He and my father went to university together. And when Felix returned from Paris, he came straight to my father, once he heard he was in London. He's always been considerate of us. You saw him at the funeral; he took care of all the arrangements, and of course he meant to be kind, finding work for Edwin. What do you suspect?"

"He's never married?"

I shook my head. "No. I think he was engrossed in his work from a young age. That's why it's so tragic and unfair—him being pushed out this way, over something that wasn't his fault."

"Yes." His face was impassive, and I felt a rising annoyance.

"You think there's more to it?" I asked. "That Bettridge had another reason for letting him go?"

"Perhaps." His tone was evasive. "I understand that Bettridge had a great deal depending on that auction's success. But if Severington had been working for them for several years . . . one mistake seems—"

"There *are* people who are terribly exacting and inflexible," I said rather sharply. "I don't know Mr. Bettridge myself. But he might be that sort."

The expression on his face was deliberately noncommittal, one I was coming to recognize. It meant Matthew knew something I didn't. "You've spoken to him, then?"

"The day before the auction," he admitted.

"What did he say?"

He hesitated. "It's more what he didn't say."

The wind whipped my hair into my face, and I pushed it back. "Go on."

"He didn't mention how much he regretted letting Severington go. He didn't give me the impression that he felt any loyalty or gratitude for his years of service."

"Perhaps he's not the sort to praise."

"Hm." His eyes were fixed on the horizon. It might have been his way of coping with seasickness, but I sensed he was avoiding my gaze.

"For goodness' sake, what is it?" I asked, worried now.

His eyes met mine and held. "Do you know why he was let go from Christie's?"

I felt a twist of uncertainty inside my chest. "No."

"He was drunk one afternoon, and ruined a painting. Put his foot right through it. He denied it, but there was a witness." He took a deep breath in. "The insurance paid, but Christie's knew it was a fraudulent claim."

"Did he ever admit to it?"

He shook his head. "According to the witness, Felix would have been too drunk to remember—and when asked, Felix admitted he wasn't certain what had happened."

I imagined gossip like that spreading like wildfire, and my heart sank.

And now Felix was drinking again.

After a moment, I confessed, "He came to my flat last night."

"Why?"

"I didn't let him in. He was well into his cups, so I brought him downstairs and put him in a cab." A feeling of disloyalty came over me, and hastily I added, "He said over and over how sorry he was."

"What for? Did he say?"

I hesitated. "Well, most of all, he wished he'd never asked Edwin to clean that painting. I'm sure he blames himself for Edwin's death." A wave threw a light spray that reached my cheek, and I wiped it off with the inside of my sleeve. "I suppose it's natural, but it isn't right."

"Unless he spoke out of turn to someone," Matthew said. "Maybe when he was drinking, he mentioned that Edwin was restoring the painting."

"Even if he was drunk, I can't imagine him saying anything to endanger Edwin," I objected. "He loved him."

Matthew looked troubled. "Whether he is drinking or not these days, his past makes him susceptible to blackmail."

"Blackmail! By whom?"

"Whoever wanted the painting—and whoever stole it," he replied. "If the thief is looking for a buyer, he'll assume Felix will know the people who'd be interested in it, don't you think?"

"I suppose so." I felt wretched. "I hate to think he's mixed up in something like that."

"I hope he isn't," Matthew said soberly.

A sudden roll of the boat made him groan. His knuckles whitened as he grasped the rail, and he blurted, "Can you leave me—quickly—I'm going to be sick."

I handed him my handkerchief and abandoned him to his misery.

Chapter 17

We disembarked, and I left Matthew to sit and recover himself while I went to the railway station to purchase our tickets. Fortunately a large map of the island hung on the wall, and beside it hung a map of Newport. The town was represented by a loose crosshatch of streets, and I found Shanklin High Street tucked behind St. Thomas's Square, right across from the platform.

I returned to the bench where Matthew sat and handed him the tickets. He already looked less pale.

"Feeling better?" I asked.

"Much." A grimace. "I'm just dreading having to go back."

After a few minutes, we heard the train clacking along. It came around the corner and slowed to a stop, and a lone porter stepped off. He blew a short blast on his whistle, and Matthew and I, the only passengers on the platform, climbed into one of the carriages. The train started up, and I anticipated it approaching a quick hum. Instead, we merely trundled along, and I began to fidget. It wasn't logical of me, of course—minutes wouldn't matter, but I felt a growing sense of urgency. Matthew raised an eyebrow. "Not the London and North Western, is it?"

I tried to smile.

He looked at me understandingly. "I know it feels there's a lot riding on this meeting, but if it leads nowhere, I have some other ideas."

I nodded. "Thank you."

The train rolled to a stop at an open platform with two benches beside a sign that proclaimed NEWPORT, and we disembarked. A dozen people occupied the square, lingering and laughing. One woman had a picnic basket, and three little children following alongside; a young man with a bicycle had paused, one foot on the ground, to admire the view.

"There's no hurry here, is there?" Matthew commented, as our own pace slowed. Perhaps he felt as I did, that we'd seem out of place if we hurried along the way we did in London.

Several streets intersected near the bell tower, but there were no signs, so Matthew stopped into a shop to inquire about Shanklin High Street. The haberdasher pointed down a road wide enough for a single carriage. We walked along until we found Charles Rawlings's cottage and passed between two stone pillars into the yard. There was a tidy garden, a white stone birdbath, and a gravel path to the entrance. At the door, we found neither bell nor knocker, and with some trepidation, I raised my hand and rapped.

It was opened by a woman not much older than I.

"Good afternoon," she said, smiling.

Matthew introduced us and asked if Mr. Rawlings was in.

A look of curiosity crossed her face. "I'm his grandniece,

Catherine Wooster. And he's here, but he's not accustomed to visitors. Would you like to come in? I'll see if he's feeling well enough."

We entered the front room. It felt warm and close, the result of the sun coming in the window for the entire morning. A multicolored rag carpet covered the floor, and the hearth was clean and ready for the fire to be lit. Two bookshelves were full. On the mantel were four framed photographs in sepia tones, all featuring groups of young men dressed in white and standing behind their rowboats. Out of the corner of my eye I saw movement, and I started. A calico cat, nicely camouflaged by a woven blanket, lay on one of the armchairs. She gazed at me through her slit eyes, stretched her two front legs straight out, and tucked them back under her chest before closing her eyes again.

"Catherine said you wished to speak with me," came a man's voice.

I turned to see a gentleman, stooped and spare, perhaps sixty years old, walking with the assistance of a wooden cane. He had a long, narrow face, a fringe of gray hair around his ears, and a pinkish pate. His brown eyes were rheumy, but his smile was pleasant, and he gestured toward the couch. "Please, sit. Sit."

He lowered himself into one of the armchairs and peered at us. "I cannot see so well anymore, but even if I could, I don't believe I'd recognize you."

"No, we've never met," I spoke up. "This is Matthew Hallam, and I'm Annabel Rowe. My brother, Edwin, went to school at Tennersley, years ago."

His smile faltered, as if a memory had snagged. And then his cheerful expression returned, as if the memory pleased him. "Ah, Edwin Rowe! Of course!"

I felt relieved he remembered.

Matthew rose and pointed to the photographs on the mantel. "Is he in any of these?"

"No-o-o." He drew out the monosyllable. "Those are some of our crew teams. In addition to my duties as headmaster, I trained all the boys." His smile was droll. "Edwin is a *very* talented young man, but he wasn't a rower."

"Mr. Rawlings," I said gently, "I don't suppose you heard. Edwin died recently."

His forehead wrinkled in deep horizontal lines. "Died! Why, that's a tragedy! So young, and such a talent."

"What do you remember of him at Tennersley?" I asked.

"Oh." He spread his hands. "He was one of our most successful students. A very talented boy. A happy boy."

I felt myself stiffen in surprise, for the one thing I'd gathered from those sketchbooks was that Edwin was not a happy boy at the school.

Matthew turned away from the photographs on the mantel. "Do you have the class picture from his year, Mr. Rawlings? I'd love to see it."

He began to push himself to standing.

"May I fetch it for you?" I asked hurriedly and began to rise.

"No, no." He waved me off, and with as much alacrity as his stiff joints would allow, he went to the bookshelf and drew out a leather-bound album. He came toward me, his elbows bent, and offered it. "Be careful, it's heavy." I placed it in my lap and opened the cover before he'd even returned to his chair.

"They're all in there," he said as he lowered himself back onto the cushions. "We hired a photographer to commemorate the opening of school, beginning my first year as headmaster."

I handled the endpapers gingerly, for they felt as brittle as
dried leaves. Then came the pages with the class pictures. Each
was covered with a thin cover-glass to protect the surface. The
first was dated 1851, and it was a daguerreotype, horizontal,
and approximately six inches by nine. It showed three rows of
boys. In the first row were the younger boys, seated on wooden
chairs, their hands folded in their laps. In the second row were
older boys, standing; the oldest boys occupied a riser at the
back.

Carefully I turned until I found the page for 1861, the au-
tumn Edwin arrived, and I scrutinized the picture. As in all
the others, the boys were arranged in three rows. Edwin was
seated second from the left in the front. He looked small and
thin compared to most of the other boys, and his rigid posture
made me wonder if he was already unhappy, or merely uncomfortable at having his picture taken.

Matthew leaned over my shoulder as I scanned the rest of
the picture. On the far right was a face I recognized. "There's
the one Edwin called Witty."

"Ah, Lewis Witt," Mr. Rawlings said.

I started. *Felix had mentioned a friend named Lewis.*

The headmaster folded his hands—large, long-fingered,
knobby at the knuckles—and rested them under his rib cage.
"The two of them were thick as thieves—although Lewis was
not always the best influence on your brother."

"He wasn't?" I asked.

He tipped his chin and his eyebrows rose in V's. "Oh, no.
We ran a proper school, and Lewis wasn't the sort of boy who
appreciated rules and order. Not a bad boy, but accident-prone
and rather a troublemaker, I'm afraid. He enjoyed his pranks

and would often lure the other boys along." He sighed. "One night, Lewis convinced Edwin to leave school grounds, and they jumped on a train for London—an action completely against school rules. We allowed Edwin to return." His lips curled a bit. "But it was Lewis's third offense. I was sorry to lose him, though. He was a good rower. In the top boat for two years."

So Edwin's close friend was expelled, I thought.

"But Lewis's departure was a boon for Edwin," Mr. Rawlings said. "Your brother immediately settled down to his studies."

"Oh?" I encouraged him.

"Edwin didn't just have talent—it was genius, and we all knew it. Even the younger boys." Mr. Rawlings rubbed thoughtfully at his chin. "Rarer still, he had a remarkable natural diligence, that boy. He was in the studio whenever he wasn't in classes. Sometimes he'd remain there after curfew." He sighed philosophically. "Perhaps I shouldn't have allowed it, but I couldn't see the harm, and Edwin made wonderful progress. He was even commissioned to do a portrait for one of the board members. Hiram Boulter was immensely pleased with his protégé."

"Mr. Boulter was the art master, then?" Matthew asked.

Mr. Rawlings's voice deepened with pride. "He was. You may have heard of him. He'd won several prestigious awards before he arrived at our school. A tremendous asset. Have you seen any of his work?" He squinted first at me and then at Matthew.

"I'm afraid not," Matthew replied.

I examined the second and third rows of the class photograph. Will Giffen was easy to find, already more a young man than a boy, with broad shoulders, features that had lost their round softness, and a riot of what looked like light brown curls.

I looked at the two boys on either side of him. One had fair hair and a squarish jaw; he didn't look familiar from Edwin's sketchbooks. But the other did. I leaned over to study him more closely, and I was sure. It was the dark-haired boy who'd been standing with Will at the river in Edwin's sketchbook—and who'd been at the auction.

"Matthew," I said softly and pointed.

"There he is," Matthew murmured.

I rose and carried the book to Mr. Rawlings, pointing at the boy. "Who is this?"

He bent over the photograph. "Next to Will? Why, that's Samuel Boulter."

"Boulter?" I echoed. "Was he the art master's son?"

He peered again at the image. "Yes. He looked very like his father."

I returned to my chair and turned another page. The following year, Edwin was in the second row, with Lewis beside him. The next two years, Edwin was in the second row, but Lewis was gone, and Will and Samuel had moved to the third row. The year after that, Edwin was gone, as was Sam. Will was the only one remaining.

"Mr. Rawlings," Matthew spoke gently. "Why is there no portrait of Mr. Boulter on the wall at the school? I noticed his was the only one missing."

He waved his right hand dismissively. "Oh, when he left, he asked to take it with him. It was his property, after all. Most people leave their portraits for posterity, but the board agreed he could have it."

"Why did he leave?" Matthew asked, his voice pleasant. "Was there some difficulty?"

"No, no." Suddenly he stiffened and his jaw came out. "Look here. You're not planning to rake all that up again, are you?"

I flinched at the rancor in his voice. Mr. Rawlings glared at us, and his brows had drawn down. Perhaps the cat heard the same harsh note I did, for she slid off her chair and slinked out of the room.

"I beg your pardon?" Matthew asked.

"We ran a *proper* school." The skin over Mr. Rawlings's knuckles had whitened, and his entire frame was braced as if for a fight. In the gathering silence, both Matthew and I sensed the story we'd come to hear was hovering thick in the air. "A good school, turning out boys with a sense of what was manly and decent and *honest*."

"Well, of course you did," Matthew said amiably. "We've heard that from everyone."

Mr. Rawlings looked mollified, and the lines around his mouth eased. "There is one thing I could not abide—a liar. And when we found one"—he poked a forefinger at the air with each word—"we—rooted—him—out."

Matthew gave a small cough. "Were there particular boys you had trouble with?"

"Alan Kane." Mr. Rawlings spat out the name, and his mouth curled in disdain. "He was a sly, manipulative boy. No one liked him." He tilted his head toward me. "He told terrible lies about Edwin."

Matthew shifted beside me. "What sorts of lies?"

Mr. Rawlings's lips pursed in disgust. "Oh, all sorts of things, none of which bear repeating. But when he slandered a teacher— well, we couldn't overlook *that*."

"Why would he do that?" Matthew asked.

"He was homesick." Mr. Rawlings grimaced. "He wanted to go home, plain and simple. So he told his father that Hiram Boulter was being cruel to him. And Alan's father believed him because he didn't understand boys." Mr. Rawlings poked his forefinger in the air again. "When Alan came to me, I *knew* he was lying. I hadn't been headmaster for over a decade without knowing how to spot the signs of truth or a lie. He hung his head, wouldn't meet my gaze honestly."

"Those are signs," Matthew acknowledged.

"Of course they are!" Mr. Rawlings nodded vigorously. "I went immediately to Hiram and asked him if he had been unkind to Alan, teased him or tormented him in any way. Naturally, he was horrified and could think of nothing he'd done." His chest rose and his mouth tightened. "Hiram had a spotless reputation! Yes, he was strict and exacting, but he was a brilliant painter and an extraordinarily dedicated teacher. He cultivated their talents, nurtured their abilities, took his time with them." Mr. Rawlings scowled. "And I will tell you, in the end, Hiram was more generous than I toward Alan. He said he forgave Alan—because it was possible that Alan had truly mistaken Hiram's strictness for cruelty."

"So Alan went home?" Matthew asked.

"Oh, yes. Good riddance. Alan left and Mr. Boulter remained."

"How long was Mr. Boulter at the school?" I asked.

"Until the spring of 1865. I remember because I left the following year." Mr. Rawlings cradled one hand inside the other and rubbed gently at his knuckles. "The board shifted the curriculum of the school toward maths and the natural sciences and away from the arts. Frankly, I think it broke Hiram's heart. He didn't even finish out the year." Mr. Rawlings gave a phlegmy cough. "His departure changed the school forever. I know Edwin was very upset. He left the school only a day or two after Hiram did. Such a shame."

I could see Edwin being upset over losing his mentor, but that wouldn't explain his general unhappiness.

Matthew was asking something about another teaching position.

"Yes, of course." Mr. Rawlings's face twisted with the effort to remember. "Hiram went to a school in Manchester, I think. I don't . . . I don't recall the name. Sam still had several years of schooling, and he went with his father, of course."

I sensed Matthew had been waiting for Mr. Rawlings to mention Sam, wanting to return to the topic with some appearance of naturalness.

"What can you tell us about Sam, Mr. Rawlings?" Matthew asked. "What sort of student was he?"

"Oh, he was clever, and a good artist, naturally. But he preferred sporting games, rowing and the like." His chest puffed out a bit and one side of his mouth curved up. "He was in our top boat three years running."

"I see."

I studied the images from Edwin's four years, and I thought I could begin to see the character of the entire class. There were boys who stood confidently and boys who seemed uncertain of themselves. Though the boys occupied different places in each photograph, Will and Sam always stood together.

"I never heard from Edwin after he left—but I do hope he found a proper situation for himself. Did he continue to paint?" Mr. Rawlings asked, hopefulness lighting his face.

"Some," I managed.

"Hm. A pity." He passed a hand over his eyes wearily. "Forgive me. Suddenly I'm very tired."

I closed the book and set it on the table. "Thank you for talking with us, Mr. Rawlings."

"Yes," Matthew said as he rose from the couch. "Thank you, sir. We can see ourselves out."

The headmaster remained seated, staring off into the distance, trapped in a reverie of his own. As we exited the room, I heard him mumble under his breath, "A good boy. A happy boy. A proper school." The way he murmured those phrases made me think of a rope worn thin with too much handling.

Matthew opened the door, and as we reached the gray stone pillars, I put a hand on one to feel its solid warmth and took a breath of the clear island air. We certainly knew more than we had an hour ago. But nothing Mr. Rawlings said shed any clear light on what I'd thought was Edwin's pervasive unhappiness. On the contrary, Edwin had a good friend in Lewis, at least for a while, and it sounded as if he had found an art teacher who inspired him.

Had I misread those sketches?

We started toward the train station and Matthew jerked his head back toward the house. "It's good we came. He might be wrong about Edwin being a happy boy, but at least we know who Lewis Witt and Sam Boulter are."

I couldn't see how that would help, but suddenly Matthew put his hand on my arm to stop me.

"Wait," he said and darted back toward the house. I waited several minutes until he reemerged from between the pillars.

He strode toward me. "I wanted to see a picture of Alan before we left," he explained.

"So you found Alan's story odd, too," I said.

"I'm always dubious when everything is proper except for one person, particularly if they're cast out."

"Like a scapegoat," I said in surprise. It hadn't occurred to me.

We fell into step and Matthew added, "He was still muttering those phrases when I went back in, like an incantation."

"Keeping less pleasant thoughts at bay, you mean."

"Rather." His tone was absent, and I gathered he wanted time to reflect. I didn't mind. For my part, I had plenty to consider as we made our way to the station and from thence onto the boat back to Portsmouth.

The night was unusually beautiful and the water serene. The sky was black and clear, the moon delicate as an eyelash among the constellations tracing their own arcs across the sky. I took a deep breath of briny air and felt the coolness in my lungs. Matthew stood beside me, bent over with his forearms resting on the rail, and I was relieved to see he didn't look quite so queasy as he had on our first crossing.

"I want to talk to Lewis," I said.

"Yes, I thought you might."

"I have a feeling he might know more about events that happened at Tennersley."

"He'd certainly provide a different perspective," Matthew allowed. "Do you know where he is?"

"No. But Felix mentioned Lewis to me once. He may know where I can find him." I hesitated. "I doubt Lewis has anything to do with Edwin's murder, or the theft of the painting, and . . . well, I don't think he'll talk to me as readily if you're there."

"Probably true." He laid his warm hand over my cold one and gave it a squeeze. "Just—be careful."

I nodded a promise, and he let his hand remain where it was just long enough that I felt the chill when he let it go.

Chapter 18

The next morning, by sheerest luck, I came upon Felix as he was leaving his flat. He looked bleary-eyed, as if he hadn't been sleeping well, and he certainly didn't seem pleased to see me. Indeed, he wouldn't even meet my gaze. I imagined his surliness was partly due to feeling ashamed of his behavior the other night.

"Where are you going?" I asked as I fell into step.

"To find something to eat," he muttered.

"Could I come along?"

He heaved a sigh that held the bitter tang of gin and squinted at me sideways. His eyes were bloodshot, and his wisps of brown hair were blown this way and that by the wind. "I suppose that inspector told you I broke into Edwin's flat," he said gruffly.

I stared. "No, he didn't. Why would you break in?"

"I wanted to see if he had the guaranty among his papers. I thought he might've signed it."

I almost asked why he hadn't simply asked me for the key. But perhaps he'd made the choice to break in when he'd been drinking. So instead, I said merely, "I understand. I should have thought of that myself."

He gave a phlegmy cough. "So what is it you want?"

His manner was so prickly I wondered if I should abandon the conversation. But I needed Lewis's address. "Let's eat first, shall we?"

He grunted and continued on until we reached a pub. "Here." He held the door and gestured for me to step inside. The establishment felt seedy, with a meager fire on the hearth and the smell of rotten meat and ale. There were two older women at small round tables, with men who might have been their husbands. At the bar, four men hunkered over their pints, drinking with a doggedness that made me uneasy, and as we made our way to a table, the barkeep nodded familiarly to Felix. My heart sank. How often did he frequent this place?

As Felix started in on his stew, I told him an abbreviated version of what we'd learned from Mr. Rawlings. As I finished, his head was bent, and he spooned the last bit of broth from the bowl. Then he took up his pint of ale and gulped most of it.

"Felix, did you know he was unhappy at Tennersley?"

"Not at the time." He set down his glass and met my gaze. "I gathered afterward that something unpleasant had happened. He never told me specifically."

"Do you know where Lewis Witt lives?" I asked.

He sat back with a skeptical look. "I doubt he'll speak with you about Tennersley. Edwin told me he was expelled."

"I won't ask him about himself," I promised. "I'll only ask about Edwin." Felix's expression remained dubious, and I

added, "For goodness' sake, Felix! Surely Lewis will understand if I want to hear about my brother from someone who
was his friend."

He held back a belch and wiped his mouth with his napkin.
"I don't know where he lives, but he works in his uncle's gallery
on Coulton Street, about a mile or so from here. Massey's."

"A gallery," I echoed.

"Tennersley provided the proper training for that, if nothing
else."

I pushed back my chair and stood. "Thank you."

He gave a "hrrmph" under his breath, and I waited. He'd
finished his meal, but he showed no signs of getting up. Instead
he sat with his eyes fixed on his empty bowl.

I nearly walked away, but instead I put my hand on his arm.
"Why don't you come with me?" I asked persuasively. "Don't
stay here in this place."

He pulled away and looked up at me sourly. "Stop it, Annabel. I'm a grown man, and you're not my keeper. I don't need
you pestering me about how to spend my time." A pause. "I've
nowhere I need to be."

Stung, I shut my mouth and backed away from the table.

I left without a word. I reached the pavement overcome with
resentment at his rudeness, when I'd only meant to be kind. But
as I walked, my anger gave way to worry. Felix wasn't acting
himself. I'd known him for years. He might be reserved, but he
wasn't churlish. Was he unwell? Or just profoundly miserable?

He certainly had a right to be, but spending his days in a pub
wouldn't help. My fear was the drink was making his misery
worse.

I proceeded toward Massey's with a mixture of curiosity and dread, and a knot in my stomach that tightened as I drew near.

LEWIS WAS OCCUPIED when I entered, and though I waited until his customer was gone, he told me he couldn't speak with me until he'd finished for the day. So I spent the next two hours waiting in a tea shop nearby, nursing several cups of tea and glancing over the papers, all the while keeping an eye on the front door of the gallery. At last, as the clock struck four, the shop door opened, and Lewis emerged. I saw him take a breath in and out; he hesitated, and in that moment, he appeared to debate whether to elude me. I nearly jumped up and ran out, but with an evident unwillingness he turned and started toward the tea shop. I watched as he entered and approached my table.

I gestured toward the empty chair. "Please."

He didn't take it but stood above me, his lanky frame restless, his pale hair falling over his brow, his gray eyes wary and watchful. He reminded me of a jumpy hare.

"How did you find me?" he asked.

"I asked Felix Severington. He told me where you worked."

He considered that for a moment, then shrugged. "D'you mind if we walk? I've been inside all day."

"Yes, of course."

I took some coins out of my reticule and deposited them by the plate.

As we reached the street, I began, "Thank you for talking to me. I miss Edwin a great deal. Felix says that you and he were good friends."

He gave me a look that was skeptical and scornful all at

once. I wasn't sure what I'd done to deserve either response, and it made me wonder how to proceed. I watched him out of the corner of my eye. He walked with his head slightly in front of his neck, like a horse reaching for the bit, and his eyes darted about, left and right. With his long legs, he walked quickly, and I wanted to slow him down, calm him down, if I could.

"I'm sorry, I can't walk this fast," I said. Sweat was dampening the back of my dress, and my rapid breathing wasn't wholly feigned.

He muttered something under his breath that might have been an apology or a curse, but the sound of passing wheels on the cobbles drowned it out.

"Lewis, *please.*"

He spun to face me. "Look here, what do you want with me?"

"I just want to talk to you about Edwin."

"Edwin." As he said the name, some of his anger dropped away, and we stood together on the pavement, just staring, each taking the other's measure.

At last I dragged in a deep breath and let it out. "He was my brother, and I just want to talk to someone who knew him. Someone who was his friend." My voice broke over the words, and perhaps he heard it, for his expression softened.

"I'll tell you what I know, if you'll tell me one thing." His voice carried a challenge. "How could your father have done that to him?"

I gaped at the degree of resentment and disgust in his voice.

His eyes—narrowed and gray and black-lashed—were locked on mine. This was no timid hare, I realized; his eyes were glittering as a snake's. Instinctively, I stepped back, realizing this wasn't a conversation I wanted to have with the distraction of dodging other pedestrians. I cast around and saw a triangle of tree-lined park nearby. I pointed. "Can we sit down? Over there?"

Reluctantly, he nodded and started toward the green. His eyes remained fixed on the pavement in front of him, and he stalked forward in a stubbornly straight line, although several times I had to step left or right to make way for the pedestrians coming toward us. At last we reached the park entrance. One of the two black wrought-iron panels was ajar, and we went inside. The park wasn't large. It would've taken only a few minutes to walk the single, sinuous gravel path among the gardens. The trees arched gracefully overhead, as if holding out a promise of some peace, and the air had the pleasing smell of old leaves. I led him to the nearest empty bench and perched sideways, so I could view him in profile. He sat with his back pressed rigidly against the wooden slats, his hands buried so deep in his pockets they strained the seams. His hair lifted in the breeze and fell over his pale brow, the late-afternoon light carved shadows under his cheekbones, and it occurred to me that he would be handsome if he ever smiled.

"Lewis, I don't know much about Edwin's life at Tennersley," I said. He remained silent, so I continued, "I went to see Headmaster Rawlings yesterday. He lives on the Isle of Wight now. Did you know that?"

He snorted. "I'd have thought he'd be dead."

"Well, he's failing," I admitted. "But he was well enough to talk with me, and he had photographs of all the classes—including yours and Edwin's. He remembers Edwin, and . . . well, he insists that Edwin was happy there."

Lewis stiffened but still did not look at me.

"But from some things in Edwin's sketchbooks, I gather he wasn't. Not at all. I just wonder if you might help me sort it out."

At that he turned to stare incredulously. "There's nothing to sort out! He was bloody miserable. Surely, you had to know!"

I stared. "How would I? I was a child when Edwin left for school, and after he left, he only wrote to me twice." I paused. "Lewis, he didn't come home except for at the holidays. And once he came back to London, he never spoke about school to me, ever."

Lewis remained stubbornly silent, as two birds in a nearby tree twittered at each other.

I tried another tactic. "The headmaster said you were one for pranks. He told me how you and Edwin once tried to run away to London."

"Pranks?" He gave a short bark of a laugh and shook his head. "Bloody Christ."

I felt a rising impatience with this young man who was making a show of having plenty he could tell me but refusing to do it. He seemed genuinely angry at my ignorance, which seemed hardly fair. Yet I also sensed underneath, he desperately wanted me to understand.

"Don't laugh at me," I said finally. "Just tell me."

He bit at his chapped lower lip.

Stifling a sigh, I propped my elbow on the back of the bench and rested my head in my hand. "Lewis, when did you come to Tennersley?"

"Two years before Edwin."

"Are you a painter, too?"

He shook his head and sniffed hard enough to pull his mouth out of shape. "Not like him. I didn't like it much. But rowing was all right."

"Mr. Rawlings seemed very proud of the school's crew teams."

He met my gaze and his smile was sardonic. "Of course he'd say that. He ran a *proper* school. Did he say that, too?"

"Several times." I paused and added pointedly, "Maybe as if he were trying to convince himself. But it couldn't have been a perfectly proper school. He told us about Alan Kane and the lies he told about Mr. Boulter."

A quick sideways glance. "Hmph." He leaned forward to pick up a dead branch from the ground, rested his elbows on his knees, and began to pick off the leaves. I waited patiently, and at last he said, "You should know about Alan, so you understand what happened later."

"All right."

"He wasn't a liar, whatever Rawlings told you. Alan was a few years older than Edwin and me, and he was talented." A deprecatory shrug. "Not like Edwin, mind you, but good enough that Boulter took him under his wing, held his work up as a model for others. That's what we all saw back then, anyway." He rolled the bare stick between his thumb and forefinger. "Boulter's son Sam hated him for it. He and Will Giffen—we used to call him Sam's henchman—would take Alan behind the boathouse and beat him."

I felt my eyes widen. "They did?"

My words were only an instinctive, unconsidered response to my shock, but he turned toward me, his eyes narrowed and furious. "You don't believe me?" He dragged up his pant leg so

I could see his white calf, with a shining scar that ran six inches along the bone. "They beat me, too, for taking Will's spot in the first boat one term. He and Sam threw me down the river-bank and left me there with a broken leg. I'd have died of cold except Edwin came to find me. They made me tell Rawlings I'd fallen in the river."

Mr. Rawlings had used the word accident-prone, I thought.

I shivered. "What did your parents say?"

He pulled his pant leg back down to his boot. "It's just my mum. But she never knew, not till later. School never told her. I spent a week in the infirmary, and a month hobbling around on crutches. Edwin kept Sam and Will from kicking them out from under me and carried everything for six weeks."

Something in the way that Lewis said their names, Sam and Will, made me think about how they were always together in the pictures.

"You and Edwin were good friends by then?" I asked.

He bent to scrape the end of the twig in the dirt. "We were friends almost right away after he came." He gave a faint gri-mace. "Even though he made me jealous, he was so bloody good at everything. But he helped me with my maths and Latin. Same way when he came back to London, he taught me how to restore paintings and build frames and gild them, so I could find work."

"That's what you do at the gallery?"

"Yah." He raised an eyebrow. "Though I've never been asked to clean anything like the Boucher."

I started. "Did he show it to you?"

He grunted. "I happened to stop by his flat the day after it came."

I took a deep breath in and tried to find my way back to Tennersley. "So what happened to Alan?"

"He went to see Rawlings." He gave a particularly vicious stab at the dirt with his stick. "People told him not to bother."

"But Rawlings said Alan accused Mr. Boulter of cruelty," I said slowly. "Why didn't he just explain about Sam and Will beating him?"

He shrugged. "Probably because he knew if he ratted on Sam and Will, and ended up staying at the school, he'd be dead."

I swallowed. "Mr. Rawlings said Alan told lies about Edwin."

My words surprised him enough that he turned to stare. "Well, he's wrong. Alan was gone by the time Edwin arrived. He left the spring before."

I stared. "Perhaps Mr. Rawlings was confused."

A snort. "Wouldn't surprise me."

"So Edwin arrived, and you became friends," I prompted him.

He nodded. "Mr. Boulter recognized Edwin's talent straight-away, same as he had with Alan. Sam hated it, so he and Will started in on Edwin. There was a river nearby. They'd push us in, hold us under sometimes."

I had a sick feeling in my stomach, for I recalled Edwin's sketches of the river, and now I understood. "How did the headmaster not notice all this . . . this . . ."

"Torture?" Lewis spat out the word. "He was gone most of the time, raising money, meeting benefactors. Left everything except for crew in the hands of the assistant, who was more interested in giving a green gown to the kitchen maids than minding the school." He grimaced. "Besides, none of us would ever say anything. Sam and the rest of them would only come

down on us harder. By the spring it was bad enough Edwin and
I tried to run away."

"What Mr. Rawlings called a prank," I said.

"Yah. We made it to the train station at Milton Keynes and
bought tickets. But the train was stopped at Bletchley, and we
were pulled off. The school had telegraphed ahead."

"So you didn't reach London?" I asked in some surprise. I'd
assumed they had.

"Nah." A sniff. "Not that time."

"You did it more than once?"

"The following year, after they broke Edwin's arm. Not his
painting arm, thank God." He gave a dry smile. "That's what
Edwin said at the time. But yes. This time we weren't just trying to get away for a while. We wanted to see if our families
would let us stay. Only this time we were smarter about it. We
paid a couple boys to keep quiet and made it to London." He
looked at me skeptically. "Don't you remember him coming
home?" He ran his hand along his left shoulder and bicep. "He
had a sling on."

Into my mind came the image of Edwin in the doorway,
the sky dark behind him. The image merged with half a dozen
other times he'd stood in the doorway. But now I could almost
see, like a white blur, something that might have been a sling
hanging from his shoulder.

"Yes, maybe," I said.

He ran his thumbnail along the bark of the stick, scraping it
away. "Edwin told me your father thought he was a liar."

"Yes."

"Edwin had a broken arm, for God's sake! Why wouldn't he
believe him?"

I shook my head miserably. "I don't know. I'm not excusing my father by any means. But Edwin and he had been having rows for years, with my father trying to force Edwin to take painting seriously. He didn't know that Edwin *was* taking it seriously at school. When Edwin returned home that time, I'm sure he simply assumed Edwin was being rebellious as usual."

A snort. "So he sent him back." His eyes staring straight ahead, he shook his head in disgust.

"What about you? Was that when you were expelled?"

"Yah. Came to the Hawley School, here in London. But Boulter put in a word for Edwin, so he was allowed to stay," Lewis replied.

And Edwin lost his one ally.

The thought of Edwin being alone against Sam and Will every day sent a shudder to my core. "It probably would've been better if he hadn't."

A short, horrid laugh. "A hundred times better. The fact that Edwin almost made it away only made Sam and Will come after him worse. Sam knew his father had stepped in for Edwin, and if he was jealous before, now it just ate him up. And with me gone, it was two against one." His expression was grim. "Edwin began spending every minute in the studio when he wasn't in class or at meals. Didn't sleep in his room because they'd find him. Boulter was teaching him—and Edwin soaked it all up like a sponge. He was painting five, six hours a day." His expression became bleak. "But that's when Boulter started coming after him. I think Edwin . . . I don't know. He didn't want to displease him. I know Edwin felt he owed him, for keeping him from being expelled, and for teaching him." His voice grew rough. "But he didn't owe him *that*."

My thoughts had halted several sentences before. "What do you mean, 'coming after him'?"

He turned then, and I saw his eyes were wet with angry tears. Finally he said it, quietly. "Boulter liked his boys. Edwin was the next in the line after Alan."

Perhaps I should have guessed, but I didn't. My horror blazed like waves of fire over my entire body, spending its most scorching heat in the center of my chest. The world around me began to turn black as ash—

"Annabel!" Lewis's hand reached out and grabbed my arm, shaking it hard enough to pull me back to sentience.

My vision cleared, and faintly I said, "Stop, please." I rubbed at my forearm as he released it. Later there would be a bruise.

I was grateful Lewis know how to be silent, and to wait. When at last I looked up, he was turned toward me, his left arm along the bench, just watching. His expression was no longer even faintly sardonic, only very sad.

After a few moments, he sighed. "He knew Rawlings wouldn't believe him, same as he didn't believe Alan."

"Did he tell *anyone*?" I asked finally.

"Yah. Mr. Wexford. He was the president of the board of directors for the school, and when he saw Edwin's work, he asked Edwin to paint his wife's portrait." The breeze blew his hair over his brow, and he pushed it back. "He liked Edwin, took an interest."

I nodded, remembering what Mr. Rawlings had said about the commission.

"It was the last day. Edwin was putting the finishing touches on it. I don't think Mrs. Wexford was there. But Mr. Wexford was, and Edwin told him what Boulter had been doing." Lewis shook his head almost wonderingly. "He was lucky. Wexford believed him."

I felt my breath rake the back of my throat. "Did Wexford confront Mr. Boulter?"

"Nah." He sniffed. "He had a better way. Wexford told the rest of the board and Boulter was thrown out the following week. They put out a notice about changing the curriculum or some such thing. But that's what really happened."

"I see," I said slowly. "Yet Mr. Rawlings said that Edwin left *after* the Boulters did. Was that true? I mean, if they were gone, why—"

"Because Sam found out Edwin had talked to Wexford." His breath caught, and he coughed before he continued, "The night after Sam and his father left, Sam sneaked back. He and Will dragged Edwin from his bed, and took him out to the woods."

My heart sank, dreading what was to come.

"Edwin told me afterward it was different from the other times. They didn't taunt him or even talk to him. They just wanted him dead. Somehow Edwin managed to get away, and he climbed a tree. He was lighter than they were, and the bottom branches weren't strong enough, so they gave up. It was pouring rain, but Edwin stayed there all night. In the morning, Edwin left Tennersley for good. Made his way to London, found our house and stayed with us until he'd recovered. My mum took one look at him and . . ."

Edwin had gone there because he couldn't come home.

A faint breeze set off a violent shudder through my entire body. "Thank God he had you."

"Yah." A leaf dropped on the bench and he flicked it away.

"Not that it did him much good in the end. They still wanted him dead."

I understood what he meant. "You think he was killed by someone from Tennersley, don't you?"

His shoulders twitched. "I'd say Will. He was at the funeral. Tall, curly hair, probably told you he was a friend of Edwin's from school."

"Something like that," I managed. "But why? After all this time?"

Lewis's hand clenched around the rail of the bench. "Damned if I know. His kind is just vicious. Does it because he can. And he's the sort who'd come to the funeral to rub it in your face, show you he got away with it."

That hadn't been my impression of Will Giffen, but we'd only spoken for a moment. Indeed, I hardly remembered it. At the funeral, I hadn't known to take any special notice of him.

"He lives here in London," Lewis said. "Bowen Street. Number 49."

"How do you know?"

"Followed him from the church, of course." His eyes were hard. "Was all I could do not to set fire to the whole bloody place with him in it." A pause. "He has two little ones, d'you know? One's a boy. And I hope to God someone buggers him someday, so Will knows how it feels."

I stared at him, the inside of my mouth dry as paper.

His entire face was twisted in an ugly rictus. "Don't look at me like that! It's the only way someone like him learns." He pushed himself up from the bench.

Any fragile connection based on our mutual grief was gone.

He bent at the waist, his face close enough that I could see the spittle at the corners of his mouth. "You should hate him more than anything." His hands were in fists. "What the devil is wrong with you? He was your brother!"

Then he spun and strode away, his dark coat flapping like the wings of an old crow.

Shaken, I sat on the bench through the tolling of several quarter hours from a church nearby. Dusk was falling before I began to take in the full meaning of Lewis's words. More than his descriptions of what happened at Tennersley all those years ago, his vicious wish for Will's son conveyed the depth of his wounds, and Edwin's. Powerless and lonely, these young men had been caught up for years in fierce struggles for respect and safety and well-being. Was Lewis right? Should I feel the sort of rage he did?

With my misery like a heavy stone inside my chest, I rose and walked home through streets whose colors were fading with the dwindling of day.

COLD AND WEARY, I climbed the stairs, and as I reached my door, I spied a dark figure. *But of course,* I thought. I should have expected Felix would come to see what had happened with Lewis. I just hoped he was sober.

I sighed. "Felix? Are you all right?"

He stepped out of the shadow and by the dim light cast by the moon, coming through the window of the landing below, I saw it wasn't Felix at all. A black scarf and a hat pulled low covered most of his face. My eyes met his—hard and glinting as obsidian—and before I could utter a sound he leapt toward me, his hand coming up swiftly to cover my mouth, the fingertips biting into my cheekbone. His voice in my ear was a low growl, and he seemed to want something, but I couldn't make out his words through the ringing in my ears and my own rasping breaths.

The man's hand shifted down to my throat, and his thumb dug into the soft spot under my chin, so I could barely squeak a sound. Pinpricks of light appeared in my sight, and the objects around me began to go dark.

"What were you doing there?" he hissed in my ear.

I had no idea how to answer. My mind had gone so full of fear I couldn't comprehend his question.

He shook me—everything shifted left and right in a blur before my eyes—but I managed a strangled inhale.

"Tell me, damn you!"

Suddenly I heard the front door open below followed by footsteps coming fast and hard on the treads of the stairs.

The man's viselike grip on my mouth loosened for a moment, and I let out a cry that was half relief and half warning, for by some miracle Matthew was on the landing just below, leaping up the stairs two at a time, his coat flying behind him. With a curse, the man flung me sideways, toward the stairs. The soles of my boots scrabbled across the wood floor. I cried out, my hand clawing for the banister but finding only air. I pitched over, my forehead smacking the wall of the stairwell. Everything before my eyes vanished into an ocean of black sparked with white. As I tumbled down the stairs toward the landing I had the fleeting impression of a man leaping over me, lunging down the stairs toward Matthew. I saw a gleam of silver—a knife in the man's right hand—

I longed to warn Matthew, but it was as futile as trying to

cry out in a nightmare. From where I lay in the corner, all I managed was a feeble croak.

Above me, the silvery moonlight coming through the window shaped the landing into a shimmering box and transformed the men into something chimerical, halfway between silhouette and shadow.

The stranger's shoulders were broad, and he crouched low, his quick hands making the blade flash like a live thing. Matthew spun, and I heard the high whirr of something slicing the air and then the smack of his truncheon against pliable flesh that gave way under the blow. The stranger let out a cry and sprang toward Matthew with his fist raised. Matthew jerked backward but not in time. The man's fist met Matthew's jaw, and then he flung an arm around Matthew's neck. But Matthew's hands were up, grasping, and he threw the man sideways into the wall, where his spine met the wooden panel with a sickening thud. Matthew's hands came to the man's collar, and for a moment they were face-to-face. It seemed the stranger was getting the worst of it, and he let out a howl that echoed in that close space—

And then he caught sight of me, and I felt him shift—change his tactic—

His foot came up to kick Matthew, and as Matthew dodged, the man scrambled sideways like a crab, and slashed his knife across my arm—

The pain was sharp as a burn from the stove, and even before the blood began to run, I let out a shriek that made the walls ring—

Matthew's gaze broke toward me, and in that moment, the man rolled sideways, eluded Matthew's grasp, and bolted down the stairs.

Matthew stood above me in the moonlight, his chest heaving, and for a single breath it seemed he was torn between racing after my assailant and tending to me. He turned and dropped to his knees, and my name came out raw and rough from between his lips. His hands ran over my legs and torso, a hasty search for broken bones, and then he pulled a handkerchief from his pocket, tore it, and wrapped one half around my arm to stanch the flow, tying the makeshift tourniquet so fiercely that the pain he caused was worse than the cut itself.

Blood dripped from his temple to his cheek, and he looked terrifying.

"Matthew."

Even as I whispered his name, his demeanor changed. He took a few deep, ragged breaths, and the fire faded from his eyes. Another moment, and he recovered enough to feel the blood dripping, for he wiped the side of his face against his sleeve.

I laid a hand on the tourniquet and winced.

"I know it's tight," he said. "But it's just for a few minutes, and it's the best thing. You're going to be all right," he said, and then again, as if reassuring both of us, "You're going to be all right."

My entire body was shaking, the tremors raking over me. My forehead was beginning to pulse sickeningly. I put a hand up to feel—but he grasped it and held it away. "No, Annabel. Leave it." Rapidly he folded the other half of the handkerchief into a square and pressed it against my forehead. Only then did I feel the sticky hot wetness of blood.

"What's happened? Who was that man?" Mrs. Trask's timorous quaver came from the landing below. A wave of sickness came over me, and I closed my eyes.

"Who was it . . ." Mrs. Trask's voice was fading.

I longed to speak, to say I hadn't seen his face, that it might have been Sam Boulter, but I couldn't be sure. But I felt as if I were dropping into a dark hole, and the words came out a mumble.

I heard Matthew say my name, but his face dissolved into darkness.

Through the wooden floor under my hands, I felt a door closing quietly, as if someone on one of the lower floors had heard the ruckus but wanted to pretend they hadn't—

And then everything went black.

Chapter 19

When I came round, I was in my bed, and Matthew was beside me in a chair. My arm throbbed, and my head ached. Gingerly, I put my hand up to my forehead and felt a cloth, coarse and much bulkier than his bit of handkerchief.

"Matthew."

It was no more than a murmur, but his eyes were open in a minute, and he bent over me, took my hand, and drew it away from my head. "It's a bandage, Annabel. Let it alone. You had stitches, there and in your arm."

I had no memory of any of it, but Matthew had a spot of plaster on his temple. "The doctor's been here?" I slurred. My tongue didn't seem to work properly.

He nodded. "I'm surprised you woke. He gave you a tonic to help you sleep till morning."

"Where is he?" I murmured.

"The doctor? He's gone," he said patiently.

"No. The man. Was it Sam Boulter?"

His jaw tightened. "Yes," he admitted. "He's gone, too. Don't worry."

I let out a soft groan. "You should have gone after him."

He gave me a look that told me what he thought of that idea. "You were unconscious—and bleeding."

"What time is it?"

"Just past midnight."

I tried to roll over and winced at the pain in my side. "Oh! That hurts."

"Your ribs are bruised. But the doctor says nothing's broken."

I reached a hand out, and he took it. "How did you even know I'd come home?" I asked.

"This afternoon, I started to worry about you seeing Lewis. I went to Felix's, and he gave me the address of the gallery. I traced you to the park."

"I can't believe you found us."

"Well, someone in the tea shop thought he looked peculiar. Often when we trail someone, it just requires asking enough people in the vicinity. It's surprising what the public will notice."

"I didn't see you at all," I murmured.

"I kept my distance. But I followed you home, and when I didn't see your light go on, I had a feeling . . ." His voice faded.

"What?"

He drew the chair closer, so he could hold my hand between both of his. "I waited too long to go after Crewe," he explained. "Now, I don't wait." He added under his breath: "I just wish I'd been quicker."

The fire in the stove sent a flickering light that cast Matthew's face half in shadow. Even so, I could see how deeply he meant it.

"Matthew, don't," I said quietly and squeezed his hand. "I'm fine."

He brought my hand to his mouth and kissed it, and in that moment my every nerve was on fire and nothing hurt. Then he laid my hand on the bedclothes and stepped to the stove. He knelt before it and added another small log, waiting until it caught before adding another.

At last he sat back on his heels, staring into the flames. "Did he say anything?" he asked.

I searched my memory. "I think he asked me something, or told me something, but I don't remember what it was." I shivered, remembering the viciousness in his voice, the way he'd shaken me so hard the whole world seemed to tilt—

Matthew rose and bent over me. "Well, I'm not leaving you here alone. Not until this business is finished. Not with him knowing where you live."

"Where should I go?"

"To my house. My housekeeper, Peggy, is there. She lives in. She'll get you settled." He paused. "But for now, just sleep."

I closed my eyes. "You'll stay here?" My words came out slurred, as if I'd been drinking like Felix.

"Yes."

"I need to tell you what Lewis said," I managed.

I felt his fingertips move gently against my temple, the part where the bandage wasn't, his palm warm against my cheek. "Tomorrow. It'll keep till then."

THE NEXT MORNING, my ribs still felt bruised, and my arm was sore, but the throbbing in my head had subsided, and after I had gathered a few things in a case, Matthew opened the door, let me pass through it, and locked the door behind us. He found a cab, asking the driver to jostle us as little as possible, which meant that our journey was slow, and I had plenty of time to tell him what Lewis had said.

Matthew's face was strained, but he didn't say a word, even after I finished.

Finally I ventured, "You were guessing this, weren't you, once you heard about Alan?"

"I'm sorry, Annabel." He winced. "Usually in the cases with men of this sort—and there are a bloody awful lot of them—it isn't ever just the one."

MATTHEW TURNED THE key and held the door so I could enter his house ahead of him. In the foyer stood a woman of middle age, her gray hair pulled severely back from her face and with plump, capable-looking hands. At the moment they rested on her hips, and her eyebrows were as high as I imagined they could go.

"This is Peggy Greaves, our housekeeper," Matthew said. "Peggy, this is Annabel Rowe. She's going to stay with us for a few days. I thought you might put her in the room downstairs. She's been hurt, and it might be best for her not to have to climb stairs, at least for a day or two."

She lowered her chin toward Matthew and pursed her lips so hard that dimples formed. But all her censure rested upon him. She turned to greet me with the air of a practical and sympathetic woman who had taken in my injuries and saw no use in wasting time with foolish questions.

"Well, let's get you settled," she said briskly and led me at a pace suited to my state through the parlor. It was an attractive but modest room with red upholstered chairs, tables full of books, and a fire that had been set early and cast a warm glow.

His sister's piano stood in the corner, its wooden lid covered by a patterned silk cloth.

Mrs. Greaves opened a door in the corner that I might have guessed was for a closet, but it led to a room, and I realized that a wall had been built to apportion part of the parlor for a guest room. It was furnished with an attractive carpet that looked as if it had been cut from a larger one, a bed, a dressing table, a comfortable chair, a washstand of the usual birchwood with a towel rail beside, and a wardrobe. One door had swung open and I saw the shelves inside, lined with paper.

"Do you often have guests stay here?" I asked.

"It was built for the nurse," she explained. "Back when Captain Hallam was ill." She grasped the door handle. "I'll let you settle in, and when you're ready, there's tea and breakfast."

"Thank you. I'm sure this is irregular."

She pursed her lips. "Goodness' sake. Matthew and Nell don't do anything much regular. I've grown quite accustomed to it."

Her tone was such that I couldn't help but laugh, though it made my ribs twinge.

"Is Nell here?" I admitted to myself I was curious about her.

"She's in Vienna for the next two weeks, for rehearsals."

Mrs. Greaves closed the door behind her, and I unpacked the few things I'd brought and settled them on the wardrobe shelves.

THE MORNING CLOUDS hung low and gray, and as we took our breakfast in the parlor downstairs, it began to drizzle. We were seated near a window, and the rain had the effect of softening the colors, of blurring the shapes of the houses across the way as if they were the background of a painting—except there was no proper subject in the foreground.

"I've been thinking about how to find Sam Boulter." Matthew buttered his toast. "It occurred to me that you might ask Felix."

"Felix?" I echoed.

"He's worked in the art world for a long time. He knew where to find Lewis straight off, and he may even have known Hiram Boulter, or had dealings with his son. We know that Boulter was in the auction room. If he is the thief, he knew how to cut a picture out of a frame. Maybe he works for a gallery too, or one of the other auction houses."

"Should I send Felix a note and give him this address?"

"If you tell me where to find him, I'll fetch him here."

Remembering Felix's irritation with me, I said that might be best.

I gave him the address, settled myself on the couch by the parlor fire, and an hour later Matthew returned with Felix and ushered him into the room. Felix didn't look well. His eyes were red, and he smelled of spirits. Matthew asked Felix if he'd like anything besides coffee, and Felix shrugged.

"Felix." I reached my hand to him.

He held it briefly but wouldn't meet my gaze and took a seat.

I saw the shame on his face and attributed it to his sharpness at our last parting. "Felix, it's no matter," I said clumsily. "I know this is terribly difficult for you."

"I'm fine." It came out a rasp, as if he hadn't used his voice for a few days. A faint nod toward the kitchen where Matthew was running water. "I'm sorry about your injuries. He told me what happened."

"We believe the person who killed Edwin and took the painting might be someone from his old school."

"Tennersley?" The smallest spark of curiosity came and went, and he heaved a sigh. "Well, if he was an art student, he'd know the value of the Boucher—although I'm not sure how he knew where to find it and why the Boucher in particular—"

"I don't think the Boucher was ever his object," I said. "I think he went after Edwin and only happened to find the Boucher."

Felix sat back and stared, dumbfounded.

"I know." I swallowed. "Something terrible happened to Edwin at Tennersley, and I think his death had something to do with it . . . but we're not certain how it all fits together yet."

Matthew entered with a tray that held three cups of coffee, steaming hot. He handed one to me and one to Felix and took one for himself, then turned to Felix.

Felix rubbed his hand over his face wearily. "He wasn't happy at Tennersley. I know that much. But aside from Lewis, I don't know anyone who was at school with him. And Lewis wouldn't have hurt Edwin."

"Did Edwin ever mention a man named Sam Boulter?" Matthew asked. Felix shook his head. "I saw him at the auction. His father was the art master at Tennersley while Edwin was there, and the son may have connections to the art world."

Felix's face remained blank. "I'm sorry. I don't know him."

I set my coffee cup aside. "Matthew, can you get me my sketchbook, please, and a pencil?"

He rose and went to the other room, returning with both. The two men sat silently as I reproduced Edwin's drawing of Sam. I turned it to Matthew. "Is this close?"

"He has a heavier jaw now, and a mustache, but yes, that's him."

I passed the page toward Felix. "Making those allowances, do you recognize him?"

He glanced at the sketch, perfunctorily at first; but his eyes widened, and he looked at me. "That's the man you call Sam Boulter?"

I nodded. "What do you call him?"

"I don't remember the name he gave. But I've seen him."

"When?"

Felix screwed up his face, trying to remember. "Two—no, three years ago, maybe a little more, at the Garrick." I had heard of it, but I must have looked mystified, for he added, "It's a gentleman's club for artists and their patrons. Millais and Leighton and Rossetti, that sort. I'd been invited as a guest." He took a breath, blew absently on the coffee. "It was after the war, when the Germans still occupied France. As you know, Parisians who could afford to leave were fleeing, and those who had valuable collections brought over paintings in order to fund their exile." He nodded toward my sketch, and his mouth curled in contempt. "That man acted as a broker, but I heard he made a practice of purchasing items below market value and then reselling them to galleries for significantly more."

"Not illegal," Matthew commented. "But it's certainly taking advantage."

"How did Boulter get in to the Garrick Club? Was he a guest, or a member?" I wondered.

"I imagine he belongs," Felix said. "Naturally, it's not acceptable to conduct business formally in the club, but members could always manage it. If Boulter's father belonged, membership is usually extended to the son."

"Do you think Boulter is secretly selling the portrait at the club?" I asked.

Felix shrugged, and Matthew asked him, "Does Mr. Pagett belong to the Garrick?"

"You think Mr. Pagett is buying his own painting?" Felix returned skeptically.

"He wants it, doesn't he?" I asked.

Felix grimaced. "I suppose. But he could make the case that it already belongs to him—that Celia was in wrongful possession. He certainly has enough proof to bring the case to court."

"But the documents were in Mrs. Jesper's possession, and a court case would open Mr. Pagett up to questions and possibly some nasty publicity," Matthew objected. "Taking a painting from a widow."

"Would Mr. Pagett be able to afford the painting, do you think?" I asked.

"Certainly," Felix replied. "His mother was a wealthy manufacturer's daughter. After she died, Mr. Pagett began attending auctions regularly."

That caught Matthew's attention. "So her fortune passed to her son, not her husband?"

Felix nodded. "I would assume her father made provisions for a trust for her, to keep the money in the family."

Matthew's eyes narrowed. "Do you have any idea about the relative value of Mr. Pagett's inheritance compared with Lord Sibley's fortune?"

Felix shrugged. "My guess is it's less. The Sibleys are an old family. Their title goes back over two hundred years. But I couldn't say for certain."

Matthew stood. "We need to talk to Mr. Pagett."

"I'd try the Garrick." Felix drained his cup; and whether it was the effects of the coffee or the feeling that he was doing something useful, he wore a more animated expression than before. "It's Saturday; typically they invite a guest speaker for the members' lunch."

"I wish I could go with you," I said.

"Well, it being a gentleman's club, this is one place you can't," Matthew said with a ghost of a smile. He turned to Felix. "I'd appreciate your help. You know more than I do."

Felix's expression when he looked at Matthew was no longer distrustful but cautiously respectful. He nodded. "Of course."

I stood at the window so I might watch them leave. As they proceeded down the street, I saw in Felix's posture and the tilt of his head some of his old self, with the guilt and shame less evident than before. And in that moment, I began to trace some of the deepest curves of Matthew's character—his willingness to observe before judging, his ability to step inside the minds of others, and his desire to shore up the heart in those who needed it most.

Chapter 20

After they left, I felt worn and my head began to ache again. Peggy was in the kitchen, and I didn't want to bother her. I retreated to my room and examined the bandage. Somewhat perversely, I longed to know what the injury looked like. Taking some care, I unwrapped the linen to reveal four black stitches, the eight ends like the legs of an ugly spider. The wound appeared to be healing, but as I rewrapped my head I felt the beginnings of nausea and lay down on the bed.

It was a long, slow, horrid afternoon and evening. My head pulsed and my ribs hurt. I dozed, but when I woke, I felt at once weary and fidgety, and my thinking felt sluggish. Peggy was brisk but pleasant, fetching me tea and bringing me a tray with soup for dinner. When the clock struck nine and Matthew hadn't returned, I prepared for bed and turned out the light, telling myself I'd wake when he returned and ask what he'd discovered. But the next I knew, the sun was etching a bright line around the curtains. To my relief, the fog in my head had cleared, and I felt almost myself again.

Peggy told me that Matthew had already left for the Yard, so I was alone at the breakfast table and, after Peggy departed for the shops, alone in the house. A good night's rest and breakfast had made all the difference. My head felt fine; my ribs were much improved; and after pacing around the lower floor, I paused by the mirror in the foyer. My countenance appeared much as usual; in fact, if I were to remove the bandage and wear a hat, there would be no sign at all that I'd been attacked.

I had an idea of something useful that I might do; I only hoped that Mr. Pagett wasn't at home, and I could somehow reach Mary, the maid who'd so clearly disliked him. It was Sunday, after all, and most servants had at least part of the day off.

And maids often had a fair inkling of the undercurrents in their masters' houses.

I LET MYSELF out the front door and found a cab on Regent Street, directing it toward the park opposite the Sibleys' home. I took up a position on a bench where I could watch for a servant to emerge. As luck would have it, I waited less than twenty minutes. The black wrought-iron gate at the side of the house swung open, and out came a young man, bearing a package. I leapt up from my seat. My ribs twinged as I did so, making me catch my breath, but I hurried across the street and reached out a hand to intercept him with a smile. "Begging your pardon, I've a friend, Mary, who works in that house. Is it possible you could get word to her to come out to see me?"

"She'll be out soon enough. I heard Wilson ask her to fetch something from the milliner's." He eyed me curiously. "I've never seen you a'fore."

"She's an old friend and I've just moved to London," I said, the lie slipping easily off my tongue. I dropped a half crown into his hand, and his eyes widened.

"Would you please let her know I'm here?"

A few minutes later the young man returned and sent a silent nod to me where I sat on the bench. Ten minutes later, Mary emerged, her eyes darting about. Her gaze caught mine, and though she turned in the other direction, she walked slowly, so I might catch up.

"Hello, Mary. Do you remember me?"

Her head ducked down a bit into her collar. "Yes'm, from when you came last week with the inspector." She turned to look behind her and then back at me, her expression wary. "What do you want with me? I've done nothing wrong."

"I know," I reassured her. "You're not in any trouble. My name is Annabel. May I walk with you for a moment? I need to ask you something."

"I s'pose." Her voice wobbled uncertainly.

We had entered an arcade. "Mary, let's stop here for a moment, all right?" I asked. "I know you're frightened. I am, too."

Her eyes grew round.

I'd had to remove the bandage to wear my hat. Now I removed my hat to reveal the stitches and bruise on my head. "The man who did this stole Mr. Pagett's painting—the one that was taken out of the Pantechnicon."

She stared at my wound for a moment, her mouth half open. Then her pale blue eyes filled with honest sympathy. "Miss, I'm terrible sorry about you being hurt. Only I don't know what *I* can tell you. I don't know anything about the painting or it burnin' up." She turned her two hands palms up. "I'd barely come to London myself when it happened." It was the most she'd spoken at once, and I heard the Midlands vowels lying heavily on her tongue.

"You sound like you're from around Birmingham," I said, trying to set her at ease. "Is that right?"

"Yes, miss. Wolverhampton," she said. "My father was a smith there."

"And how did you come to be here?" I asked.

The tension in her shoulders eased a bit. "I started working for the Sibley family at their country house in August, four years back. I'd been with them only a few months when they asked me to come to London for the start of the season." Her expression was earnest, as if searching for understanding. "I said I would, o' course. I like the country better, but I didn't want to displease them straight off, and here is a good place for a girl like me."

I smiled reassuringly. "Of course. It's a beautiful house."

"Well, it has its troubles like anywhere."

"It isn't the same since Lord Sibley died, is it?"

"No, miss. He was kind to me," she said fervently.

"Was he?" I asked. "In what way?"

Her gaze skidded sideways as if she was ashamed. "I'd come to them without a character. But he wanted to gi' me a chance. He said that he alwus believed in giving folks a chance, so long as they were willing to work."

"What about his stepson? Did they get along?"

Her lips twitched, and she didn't reply. I had a feeling it was out of loyalty to the father.

"Everyone quarrels sometimes, Mary."

"Miss, this warn't just sometimes." She cast a quick look

around her and lowered her voice to a murmur. "I heard they got on better back when Lady Sibley was alive. And I don't mean they warn't fond of each other, but so far as I saw, they quarreled most every week."

"Really?" I kept my voice even. "Over what? The paintings?"

"Sometimes," she admitted. "Mr. Pagett said he should be given a free hand, you see, with the collection, seeing as his father was occupied in Parliament. Said it was his responsibility to cor—to—"

"Curate the collection?" I supplied.

"Yes'm. To improve it, 'specially the French paintings. They were his favorites."

"What about the Boucher painting? The one that supposedly burned in the Pantechnicon."

"Oh!" She grimaced. "They had terrible rows over that one. Lord Sibley bought it from the LeMarcs, you see, and Mr. Pagett had it hung. But Lord Sibley wanted it kept separate, so he had Mr. Franks take it down again."

"What did Mr. Pagett do when he discovered the Boucher hadn't burned in the Pantechnicon? Was he happy?"

"Happy?" she echoed, her eyes large with surprise, followed by something like amazement at my foolishness. "Hardly! I warn't in the dining room, o' course, but Edith was, and she said he nearly flew out o' his chair. Upset the dishes, broke one of the crystal candlesticks, spilt the tea every which way. It was all she could do to clean it up before it stained the table." She shivered and rubbed at her eyebrow with the heel of her hand. "That was an awful few days. Worst I ever saw, and he was certain the LeMarcs had played his father false. We were all on pins and needles, and him in a temper the whole time."

I winced. "I'm sorry. That sounds wretched. Why did he have such ill feeling toward the LeMarcs?"

The blood rose to her cheeks, and she didn't answer at first.

"Mary, please. This is important."

She sighed. "'Twas on account of Mademoiselle. That's what Lord Sibley and Mr. Pagett fought about mostly, at least so far's I could tell."

"Do you mean the LeMarcs' daughter?"

"Her name was Hel—Hel-leese." She shook her head. "I can't pronounce it proper. It's French."

"Heloise?" I asked.

She nodded, relieved. "That's it."

I began to have a guess what the problem might have been. "Is Heloise pretty?"

She leaned her back against the wall. "Oh, yes—and just about Mr. Pagett's age, which I'd guess was part o' the reason he was so peevish about her, 'specially when she paid all her attention to Lord Sibley. When the Germans left, and it was time for them to go back to Paris, we all thought he'd ask her to marry him—"

"Wait," I interrupted. "I'm sorry. *Who* would ask her to marry him?"

"Lord Sibley," she said impatiently. "He was besotted with her! And with him maybe having a son, he wouldn't inherit anything—"

Mary's pronouns were presenting a challenge, but the message was clear enough, along with its implications.

"You mean that if Lord Sibley married Mademoiselle Heloise, and she had a child, Mr. Pagett would be cut out of any inheritance."

Her eyes were round and serious. "And the paintings, miss. He'd already lost the Boucher, seeing as Lord Sibley planned to sell it back to the LeMarcs. But if they married, he'd lose them all. I'd say they mattered more to him than the money." She paused. "I've caught him myself, standing in front of 'em, whispering to 'em like—like they was alive."

And there it was. A fear of being displaced and disinherited. The nugget of Mr. Pagett's resentment, as simple as that.

My thoughts whirled, and I struggled with what to ask next. "The LeMarc family—did they return to France?"

"Yes, miss. First week in January. Lord Sibley went with 'em."

"But they didn't take the Boucher?"

"No, just their trunks and boxes. They'd have it shipped later, along with some other special things that needed crates and such."

So perhaps that was why Stephen Jesper had it. He'd been entrusted to ship it to France.

"That must have made Mr. Pagett angry—to lose that painting."

"Oh, he was furious. He said—well—" Suddenly her face went crimson. "Oh, I ain't going to repeat it, but he and his father had a row we could hear all the way down in the kitchen . . ." Her voice faded and she shivered, as if even the memory of the words jabbed at her.

"And then Lord Sibley returned from France?"

"He came back in March, but that's when he got sick." A church bell chimed nearby and she started. "Miss, I can't keep talkin' to you. I took my half day yesterday instead of today, and I have to stop at the bakery, and pick up something at the milliner, and get back before tea. I'll catch it if I'm late."

"Of course. Thank you, Mary." I reached out my hand and squeezed hers. "You've been so helpful."

She scurried off, and I turned to survey the street. There were dozens of people walking along the pavement, and no one seemed to be taking particular notice of Mary or me. But I had the unsettling feeling that had I turned a moment earlier to look, I might have seen someone who was.

Chapter 21

*M*y thoughts occupied with all that Mary had told me, my feet instinctively headed back to Matthew's house in Mayfair. Halfway there, however, I realized I wanted to see someone first.

At Felix's rooms there was no answer to my knock. But I could see a faint light coming under the door, so I knocked again.

I expected to hear his voice or his footsteps, but still there was nothing. Finally I tried the handle and pushed at the door. To my surprise, it was latched but not locked, and I went inside.

By the daylight coming through the open window, I could see into all the corners of the room. I hadn't been to his flat in over a year, but the disarray shocked me. Felix had never been fastidious; he liked his papers and books piled about him, close at hand, and he didn't discard anything, out of fear it might someday be useful. But I'd never seen clothing or newspapers thrown around like this. I couldn't even see the two chairs for everything strewn over them.

And then I saw something that stopped me cold: his father's gold pocket watch, glinting from the floor. I knew the timepiece was one of Felix's most prized possessions, and one of the few items his father had bequeathed him before he died. I bent over, picked it up, and searched for the walnut watch stand upon which it always hung. That, too, was on the floor. I picked it up, found a flat space on a table for the stand, and hung the watch on its hook. With a feeling of misgiving, I started toward the bedchamber.

"Felix?" I called softly. I went to the door and pushed it open, dreading what I might find. This room was also untidy, but I could tell at a glance that he wasn't in it, and I gave a sigh of relief.

I stood between the two rooms and scanned the living area. Was this squalor because Felix was unhappy and disheartened? Or was it because the room had been searched? I couldn't tell. But if it was searched, why wouldn't the person have taken the watch? Any pawnshop would accept it.

Well, there were no answers here. The best I could do was leave him a message to come to Matthew's as soon as he could, for I had important news to share. I went to the desk to search for an empty piece of paper. As I shifted a stack of circulars, I nearly knocked his precious meerschaum onto the floor, but I snatched at it in time. I cleared a small space on the desk to write a few lines—

And there, caught on the edge of the blotter, was something that made my breath catch.

An envelope, addressed in Edwin's handwriting. But the name scrawled in Edwin's heavy slanted hand across the pale rectangle wasn't Felix's. It was mine, in care of the Slade—although he'd written the address so poorly that it might well have been misdirected.

Slowly, I took it up. As I turned it over to peel off the sealing wax, I felt a stinging sense of dismay and betrayal. It didn't seem to have been opened, but Felix had kept this from me, for goodness knows how long.

Still, there was part of me that leapt to his defense. Perhaps Felix had done it out of kindness. Perhaps he feared that Edwin's letter contained something he thought I shouldn't read. Something cruel or accusing. I could understand Felix keeping that from me, perhaps giving it to me later, when Edwin's death wasn't so recent.

I held the missive in the palm of my hand, feeling the near-weightlessness of it, in such contrast with the heft of what it might reveal, and my fingers trembled as they unfolded it.

The letter was only a few lines, scrawled on a single page that, given its thickness and texture, was probably torn from a sketchbook. It was dated two Saturdays previous, only a few days before his death.

Bel—

I found something important today, and it's made me uneasy. Would it be possible for you to come see me tomorrow? If not, I'll see you on Tuesday as usual, but—just in case—I want you to know about it. Remember our Caesar.

E

I read it several times over, bewildered not only by his use of my childhood nickname, which he hadn't called me in years, but also by what "it" could be. And his entreaty to "remember our Caesar" made no sense to me at all. Edwin had read Caesar's *Gallic Wars* under the instruction of his Latin tutor, and some days I'd been present incidentally, sitting in the same room, but I'd been only seven or eight, and I certainly didn't learn much of it. Although, to be fair, I'd taken in a good deal of Edwin's early maths and history that way, so perhaps he thought that I'd absorbed Latin that way as well. I groped desperately for what I remembered about Julius Caesar and why his works, or the man himself, would have been on Edwin's mind at the moment of writing this letter. What emerged from my memory first were some phrases from Shakespeare's tragedy, rather than anything I recalled from Edwin's lessons—phrases I'd loved for their sound as much as their sense. But Edwin wouldn't know the phrases that I'd committed to memory, and so far as I could remember we'd never discussed the play.

More to the point, what had he discovered that disturbed him so?

I reread the letter again. Did Edwin intend that I connect Caesar with a place where the important thing might be hidden? Or perhaps with a painting of Caesar or of a place connected with him? But I couldn't recall any painting in Edwin's room that featured Rome or Pompey.

Or—my heart stopped—in referencing Caesar, was Edwin thinking of *himself* as Caesar? Wretchedly, I took a seat in the desk chair. Caesar was killed by conspirators who were close to him, including members of his family. Is that how he saw me? Someone who betrayed him? Did the "something important" mean something that he had hidden from himself, in his mind or heart, that he wanted *me* to discover? But "uneasy" seemed too faint a feeling for that.

I read the letter yet again.

No, I decided. That wasn't Edwin's tone at all. Those first lines conveyed a sense of tamped urgency; they were scribbled hastily, but didn't have the unevenness of ink that would accompany bitterness or anger. And Edwin wasn't prone to elaborate conceits. He was practical and spoke directly, and in these written words, I could almost hear the tone in his voice.

I closed my eyes, trying to feel my way into my brother's thoughts. What did Caesar mean to Edwin? He didn't even like classical Latin. In fact he'd *hated* studying it and found it a waste of his time, as he couldn't see how it would help in his painting—

My eyes flew open, and my breath caught in the back of my throat.

Of course.

Caesar was Edwin's *dog*. A sweet reddish-brown spaniel. The whole reason he was named Caesar in the first place was because my father insisted that Edwin *learn to love his Caesar*. When my uncle brought the dog for Christmas, Edwin named him Caesar. That sort of sly ruse was exactly the way Edwin managed my father. He would acquiesce to the letter of his commands but skewer the spirit of them.

The spaniel wasn't a puppy, I remembered; he had belonged to a friend of my uncle's who couldn't keep him, and Caesar only lived with us a few years. Indeed, I scarcely remembered him. But Edwin had often taken him as a subject for his paintings back then.

As I drew on my coat, my mind raced, recalling the day Edwin had died, when Matthew and I had searched his room. I didn't remember seeing a painting of Caesar among his others, but there might have been.

My coat still unbuttoned, I penned a hasty note to Felix, shoved Edwin's letter into my pocket, and hurried down the stairs. Dusk was beginning to fall, and as I started toward my brother's flat the church bells rang half past the hour.

Time had slipped away when I wasn't watching.

AT EDWIN'S, I opened the door with my key. The room was shadowy and cold, with no residual warmth, and the air was stale.

I lit three lamps and two candles to dispel the gloom and went straight to the stack of Edwin's original paintings, where I thought I'd be likely to find one of Caesar. There was nothing there, nor was there one in the second stack, but at last I found one in the third, toward the back. It was still unframed and with the background unfinished, as if having finished Caesar, Edwin had lost interest. I pulled it out, laid it upside down on the table, and began to search for a note or something tucked underneath or around the stretcher bars, or for a sign of Edwin having hidden a message somewhere. There were no stray pencil marks, no scratches in the paint, no sign that the staples had ever been removed from the stretcher bars and replaced. Nothing.

I turned the painting over and inspected it for any indication that Edwin had recently tampered with the original paint but found none. My heart sank. I'd been so sure. Was there another painting of Caesar? My eyes cast over the room, across the different piles of canvases—

Swiftly, I went to the stack closest to the bedroom. The portrait I'd done of Edwin at his easel was still turned with the unpainted verso toward the room, just as Matthew had placed it.

I took up the painting and turned it over to be sure I had the correct one. Yes, Caesar was there, underneath the easel, but just a suggestive russet blur. No doubt I intended to finish the dog later and never did. Still, this painting was more "our Caesar" than the other because it was by my hand, and I examined it with care. But again, I found nothing, either on the painted canvas or on the verso.

"Oh, Edwin," I whispered in frustration as I stared at Edwin's animated face, his boyish grace in front of his easel. "What were you thinking?"

And then, it came to my mind, clicking in a sequence. Edwin good-naturedly chiding Caesar for dashing around the three wooden legs of the easel; Edwin with his brush raised, threatening to paint stripes on Caesar's tail; Edwin throwing his head back and laughing—and I?

I had been giggling myself, so hard that my stomach hurt, because Caesar looked so silly—

And Caesar had knocked the easel over, bringing it crashing to the ground. Our father had found us some minutes later, shrieking with laughter, as Edwin was wiping blue paint off of Caesar's paws and his tail. Following the incident, Edwin had taken some pains to teach Caesar to be mindful of his easel. Eventually Caesar learned to curl himself into a ball between the three legs and remain quiet. And when he was close to the end of his life, that space became Caesar's lair. He spent hours there, sleeping and serving as Edwin's sole companion while he worked.

Edwin's easel stood in the corner.

I circled it, looking for signs of writing or anything out of the ordinary. This wasn't Edwin's childhood easel; he probably acquired it after he was released from prison. The legs were a bit wider perhaps and the bolts sturdier than his old one, but it wasn't heavy, and I rapped on one of the legs and heard a hollow twang. Carefully, I tipped the easel on its side, bringing it gently to the ground so that I could inspect the bottoms of the legs, which were capped with a felted fabric. I ran my fingers around the cloth, but I felt no gaps. Nevertheless, I peeled the felt away from the first leg and slid my fingers inside. There was nothing. Nor was there anything in the second. But the third piece of felt was more difficult to remove, as if it had recently been glued tightly back in place. I went to Edwin's table where I found a knife he employed to cut canvas and used the blade to pry the felt away. I reached inside the hollow space, and my fingertips brushed against something that felt like paper, coiled tightly into itself.

My heart pounding, I teased it out from its hiding place. Still sitting on the floor, I unrolled it to find two pieces of paper. The first was a notarized receipt, of a sale of the Boucher painting, for one pound sterling, from Lord Sibley to Mme. Heloise Le-Marc, on December 21, 1873. The second was a bill of lading authorizing the Jesper Shipping Company to handle the painting. The space for the date was left blank, but the stamp on the lower left corner indicated the shipping fees had been paid for carriage all the way to Paris.

I sat there on the floor, the papers in my skirt for a long minute. The price paid suggested that Lord Sibley intended the painting as an engagement present, but this receipt proved beyond a doubt that it belonged to her. And Edwin? Where had he found these papers? Moreover, where had they been that Felix *wouldn't* have found them?

I crawled over to the wall, where someone—perhaps Matthew—had stacked the pieces of the broken frames. I found the two sections of the heavy gilt one that had likely held the Boucher. A wide molding overlaid with gilt, it had broken on the diagonal, at the upper left and lower right joints. I fit them properly back together, in their usual shape, on the floor. By the light from the lamp, I saw that this frame was a piece of art in itself. I found one of Edwin's magnifying glasses and peered through it. The gesso had been applied to the wood in very thin layers and with care, and the recutting, prior to the application of bole and the gold leaf, had been performed with exquisite attention to the delicate details of the leaf stems and the crosshatch of the diaper pattern. I flipped the frame so I could examine the back, and began to run my fingers very slowly over the unpainted wood, feeling for any anomaly in the fine workmanship.

It was on the second pass that my right forefinger felt a crack, no wider than an embroidery needle. Through the glass, I could see what I missed at first: a small door inside the rabbet, the section of frame a quarter inch wide and, on this frame, nearly two inches deep that created space for the canvas behind the molding. I'd never seen something like this in a frame before. It made me think of the hidden compartments in the headboards that Mr. Radermacher had described to Matthew.

Still, I couldn't find a way to open it. I picked up one of Edwin's knives and tried to slide the blade in, thinking to wedge it open. But even that slender blade was too thick, and there was no nick or scrape to suggest Edwin had used that method. I began to press on it, gently—toward the top, toward the bottom—

And then, silently, it swung open on its hinge.

The door was perhaps an inch wide and eight inches long, concealing a compartment an inch deep. The mechanism was simple—only three metal pieces: a tiny metal hinge so precisely attached inside a groove as to make it invisible from the outside and two pieces of a latching mechanism that held the door closed.

This wasn't a Régence frame like those in the Sibleys' parlor, but a Salvator Rosa, which meant that it was probably original to the work. Did the LeMarc family know about this hidden pocket?

I sat back on my heels, staring at the neat little mechanism, my thoughts scrambling for a logical version of events. I could see why Edwin found the compartment. Once he'd removed the canvas, he'd no doubt have examined the frame for wear and damage. But why would Lord Sibley have hidden these papers here? Why wouldn't they be with the other papers that showed the provenance?

The only reason I could surmise was that he was afraid his son might destroy them.

But why wouldn't Edwin show the papers to Felix? Why had he removed them and hidden them?

My heart sank as I reached what seemed to be the only possible conclusion: Edwin wasn't sure what Felix would do with them. Perhaps he was afraid that Felix would destroy them, out of affection and loyalty to Celia Jesper. Or—a more disturbing possibility—Felix would know that the painting wouldn't be sellable at the Bettridge auction. The jewel of the sale, gone, because of these two pieces of paper, which revealed the true reason it had been in the Jespers' house.

The room had gone very cold, and I found myself shivering. I wished to see Celia, and suddenly I very much wanted to hand all this over to Matthew. I stood, folded the pieces of paper without creasing them, and slipped them into my bodice. I would take no chances with these. I extinguished the lamps, locked the door behind me, and then—even as I turned away—replaced the key in the lock and went back in. I selected a stretcher bar from Edwin's box. It wasn't much, but I felt better with that solid piece of wood in my hand as I made my way to Celia's.

Chapter 22

The upper floors of Celia's house had a strangely vacant appearance, and it took a moment for me to realize what the difference was: the curtains were gone. With the downstairs windows bare, even the dim light from a few lamps shone starkly through. From deep inside me came a sound that was half a cry and half a sigh of relief—the removers had come but someone was still home. I knocked at the door and it swung open to reveal Celia, her coat and shawl over her arm. "Why, Annabel!" she said in surprise. "I was just about to leave for my sister's."

My eyes fell on the empty hallway behind her. The sight made me think of a hollow log, scraped raw.

"Annabel?" Her expression was one of concern. She reached out and took my hand to draw me inside. "What's the matter? My goodness, you're freezing!"

I hadn't even noticed, but as I stepped into the comparative warmth of the house, I began to shake, and her hand felt almost feverish by comparison with mine. Still, I didn't reply; inside me rose the feeling that I longed for Celia to know everything without my having to speak the words.

My breathing echoed in the barren space.

Numbly, I let her guide me to the stairs and push me onto the second-to-last step. "I'm afraid it's the only place left to sit," she said. "The removers are coming for the last few paintings tomorrow."

"It feels so empty," I said.

She sat on the step beside me. "What is it?" She peered at me, and her expression became alarmed. "And what happened to your head?"

I put my hand up. "Someone—probably the man who killed Edwin—was waiting at my flat the other night. Matthew was there, too, so I'm all right. But he got away."

Her breath sounded like a soft scrape, and in the ambient light from a hallway sconce, I saw the whites of her eyes. "Good Lord, Annabel."

"I'm staying with Matthew until this is over." I attempted a smile. "And don't worry, his housekeeper is there as well, so there's no impropriety. I think he just didn't know what else to do with me."

"Of course," she murmured.

I reached inside my bodice, drew out the two pages, and offered them to her. "I found these in Edwin's room."

Her eyebrows raised, she took them from me and studied them silently for a moment, her mouth forming a small O. When she looked up at me, her eyes were enormous. "So it was here to be *shipped*. No wonder! Stephen . . ." Her voice faded, and I could see her beginning to assemble events in her mind, her mouth opening to ask questions—

"Will you come with me, please?" It came out a choked plea. "To see Matthew, at his house. I have things to tell him, but I want you to know, too, and—and I don't want to explain it all twice."

She didn't demur for a moment. Silently she donned her coat, drew a key from her pocket, and locked the door behind us. She signaled a cab at the corner, and we climbed in.

"You look exhausted," she said softly. Inside the cab was just as cold as outdoors, and I felt every muscle clenching. She reached out a gloved hand, and I clung to it like a lifeline all the way to Matthew's house.

To my relief, I saw his bulky silhouette moving across the window and then back, as if he was pacing.

"He's home," I whispered.

"Yes, he is," she said quietly. "Thank goodness."

And I realized her curiosity was at least as great as my desire to share what I knew. I hated the feeling of holding it all alone.

As the carriage drew up, I saw Matthew halt and draw the curtain aside. His face appeared at the window and then vanished. The door was open before I reached it, and I gazed up at him. His face was white to the lips, his eyes dark with what looked like a potent mix of fear and fury. His words came out jerkily, as if they might explode out of him, and he was trying to mete them out in some reasonable way: "Where—the devil—have you been?"

Wordlessly, I thrust the papers at him.

He didn't even glance at them.

"Mr. Hallam, she's done in, and she's freezing." Celia's gentle voice behind me carried a note of caution.

His jaw clenched, he stepped aside and held the door for us to enter.

My teeth were chattering, and the wound on my head began to pulse. Stiffly, I made my way toward the fire and held out my hands. Far from soothing them, the warmth made them itch.

From behind me, I heard the squeak of a cork and the sound of pouring, and Matthew was at my side, holding a cut-crystal glass of something golden brown. "Here."

"What is it?"

"Good brandy," he said tersely. "Get it down."

Dutifully, I sipped and felt the burn of it like a fire down to my belly.

Matthew dragged a chair closer to the fire, and then left the room.

"You'll warm faster without your coat," Celia said.

I set the glass down on the small round table beside me and reached for the top button, but the ends of my fingers felt numb.

"Can you manage?" Celia asked when she saw me fumbling, and then she gently moved my hands away, undid the buttons, and eased my arms out of the sleeves. She set the coat aside and drew the chair and a footstool closer to the center of the hearth, where it was warmest.

"He's so angry," I said as I sat down. "What did I do wrong?"

"He's not angry," she corrected me. "He was afraid." She found a warm woolly blanket and tucked it around me as if I were a child. "Now I'll go help in the kitchen. Just stay there and get warm."

I closed my eyes and put the soles of my boots as close to the fire as I dared.

A few moments later, I heard footsteps. The brandy had begun to work its magic, and the sharp edges of my exhaustion and emotions had begun to blur into a pleasing softness. I turned to see Matthew and Celia reappear with Peggy in tow, and I smelled the rich aroma of chocolate. Matthew carried a bucket of coal to heap on the fire. Celia was unfolding a second blanket, and Peggy bore a tray with three cups and some biscuits on it. Peggy frowned at the glass of brandy. "Hmph," she said. "Chocolate will do you a world of good, better than that vile stuff."

I said gratefully, "It smells wonderful."

She gave a nod as if she'd proven us all wrong about something. "I'll finish the stew," Peggy said, "and set another place. We'll have supper in an hour."

"Thank you, Peggy," Matthew said. To my relief, I noticed that his expression, while still unsmiling, reflected some of his usual equanimity. I sent a small, appreciative smile toward Celia, for I had a feeling she had something to do with it. He and Celia each drew a chair close on either side of me, and Matthew brought over a lamp and took up the pages I'd brought.

He separated them carefully and smoothed them, and while Celia and I sipped our chocolate, he read them over, each one twice. He didn't raise his head for several minutes, and when he finally did, he looked at me.

"Where did you find these?" he asked soberly.

"Inside the leg of the easel in Edwin's room."

His eyes narrowed, and before he could ask, I blurted out, "I'll tell you everything." I glanced at Celia and then back to him. "But it will make far better sense if I tell it in order."

Out of the corner of my eye, I saw Celia nod encouragingly.

Matthew picked up his chocolate with his right hand and turned his left palm up in a gesture of acquiescence.

Our chairs were in a tight little triangle, and I leaned back in mine, so I could see them both without turning my head as if I were watching lawn tennis.

Both of them looked at me expectantly, and I began:

"I went to the Sibleys' house this afternoon, to see Mary, the maid . . ."

As I related the events of my day, Matthew's eyebrows rose at parts, and Celia shivered in sympathy, but both of them remained silent until I gave the conclusion I'd reached: "I think that Mr. Pagett is going to try to get that painting back somehow, even though he probably guesses that it doesn't rightfully belong to him."

"I think you're right," Matthew said as he set his chocolate back on the tray. "What's more, I think Boulter knows about Mr. Pagett's interest."

Suddenly I remembered where he'd been heading last time I saw him. "Did you find him at the Garrick Club?"

He shook his head but his eyes were keen. "Boulter isn't a member, but Mr. Pagett is, and the valet told us that he delivered a letter from Boulter to Mr. Pagett this past Tuesday."

I heard Celia's soft gasp beside me.

"The day after the auction," I said in surprise. "Perhaps Boulter knew to contact him because he saw him in the auction room."

"Or because of the *Beacon* article," Matthew countered. "Boulter was likely Fishel's source for it. And I think he fed Fishel that information because he knew an article like that would send a message to whoever wanted the painting that it was available for sale." He raised an eyebrow. "Remember the lines about experts believing it's still available for a price?"

I nodded thoughtfully. "If Mr. Pagett saw the article, he would call upon Fishel, wouldn't he?"

Matthew shrugged. "I would if I were him. And Fishel would pass along his information to Boulter. Hence Boulter's letter to Mr. Pagett at the club."

"My God," Celia said under her breath and set her half-drunk chocolate on the tray with a clatter.

"What is it?" I asked.

Her eyes were wide and dark with apprehension. "I just wonder how far Mr. Pagett would go to obtain that painting. If he's willing to deal with someone like Sam Boulter, then who's to say he didn't threaten Stephen last year, to keep him from shipping it out?"

"You're wondering if Mr. Pagett had anything to do with your carriage accident?" Matthew asked guardedly.

Her fingers were knotted together so tightly the knuckles were white.

"Celia?" Matthew's voice was quiet. "I can't see Mr. Pagett involved in a murder. He just doesn't seem the sort. But why—"

"I know how Lord Sibley and Stephen knew each other," Celia blurted.

"You found the second link, then. The professor in Leuven?" I guessed.

She nodded. "After you left the other day, I wrote to him, as I said I would. His reply arrived last night in the post." Her gaze shifted from me to Matthew. "He wrote that he gave Stephen the keys to his house, for a series of private meetings beginning in February of 1871."

"In Leuven?" Matthew clarified.

"Yes." She bit her lower lip and let it go. "Five men attended. Two Frenchmen and two Englishmen besides Stephen. One was an MP and the other was a gentleman"—she glanced at me before returning her gaze to Matthew—"from Birmingham."

So this is why Stephen had made those trips, I thought with a twinge of relief for Celia. She had been right not to suspect a mistress.

Matthew shifted. "Was the Jesper company shipping guns?"

I nearly choked on the last of my chocolate. I stared incredulously at him and turned to Celia, expecting her to deny it. But to my surprise she was nodding, albeit reluctantly. She leaned forward in her chair, her hands clasped tightly in her lap, her expression pleading. "Truly, I didn't know about Stephen's trips to Birmingham until this past week. He never told me, probably because he knew I'd ask if he was conveying weapons."

"Why would you assume that?" I asked, bewildered.

Matthew rubbed his fingertips over his mouth. He removed them long enough to say, "Because Birmingham is the gun-manufacturing center for England. And for most of Europe."

"Oh." I frowned. "But how many guns was Stephen's company shipping? Lord Sibley's a wealthy man, but—"

"Oh, I don't think he funded it himself," Celia corrected me. "A man in his position could channel money from a Parliamentary account. Indeed, this entire plan could have been accomplished sub rosa, without Parliament's knowledge—or the knowledge of the prime minister."

I stared. "Surely there's more oversight in the government than that."

"Celia's right." Matthew rose, took up a poker, and nudged at the coals. "Scudamore managed it. Two years ago, he diverted over a million pounds to keep the telegraph system going. He was found out, and he wasn't even censured by Parliament."

I vaguely remembered reading about it in the papers. "But that's different," I said. "That time, the money was staying in England."

"Some would say that keeping our nation safe from invasion was even more critical than keeping the telegraphs going," he replied. "And I can imagine how Sibley would justify obtaining the guns secretly. As soon as people knew the government was in the market to buy, the prices would double." Matthew sat back on his heels, eyes on the fire. "The new prime minister would never condone this sort of interference. Disraeli likes von Bismarck."

Celia stood and paced about the room, drawing her shawl close around her. "Well, perhaps Mr. Pagett had nothing to do with the accident. But I still think it's a strange coincidence that Lord Sibley and Stephen died within weeks of each other."

"To be sure, I'll be in a position to question Mr. Pagett soon, and we'll look into your husband's death further," Matthew said as he replaced the poker, and there was enough decisiveness in his voice that Celia was satisfied and nodded gratefully in reply.

He sat down, settling his elbows on his knees, and tapped his thumbs against his mouth. "But for now, our surest strategy is to confront Mr. Pagett with what we know for certain—the painting never belonged to him at all—and that he probably knew his father intended to return it to the LeMarcs." He frowned. "With the family back in Paris, maybe Mr. Pagett assumed they'd never hear about its reappearance—because it was Bettridge's auctioning it, instead of one of the other houses."

"I don't think he would have thought so," I disagreed. "It's an important painting. Surely he knew someone would mention it to the LeMarcs. The art world isn't large, and the market for these paintings—"

"I agree with Annabel," said Celia. "I think they'd hear of it."

"All right, then." Matthew stood and rested his right forearm heavily on the mantel. "So the painting has to remain stolen, or it goes to the LeMarcs. But still, Boulter has to sell the painting to Mr. Pagett."

I frowned. "But Mr. Pagett wouldn't be satisfied with merely owning the painting." I looked up at Matthew. "You remember that room. He'll want to display it, make it part of his collection, show people that he owns it. So he must do it legally, somehow." I shrugged. "Maybe he'll say it's a reproduction."

"No," came Celia's voice from the other side of the room. She had halted by the window, and the black of her dress and shawl made her appear almost a silhouette against the green curtains. Her words came slowly: "Mr. Pagett could display it legally—could own it legally—so long as he buys it under the rules of *marché ouvert*."

"What?" I asked.

She looked at Matthew, as if she expected him to know, but he looked mystified as well.

She returned to the chair, resting her fingers lightly on the wooden back. Her voice was quiet but certain. "It's an English law that's been on the books since medieval times. It states that for any item sold in a designated open market—free to the public—between the hours of sunrise and sunset, its provenance cannot be questioned, and it is irrevocably and legally the property of the buyer."

I stiffened with surprise. "Even if the goods are stolen?"

She looked for confirmation to Matthew, and he was nodding, though he wore a stunned look on his face. "The open market law, yes. I've heard of the odd case when it comes to a cow or a pig." He spread his hands. "But not something like this."

It was on the tip of my tongue to ask how Celia knew about the law—until I remembered her father had been a barrister.

Celia's eyes were glistening in the light of the fire. "Some years ago, my father handled a case in which a medieval manuscript was stolen from a print shop and sold for only a few pounds in an open market. The rightful owner had no recourse, although he made things unpleasant for the buyer. No doubt the law will be revoked someday, but it's still valid."

I leaned back against the cushion again. "So if Sam Boulter sells the painting to Mr. Pagett in the open market—"

"It's a legal purchase," she said, her voice steady and certain. "Today is Sunday. The market in Islington occurs every fortnight. It's open on Tuesday at dawn."

"Are there designated markets besides this one at Islington?" I asked.

"Yes, but not here in London, and not this week."

"Any time between dawn and dusk, you say?" Matthew asked.

She nodded. "Don't you think we should tell Felix?"

Matthew winced and his eyes darted from Celia to me. "I've something to tell you, about Felix."

I felt a beat of fear. "Has something happened?"

"He's alive," he replied hurriedly. "But he's in hospital. I saw him earlier today."

My hands gripped the arms of the chair. "Why? What happened? Did Boulter try to—"

"No," he interrupted. "I don't think Boulter had anything to do with this, except incidentally. Felix fell in front of a cab in the road last night."

A groan escaped Celia's lips. "Was he intoxicated?"

I felt a jab of surprise that she'd guessed.

"I'm afraid he was," Matthew said.

"How did you know to go looking for him—and in hospital?" I asked.

"I didn't. The hospital found my card in his pocketbook. From the day we went to see him at Bettridge's. They called the Yard."

"Was he conscious when you saw him?"

"No," he said. "He was sleeping."

"Is he badly injured?" Celia asked.

He hesitated. "They said he's slightly concussed. But they were more concerned about his inebriation."

I swallowed past the tightness in my throat. "Poor Felix. When I saw him a few days ago, to ask for Lewis's address, he was . . . difficult. And when I went to his rooms, I knew straightaway that . . . well, I wasn't sure if they were disordered because someone had searched them, but there was a valuable pocket watch that a thief would have stolen, and my guess was Felix hasn't been taking proper care of himself. His flat was positively squalid." I paused. "It's only the sheerest luck I saw Edwin's letter."

Matthew put out a hand. "Can I see it?"

I went to the rack where Celia hung my coat and fished in the pocket. For a panicked moment, I thought I'd lost it, but there it was, flush against the lining. I handed it to Matthew and he read the few lines. At last he looked up. "You said this letter told you where to find the papers, but this message says nothing about looking in the leg of his easel."

"It took me a while to realize what he meant," I said. "Caesar was his dog when he was a boy. He used to spend hours under Edwin's easel." The memory of it caused a tightening in my chest, and I felt my eyes begin to burn. "There are things from my childhood that I hardly remember—*happy* things." I gulped and blinked the tears back. "Like when Edwin and I could still laugh together. And it doesn't feel *fair* that it's more difficult for me to remember those things than the times that were awful and frightening. It's a rotten trick."

My voice shook, and Celia reached out a hand to hold mine. "I think it's human nature," she said gently.

A sob burst from me. "I was so angry with him for what he'd done—all the times he'd leave, and—and—well, you'd think your heart would get used to it, or the worry would diminish, but it never did. Not *ever*. I was always just as scared, every time, that he'd die." I knew I sounded incoherent, and the tears spilled over onto my cheeks as fast as my words, but I rushed on. "Because under it all were memories of a brother I knew. The kind of boy who would laugh when a dog knocked over his painting, instead of kicking him. I *hate* that I never told him I forgave him—or at least that I mostly had. He never knew I was just waiting until I was sure. That I had never given up on him, and I'd always just been waiting for him to come back."

I was sobbing too hard to speak another word, and Celia held my hand in both of hers while Matthew passed me a hand-kerchief in sympathetic silence. Eventually the tears slowed. I wiped my cheeks once more with the sodden square of linen, and tried to steady my breath.

"For what it's worth, Annabel, I think he knew," Celia said softly.

"I do, too," Matthew said. "Just from his letter."

I sniffed, an ugly rasping sound at the back of my throat.

"He knew he could trust you with something important," Matthew said. "Otherwise, he'd have told Felix, or Lewis, or even the vicar. But he sent it to you."

The very reasonableness of his words forced itself into my consciousness. Yes, Edwin had chosen me. The realization surprised me out of any more tears, and by the time Peggy called us for dinner, and I slid the letter into my coat pocket, the fierce knot of self-loathing I'd had in my chest since Edwin's funeral had loosened. Not much, but a little.

Because, though I had disappointed my brother in many ways, I had not failed him in this.

IN THE AFTERMATH of my outburst, dinner was a quietly cheer-ful meal, for which I was grateful. Celia embraced me warmly before she left, and I watched from the window as Matthew handed her into a hansom headed to her sister's. She peered through the cab's side window and smiled, and as I waved goodbye, I remembered what she'd said about Matthew being afraid.

He entered the house, and I felt the cold outdoor air come in with him. He stood at the threshold of the parlor, taking up most of the doorway. "You're all right?"

I moved away from the window and toward him. "Yes. Thank you."

He was silent for a moment, and then he shifted his weight, as if he might excuse himself to go upstairs—

"Wait." The word burst out of me. "Matthew, I'm sorry I worried you." He didn't move or speak, and I hurried on. "I know Boulter is still out there. And perhaps I should have been more cautious, but . . . well, London is enormous, and I didn't think he'd find me."

Slowly he came into the room and approached a table. On it stood a carved jade box, and idly he shifted the lid, his thumb making it flush with first one side and then the other. "No," he said at last. "I don't think Boulter knows this house, although men like that do have ways of ferreting out information. Still, I shouldn't have been so angry with you. It's just that I knew he couldn't have dragged you out of here, and I couldn't imagine where you'd have gone, or why. Peggy had no idea, either. You simply . . . vanished."

At that word, a wave of remorse flooded over me. "Matthew, I'm sorry. It was stupid of me. I truly thought I'd only be gone for an hour or so, to see Mary, and I'd be back hours before you returned."

His hand dropped away from the jade box and fell at his side. "I understand."

I stepped closer. "I didn't think about how especially unsettling it might be for you, finding me gone with no explanation, and I should have."

He looked askance. "That's asking a bit much, don't you think? For someone you've known only a matter of weeks?"

I shook my head slowly. "No. In fact, I don't think it's too much to ask at all."

Perhaps it was the aftereffects of the brandy, or the turmoil of the past weeks, or the knowledge that I'd waited too long to speak truthfully to my brother, but the words rose from somewhere inside me and I let them fly out: "Naturally, no one can be expected to know all of another person's fears and—and—experiences and sensibilities in a short time. But your mother vanishing without a word?" His expression altered, but I rushed on. "Surely I can remember *that* much of your experience, and avoid doing something similar to you, if you matter to me in the least—and of course you do—"

One swift step toward me, and his arm was around my waist, and his mouth was silencing mine with a kiss that was at once fierce and tender. The brutal beat of the day's anxiety and sorrow was stilled, and in its place came a race of feelings that I couldn't even name, like a river fed by half a dozen streams and tumbling full tilt down a hill.

When he finally drew away, we were both taking ragged breaths. His forehead dropped to mine. "Next time, leave a bloody message somewhere, all right?"

Mutely, readily, I nodded.

A spark of humor came into his eyes. "Next time, that is, you decide to go running off and doing my police work for me."

My laugh was shaky. "I think it's time I went back to the Slade. At least there's less risk of bodily harm."

His hands held both of mine, and his eyes darted briefly to the wound on my head. "How is it?"

"Better. I hardly feel it."

"That may be the brandy."

I touched my thumb to his mouth. "Or this."

His lips curved, and he pulled me close again. This time his kiss was slower and deeper, and when at last he let me go, he took my hand and drew me to a settee, pulling me close beside him.

His arm around me, I rested my head on his shoulder, and for that precious hour, time stopped its demands, the world dropped away, and it was just the two of us speaking in murmurs and watching the flames dance. Was this the beginnings of love? Not having seen any notable signs of it with my parents, I couldn't say with any certainty. But if blithe contentedness and a feeling of expansive possibility were signs of it, well then, perhaps it was.

I began to feel drowsy, and eventually the clock struck. It was late, and I felt him take in a breath, as if he were preparing to speak.

Before he could, I said, "Matthew, I'm coming to the market Tuesday. Celia and I can be there together."

I felt his shoulder tense, but I forestalled his protest by sitting up and pulling away so I could see his face—and he could see mine. "There won't be any danger," I promised. "We'll stay exactly where you tell us, and there will be dozens of people about." He still appeared dubious. "Remember, I am one of the only people who knows what both men look like."

He rubbed roughly at his face. "I know. Every instinct I have is to keep you away from there, but you're a valuable pair of eyes."

He stood and went to the window. At last he turned back, and his tone was decided. "Celia and you can't separate. And if at any time you see either of the men, you don't go near them. You find a plainclothesman."

"Agreed," I said. "And tomorrow I'd like to go see Felix."

"Let me send a message to the hospital. If he's awake, I'll take you there myself. If the doctors say he can't be seen, I'd rather you stay here." He frowned, as if I'd objected. "I mean it. As you said, Boulter is out there, and if his plan is to go to the market, we'll find him there. It's only a day to wait."

I nodded. "Fair enough."

The fire no longer danced but had diminished to a few orange-edged coals, and the room was full of shadows.

"It's time we went to bed," he said softly. He took my hands in his, drew me to standing, and pressed his warm lips to my fingers.

He left the room, and I went to mine. Leaning against my closed door, I felt my heart beat an unsteady rhythm against the solid wood behind me. I touched the fingers he'd kissed to my mouth and felt the lingering heat. The floors in this house were old enough to creak, and I could follow his steps up the stairs and along the hall. It was only when I heard his door close that I pushed myself away from my own and began to undress.

Brandy or no, it took a long time for me to fall asleep that night.

Chapter 23

*M*onday was rainy and cold. Matthew's message to the hospital had received the reply *No change. We regret Mr. Severington is not available for visitors.* I remained indoors the entire day. Matthew was away until after I retired for bed, but I left a message beside the coat rack for him to wake me when it was time to depart for Islington. Half suspecting he would leave me behind, I slept anxiously, waking nearly every hour. When his knock came at my door at three o'clock, I was already lying awake, waiting for it.

In the foyer, I found Celia looking pale but wide awake. I felt grateful for the closed carriage, as well as the blankets and hot water bottles that kept our feet from freezing. Two lanterns hung on the outside of the cab, one by each window, swaying and sending their light against the cobbles and catching the metal fastenings on the gates and doors as we passed. Celia and I sat facing backward, and by the light from the lanterns, I could glimpse Matthew well enough to see that he was unshaven. I wondered if he had slept at all.

"I studied the map," he said to us both. "The market is roughly triangular; it comprises a grid of barns and booths. The west side is primarily for livestock, as there's a railway station nearby for the loading of cattle and pigs. The east side includes booths for everything else—candles, food, vegetables, potatoes, bread, clothing, soap, and the like."

"Is Boulter required to have a booth in order to sell the painting, or can the transaction be done anywhere?" Celia asked.

"He must have permission from the owner of a booth, if he hasn't taken one himself. If Mr. Pagett leaves the market, the transaction will be considered finished."

Celia shifted beside me. "Are there established entrances and exits?"

"There are several ways in and out."

"How on earth are we going to manage?"

"I've thirty policemen meeting us," Matthew replied, his voice breaking as we bounced over a rut in the road. "I had a copyist at the Yard make versions of Annabel's sketch yesterday; everyone will have one."

I felt sorry for whoever had been given that task.

The carriage bumped again over a ridge in the road, throwing Celia and me sideways. I felt the hard edge of the wall against the bruised part of my shoulder and winced.

"At our back, time's wingèd chariot hurrying near," Celia muttered.

"What?" I asked.

Celia's voice was wry. "I feel like we're in a race against the sun."

"We're not," Matthew said easily. "The gates don't open until half past four. We'll be there in plenty of time."

Was he genuinely as tranquil as he seemed? I found my

stomach knotting, but at last we arrived at Islington and drew up to the market. Matthew was right. The church nearby was only striking a quarter past.

We dismounted from the carriage, and the driver pulled away, leaving us in the shadows of an enormous cattle shed by the gate. From the darkness came the sounds of animal rustling, an occasional grunt, and the unmistakable smell of cows and swine. But so far as I could tell, we three were the only humans here.

"I thought you said . . ." My voice faded as men began to emerge from around the corner of the shed. Some carried lanterns that dropped puddles of gold against the dirt. The light sparkled in the eyes of a few cows that surveyed us with a mild, silent curiosity.

Not one of the men wore the usual buttoned blue police uniform. Indeed, they might have been farmers or laborers or costermongers, although all wore caps that could be pulled down low over their faces if need be. They gathered around Matthew, and as he began to speak the murmurs and whispers went silent. They all studied Celia and me but seemed to accept our presence without question.

"We're looking for two men with a painting," Matthew said. "You've seen the sketches of them both."

Briefly I wondered where they'd seen a sketch of Mr. Pagett, but then I realized his image would be easy to find in the society papers.

"How big is the painting?" one man asked.

"About so big"—Matthew's hands sketched a rectangle—"but it most likely won't be in a frame; it will be rolled, or concealed in something roughly a yard long."

"Something like the size of a quiver for arrows, then," one man spoke up.

"Are those sold here?" another asked.

"I've seen them in the past," came the reply. "I'm just trying to think how they might smuggle it out."

With relief, I realized that these men were already anticipating the difficulties. Though clouds hung heavy, a dim light appeared behind the stock building, and Matthew said, "It's time to scatter. We're here until dusk, or until we find him."

The men with their lanterns melted away, leaving two behind. Matthew kept one for himself and handed one to me.

"What can we do?" Celia asked.

"Shop," he said with a small smile. "Stay together. Remember, don't approach either of the men. It isn't worth it. If we don't catch them here, we'll find them somewhere else."

I wished I felt as certain.

"I wouldn't bother with the livestock pens. Spend your time at the booths."

"How will we know if someone's a plainclothesman?" Celia asked. "I couldn't see most of their faces in this light."

"They're wearing the same brown caps." Matthew touched his own. "We've used them before to help identify each other. And if you're in doubt, look at his shoes. Most of us wear these boots. They stand up to a chase."

Celia and I peered at his footwear, then she linked her arm in mine and watched as he set off. The sun pierced the morning clouds enough for us to see where we were going, and we both paused by the livestock. The cows were clustered together, and I could feel the bovine warmth emanating from the pen. The metal trough of water had a gleam of thin ice near the edges.

"Poor things, standing about," Celia murmured. "Though I think they're warmer than we are."

I shivered and made a sound of agreement. "Do you think Matthew is correct, and Boulter wouldn't try to sell the painting somewhere near the pens? It seems to me that it's precisely where he would sell it—just because no one would expect it."

"The transaction must be done at a booth," Celia reminded me. "Besides, I don't think they'll feel the need for that much caution. You forget that they have no idea we'll be here."

"It's only because of you that we are," I said.

"Well, if I'm right," she amended with a grimace. "If I'm wrong, I'll have wasted time for all these men."

We started down one of the rows of booths, which were tables nominally separated by wooden posts and the occasional lattice. Most were still unoccupied but here and there, the proprietors began to set out their wares. The sun remained hidden behind gray clouds.

Celia and I wandered up and down the aisles, surveying the displays. She exaggerated her limp to justify her keeping her hand tucked in my elbow. Every so often we saw one of the men in brown caps, but he took no notice of us, and we kept our gazes elsewhere. There was plenty to see: soaps and candles, scarves and woolens, carrots and peas, linens and quilts, mourning bands and veils, ceramics, copper goods, glass, knives and scissors, brooches, books and maps, harmonicas and zithers, pillows, onions and potatoes, umbrellas and walking sticks.

"Have you ever seen such a miscellany?" Celia asked under her breath. I didn't bother to make the obvious reply. "What are you thinking?" she murmured idly as we paused by an array of soaps in the shape of flowers and turtles and bumblebees.

The pale yellow ones looked almost like butter, and I resisted the urge to reach out and touch them.

"I'm looking for boxes or bags large enough to hide a painting," I replied under my breath. "But so far, aside from some boxes for long knives, I haven't seen any."

It seemed an unending day, damp and raw and unpleasant. The apprehension and suspense of the morning had worn off, and now I was beginning to feel the queasy fatigue that follows upon a poor night's sleep. We rounded the end of the sixth row for what must have been the fourth time. It was nearly two o'clock, and we paused to watch as a railway train drew up to the station. We covered our ears to dull the shriek of the braking wheels and the lowing and squealing of cattle and pigs, shifting uneasily in their pens.

We turned away, and as we dragged ourselves down the first row yet again, I became aware that my feet hurt, and I was becoming desperately thirsty. I spied a selection of apples and led Celia toward the booth. I took out some coins and paid. The apples were sweet, tangy, and deeply satisfying, and we walked and munched in silence, making our way up the middle of the aisles, with people bustling and dawdling at the booths on either side of us, Celia looking one way and I the other.

"Don't give up yet," Celia replied, her voice hopeful. "There's nearly two hours before it closes."

"Celia!" came a man's voice. "What a pleasant surprise!"

We both turned to find a tall, clean-shaven man in his forties smiling jovially down at my friend. "I haven't seen you in months."

"Carl Fowler." She smiled up at him and extended her hand cordially. I was bumped from behind, and I edged sideways to be out of the way. She turned to me. "He owns my favorite gallery in all of London." She withdrew her hand—I detected some reluctance on his part to let it go, which made me smile, despite everything—and she used it to gesture toward me. "And this is my friend Miss Annabel Rowe, who is a painter at the Slade. She's never been here, so I thought we'd take in the market today."

He looked up at the sky. "The weather is unfortunate, isn't it? Have you just arrived? Are you here looking for anything in particular?"

Celia ignored the first two questions. "Not really. It's more an excuse to be out of doors. And, well, my house is uninhabitable at the moment."

"Of course," he said, the smile slipping away. "I'm so sorry. I had forgotten. When will you be moving to Gwendolyn's?"

"In a few days. No doubt she'll have you to dinner soon."

His eyebrows rose, and he chuckled. "Your sister does love her parties."

"I don't think she knows how to dine alone." Celia smiled up at him.

"Well, I shall look forward to it," he said, and with a bow, he left us.

I turned to watch him go, and my eye was caught by a figure I knew—

Mr. Pagett was making his way toward us, slowly, one hand holding a walking stick.

I turned toward Celia, positioning myself with my back to him. "He's here," I said breathlessly. "Look over my shoulder."

Her eyes darted, and I heard her quick intake of breath as my eyes began searching for a plainclothesman.

It seemed there was none in sight. I spun, frantically, to see if I might find a telltale cap.

After all this time searching, to let our chance slip away—

"I see him," a masculine voice murmured in my ear.

Celia and I turned to find not one but two brown caps.

"Now we just need to wait," the other said. "Stay here."

We both nodded our assent, and I saw Mr. Pagett dawdling beside a booth that displayed bolts of cloth, examining the collection of woolens. He moved on to the next, which carried a range of scientific instruments. Suddenly, I saw another man proceeding along the row. He had a mustache and beard and walked with a stiffness that might have been due to an injury from his struggle with Matthew. But it was Sam Boulter, and tucked under his arm, as nonchalantly as if he carried this sort of parcel every day of his life, was a wooden box approximately a yard long with the words E. BUK, LTD. TELESCOPIC APPARATUS stamped in large black letters on the side.

We'd been ordered to stay where we were, but I hurried toward the policeman and bumped him with the left side of my body. "Telescope box," I said, as loudly as I dared in the direction of his ear, and continued on my trajectory away from him.

I couldn't be sure he'd heard me, but not wanting to attract notice, I strolled toward a booth that sold homemade preserves and butter. The crowd had thinned as the day waned, and God forbid either Mr. Pagett or Sam Boulter caught sight of me. My heart beating in sickening thuds, I fixed my eyes on some jars of strawberry preserves, straining to hear above the low chatter of market-goers, the clinks of jars, the bark of a dog.

Waiting—

Waiting—

Waiting for voices raised in protest, a crash as someone was shoved into a table, the clatter of Mr. Pagett's walking stick as it fell, the scream of an onlooker—

At last I could stand it no longer. Warily, I turned, craning my neck to peer down the aisle—

And I saw evidence of none of those things.

Celia appeared at my side. "There." She nodded, and I followed her gaze. The aisle was nearly empty, and I could see them, three-quarters of the way down the row, a tidy group of seven: Mr. Pagett walked between two policemen while Sam Boulter walked between two others, and Matthew brought up the rear, the telescope box under his left arm.

With a profound feeling of relief and anticlimax that almost made me want to laugh, I watched them go.

And then, suddenly, coming toward them with a bold, purposeful gait, was a man, tall and handsome, with brown hair and a face I'd seen before—

A warning bell sounded in my head, loudly.

Still, I couldn't place him—and yet it seemed terribly important that I remember who he was—

Then I knew:

Will Giffen. Sam Boulter's best friend.

His hands had been down by his sides, but now one was unbuttoning his coat.

My feet moved of their own accord, and I raced toward them—

"Matthew!" It came out as a shriek that sliced through the rumble and mutter of the market.

He whirled, and I saw his eyes searching desperately for me.

My arm was stretched straight out, my hand pointing—

Even as he turned away, his left hand dropped the box and his right drew a pistol.

Not ten steps from Matthew, Will Giffen jerked to a stop, his hand reaching inside his coat—

But Matthew closed in with long strides, and Will Giffen froze as Matthew's hand grasped his arm. In an instant, one of the other policemen was beside the pair, surreptitiously drawing Will Giffen's arms behind his back and clasping metal cuffs around his wrists. Now it was Matthew's hand slipping inside the man's coat at the waist. When it emerged, his fingers were wrapped around something dark and shining, and he slid it into his coat pocket without a glance.

Celia had reached my side. "Who's that?" she asked between gasps.

"Will Giffen," I said. "He came to Edwin's funeral, but they weren't friends. Lewis called him Sam Boulter's henchman." In the aftermath of my terror, my heart was pounding uncontrollably. I put my hand to my stomach, fearing I'd be ill.

A pair of women peered curiously at me.

"Be you all right?" one of them asked.

I nodded. "Yes. I thought I saw someone I knew."

Her thick brown eyebrows rose and she turned away muttering under her breath to the other, something about seeing folks you know without screaming like a banshee. The other woman chortled in reply.

Celia's hand grasped mine, and together we watched as two more policemen appeared. Each took one of Will Giffen's arms and steered him away. Matthew retrieved the box—which had remained intact, thank goodness—and I watched as they all vanished around the corner.

The very lack of furor, so in keeping with Matthew's usual equanimity, stunned me. How could anyone think that plain-clothesmen weren't superior at their work? I glanced around at the cheerfully mundane scene—a woman packing carrots and potatoes into a crate, another woman tugging at her two children, a man examining some old books at the next booth—and marveled.

A thief, a murderer, an accomplice, and a museum-quality painting had been removed from the scene, and no one was the wiser.

Chapter 24

$\mathcal{T}$he knowledge that the men had been caught and the painting found permitted me to slumber heavily, and for the first time since the attack, I woke without feeling the flare of anxiety along my nerves.

I drank my tea and dressed quickly, and soon arrived at the Yard. The men to be questioned had already been put into separate rooms in the back hallway. I sat on the same bench that I'd occupied twice before, the wooden seat at the junction of the hall and the main room. That morning it seemed to me there was a heightened intensity about the entire division, and no one paid a whit of attention to me as I waited for Matthew to emerge from the chief inspector's office.

At last he did, and I rose to meet him. I laid a hand on his forearm and under my breath, I pleaded, "I want to talk to him. Just for a few minutes."

Matthew shook his head. "Annabel, you can't. He's in custody. I'm sorry."

"You might not even have found him without me," I

whispered. "Edwin was my brother. I've a right to know what Boulter did, to hear it from him."

"I understand." His gaze met mine. "But there are procedures. Having you speak to him could jeopardize any evidence he gives."

He'd said the one thing that would stop my protests. I eyed him suspiciously. "Is that the truth?"

He nodded. "But you can listen from the monitoring room. I convinced the chief you might catch a lie that the two of us might not. It's the best I could do. All right?"

My disappointment faded. "He won't know I'm there?"

He shook his head. "There's only a vent connecting the rooms. You'll be able to hear, though you can't see. And you can't make a sound."

"Of course," I agreed hastily, grateful for the concession.

"We've already questioned Giffen and charged him as an accessory, but he claims he didn't know anything about the painting or Edwin. The chief and I will question Mr. Pagett and then Sam Boulter in turn." He hesitated then added haltingly, "You may hear . . . well, some things that will surprise you—and upset you."

"I'd still rather hear them than not."

"All right, then." He led me through the middle door of the three, and I sat in one of the wooden chairs.

A few moments later, I heard footsteps in the corridor, and a door opened and closed.

"Mr. Pagett, Chief Inspector Martin," Matthew said.

"It was not necessary to keep me overnight when I'd have immediately answered any question you asked. I've done nothing unlawful." Mr. Pagett's voice sounded icy. "I was purchasing a painting that by rights belongs to me already. The only person injured is myself."

The sound of scraping allowed me to imagine Matthew and his chief drawing out chairs and sitting down.

"That isn't true, is it? I believe your father intended to return the painting to the LeMarc family," Matthew said.

"That was never definite. At one point he also considered taking the painting to our estate in Salisbury."

"Not by the time he was planning on accompanying the LeMarcs to France," Matthew replied.

A heavy sigh. "If that's true, it was only because he was being tricked out of it."

"Tricked out of it," Matthew repeated. "You make your father sound like a gullible fool. Isn't it true that he was in love with Heloise and wanted to return it to her family as a gift? That's hardly a trick."

"Oh, for God's sake," Mr. Pagett burst out. "There is no one on this earth who thought more highly of my father than I, and he was no fool! But in later years his judgment was . . . compromised. Naturally, he was lonely after my mother died and susceptible to being infatuated with a beautiful young woman. Surely you've heard of that situation."

"Indeed, I have," said a third voice, regretful but eagerly conciliatory. "A young woman will sometimes play to an older man's need for companionship, make his evenings more pleasant."

I stiffened with annoyance. Why was the chief inspector being so solicitous?

"Exactly. She quickly discerned his preferences. She played whist with him, read the books he liked, and purposefully cultivated his affections."

The entire timbre of his voice had altered, and I could tell from its volume that Mr. Pagett had turned away from Matthew toward the chief.

"You don't think it's possible there was sincere affection on her side?" Matthew asked, his voice skeptical. "By all accounts, your father was a personable man."

"He *was*," he said earnestly, and his voice carried an edge of pain. "Personable and brilliant and cultivated. Heloise wasn't his equal in any way—in intellect or understanding or character. The truth of it is she wanted a comfortable place to stay while her country was overcome with turmoil. And she's the sort who enjoys conquests." His voice soured. "She plays with men like other women dabble in needlepoint."

"Was there perhaps some jealousy on your part?" Matthew asked.

A silence, and then he replied stiffly, "When she first arrived, she made clear her interest in me. When I rebuffed her—as tactfully as I could, for I had no desire to stir up animosity between the families—she turned her attentions to my father. At first, I thought the disparity in their ages would lead her affections to a natural death, and he would recognize how shallow and stupid she was. But he didn't."

"Was she really so shallow and stupid?"

A snort. "Heloise would take a fancy to one portrait or another, for no reason other than she thought some carved flowers on the frame were pretty, or because she liked the lace on a woman's dress and might see about having some made in Brussels. That was the extent of her understanding." A pause, and then, as if he realized how narrow that perspective was, he added, somewhat impatiently, "That is only one example."

"And yet your father was drawn to her."

"Yes." He admitted, reluctantly, "She *is* beautiful, and as I said, she was attentive."

"But you don't think she was attached to him? He went back to Paris with them."

"I watched her. As soon as she learned they'd be returning to Paris, she began to draw away from him."

"Oh?"

"It hurt him," he said, his voice brittle. "But he ascribed her growing indifference to anxiety about returning home. It was only after they left that I discovered that she'd had relations with one of our footmen. My father was in love and wouldn't have believed me." His voice dropped so far I had to strain to hear. "I never told him."

Matthew coughed. "You were angry that he was giving away this painting."

A sigh. "I don't expect you to understand. If it were going to someone who would appreciate it, I wouldn't mind half as much. But it is an *extraordinary* painting, the sort of painting one builds a collection around—a collection that transcends one person's life, a tangible manifestation of intelligence and knowledge—" He halted. "It shouldn't be used as a mere token in a doomed romantic scheme with a shallow, grasping woman."

"I understand," the chief interjected. "You want to create something that will last—something that will survive into posterity, something valuable that will stand up against time."

"Yes." Mr. Pagett sounded relieved. "I do."

"When your father returned from France, in March, he became very ill," Matthew said.

"Yes. He had influenza," Mr. Pagett replied.

"It appeared to be influenza." Matthew's voice was perfectly calm, the way it often was when he had something shocking to reveal, and I felt myself tense. "In fact, we now believe your father was poisoned."

Even as I felt the rush of surprise, I remembered I must stay quiet, and I silenced my gasp with my palm.

"But—but the doctor—but he—" Mr. Pagett sputtered.

"One of our specialists, Dr. Dunning, recently reviewed your doctor's notes," Matthew said. "And we consulted with an apothecary."

There was only silence.

"Mr. Pagett?"

"I—I—" His voice caught. "What—was it arsenic?"

"Not arsenic," Matthew said. "There was vomiting, head-ache, and tingling in the hands and feet, which could be due to either influenza or poison. But with a toxin such as arsenic, there are usually signs on the skin—lesions, redness and swell-ing, and a darkening of the skin over time; your father didn't have any of that."

"So it was something else?"

"Yes. As Dr. Dunning continued reading the list of symp-toms, he noted that Lord Sibley was having problems swal-lowing his food, his vision blurred, and his hair and eyebrows had begun to fall out. The apothecary described a recently discovered poison named thallium that dissolves in liquid and causes not only symptoms of influenza but also dysphagia—difficulty with swallowing, sometimes caused by injury to the esophagus—as well as injury to the eyes, and hair loss."

The thought of suffering those symptoms made me shudder.

A groan from Mr. Pagett. "My poor father."

Silence.

"Just how much did you want the Boucher?" Matthew's voice was soft.

I heard the shrill scrape of a chair against the floor, as if Mr. Pagett had pushed back from the table. "I *loved* my father! I would never, ever do something like that! Certainly not over a painting!"

"He was your *step*father," Matthew said quietly.

"Stepfather or not, he was the only father I ever knew! My mother married him when I wasn't yet two years old!"

"But it wasn't merely the painting you'd lose," Matthew pressed. "If your stepfather remarried, and Heloise had a child, you'd lose the Sibley inheritance and the entire collection, wouldn't you?"

His voice was hard. "You're right, most of my father's wealth would probably go to his new wife and heir. But I have my mother's inheritance, and it's plenty for my needs—including purchasing other paintings."

"How much was it?"

"Nearly twenty thousand pounds per annum." His voice was clipped.

I caught my breath. *Felix had been mistaken. It was a substantial fortune.*

The room was silent, and I understood that Matthew was temporarily nonplussed.

"My mother was an heiress," Mr. Pagett continued. "What I might inherit from Lord Sibley is less than a third of what

I inherited from my mother. I would certainly never kill him for it." His voice sharpened. "But who would have wanted to poison my father? And why?"

"I can't say," Matthew said. "It's part of an ongoing investigation."

"Damn your talk of investigations!" Mr. Pagett burst out. "He's my father! You can't merely tell me he's been poisoned and nothing else!"

"Mr. Hallam, I'd like to speak with Mr. Pagett alone," the chief inspector's authoritative voice broke in.

After a moment, I heard the scrape of a chair, and the door opened and closed.

"Mr. Pagett," the chief inspector said. "I assure you, we will share the truth when we know it. But we want to be very sure of our facts first. I'm sure you can understand. Believe me, we want justice for your father as much as you do. We have our eye on someone, and the man who did this will not go unpunished."

A heavy sigh. "It's just . . . oh, for God's sake. I feel like this is all because of that bloody portrait. I almost hate it now."

There was a long silence, and then the chief inspector said mildly, "My grandfather was a great admirer of portraits. We spent hours in the National Gallery together. He particularly liked the Old Masters."

Mr. Pagett made a noncommittal sound.

The handle to my room turned with a soft click, and Matthew stepped inside the room, his finger to his lips. I nodded, for I understood. The clouds of suspicion were clearing from around Mr. Pagett, and the chief inspector wanted to treat him as an ally—a task more easily done with Matthew out of the room.

The chief's voice continued, "It was he who taught me the difference between a half-length, a kit-cat, and a full-length, and to understand the iconography of the globe, the books, or the pointers at a man's feet. He impressed upon me from a young age how art was a record of history, not only an indelible record of an individual's pursuits and interests but also representative of the politics and mores of the time."

The echo of my own words—knowledge I'd gained myself from Mr. Poynter's lectures—made me turn to stare at Matthew. There was a glint of acknowledgment in his eye, but his face remained intent. He was listening with every bit of his being.

"My father and I also spent hours together looking at paintings," Mr. Pagett said, and his voice was low. "One of my earliest memories is of sitting on his knee in the study. He was showing me his grandfather's portrait and explaining to me what the painter had done and why."

"Do you have any idea who might have wanted to injure him?" the chief inspector asked. His voice was sympathetic. "A personal quarrel, perhaps something to do with his politics?"

Mr. Pagett gave a choking sort of gasp. "Father had his enemies in Parliament—particularly those in favor of strengthening ties with Germany. He thought they were shortsighted fools, and my father was accustomed to making his feelings known."

"Anyone in particular?"

He shrugged. "Lord Bartleston. Lord Chelmsley. Those are the two who come to mind."

"Thank you."

"Of course," he said despondently.

"Mr. Pagett, I have just a few more questions. First, did you ever speak with Mr. Fishel of the *Beacon*?"

"God, no. I hate newspapermen."

"And how did you find Mr. Boulter?" the chief inspector asked.

"Oh." A sigh. "I didn't find him. He found me. He sent a letter to my club, suggesting we meet."

"Where was that?"

"At a coffee shop in Islington."

"What price did he name?"

A brief hesitation. "One thousand pounds."

"One thousand pounds!" The chief's voice registered astonishment. "The painting was worth several times that, wasn't it?"

"Not with the controversy surrounding it," Mr. Pagett replied. "If there's even a doubt as to its legitimacy—and very few people other than myself would be able to distinguish the original from a copy—no one would pay full price for it."

"And how did you imagine that Mr. Boulter had the painting in the first place?"

The answer came reluctantly: "I assumed that he had been commissioned by Heloise LeMarc to sell it. It's well known that he frequently sells French art here. But I didn't ask. Frankly, I didn't much care." A pause. "How *did* he obtain it?"

"It was stolen from the flat of the man who was restoring it for auction."

Dead silence. And then a whisper: "Oh God."

"In fact, Boulter at first tried to tell us that you stole it and murdered the man who was cleaning it," the chief inspector said quietly. "And you knew him because he'd cleaned a painting for you several years ago."

"That's absurd!" He hesitated, then asked, "Who was the man cleaning it?"

"Edwin Rowe."

"The man in the newspaper," he said slowly.

"Yes."

"I never met him," Mr. Pagett said. "When was the painting stolen?"

"Two weeks ago, on Monday, in the late afternoon or evening."

A sigh. "Well, there you have it. I was in France."

"What?"

"I can find you the canceled tickets. I went to Paris to see the LeMarc family because I had reason to suspect they had commissioned the sale."

"How did they receive you?" the chief inspector asked.

"They were civil enough, at first."

"At first?"

"Yes, until I asked Heloise outright if she'd put the painting up for auction at Bettridge's," Mr. Pagett said. "She flew into a temper and told me my father had sold it back to her for a pound, as a present, but she insisted she hadn't seen the Boucher since they'd left England. I assumed she was lying."

The chief inspector remained silent, and I wondered if he was imagining what I was: how angry Mr. Pagett would have been, believing that Heloise had sold Lord Sibley's gift to her—especially after he had done her family the kindness of providing them with a safe haven for nearly two years.

"She wasn't lying," the chief inspector said. "We found a notarized receipt of sale signed by your father."

A sharp intake of breath. "You did? Where?"

"I can't say at the moment. But it is most assuredly authentic."

There came a sound halfway between a snort and a sigh. "Very well." His voice was heavy with resignation. "Then it's hers by rights."

"One more thing," the chief inspector said. "Does the name Stephen Jesper mean anything to you?"

"I assume he's related to Mrs. Celia Jesper, who consigned the Boucher."

"She had it in her house because his firm had been hired to ship the Boucher. We found a bill of lading to that effect." The chief inspector paused. "Would you have had a quarrel with Jesper for heeding your father's request?"

"Of course not," Mr. Pagett scoffed. "If Father had ordered it, the shippers certainly weren't to blame. But I've never spoken to Mr. Jesper in my life, much less quarreled with him. If you don't believe me, ask the man."

"Thank you, Mr. Pagett. Would it be possible for us to send a policeman round to your house for those tickets? It would be most helpful."

"Of course. They're in the top right-hand drawer of my desk."

"That will be all for now," the chief inspector said. "I'll be back shortly."

The door opened and closed.

I saw Matthew's chest expand with a sigh of relief, and he wore a look of satisfaction. From the room we heard a soft groan from Mr. Pagett followed by a whispered "damn."

Matthew came forward to touch my elbow, and his expression seemed to ask for understanding. He tipped his head toward the other room; it was time for him to speak with Sam Boulter. I had a feeling this interview would be more difficult for me to hear. But I nodded, and he closed the vent to Mr. Pagett's room then left. A moment later, I heard a door open and close. I went to the vent on the other wall and soundlessly slid the lever all the way up, my heart hammering.

"Mr. Boulter."

Silence.

"Do you have anything you'd like to say, before we begin?" Matthew asked.

"Only that Mr. Pagett wanted that painting." His voice was churlish. "He would have done anything to get it back."

"Let's set the matter of the painting aside for a moment," Matthew replied. "I want to know about Edwin Rowe. You knew him from school?"

Silence. I imagined the look he was giving Matthew, for asking a question to which the inspector knew the answer.

Matthew's voice was conversational: "He must have done something to make you angry, all those years ago."

Still, silence.

"Your father was the art master there, wasn't he?" Matthew continued.

"Yes."

"And he took a liking to Edwin."

"Perhaps. I don't recall."

"Right now you're going to hang for murder," Matthew said, his voice nonchalant. "If you want any chance at prison instead, you'll answer the question."

"You've no proof, or you wouldn't be asking," he said flatly.

"Aside from the fact that you had in your possession the Boucher that was in Edwin's room, we have a witness who puts you in Edwin's rooms that night, and we can probably make a case that it was your knife. You dropped one of the proper length and width in the stairwell the other night."

I felt myself freeze in my chair. Was Matthew lying? Or telling the truth?

A long pause.

"There are plenty of knives like that," Mr. Boulter said coolly. "You can't prove I used it on him."

"Well, whether you did or didn't, there's a factor you're not taking into account. The painting belonged to Lord Sibley, and he had plenty of friends in legal circles who'd like to see justice done. I've seen cases like this, and I can tell you there's enough evidence that a judge will convict, if only to hold someone accountable," Matthew said calmly. "But if you tell me how it happened, I will have a word with him. It usually makes a difference in sentencing. Might even be mitigated to transportation."

Another long silence, as if Mr. Boulter were running through some internal calculation. I prayed that he would resign himself to having nothing left to lose.

"Why did you hate Edwin so?" Matthew asked curiously. "He must have injured you in some way at Tennersley."

A sigh. "Rowe was an arrogant little ass. No more talented than any of the rest of us."

"Your father thought otherwise, didn't he?"

He remained silent, and my spine was pressed cruelly against a spindle in the back of the chair as I waited, wanting to know everything Sam Boulter could tell me but dreading it all the same.

"In fact, he thought a great deal of Edwin," Matthew said. "They spent hours together in the studio."

"My father didn't do those vile things Edwin said he did," Boulter said, his voice low and defiant. "But Wexford was the head of the school board, and he hated my father, so he *wanted* to believe Edwin's lies. No one could stand up to Wexford. He led that entire board around by the nose."

"There were other boys your father took an interest in, weren't there?" Matthew asked.

"Not like Edwin."

"How did you find him, two weeks ago?"

"Saw him on the street by chance," Mr. Boulter replied. "That hair of his makes him easy to spot."

"And you followed him," Matthew said.

A grunt.

"And went upstairs?"

"No . . . not that day." A pause. "I lost him in the crowd. It took me two days to spot him again."

"What happened when you confronted him?" Matthew's choice of word sounded deliberate, and I understood he was coaxing answers from Mr. Boulter while trying to protect me from the worst of what I might hear. I felt a pinch of regret about the additional degree of complication for Matthew, but there was no possibility I would leave. Not yet.

A long pause, and the sound of a chair creaking. "I didn't intend it to be a confrontation," Mr. Boulter said. "Not like that! I wasn't looking for a row. I just wanted him to admit he'd lied. It didn't have to be public!" His voice frayed around the edges. "I just wanted him to admit it to *me*, that he shouldn't have ruined our lives."

"Ruined your lives?"

I heard the authentic surprise in Matthew's voice.

"It took my father months to find another position. Finally ended up at a school in bloody Manchester," Boulter spat. "It was hell."

"I see," Matthew said, dragging out the syllables. "And what did Edwin say?"

A nasty little laugh. "He wouldn't do it. Stubborn little bastard."

Matthew had been keeping the conversation moving forward, as if he were easing Sam toward an edge. But at those words, time seemed to stand still. I felt my anger spike straight from my heart toward Sam Boulter. And then, the following instant, the anger ricocheted toward Edwin, who might still be alive, if he'd just been willing to lie—

"What if he wasn't lying?" Matthew asked. "What if Edwin was telling the truth?"

"He was lying, I tell you," came the response through gritted teeth.

"I don't think so," Matthew said.

A snort. "Believe what you like."

There was a long pause during which I found myself holding my breath.

Matthew asked, "Why did you torment boys like Alan and Edwin and Lewis? You were years older and twice their size."

There was the screech of metal against wood, as if he'd pushed back from the table. "Bloody hell! That was years ago! What does this matter? They were sniveling little brats!"

Boulter's remorselessness made tears burn at the sides of my eyes.

"All right," Matthew said resignedly. "There's no point in

this. But I'll have you know you're being charged this after-noon."

I heard footsteps and the sound of the door opening, when suddenly Boulter's voice sheared through the vent—

"He wasn't innocent, you know! Edwin. He *wanted* things from my father! Things he had no right to. *Hours* of his time. *All* of his attention. You should have heard his incessant whing-ing." Boulter's voice rose several registers in imitation of a young boy. *"Professor, won't you look at this painting? Professor, is this a proper line?"* A pause filled with labored breathing. "He was *my* father! Not Edwin's!"

Against my every impulse, I felt a glimmering of under-standing for the man. If this was truly what he believed, no wonder he hated Edwin so.

"You didn't kill him for the painting, did you?" Matthew asked softly. "You killed Edwin because you felt he took your father from you. The painting was only incidental."

"Wouldn't *you*?" burst from him. "And of course I took the painting! It was lying out in the open, and it's the *least* he owed me! After all that?" There was a sound that might have been a sob. "For God's sake, he bloody well owed me *something*!"

The last word was a cry, as if from the deepest recess of his heart, and it came to me that Sam Boulter knew Edwin wasn't the one who owed him. There was a long silence, and then, heavily and slowly, as if each word were a stone he had to heave out of a river, he repeated, "He owed me something."

Perhaps if I'd been able to see Sam Boulter, I might not have been so attuned to the nuances of his voice. But sitting there, in that bare room, stripped of every sense but hearing, I caught the tones that thickened the air: the fierceness of a boy's love and loyalty toward his father; the despair at being abandoned; and the shame over the secret that Sam Boulter wouldn't admit even to himself.

And though this man had killed my brother, God help me, my heart broke for him.

Chapter 25

I left the Yard, not wanting to hear any more. Matthew remained away until late that night, but I stayed awake in the parlor, adding coals to the fire, waiting for him. At last, the key turned in the lock, and I met him at the door. He looked drained, and I helped him with his coat.

"Do you want something to eat?" I asked.

"I'm not hungry." He took my hand, drew me to the settee, and pulled me beside him. "I know that wasn't easy for you to hear."

I turned sideways, so I could face him. "I know that wasn't easy for you to *do*, trying to obtain answers while you knew I was listening."

A brief nod acknowledged the truth, and his eyes showed a glint of surprise. "Is that why you left?"

"Partly." I swallowed. "Mostly because I didn't want to hear any more just then."

For a few minutes we just watched the fire burning in front of us, every shade of red and gold there ever was. Around us, shadows hovered, but they seemed benevolent rather than eerie.

At last I asked, "Did he say much more?"

"Some."

"Did he tell you why he attacked me?"

"Mm-hm." His hand reached over to touch my hair. "He says he didn't intend to harm you, only wanted to frighten you, to keep you from learning about his father. Hiram Boulter is still alive, although he's ill, and here in London. His son didn't want him to spend his last few months answering questions about old crimes."

"Still protecting him," I murmured. "Despite everything."

"Yes."

"Did he know about my brother having the Boucher?"

"He had no idea. But apparently it was in plain sight, and after he fought with Edwin, he recognized immediately what it was. So he cut it from the frame and left." He paused. "I think he did it partly for the money, of course, but also just to throw another shade of suspicion on your brother, even after his death."

The viciousness of it made me shiver. "He's so angry. Like Lewis."

"Lewis?"

I nodded. "One of the last things he said to me was Will Giffen has a little boy, and Lewis hopes someone would do to him what Boulter did to Edwin. Maybe to Lewis, too, I don't know. He didn't say, but he was so bitter I have to imagine . . ."

He drew a deep breath. "My God."

"I know. The cruelty just seems to go on and on. Maybe now

it can stop." I spoke hopefully, but he made a noncommittal noise, and I eyed him with concern. "There's more to this, isn't there?" And then I remembered. "What you said about Lord Sibley being poisoned, was that true?"

He studied me for a moment. "If I tell you, can you promise not to say anything—even to Celia when you see her?"

"Of course."

"It involves a case that began before I came to the Yard, so I've only just learned about it myself." A dark eyebrow rose. "But you'll recognize the gist of it."

I leaned an elbow along the back of the settee and rested my cheek on my hand, watching his face intently.

"Several years ago, one of our inspectors intercepted a shipment of guns bound for France. There was no bill of lading and no identifying marks on the guns, but the vessel belonged to the Jesper Shipping Company."

I stiffened.

"Naturally, this raised questions, but almost immediately the head of the Yard halted the investigation. The order came from the highest levels of government."

"So someone was condoning it," I said slowly. "And Lord Sibley was involved?"

He nodded. "He had arranged for the funds outside normal channels."

I frowned. "But why was he poisoned?"

"The gunmaker died and left the business to his son, who recognized that if this ever came to light, he'd never receive another government contract again—because while Gladstone might have looked the other way, Disraeli wouldn't."

"And Disraeli was elected in February of last year," I recalled. "So the son had to silence Lord Sibley when he returned in March—" My voice broke off and I realized with horror what this meant. "What about Mr. Jesper? He died at the end of February."

Matthew's eyes were dark with regret. "February twenty-fourth, to be precise. I know. We've no proof his death was anything other than an accident, but . . ."

"Oh, Matthew," I breathed. "Are you going to tell her?"

"She already suspects something," he reminded me.

"That's why it would be kindest to tell her," I insisted. "Otherwise she'll always wonder."

"I may not be allowed to, Annabel." He shrugged wearily. "I need to wait, in any case. I shouldn't even have told you this much."

"I'm sorry," I said, regretting I'd pressed him. "I won't say a word. Not to her or anyone," I promised soberly. Nothing good would come of it, certainly. I drew close and rested my head on his shoulder. The linen of his shirt was soft against my cheek.

He wrapped his arm around my shoulders and gave a sigh that expanded his ribs. "In any event, this marks the end of my work on the case. Martin is sending me to Bracknell tomorrow on the two-oh-six with another plainclothesman on another matter. I expect to be gone for at least a fortnight."

I felt a pang of unhappiness at the thought. Until everything was settled, I wished he were staying in London. But I kept that feeling to myself.

His hand was gentle on my hair, and we stayed like that for a good while. And then Matthew's breathing deepened, and I realized he was asleep. I shifted, and touched his face. "Matthew."

His eyelids flickered, and I stood and took his hand to help him up.

"Matthew, you should go to bed."

Fumblingly he stood, drew me close for a moment, and started up the stairs. As I listened to his heavy steps, my heart went out to him. After all his work, this seemed such an unsatisfactory result, especially as he'd unearthed additional crimes. But he'd discovered some bits of truth, and perhaps he could be content with that.

WE'D HEARD NOTHING from the hospital regarding Felix, but at the breakfast table the next morning, as I poured the last of the tea for us, a message arrived that he could see visitors. Matthew said he had time to visit Felix with me before he was due at the train station, so we finished up hastily and set out for Agar Street. At Charing Cross Hospital, a nurse directed us to the upper floor, and we walked into the ward.

I hesitated outside the curtained area, thinking of Felix's weakness for spirits and the shame he might feel. But I hoped the news we brought might help.

His head was wrapped in a white bandage that failed to conceal the curved edge of the purpling bruise over his temple. His face was slack and pale, but his eyelids fluttered as I approached the bed.

"Felix." I rested my hand briefly on his shoulder. "I'm glad you're going to be all right."

He turned his head away with a low moan and closed his eyes. "Please. I'm tired."

I kept my voice soft. "Felix, Boulter has been caught, and the painting's recovered."

At that he opened his eyes again, and his dull gaze shifted from me to Matthew, who nodded. Still, there was barely a spark of feeling, and I realized what might help most of all.

I sat down close to his bed. "I want to apologize, Felix. I never thanked you for your kindness to Edwin and to me, for years now. The day of his funeral, I couldn't have managed anything for myself—and you did all of it. I've been so consumed by my own grief that I've completely ignored how painful it was for you, losing Edwin. I know you loved him."

He was staring up at the ceiling. Slowly, tears rose to his eyes and rolled down the sides of his slack cheeks onto the pillow. He didn't even look at me, but he let them come. "Yes, I loved him." A juddering sigh. "We understood each other."

"Edwin was unhappy for a long time," I said. "At least he seemed to find some peace—and trust—with you . . . and me, too, at the end."

He turned to me, a question in his eyes.

"Felix, I went to your rooms the other day, intending to leave you a message. And while I was at your desk, I found a letter from Edwin, addressed to me."

His eyes widened in bewilderment, and then his expression changed to one of horror. "Oh God. I'm sorry—"

"It's all right," I assured him and laid a hand on his arm. "Truly. Please don't distress yourself!"

He struggled to sit up. "But I completely forgot! Mr. Poynter gave it to me at the funeral. He felt it would upset you, coming so close to Edwin's death." A sigh as he lay back against the pillow. "I should have given it to you right away."

"No, you did the proper thing, waiting," I said. "If you'd

given it to me earlier, I doubt I'd have paid it any attention. Instead, it gave me what I needed, at the right time."

He frowned. "What do you mean?"

"He told me where to find the receipts and shipping information for the painting. They proved the late Lord Sibley had sold it back to the LeMarc family, and it was rightfully theirs. Stephen Jesper had it in his house only because he was supposed to ship it, once Lord Sibley sent word that the LeMarcs were settled again. But Lord Sibley became ill and the order never came. If it had, Celia might have looked for the painting earlier. As it was, the LeMarcs thought it was in the Pantechnicon, like everyone else."

"Where is the painting now?" Felix asked.

Matthew spoke up. "It'll be sent to the LeMarc family. We'll ensure it arrives safely."

Felix's chest heaved with a sigh. "Well, Annabel, I am glad for your sake."

I was about to protest that this mattered for his sake, too, but suddenly Felix's eyes were wide, and his head was moving as if he were trying to track a moving fly. "I'm going to be sick."

Hastily I reached for a metal bowl nearby and held it for him. When he'd finished, I went to the washstand and submerged a small towel in water and wrung it out. "Here."

He pressed the cold cloth to his face, and took a deep, shuddering breath.

A nurse appeared and spoke officiously, "You need to rest, Mr. Severington. Your visitors can come back tomorrow."

I put a gentle hand on his shoulder. "She's right, Felix. Just rest. Everything will be all right."

He drew away the towel, and his expression was incredulous. "How can it be? My reputation is gone, and I'll never find employment. Bettridge's told me on Saturday that I was finished for good." He shook his head hopelessly. "I've still no idea . . ."—his voice faded until it was almost inaudible—". . . how I'm to live."

The two meanings of that phrase struck me with the force of a stone against my chest. I knew Felix had been inebriated when he'd fallen in front of the cab, but had there been a part of him that *wished* it would kill him?

Felix turned his head away and closed his eyes. His fingers waved me off.

"Annabel," Matthew said quietly. "Let him be."

And so we left. But as we descended to the street, I felt how deeply unfair this was, and as we reached the pavement I pulled Matthew to a stop beside me. I'd been prevented from accusing Sam Boulter, of staring into his face as he was forced to acknowledge what he'd done. But John Fishel was a public figure, and accessible—and I despised him for the despair that he'd sown in a man who wasn't to blame for Edwin's death, or for any of this mess. I felt my fury rising. "I want five minutes with John Fishel."

Matthew's blue eyes met mine. "I can get you that," he said. "But I'll warn you—and I'm not jesting—you'll probably make no impression upon him whatsoever."

"That may be," I said shortly. "I want it anyway."

THE OFFICES OF the *Beacon* weren't far from those of the *Falcon*. This newspaper occupied all four floors of a large, prosperous-looking building made of a pale brown brick that showed a gray film of filth near the foundations. I gave a grim smile at the aptness of it.

We entered, and I asked the clerk at the desk for Mr. Fishel.

He never looked up from his ledger. "Sorry, miss, he's busy."

Matthew drew a card from his pocketbook and slid it across the wood surface. "He'll see us," he said smoothly. "Or I shall take him to the Yard in cuffs. It'll save time, if we can speak to him here."

The man's eyes darted to the card; his eyebrows leapt up and he hastily pushed Matthew's card back the way it came. "A'right, guvnor. No need to be tetchy. He's upstairs, first room on the left."

We started up the flight of steps along the wall. The staircase had only a banister to the right, and halfway up, I glanced back and saw the man staring at us and gnawing his lip. I could feel his desire to warn Mr. Fishel, but I glared at him, and he turned away with a shrug.

As we reached the top of the stairs, we heard the sound of men's voices shouting and laughing. The door was ajar, and Matthew pushed it open. The creak silenced the three men in the room. They all turned, but it was the man standing behind the desk who said, "What do you want, Hallam?"

So this was Mr. Fishel.

I'd imagined him toadlike, but he wasn't a particularly ugly man. He was of medium height and sturdily built, with round cheeks, brown eyes, and a shock of dark hair running to gray. His expression, however, was repellent.

One of the other two men chortled. "Well, it's Scotland Yard payin' a call. That's always an int'resting break from routine."

"Not to mention the lady," muttered the third man.

"He's too scared to come here by hisself, has to bring an escort," said the second man laconically. He leered at me as he walked past, and I resisted the urge to shrink away from him. I felt my skirts catch on the cloth of his trousers, and with a sort of half-mocking courtesy, he said, "Good day to you, miss."

Matthew shut the door behind them.

"For Christ's sake, Hallam. There's no need for secrecy." Fishel sat down behind his desk and picked up a pen with an air of weary indifference. "Unless you're planning to horsewhip me."

"I would if I could," I said.

His gaze shifted, and his eyebrows rose. "Who the devil are you?"

"Annabel Rowe. I'm a friend of Felix Severington's."

"Ah." He sat back a bit. "Well, you might not have liked what I wrote, but we didn't print anything that wasn't true."

"True in the letter, perhaps," I retorted. "But you all but ruined his reputation with innuendo and speculation."

He turned to Matthew. "Tell her it's not illegal to propose possible explanations."

I took a step toward him. "You've deprived him of his position and driven the poor man to despair," I said incredulously. "Have you no compunction at all? Doesn't it matter to you how badly you injured him—and without cause?"

He spread his hands. "It's my duty to tell the truth as it unfolds."

"The *truth*?" I echoed in disbelief. "You only tell the aspects of the truth that would stir people up. You're worse than a bloody sensation novelist!"

He gave a laugh. "Your insult is thrown away on me, my dear. Sensation novelists are highly successful. Have you looked at any of the railway stalls lately? Smith's isn't selling sober works of philosophy. They sell what people want to buy. It's the power of the market—and it's the very same power your brother listened to. He didn't try to sell paintings people didn't want, did he? How could he survive?" A pause. "We're all selling something, miss."

"My brother didn't drive people to despair with his paintings," I said between gritted teeth.

His eyes narrowed. "Well, he caused plenty of people distress when they found they'd bought his worthless copies." He dropped his chin and looked up at me. "And that's a crime, miss. What I've done isn't." He turned to Matthew. "You should have told her. I've done nothing against the law. Fully within my rights."

"My brother paid for his crime. And you're vile," I spat.

A genuine laugh burst from him. "What's vile is the corruption and deception of the auction world! You're just angry because I pointed to the muck sticking to your friend's shoes."

I longed to pick up the inkwell and throw it at his smirking face. "If you're trying to expose the deceit in the auction world, then at least marshal public venom against the proper person. Felix had nothing to do with the painting's disappearance. The man who stole it didn't even know Felix!"

His eyes narrowed. "But if my story heightens scrutiny toward the auction houses, I've provided a service." Elbows on his desk, he leaned forward and pointed a finger at me, and I noticed how coarse his hands were, how heavy the knuckles. At some point in his life, he'd labored with them. "People like you may not care how corrupt practices plague this bloody city, but the public has a right to know when they're being swindled. I've done my duty getting this story into their hands, and they're not stupid. They want to hear the truth more than puffery and lies." He pulled a face and shrugged, giving a sideways glance at Matthew. "Perhaps if we had more information—if the Yard didn't hide its every move, we wouldn't be forced to speculate now and again."

There was a glint in his eye, and suddenly I understood the larger stakes at hand. Felix had merely been a marker in a game between the police and the popular press.

The realization left me speechless.

Matthew approached the desk. "We want an amendment in which you make it clear that neither Edwin Rowe nor Felix Severington had anything to do with that painting going missing."

All signs of sardonic humor vanished from Fishel's face. "You can't tell me what to write, Hallam. I refuse to print an amendment."

"Why?"

"Because no one's going to care."

Matthew put his two hands on the edge of the desk and leaned in. Fishel didn't flinch. He was no coward; I'd give him that.

"Do you think your wife and her father would care to know about Lucille Vesey?" Matthew asked, his voice gentle.

Fishel's eyes remained locked on Matthew's, but I saw a telltale slackening along the newspaperman's jaw.

"The French actress who lives on Partridge Street, second floor?" Matthew continued. "Or perhaps her husband might care."

Fishel's cheeks flamed red. "You've been spying on me, Hallam? Creeping around at night, looking through my windows? Is that what you do now?" It came out a snarl.

Matthew straightened and headed toward the door. He opened it and waved me into the hallway. His hand was still on the knob and he turned back. "Print an amendment," he said mildly. "And I'll forget all about her. Otherwise, I think it's my duty to tell the truth as it unfolds."

Chapter 26

I'd forgotten to close my curtains the night before, and I was roused by the first slant of sun flooding my room.

With Boulter in custody, I'd returned to my own rooms and my classes at the Slade, and life was gradually reverting to its normal shape. My grief was still present, but it was no longer the same sharp, stabbing pain as it had been, for now it was softened by a profound gratitude that Edwin had had faith I'd do the best I could for him. The brief letter he wrote me was now the most precious thing I owned. I'd tucked it into the corner of my mirror, so I'd see it every morning.

I rolled over onto my back and listened for the mundane sounds of the world outside rising to my flat, muted by the glass. The clop of a horse's hooves, the tones of several male voices shouting, the repeated scrape of a shovel against stones, the clunk of a door closing solidly against a wooden frame.

I pillowed my head on my arms and looked up at the ceiling. It had been over a week since our visit to John

Fishel. He had printed the revised story, clearing Felix of any wrongdoing and casting all the blame on Mr. Boulter, whom he described in terms worthy of a villain in one of Mrs. Henry Wood's sensation novels. Felix was still in the hospital but mending, with respect to both his head and his spirits. I'd received a telegram from Matthew two days ago, to the effect that he would be away at least another week, but Edwin's case was near completion and we might tell Celia everything when he returned. So yesterday I'd sent a note asking if we might visit her at her sister's home, and Celia had returned an answer promptly that assured me we'd be welcome. She mentioned she'd visited Felix in hospital and offered him a position in a gallery owned by a friend. She'd also included a ticket to a private art exhibition in a fortnight, with a postscript that made me smile: *I do hope you can join me.*

There was only one more person connected to Edwin whom I wanted to see.

I SPENT THE morning at my easel, but at midday I set out. The sky was a cornflower blue and the breeze warmer than usual for early October. I found a cab in Charing Cross and took it north on Tottenham Court Road far enough for it to change names to Hampstead. Just after we crossed over a pair of railway tracks, the driver turned right and we continued on until he let me out at a church with the name engraved on a square wooden plaque out front: ST. PANCRAS.

I liked it on sight, and I could understand why Edwin would. It had neither the lofty, elaborate steeple of St. Martin's nor the flying buttresses of Westminster. Instead, it was reassuringly compact, solid, and low to the ground. Made of light brown stone, the entrance was a sturdy arch with a rose window above. The square bell tower bore clocks on each face, as if welcoming people from all directions. Rather than a typical rigid wrought-iron fence, low boxwood hedges separated the churchyard from the street, and the branches of trees arched over the church's roof, lending it grace. To the right of the door was a niche, with the carved figure of the saint, a young boy, his right hand turned palm up and fingers slightly curved, as if around a ball that the sculptor neglected to include. Below the figure was a stone bearing the inscription: *To the sacred memory of St. Pancras of Rome. He who holds everything. Martyred 303 A.D.*

I pushed at the heavy wooden door. Inside I found a narrow and unadorned room with one aisle down the middle and wooden pews on either side. The altar was plain but neat, with a white cloth draped over it. The room held a faint but not unpleasant scent of burnt candles. In the wall a stone bore a carving. At first glance, I thought it said *A.D. 1625.* But as I drew closer, I saw there was no numeral one before the six. My fingertips traced the digits. If this date was accurate, there had been a church of some sort here for over a thousand years.

I walked down the aisle, looking for a door that might lead to the vestry. When I found it, I knocked, and a young deacon opened the door.

"May I help you?"

"I'm looking for the vicar, Mr. Pascoe. Is he here?"

"Yes, miss." He pointed to a door opposite. "You'll find him in the garden. He's usually outside on a day like this."

I thanked him and went out into the churchyard. The afternoon shadows had begun to fall across the grass, and the tree limbs shifted above, but the sun wouldn't set for several more hours, and the air was still pleasant.

I followed a gravel path around to the back and although I didn't see Mr. Pascoe, I saw black vestments hanging on a low branch and flapping gently in the breeze. I headed toward them and rounding a hedge, I caught sight of the vicar. He was in plain black trousers and shirt, kneeling on a bit of carpet and weeding at the edge of a large square bed. I continued along the path, past several headstones: *Paul Bannister,* I read. *1811–1851. A beloved father, taken too soon. Ellen Bannister, 1819–1854. A treasured wife, a tender mother, and a devoted sister. Joseph Bannister, 1834–1855. Killed in Crimea. His soul was equal parts bravery, honour, and faith.*

"Hello, Miss Rowe."

I turned to see Mr. Pascoe, still kneeling but with his hands resting on his thighs, smiling as if he'd half expected me. Perhaps in his profession, very little surprised him. He set aside his trowel and brushed his hands on his trousers preparatory to rising.

"Please don't get up, Vicar," I said hurriedly. "If you don't mind I'd rather stay out here. I could help you. As a child, I'd help my mother with our garden, once I learned the difference between penstemon and the weeds."

He nodded cheerfully and I sensed that he understood it would be easier for me to talk if I had something to occupy my hands. "Very well." He picked up his trowel. "With all the rain, I'm afraid the weeds have run riot. I'm trying to pull them out before I put in the spring bulbs." He rummaged in the wheelbarrow beside him and handed me a trowel and then, after a look at my skirts, he found a rough sack. "That should do to save your clothes."

"Thank you." I folded the sack over twice, knelt on top of it, and began to turn over the dirt, taking care to pull the weeds down to the root. He'd brought a bucket to collect them, and he nudged it closer to me.

"How are you?" he asked.

I smiled. "Fairly well."

"I'm glad to see you." He paused. "Has your inspector made any progress?"

I dug my trowel down farther into the soil. "Yes. Things have been mostly sorted." I paused. "Mainly because Edwin left a letter for me."

"Did he?" He sounded genuinely surprised.

I nodded. "The painting will be sent to the LeMarc family in Paris, where it belongs. And a man named Sam Boulter confessed to killing Edwin and trying to sell the painting illicitly."

I watched him closely as I said the name, but he gave no sign of recognition. The sigh he heaved shifted the cloth over his chest. "I suppose I should be pleased at a resolution, but what a wretched, terrible thing."

We weeded in silence for a minute or two, and having finished with his half of the plot, he dug a hole approximately four inches deep. He reached into a sack, removed a bulb, and placed it carefully before covering it with dirt.

"What sort of flower?" I asked.

"Daffodil," he said. "I've crocus bulbs, too, but I'll put them over that way." He waved his trowel.

I worked away at a fibrous root as I gathered my courage to say, "Sam Boulter went to Tennersley with Edwin."

"Oh?"

I couldn't read much meaning in that monosyllable, but

one look at the vicar's face, and I knew I could ask. My trowel rested immobile on the dirt. "You knew, didn't you? What Sam Boulter's father did to Edwin."

His eyes were cast down, watching his fingers press the soil into place. "Was he Edwin's art master?"

"Yes."

"He never told me the man's name. But yes, I gathered he'd experienced something . . . heinous." He shook his head and his eyes met mine. "When I first met him, your brother was in terrible distress. Pain like that seeps from a deep wound. An act of cruelty or betrayal, or both, by someone we love." He paused. "You asked about the sketchbook that was missing."

"Yes."

"It told me what he couldn't bring himself to say." He swallowed hard. "And he asked me to destroy it."

"Did you?"

He nodded.

"Why? Did he want to pretend it hadn't happened?"

"No. I think he wanted to believe the events from that time weren't going to determine his life going forward."

"But they did." My voice grew brittle. "He was killed because Sam Boulter saw him on the street, and when he tried to make Edwin say he'd lied about what Mr. Boulter had done, Edwin wouldn't do it."

The vicar sucked in his breath, his eyes widened, and his hands went still as he took this in. In the silence, I heard the leaves rustling overhead and the bustle of the world beyond the boxwood.

"And now you're angry, aren't you?" he asked gently. "You think Edwin should have lied."

"Why couldn't he? Just to stay alive?" I pleaded. "If Edwin had told me the truth, I'd have believed him. What did it matter if he had to deceive someone like Sam Boulter?"

His eyes held a world of compassion. "You know the answer to that, don't you?"

I was silent for several minutes, and at last, reluctantly, I voiced my thoughts: "I suppose it's because he was tired of concealing it. He'd lived with the secret for so long." I hesitated. "And—given that he vowed to start living differently—he wouldn't want to take the smallest step back toward lies and pretending."

He picked up his trowel, though it lay motionless in his hand. "He'd have been repulsed by the idea."

A leaf dropped onto my skirt, and I brushed it away. "Do you think he was right to feel so strongly?"

"I couldn't say," he replied. "I know that sometimes people are so broken they cannot mend enough. But he preserved his integrity, what I might even call his soul"—he spread his hands—"at the expense of his body." He shook his head. "I can't fault him for that."

"No." I gave a heavy sigh. "But it's terribly sad . . . for me."

"I know. I'm sorry."

The misery swamped me. "It's just . . . I wish I'd been able to tell him I believed him. But he never really gave me a chance! I wish I'd been more of an ally to him after he got out of prison. Felix was, and you were. But I wasn't."

He did me the favor of not offering insincere reassurances. "Well, it was complicated," he admitted. "I do believe as we grow older, it's our responsibility to serve as an ally when someone needs us, if we can." He took up another of the bulbs, placed it in a hole, and covered it. "There are advantages some-times to our being observers, holding ourselves out of the fray. But that isn't truly living, is it?"

"No," I owned, and he smiled beatifically, as if the most important matter had been resolved. Yet I had one remaining question. "Vicar, in his last letter Edwin asked me to do some-thing for him—something important. So I know he trusted me to behave responsibly. But . . . did he ever tell you . . . well, do you think he knew I loved him?" I heard the wistfulness in my voice.

His head tipped, he surveyed me thoughtfully before he re-plied, "Yes, I believe he did." I waited, holding my breath and hoping he could offer me something less equivocal. After a mo-ment, he continued, "In my experience, love looks different to everyone. Edwin told me about your Tuesday visits, and several times he made a point of saying you'd never missed one. Never even been late. Not once."

"That's true," I said.

"I think particularly for Edwin steadiness and reliability were very important signs of love. Instinctively or not, you gave them to him, and so"—his smile was warmly reassuring—"yes, I'd say he knew."

I felt a wave of relief. "Thank you."

The sun had dropped behind the church, sending long, cool shadows over this part of the garden. He peered up at the clock and then down at his sack of bulbs. "The rest of these must wait, I'm afraid."

Together we stood and brushed off our clothes. He disen-tangled his robes from the branches of the tree, draped them over his shoulder, and grasped the handles of a nearby wheelbarrow. We started down a flagstone path toward the vestry. "Watch yourself on that stone," he said. "The tree roots have pushed it up."

What a good man he is, I thought as I stepped over the uneven edge. And while I was not in the habit of praying, here amid the gardens I felt it fitting to send up a few words of thanks for this man who had given Edwin back some peace and faith.

As we started down the path I asked, "Father, how many people do you visit in prison every month?"

"Seventy or eighty."

I shook my head. "I imagine some of them are difficult to influence. Even Edwin took weeks. How is it you're so patient?"

He gave a look that was equal parts rueful and humorous. "By remembering my own mistakes. There are plenty to choose from."

I smiled by way of reply.

We reached a wooden door, and he said, "Will you come inside? I have something for you."

He set down the wheelbarrow and as we stepped into the vestry, I smelled a faint trace of wine and bread. He led me to a separate room and opened a wardrobe. Inside were black robes hanging from hooks, and on a pair of shelves were hats and other items for cold weather. From the top shelf he took a scarf and held it out to me. "He gave this to me, but I think you should have it."

I put up a hand to refuse. "No. No, he meant it for you."

"You can always return it, but perhaps for a while, you could have it with you. Something fine and beautiful, to remind you of all the good that was in him." He fumbled with the edge of the scarf and turned it so I could see a small silver disk. "Do you see? Here's a medal sewn in, of Saint Catherine of Bologna."

I looked at him questioningly.

"She's the patron saint of art," he said with a smile and offered the scarf draped between his open palms. "So you see, it's more suitable for you."

A lump rose in my throat, and I was about to refuse again when I saw the eagerness in his expression. I recalled how he'd offered Edwin food and books, comforts in tangible forms, and how regretful he'd been that Edwin refused them at first. So I took it.

The scarf was made of lovely wool, soft and dyed in shades of blue and purple that might have found their sources in pulverized lapis lazuli and murex shells from the eastern Mediterranean. I had nowhere to carry it, so I unfolded it and draped it around my shoulders, then I offered him my hand. "Thank you, Vicar, for everything you did for him," I said and hoped he could hear how sincerely I meant it. "And for me."

To my surprise, he ignored my hand. Instead he put his hands to my temples and bent forward to kiss my forehead. "God bless and keep you, my dear."

As I left the church I took a deep breath in and smelled the boxwood, a dusty, acrid smell that could never be mistaken for anything else. With a feeling of newfound grace, I secured the scarf around my shoulders and walked away from my shadow toward the dropping sun.

Chapter 27

I had a particular reason for going to the Slade the following afternoon. A painting had been taking shape in my mind for several days and I felt a growing but pleasant sense of urgency about committing it to canvas. As I entered the studio, my nose stung with the familiar smells of linseed oil and turpentine, scents that would fade in a moment. Two other students—Mr. Wolfe and Mr. Stephenson—were at their easels; they glanced up and nodded, but they were absorbed and I let them alone. I hung my coat on the hook near the door, took my paint box and brushes out of my drawer, set them down on the stool near my usual easel, and went to the stack of blank canvases. I looked several over, rejecting two for imperfections, before choosing one approximately one and a half feet by two. Then I set it on the easel, tied on my apron, and began.

Over the years I learned to understand the connection between my mind and my brush, to balance intention and play, to abstain from both arrogance and timidity. With daily work, a more certain connection had formed between what was in my mind's eye and what my fingers could accomplish. That day, I only needed to hold the image still inside my head for the shapes to appear on the blank canvas in front of me. The outlines emerged easily and almost full-blown, without struggle or frustration. The finer particulars might come later, I knew, along with revisions—but for now, the brush did as I bade.

I painted for several hours, until the light began to dim, and I looked up to find that my two fellow students were cleaning their brushes at the sink, talking in low tones. I studied my canvas with a critical eye but was pleased with it so far. I wasn't tired in the least, but I tightened the caps on my pigments and brought my brushes to the sink.

"Hello," I said.

They glanced at each other before replying. "Are you all right?" Mr. Wolfe asked cautiously. "We were wondering when you might come back."

I offered the simplest version of the truth. "I've been taking care of my brother's affairs."

They both winced. "We're very sorry," Mr. Wolfe said, and he reached a hand for my brushes. "I'll take care of those if you like."

I thanked him and returned to my easel, just to take one last look. I was far enough along that I'd have time to finish it before Matthew returned.

"We were going to find some dinner. Do you want to come along?" Mr. Wolfe asked.

"Perhaps another time. I have a few things to do tonight."

They nodded amiably, and we parted at the door. I headed for Edwin's flat, letting myself in with the key.

I'd sorted through most of his things over the past few days, discarding some of his old art supplies and packing up his few boxes of clothes and books. I'd moved all his original paintings to my rooms, except for the last few on his walls. One of these was mine—the girl, the father, and the woman at the market. I took it down and studied it. It really wasn't very good. The expressions were drawn too sharply, as if I didn't trust my viewer to see them; the lighting was too stark in some places and too yellow in others. Edwin had been in the room at our parents' house when I had been painting it. It was he who had helped me with the shadows near the edges. I turned it over to wrap it in a section of old sheet I'd kept aside for the purpose. On the back, on the part of the canvas that wrapped the stretcher, Edwin had scrawled: *Annabel, Feb 1867.*

The sight stopped me, for I thought I'd been younger. That month, I had just turned fourteen, and he'd been seventeen.

I laid my fingertips on top of the letters, feeling the faint indentation made by the nub of his pencil. My throat tightened and I swallowed down the lump. By fourteen, I had given up hope that my father would take an interest in my painting. But apparently Edwin had been paying attention, even during that troubled period when he'd been home so irregularly. He'd kept my work and noted the date perhaps so that he—and I—could see my progress. He'd expected me to keep on.

And it occurred to me, as I closed the door to his rooms for the last time, that Edwin would always be behind my painting, in one way or another.

By staying late at the Slade every day, I'd nearly finished the painting I wanted to give to Matthew. On Saturday afternoon, when I put on the finishing touches, Mr. Wolfe, Mr. Stephenson, and Miss Stokes were at the studio as well, hard at work, and this time when Mr. Wolfe asked if I wanted to have supper with them, I said yes. The four of us together made a cheerful group, and I went home satisfied with how I'd spent my day.

On Monday evening, the paint was dry enough. I wrapped my painting in brown paper, tying it closed with string, and took a cab to Matthew's house. I knocked, and Peggy invited me inside.

"He's just home, miss. I'll tell him you're here," she said and gestured toward the parlor. "The fire's laid."

A few moments later, I heard his footsteps on the treads, and he crossed the room to where I stood. The touch of his hand on my wrist was enough to set my pulse thrumming, and I was acutely aware of his every breath, the warmth coming off his skin. His voice was husky when he spoke my name.

"How was Bracknell?" I asked.

"Difficult but worthwhile." He nodded to the parcel. "What's this?"

I handed it to him. "It's for you."

He smiled and set it on a table, untied the strings, removed the paper, and turned the canvas over.

His hands went still, and I heard his quick inhale.

It showed the two of us in a railway car. I'd sought to depict us in a private space while keeping us firmly in the world. The landscape outside the window held fields, a barn, and some distant hills in muted greens and golds; the sky was a pale blue. The interior of the carriage was as true to what I remembered from our trip north as I could make it, down to the faded sepia cushions. A valise rested on the floor in the foreground, and

Matthew sat forward, with his elbows on his knees and his eyes on me. I held a sketchbook on my lap, my fingers curled around the edge, and I was meeting his gaze. I'd worked attentively over the expressions and postures, seeking to portray the complexity of our feelings—the vulnerability, the growing trust, and the genuine pleasure in each other's company.

He looked up from the canvas. "It's us," he said, surprise lighting his voice, "though it doesn't look like the countryside around Milton Keynes—or the Isle of Wight, for that matter." His eyes, very blue today, held mine, and a slow smile curved his mouth. "But we look happy."

"Well, no, it isn't either place," I admitted. "But it *is* the two of us, happy." A laugh bubbled up from inside me as he set the painting aside and pulled me into an embrace. And for a moment, before he was kissing me, my mouth was close to his ear, close enough that I only had to whisper:

"And we're on our way somewhere."

Acknowledgments

$\mathcal{I}$ do believe there is a trace of deceit in most of our memories, but deep feelings such as pain and love and gratitude often anchor the truth. I want to express my gratitude here to all those who have supported me in the making of this book.

First, my sincere thanks to my readers: Wendy Claus, who has been an unfailing supporter and was a falcon when I needed her; Kate Fink Cheeseman, Lisa Daliere, Tina Miles, Anne Morgan, Carrie Regan, Deborah Spitz, and Filiz Turhan, who provided invaluable feedback on early chapters and drafts; and my daughter Julia, who has read this manuscript at least four times and has been an insightful and thoughtful guide.

I'm a fan of using a lifeline to phone a friend when I have questions on topics outside my purview. Special thanks to Melissa Orlov for talking me through the psychology of vengeance, Dr. Evan Leibner for sharing information about poison (he's always good for the morbid topics), and Hallie Mueller for letting me get inside her artist head. All factual errors are my own. A special thanks also to Amanda Stefansson for creating a lovely website and being patient while I learned how to navigate it.

My sincere thanks to the keen editorial eye of Masie Cochran, who has been a help from the beginning, before "the Elizabeth book" turned into *A Lady in the Smoke*; and to my agent, Josh Getzler, for his constant support and for pointing out early that I really had two separate books in the first draft of this one. A special thanks to Priyanka Krishnan, my first editor, who brought me to HarperCollins, and to the entire HarperCollins team, including my wonderful editor, Elle Keck; the marketing and publicity team of Amelia Wood and Kayleigh Webb; my copyeditor, Karen Richardson; and Elsie Lyons and Diahann Sturge for the lovely cover and page design.

My gratitude overflows toward all those who responded warmly to the publication of *A Lady in the Smoke* and *A Dangerous Duet* and offered their encouragement and support to a new author. Thanks to Barbara Peters of The Poisoned Pen Bookstore in Scottsdale for her kindness and for drawing me into a community of mystery writers and readers. I think of her marvelous shop as my literary home. Gratitude to all the bookclub leaders who have graciously welcomed me to their meetings, including Patty Bruno, Donna Cleinman, Amanda Goosen, Ruth Lebed, Phyllis Payne, and Rebel Rice. Thanks also to Ann Marie Ackerman, Rhys Bowen, Denise Ganley, Hank Garner, and Marshal Zeringue for hosting me on their blogs and podcasts; and to Bill Finley for inviting me to participate in the extraordinary Tucson Festival of Books. Thanks to those mystery writers who have read and supported my work including Donis Casey, Susan Elia MacNeal, G.M. Malliet, Anne Perry, and Rosemary Simpson.

Lastly, I am grateful to all those who have supported me in my writing career over the years, in the myriad of ways dear friends and family do: picking up the slack, reading drafts, talking through scenes and characters, road-tripping to attend my talks, spreading the word, and cheering me on. My heartfelt thanks especially to Jules Catania, Mame Cudd, Alice Cunningham, Tami Dairiki, Heidi Dauphin, Cara Denby, Kristin Griffin, Nancy Guggedahl, Claudia Gutwirth, Jody Hallam, Allison Hodgdon, Abbe Hugon, Denise Kantner, Dottie Lootens, Jennifer Lootens, Christie Maroulis, Nancy Odden, Libby Patterson, Stefanie Pintoff, Kathy Samuels, Cindy Schneider, Laura Schwartz, Lori Stipp, and Anita Weiss—and always, always, always to George, Julia, and Kyle. I feel you like the wind at my back.

About the author

2 Meet Karen Odden

About the book

3 Behind *A Trace of Deceit*

7 Further Reading

9 Reading Group Guide

Insights,
Interviews
& More...

Read on

11 An Excerpt from *A Dangerous Duet*

Meet Karen Odden

Tina Celle

KAREN ODDEN received her Ph.D. in
English literature from New York
University and has taught at the
University of Wisconsin–Milwaukee
and the University of Michigan–Ann
Arbor. She formerly served as an assistant
editor for the academic journal *Victorian
Literature and Culture*. Her debut novel,
A Lady in the Smoke, was a *USA Today*
bestseller. Her second novel, *A Dangerous
Duet,* was published by HarperCollins in
November 2018. ༄

Behind
A Trace of Deceit

When I lived in New York City in
the mid-1990s, I worked at Christie's
auction house. Their current offices are
in Rockefeller Center, but at the time,
they occupied the building at the corner
of Fifty-Ninth Street and Park Avenue.
I lived on the Upper West Side, and as
long as the weather was fair, I'd cut
diagonally across Central Park, pass the
Russian antique store A La Vieille Russie,
and head east on Fifty-Ninth. The public
entrance was on Park Avenue, where
Gil Perez, the doorman, was a fixture.
Everyone knew Gil, with his silver
mustache, broad smile, white gloves
and tails, and a cap that made me think
of a railway conductor.

I went in at the employees'
entrance—the back door, both literally
and metaphorically. I never took a single
art history class in college. In fact, one
of my nightmares is that I signed up for
one, forgot to drop the class, and found
out the night before the final exam that
I had five hundred paintings and artists
to memorize. (Is that a universal dream?
The college class you forgot to drop?)
But after college, I had worked in
marketing and with that experience,
I found a position buying ad space for
Christie's print ads in publications such
as the *New York Times, Architectural Digest,
Art & Auction, The New Yorker, Magazine
Antiques, Antiquities, Beaux Arts, The
Newtown Bee*, and some little-known
publications for rare books, stamps, and ▶

coins. Because I worked with all forty-some departments, from American Furniture to European Silver to Impressionist and Modern Paintings (Imps & Mods, as we called it), I rapidly became familiar with a wide variety of art. When I arrived, I didn't know the difference between a Manet and Modigliani. I'd never seen a Fabergé egg up close, or a Russian crown. I didn't know that so long as you are discussing handmade items, a carpet and a rug are the same thing. I had no idea what a "verso" is, or why a maker's mark on the bottom of a candlestick is important. Four months later, with the help of numerous visits to NYC museums, I did. It was a bit of a crash course—almost as daunting as my nightmare.

Because I was buying ad space, I was reading many art magazines, and I found myself deeply intrigued by the stories I found— some of which involved ridiculous wealth, scandal, deceit, thieving, smuggling, or forgery. I still remember an article I read in the *New Yorker* about several pieces of art smuggled back to the US by a WWII soldier, only to be discovered by his children after his death. Another compelling account concerned a sting operation that exposed the practice of smuggling Old Master paintings out of Italy, told by the investigative journalist Peter Watson in *Sotheby's: The Inside Story*. But little did I know there was a story of corruption unfolding under my nose. During my tenure at Christie's, Dede Brooks (head of Sotheby's) and Christopher Davidge (of Christie's) were caught illegally colluding in order to manipulate the various economics around the sales—the percentages given to sellers, the reserve amounts, budgets for ads, and so on. This story would later be told in *The Art of the Steal* by Christopher Mason, which doesn't paint either auction house in a particularly attractive light.

However, along with the dark side of auctions, there was magic and glamour, including sightings of famous people. (I nearly bumped into Alec Baldwin and Kim Basinger one day on the sidewalk.) The art was astonishing in its diversity and value. In 1994, branches of Christie's around the world sold works as varied as Degas's *Danseuses se baissant (Les Ballerines)*; an Assyrian relief from the Northwest Palace of Ashurnasirpal II at Kalhu (883–859 B.C.); and Charlie Chaplin's bowler hat. And on November 11, I was in the room when Stephen Massey auctioned off the Leonardo da Vinci Codex Hammer to Bill Gates (by phone) for $28 million. As the bid rose and rose and rose, Massey's eyes darted back and forth between the showroom and the phone bank, where a proxy bidder repeatedly raised her hand to signal yes. The room was thick with murmuring, and I held my breath until the gavel fell.

In art, we find the world writ large—more beautiful, more tragic, more passionate, more inspiring, more curious, and more intense than our daily life. Artists create works out of their pain and longing and love and desire to communicate something of their truth or imaginings to others—and the consumers of that art often find themselves with correspondingly deep feelings of profound sympathy or perhaps a fierce desire to possess, particularly if a collector is passionate about certain artists or periods or styles.

In the nineteenth century, many London families had collections that had been built up over generations—and the destruction of those legacies could be devastating. While my interests nudged me generally toward writing a novel that involved art, one of my specific starting points was the 1874 Pantechnicon fire in London, one of the greatest tragedies in the art world during the Victorian era. Beginning in the 1830s, the Pantechnicon, whose Greek façade with Doric columns stretched along a full block in Belgrave Square, provided a place for the wealthy to store their expensive paintings, furniture, and objets d'art when they were traveling or had retired to their country estates. Some people also used it as an annex for their art collections, for example, if they had more paintings than available wall space. The building was advertised as impervious to water, theft, fire, and any other disaster, but—alas!—it was not. Despite its metal framework and doors that could close off sections of each floor, the entire building went up in flames in three days. Nearly every fire truck in London came to try to put out the fire and save some of the treasures—to no avail. Millions of pounds' worth of art and furnishings were destroyed, including a significant portion of Sir Richard Wallace's fine art collection valued at £60,000 (roughly £6.7 million today). But I began to wonder: what would happen if a painting that was believed to be inside the ruined Pantechnicon suddenly reappeared? How and why would that happen?

This question drove the backstory of *A Trace of Deceit*. Mr. Pagett, stepson of the MP Lord Sibley, considered a François Boucher portrait that his family owned as the centerpiece of the collection; he despaired when it burned in the fire. When the painting suddenly appears on the front of an auction catalog in 1875, he nearly becomes unhinged.

My second starting point was the Slade School of Art, which ▶

eventually became part of the University College London. It was founded in 1871 by Felix Slade, a farsighted man who perceived the value of men and women studying art together. (This was scandalous at the time, given the question: What should we do about the anatomy classes with male nudes? The answer, for many years: Drape the loins.) The first Slade professor was Sir Edward Poynter, who trained in Paris. In chapter 1 of *A Trace of Deceit*, we meet both Mr. Poynter and our protagonist, Annabel Rowe, a student at the Slade and an accomplished painter. I am always drawn to strong women protagonists, and Evelyn De Morgan (1855–1919), who entered the Slade in 1873 and won the prestigious Slade scholarship, became my partial inspiration for Annabel. As the novel opens, Annabel has finished her work for the day and is going to visit her older brother, Edwin, at his flat. A wildly talented painter, Edwin was recently let out of prison after serving a year for forgery, and he insists that he has reformed. But when Annabel reaches his flat, she finds two Scotland Yard inspectors who tell her that Edwin is dead. When she discovers that a valuable Boucher painting that Edwin was cleaning for an upcoming auction at Bettridge's is gone, she goes to the Yard and offers to assist with the investigation—and because of her expertise in art and knowledge of the art world, Matthew Hallam accepts her help. (Historical note: While François Boucher did paint Madame de Pompadour several times, the painting stolen from Edwin's room is my invention.)

So really, my work on this novel began nearly twenty-five years ago at Christie's. This seems fitting for a novel in which the murdered man is twenty-five, and the seeds of his tragic death are sown in his childhood. As in *A Lady in the Smoke* and *A Dangerous Duet,* the foundations of the personal tragedies are laid years before the book begins—in the pain and difficulties inherent in families. When I think about it, my whole narrative drive is toward the past. Indeed, mysteries are my chosen genre because they are really all about the backstory: if there is a dead body on page five, the next three hundred pages are about how it got there. And my interest in art—an interest that persisted long after I left Christie's—may derive in part from my fascination with the ways that old objects—traces of the past, like our shifting, shadowy memories—still have meaning and value in our present. ∽

Further Reading

ON ART AND AUCTIONS

The Vanishing Velázquez: A 19th-Century Bookseller's Obsession with a Lost Masterpiece by Laura Cumming

"From Inventory to Virtual Catalog: Notes on the 'Catalogue Raisonné'" by Jonathan Franklin in *Art Documentation* (Spring 2004: 41–45)

"A Night at the Museum" by Jake Halpern in *The New Yorker* (January 14, 2019: 30–39)

"The Bouvier Affair" by Sam Knight in *The New Yorker* (February 8, 2016: 62–71)

The Art of the Steal: Inside the Sotheby's-Christie's Auction House Scandal by Christopher Mason

"The Perfect Paint" by Rebecca Mead in *The New Yorker* (March 18, 2019: 34–39)

The Private Lives of the Impressionists by Sue Roe

"Blue as Can Be" by Simon Schama in *The New Yorker* (September 3, 2018: 28–32)

"Rembrandt in the Blood: An Obsessive Aristocrat, Rediscovered Paintings and an Art-World Feud" by Russell Shorto in *The New York Times Magazine* (March 3, 2019: 34–51)

The Expert Versus the Object: Judging Fakes and False Attributions in the Visual Arts edited by Ronald D. Spencer

Sotheby's: The Inside Story by Peter Watson

"Swimming with Sharks" by Rebecca Mead in *The New Yorker* (July 4, 2016: 42–51)

ON VICTORIAN HISTORY

The Lion and the Unicorn: Gladstone vs. Disraeli by Richard Aldous

British Gunmakers Volume Two: Birmingham, Scotland and the Regions by Nigel Brown

"The 'Fire-Proof' Pantechnicon" in *The Spectator* (February 21, 1874)

"The 'Fire-Proof' Pantechnicon Burnt" in *Nelson Evening Mail* (April 24, 1874: 2)

The Gangs of Birmingham: From the Sloggers to the Peaky Blinders by Philip Gooderson

Further Reading *(continued)*

The Railway Detective by Edward Marston

The Good Old Days: Crime, Murder and Mayhem in Victorian London
    by Gilda O'Neill

*The Profligate Son: Or, a True Story of Family Conflict, Fashionable
    Vice, and Financial Ruin in Regency Britain* by Nicola Phillips

"The Controversial Rule of Market Overt" by Anna O'Connell in
    Art Loss Review (archived from the original on October 8, 2007;
    retrieved August 31, 2007)

Historic Arms Resource Centre, rifleman.org.uk

*The Ascent of the Detective: Police Sleuths in Victorian and Edwardian
    England* by Haia Shpayer-Makov

Disraeli, Gladstone, and the Eastern Question by R. W. Seton-Watson

A Victorian Hospital by Katrina Siliprandi

A History of Birmingham by Chris Upton

"The Post-Office Scandal" in *The Spectator* (August 2, 1873, archive
    .spectator.co.uk/article/2nd-august-1873/7/the-post-office-scandal)

For further historical context, please visit Karen Odden's website,
www.karenodden.com, where you will find blog entries on a variety
of subjects pertaining to Victorian England. ∽

Reading Group Guide

1. One of the questions at the heart of the story is whether or not Edwin truly reformed before he died. Why does Annabel want so badly to believe he did? To what extent do you think he did or did not?

2. At one point Annabel acknowledges that she finds it easier to recall the painful events in her past than the happier ones. Celia comments that she thinks it's human nature. Do you agree, or do you think there is some element of choice in what we remember? Why or why not?

3. The group of French painters eventually known as the "Impressionists" included Degas, Monet, Renoir, Pissarro, Sisley, Morisot, Cézanne, and others. With their works rejected by the established Salon de Paris, they staged their own "Salon of the Refused" in April 1874. Public response was mixed. In a critical article, Louis Leroy mocked the work as "impressionist." The artists appropriated the term, claiming it for their own, and now their works are among the most popular in museums. What other cultural trends do you know that were mocked initially but later became mainstream or popular?

4. At several points, Annabel shows Matthew how to "read" a painting. Do you see any ways that Matthew appropriates her ideas to his investigation? When do various characters reflect on their own ways of gathering information? Do you see any parallels in the way you perceive the events or people in your life?

5. Annabel and Matthew have two different ways of defining truth. Annabel defines it as capturing the moment when people's expressions and gestures betray their truest feelings and motives. Matthew believes truth is gathered mostly by putting events in order. To what extent do the two of them borrow from each other, or resist each other?

6. Matthew tells Annabel he believes our memories naturally have "a trace of deceit" in them. What other books have you read in which memories are shown to be inaccurate, deceptive, motivated, or simply fragile? ▶

Reading Group Guide *(continued)*

7. In Victorian England, the roles of the police and the press were intertwined. Both constructed stories about events, although to different ends. John Fishel of the *Beacon* claims he provides a service by alerting the public to potential frauds and the actions of police. What differences or similarities do you see with respect to the relationship of the press and law enforcement today?

8. In 1854, Coventry Patmore wrote a poem called *The Angel in the House* that was widely read. In it, he presented his version of the ideal Victorian woman—meek, self-sacrificing, graceful, sympathetic, powerless, passive, and above all pure. The poem also promoted the notion of "separate spheres," in which men went out to work in the world and women tended the home and the children. To what extent does this book adhere to these ideas and/or overturn them?

9. Mr. Pagett deplores the way that art is treated as a commodity, "like a plank of wood or a pig," and claims to perceive it as a transcendent object of beauty. But in this book, art is not just an object of beauty. For Bettridge and others it is a commodity, for Sam Boulter it is a tool for revenge, and for Mr. Pagett it is a plausible way to sustain a connection to his stepfather. What other roles does artwork play? What qualities of art enable it to serve all of these different roles? ⌒

An Excerpt from
A Dangerous Duet

Chapter 1

London, 1875

The back door of the Octavian Music Hall stood ajar, and a wedge of yellow light streamed out into the dark, crooked quadrangle of the yard. I picked my way toward it across the uneven ground, glad that I was in stout boots and trousers instead of my usual skirts. It had rained all day, and I tried not to think about what might be in the muck under my feet.

A tall, broad-shouldered figure stood silhouetted in the doorway: Jack Drummond, the owner's son, a stolid and taciturn young man who helped build scenery and props and fixed things when they broke. As he'd never said much more than "Good evening" to me, I knew very little else about him except that he let us performers in at the back and then went round to the front door to keep the pickpockets from sneaking in. I felt a secret sympathy for those ragged boys, desperately in need of a few pence for supper. Once the curtain rose, the men in the audience, most of them well into their cups, would be staring agog at a Romany magician or a half-naked songstress or some flame-throwing jugglers. It would've been child's play to find their pockets, and chances are most of the men wouldn't have missed a coin or two. ▶

An Excerpt from *A Dangerous Duet* *(continued)*

Jack touched his cap briefly as I approached. "Mr. Nell."

"Evening," I muttered. My voice was naturally low, but to bolster my disguise I pitched it even lower and hoarser.

"Mr. Williams needs to see you before the show."

My heart leaped into my throat. I'd done my best to dodge the foul-tempered stage manager since he'd hired me weeks ago.

"Did he say why?"

"No. But don't worry. He didn't look mad." His dark eyes met mine, and he gave a faint, wry smile. "Leastwise, no madder than usual."

I snorted. "Good."

From the bell tower of St. Anne's in Dean Street came the chimes for three-quarters past seven. Fifteen minutes until curtain.

"He'll meet you at the piano," Jack said.

I hurried down the ramp that led to the corridor below the stage, feeling inside the brim of my hat to make sure that no stray hairs had escaped my phalanx of pins. Then I turned toward the flight of stairs that led up to stage right. The hall above, where the audience sat, had been elegantly renovated a few years ago when the Octavian opened, with crystal chandeliers and paint in tasteful hues of blue and gold. But the rabbit warren of passages and rooms underground was original to the hodgepodge of buildings that had stood here a hundred years ago, when the entertainment on a given night was likely to be bearbaiting and cockfighting, and the animals were brought up from below. The air stank of mold and rust; the plaster was crumbling off the brickwork; and the wooden steps had been worn down so far that the nailheads could catch a misplaced toe or boot heel and send one sprawling—as I knew from experience.

Slow footsteps thudded above me. Jack's father—whom everyone called by only his surname, Drummond—was coming down. He was a burly man, a full head taller than I, with the same unruly black hair that Jack had, thick black eyebrows, and a cruel mouth. I smelled the whiskey on him as he drew close, and I put my back against the wall to let him pass.

"Evening," I croaked, same as I'd said to Jack.

He didn't even glance at me. Motionless, I watched as he descended and vanished into the lower corridor; then I allowed myself a deep breath and continued on my way.

At the top of the stairs, I ducked through a set of curtains to enter the piano alcove where I'd spend the next two hours. My spot was in the corner of the hall near stage right, with a second pair of curtains to separate me from the audience until the show began. The stage, which I could see from my piano bench, was elevated off the hall's plank floor—wooden boards that had no doubt once been glossy, back before they'd absorbed hundreds of nights' worth of spilled gin and ale.

From the sound of it, members of the audience had already spilled a good deal of gin and ale down their throats, for they were more boisterous than usual for a Wednesday night. Curious to see why, I parted the curtains slightly and peered out, but nothing seemed out of the ordinary. Some of the men had found seats at the round tables; the rest were still gathered at the bar, where beer and wine and spirits were being distributed from hand to hand.

The room was large, with walls that curved at the back so it resembled a narrow U. According to Mrs. Wregge, the hall's cheerful purveyor of costumes and gossip, the builder believed that keeping everything in eights would protect against fire—hence the "Octavian." He was so persistent in this belief that he moved the walls inward by a yard, so that the seating area measured sixty-four feet at its longest point. Eight gas-lit chandeliers sent their glow flickering across the room; eight spiraling cast-iron pillars supported the balcony; and each pillar had twenty-four turns from bottom to top. Perhaps the spell of eights worked because during every performance, glowing ashes from the ends of cigars and French cigarettes dropped onto the floor, and still the building remained intact.

As I did every night, I said a quick prayer that the magic would hold. This job not only paid three pounds a week; it let me finish by just past ten, which meant I could arrive home before my brother, Matthew, returned from the Yard. The coins I earned were forming a satisfying, clinking pile in the drawer of my armoire, and combined with other money I'd saved, I now possessed over half of the Royal Academy tuition that would be due in the fall. Provided, of course, that I succeeded at the audition in a fortnight.

A flutter of apprehension stirred beneath my ribs at the thought, and I suppressed it, turning deliberately to the piano, lifting the wing, and fitting the prop stick into the notch.

It was a good instrument—surprisingly good for a second-rate hall—a thirty-year-old Pleyel, with a soft touch and an easier action than my English Broadwood at home. The problem was that the ▶

French piano didn't care for our climate; it fell out of tune easily, especially when it rained.

I untied the portfolio ribbons and laid out the music in the order of the acts. First came a man who called himself Gallius Kovác, the Romany Magician, and his assistant, the lovely Lady Van de Vere. He was no more a magician who'd learned his trade from his Romany grandfather than I was, and his accomplice's real name was Maggie Long. She was exactly my age—nineteen—and the natural daughter of a wealthy tea merchant and his mistress.

After their last trick, I would play a selection of interlude music while stagehands rolled the magician's paraphernalia off the stage. Then I'd accompany a singer who called herself Amalie Bordelieu. Her songs were French, but her accent offstage was pure Cockney, and her curses came straight off the London Docks. I'd heard them one night when she and Mr. Williams had a heated row in her dressing room. From the tone of it—caustic on her side, surly on his—it seemed to me that her anger derived from a long-standing resentment. Amalie was the only one of us who dared confront Mr. Williams; she had that luxury because she was too popular with the audiences to be turned out.

Gallius and Amalie were our only permanent performers; the next few acts of the program varied. To remain novel and exciting, most entertainers traveled among the hundreds of music halls in London, remaining in each for anywhere from a week to a few months before moving on. This week, Amalie had been followed by a group of jugglers, who rode strange little one-wheeled contraptions and threw flaming candlesticks; next came my friend Marceline Tourneau and her brother Sebastian, with their trapeze act; and then, a one-act parody of marriage, complete with a deaf mother-in-law and six unruly children. Over the past two months, I'd also seen a ventriloquist, a group of six German knife throwers, trained dogs, men on stilts, an absurd dialogue between two actors playing Gladstone and Disraeli, three women singing a rollicking verse about the chaos they'd unleash if only they had voting rights, and an adagio in which an enormous man juggled two girls. The final act was always one of London's *lions comiques*—groups of men who dressed as swells, in imposing fur coats and rakish hats, twirling their walking sticks and singing about gambling and whoring and drinking champagne. They brought the crowd to their feet every time.

From backstage came the clang of bells, signaling that the show would begin in ten minutes. Where was Mr. Williams, if he needed to see me so badly? And what could he possibly want? I searched my memory for anything I might have done wrong the night before. The show had gone mostly as usual. He'd shouted himself apoplectic because Mrs. Wregge's cat Felix had streaked across his path backstage, twice. But he was always ranting about something.

I sat down on the bench and lifted the fallboard. The ebony keys had scrapes along their surfaces and the ivories had yellowed. Still, they were keys to happiness, all eighty-eight of them.

I ran a quiet scale to warm my fingers. I hadn't played more than a dozen notes when I realized that the E just below middle C was newly flat. And what had happened to the B? I pushed the key down again: nothing, and the silence made me groan aloud. Not wanting to risk Mr. Williams's wrath, I'd bitten my tongue as, with each passing week, I'd had to shift octaves and rework chords to avoid the flat notes. But this was absurd. I would have to convince Mr. Williams to hire someone to fix it, despite his being a relentless pinchpenny.

I put my foot on the damper pedal, heard a clink, and felt a scrape on the top of my boot.

What was that?

Ducking my head underneath, I saw that a long screw had come loose from the brass plate, which now rested on top of the pedal, rendering it useless. With a sigh, I reached in my pocket and took out a farthing coin that had thinned around the edge; it had served as a makeshift tool before. I crawled underneath, pushed the plate into place, and used the coin to turn the screw until it bit into the wood. I ran my thumb over the head; it wasn't quite flush, but it would have to do for now.

"Ed! Ed Nell!" Mr. Williams barked. "Damn it all! Where the devil is he?"

I scrambled out from under the piano. "I'm right here."

"Oh!" Mr. Williams scowled down at me, his bald pink pate shining in the light from the two sconces. "There's a new act tonight. A fiddler. Found him yesterday, busking at Covent Garden."

Was that all?

"He's not expecting me to accompany him, is he?" I asked, as I stood and brushed myself off. It was no business of mine who Mr. Williams brought in, but most of the musicians who played near Covent Garden weren't much to speak of.

"Nah. He'll be after Amalie. Just give him a few chords." ▶

15

I kept my surprise in check. Mr. Williams must think pretty highly of the man to insert him when people were still sober enough to be listening.

"What's he playing?" I asked.

"How would I know?" He waved a hand toward the audience. "Hope he can make himself heard over that."

"They're louder than usual tonight."

"It's because of Jem Ace."

"Who's—" I started to ask, but fell silent as the curtain parted and Jack appeared, a troubled expression on his face. His gaze brushed over me and fixed on the manager.

"The Tourneaus aren't here," he said.

"What do you mean, they're not here?" Mr. Williams demanded.

I felt surprised myself. Marceline would've told me if she and Sebastian were leaving for another hall. They had never missed a show before.

Jack shook his head. "That's all I know. And Amalie needs to see you. Her new costume is falling off, and Mrs. Wregge says there's no time to fix it."

The stage manager turned away, muttering under his breath.

"Mr. Williams—wait—please!" I said hastily. "Is there any way you could have the piano tuned? The keys are horribly flat. Listen." I played a rapid scale. "And the B isn't even working."

He waved a hand. "Jack'll look at it later."

Jack sketched a nod.

I bit my lip, not wanting to be rude, but also not wanting to damage the piano further. "Well, you see . . . it needs someone who's specially trained and—"

But he was already pushing aside the curtain. "Put up with it," he said over his shoulder. "Nobody but you's going to notice." He turned back, his expression sour. "And be ready to switch Amalie out of order—maybe after the fiddler—or she can take the Tourneaus' spot, if they don't arrive. Blasted tart and her costumes. More bloody trouble than she's worth." Then he and Jack were gone.

Somewhat exasperated, I tugged at the cords that drew back the curtains separating me from the audience. It was mostly working-class men, still jostling into their seats and shouting good-naturedly to the boys who hawked cigars and cheap roses from trays that hung around their necks. As I surveyed the crowd, I realized Mr. Williams was right: no one would notice a piano out of

16

tune, much less a missing note. And why should I care if it sounded horrid, so long as the audience was satisfied?

You're not playing Beethoven at St. James's Hall, I reminded myself as I took my seat. *And what's more, you never will if Mr. Williams decides that you're more bloody trouble than you're worth. You're not irreplaceable the way Amalie is.*

At eight o'clock precisely, two men on the catwalk pulled the ropes to swoop the curtains in graceful waves toward the ceiling. The sapphire-colored velvet with its gold trim had been mended a dozen times by Mrs. Wregge—I'd seen her perched on a stool, her needle flying across the fabric gathered in her broad lap—but in the flickering light, the patched bits were invisible and the velvet looked rich and elegant.

I struck up the dramatic prelude as Gallius Kovác strode onto the stage, his black cape flapping, his tall black hat—rumor had it he'd stolen it from a police constable—shining under the lights, his mustache waxed to fine curled ends. He extended his hand to stage right, and Maggie pranced out in a costume that never failed to elicit whistles from the crowd—a green-and-gold dress cut low to reveal the curve of her breasts. Her black hair was curled into ringlets and pinned up with sparkly combs. Her lips were painted red and her lashes darkened, like the ladies on the postcards from Egypt that hung in the window of Selinger's Stationers.

Gallius's first feat was to pull two birds out of his hat. But nine men out of ten were looking at Maggie, not the birds. The feathered creatures flapped up to the rafters unnoticed, while Maggie preened and strutted and winked at the audience. At her feet landed a small storm of roses, sent flying toward her by men who probably thought she treasured the blooms. After her performance, she returned them to the rose boys to sell again, and they split the two-penny profits.

I knew Gallius's routine well enough to match the music with the tempo of his tricks. So when he pulled a rainbow of handkerchiefs out of his hat, I rolled the chord. When he made Maggie disappear, I made the piano notes deep and trembly. And the crescendo came when she reappeared out of a box that vanished in a cloud of smoke.

His final trick was to run a sword through Maggie's neck. I asked her once if he ever poked her by accident, and she gave her sly smile. "That sword bends right through the metal collar. I made him show me 'afore I let him get anywhere near me with it—or with any ▶

17

other part of him that pokes, neither." She laughed out loud, and I felt my cheeks grow warm.

"Well, ain't you the innocent," she teased me, winking.

"I'm not innocent," I muttered. But she was right: I'd flushed again the following night, when I came upon Maggie and Gallius in the murky gloom of the back hallway, him with his hands inside her skirts and her with her arms wrapped hard around his neck.

Gallius and Maggie left the stage, and I played some interlude music, a medley of popular tunes, all the while keeping my eye out for Amalie, or for whoever might appear next. It turned out to be the new violinist, entering from stage right, and I wound up hastily so he didn't have to stand there waiting to begin.

He was handsome as anything—tall and slender, with silvery blond hair combed back from his forehead, a well-cut mouth, and bones that showed fine yet strong under the stage lights. I put his age at a year or two over twenty. He was dressed in a tailored coat and pants that bore no sheen from wear at the knees or cuffs, which made me wonder what he was doing playing here—or busking in Covent Garden, for that matter.

There was an air about him that made even this audience give him something approximating real attention. He offered a small, formal bow to the crowd; then he set his bow on the strings and began.

It was a piece I'd never heard, beautiful and haunting—and he could *play*. His bow stroked smoothly and powerfully across the strings, bringing forth the instrument's sweetness with none of the shrillness produced by a mediocre violinist.

But it was the wrong piece for this audience. These men didn't want beautiful and haunting. They wanted fast and loud, bright and bawdy, or downright silly. I felt their indifference flare to irritation, even before the grumbling began, and I prayed they'd give him a chance to finish.

Something small and white—a dinner roll—flew past his ear. He looked out at the audience, and I could tell he was surprised. Clearly, he wasn't used to this sort of reception, but he played on until a turnip hit him square in the stomach. His bow popped off the strings, and across his face flashed a look of uncertainty, followed by a hot flush of shame and anger as the groans and hisses turned to catcalls and laughter.

The sounds made me flinch, and he turned to me, glaring, as if he expected I'd join in the abuse. Once, I would've sat there, feeling as helpless as he. But a few weeks ago, when one of the dancing dogs had gone missing and I'd had to fill the time between acts, I'd played "Libiamo ne' lieti calici," the drinking song from the first act of *La Traviata*. The popular opera by Verdi had just returned to London, so the melody was on everyone's lips, and the audience had cheered lustily for a full minute afterward.

I riffled through my portfolio quickly, hoping that he knew it.

I couldn't see his expression as I played the opening chords, but by the fourth measure, he was with me, his bow flying across the strings. The words in their English translation ran through my head: *Let's drink for the ecstatic feeling / that love arouses . . . / Let's drink, my love, and the love among the chalices / Will make the kisses hotter . . .*

It was a fine piece of music for a violin, and I softened my playing so that his could be heard, falling completely silent as he drew out the last brilliant chords.

Above the sound of stamping feet came cries of "Bravo! Bravo!" The violinist pointed his bow toward me and inclined his head toward the audience. They roared their approval, and he bowed again and left the stage.

With a small feeling of triumph, I found myself smiling as I played some interlude music to fill the time until the next act—

And then Amalie fluttered in from stage left, wearing a costume that seemed composed entirely of dyed feathers floating at her bosom and around her waist and thighs.

It was outrageous, even for her.

Like every man in the theater, I caught my breath. My fingers fumbled her introduction, even missed a few notes. But the audience couldn't have cared less. They went wild for her, cheering and shouting. She sang four songs in French, and as usual, dozens of men hurled roses at her, which she gathered up as she exited stage left, amid a rain of pink paper petals dropped from above.

THE SHOW FINISHED at a quarter past ten, and I put the music into my portfolio and started down the stairs, hoping it wasn't raining, as I'd left my umbrella at home.

Mrs. Wregge was on her way up. "I say, have you seen Felix?"

"No. Has he escaped again?"

"I had the door open for not half a second, and he dashed out!" She shook her head so vigorously that her chin wobbled. "If Mr. Williams sees him, he's going to wring his neck—and mine, too." ▶

19

"I would think he'd be grateful that Felix catches the mice."

"And so he should!" she said in a stage whisper. "He has the benefit of a fine mouser, while I have all the worry of keeping the two of them apart."

I couldn't help but smile. "It's your own version of cat and mouse, isn't it?"

She chuckled ruefully and pointed up the stairs. "He's not up there, is he? Mr. Williams?"

"I haven't seen him."

With a huff, she moved to continue her climb, but I put a hand on her arm. "Do you know what happened to Marceline and Sebastian? They weren't here tonight."

"No." Her kindly brown eyes sobered. "And it isn't like them to miss a show."

"No, it's not," I agreed, my feeling of misgiving growing. "Well, good night."

Turning away, I hurried down the stairs—and caught my heel on one of the treacherous nails near the bottom. With a cry, I pitched forward, nearly tumbling to the ground.

"Are you all right?" came a male voice.

Startled, I peered into the dark corridor.

"I'm sorry. I didn't mean to frighten you. It's Stephen Gagnon. The violinist." He came out of the shadows, his pale hair gleaming in the dim light. "And you're Ed Nell, the pianist."

My heart began to fall back into its normal rhythm. I cleared my throat. "Yes, that's right."

Two stagehands approached carrying a load of bulky wooden planks, and Stephen and I squeezed back against the wall. "We should move," I said. "They have to bring all the properties through here."

He motioned for me to lead the way, so I walked toward the ramp that led out to the yard. This part of the corridor was hung with metal lanterns, and by their light I could see him clearly. He was taller than I; his face was clean-shaven, his eyes a rich hazel. He stood with an easy elegance that spoke of time spent in drawing rooms.

"Thank you for what you did," he said. "I'd have been turned into mincemeat out there."

"I'm just glad you knew the song," I said.

"You play very well. I must say I was surprised." He glanced around us and tapped a few fingers against the water-stained plaster. "This isn't exactly—"

"Yes, well, I'm here for the money."

He grimaced. "So am I."

There was a story there, evidently, but I could hardly ask directly. So instead, I said, "Mr. Williams mentioned that he found you in Covent Garden. Have you studied somewhere?"

"At the Royal Academy, here in London."

I felt a stab of envy. "You're lucky."

"Yes, I suppose I was." There was a slight emphasis on the last word. "Where do you study?"

"Just—just privately, until last year." The thought of Mr. Moehler's passing still pained me.

"Do you play here every night?"

I shook my head. "Mondays, Wednesdays, and every other Thursday. Carl Dwigen, the other pianist, plays the rest."

His eyes lit up. "Will you be here tomorrow, then?"

I nodded. "I take it Mr. Williams asked you back?"

"Thanks to you. Wednesdays, Thursdays, and Sundays for now." He shifted his violin case under his arm. "Say, I don't suppose you could help me pick a few other songs that the audience would like."

"Of course." As I looked at him, a thought occurred to me. "You don't happen to know how to tune a piano, do you?"

"No. I noticed some of the notes were off. Bad luck." He flashed a consoling smile.

"It gets worse every week. Jack Drummond is supposed to take a look at it, but—"

"Jack Drummond?" he interrupted. "Who's that?"

"He's the owner's son. He does all sorts of work around here. I'm sure you'll meet him at some point."

Stephen's face wore an odd expression.

"Do you know him?" I ventured.

"No, not at all. But I—well, Mr. Williams led me to believe the music hall was his."

"In a way, it is," I said with a shrug. "Mr. Drummond is the owner of the building, but he doesn't have anything to do with the performances. Mr. Williams manages all of us."

The back door opened, and a uniformed police constable hurried in, leaving the door ajar behind him. He passed us without a glance and headed down the corridor.

"Wonder what he's here for," Stephen said. ▶

We leaned around the corner and watched as the constable entered Drummond's office without knocking.

No one ever did that, so far as I'd seen.

"Could you meet me here tomorrow, before the show?" Stephen asked. "At seven o'clock?"

"I'll try. I should go now, though."

"Well, good night, then." He held out his hand for mine.

I stared at it. Until now, I'd managed to avoid shaking hands in my disguise. But if I ignored his gesture, what would he think? My hands weren't small, and they were strong with practice, so I took his hand firmly, trying to perform the act as a man would. However, surprise flashed over his face, and he trapped my hand between both of his, turning it over so he could study my palm. My heart sank. I pulled away, sharply regretting that I'd stopped to talk to him.

His teasing grin faded. "What on earth's the matter? I'm hardly going to snitch on you, seeing as I need your help."

I recognized the truth of his words. "I'm sorry. It's just— they'd only pay me half as much if they knew."

"If they even kept you on," he added bluntly. "From what I know, there's a distinct prejudice against lady pianists. How long have you been here?"

"Nearly two months."

His expression became admiring. "Well, I hope I'm that lucky." He bent his head toward me. "What's your name? Your real name, I mean?"

I kept silent.

"Come on," he coaxed. "I can't call you 'Ed' now."

"It's Nell," I said reluctantly. Marceline was the only other person who knew the truth. But admitting it to her had been a relief, for we had commiserated over the ways young female performers were at a disadvantage. With Stephen, I only felt a new inequality, a disadvantage that existed on my side alone.

"Short for Ellen?" he guessed.

"Elinor." I paused. "I go by Ed Nell here."

"Ed Nell," he said, trying it out with a grin. "It's perfect. I could even call you Nelly in front of people, and no one would suspect."

I gave him a look that made him instantly turn penitent.

"I won't say a word," he promised. "I think you were clever to come here looking for a job." And then, sincerely, "*I'm* certainly glad you did."

He intended his words to reassure me, and I managed a smile.

"Well"—he shifted his violin case again—"I'm told I have to find the wardrobe mistress for a proper costume. I'll see you tomorrow?"

"Yes. Good night," I replied and started up the ramp.

The constable had left the back door cracked open, and as I crossed the yard, the church bells chiming three-quarters made me start.

How had it gotten so late? And what if this were the one night Matthew came home early?

I quickened my pace along Hawley Mews, trotting past the Crown and Thorn, where jangling piano music and masculine laughter spilled out the open windows. At the corner, a prostitute called out from below the awning of the chandler's shop. I had already passed her before I realized that her invitation was meant for me. I moved faster, dodging around a pile of refuse before halting at the corner of Grafton Lane.

Usually I went home by way of Wickley Street because it was lit by gas lamps. Grafton Lane was narrow and poorly lit, but a good bit shorter.

Dare I risk it?

A night-soil man, his cart pulled by a nag with heaving flanks, came out of the alley, and after he passed, I peered in. The passage was eerily empty of people, but the clouds from earlier in the evening had mostly dispersed, and the moon, nearly full, cast a generous silvery light. I thought again of Matthew coming home, checking my bedroom, and not finding me there—and I turned in. Following a series of narrow streets, I worked my way roughly westward until I reached quiet Brewer Street, where all the inhabitants' windows and doors were closed to the night air and its miasmas. With only another few hundred steps, I'd reach Regent Street. There, gritty Soho ended and fashionable Mayfair began, the boundary marked by Mr. Nash's famous pillars, the ones that looked like something out of ancient Greece but were only stucco painted to look like rare white marble.

I was almost there when a low cry, quavering and full of pain, sounded from a dark pocket between the buildings to my left. My steps slowed. Wary of lingering—I knew enough from Matthew about the tricks that cutpurses could play—I strained to see who had called out. It could be a prostitute, or a beggar, or some unfortunate drunken soul who had fallen on the way home from a pub.

But the next cry was pitched high, like that of a woman or even a child, and it held a note of fear as well as pain. ▶

An Excerpt from *A Dangerous Duet* (continued)

The moon had edged behind a cloud, but I could just make out a small still form huddled beside a drainpipe. "Who's there?" I said softly. "Are you all right?"

The only answer was a ragged breath.

I moved forward cautiously, and when the figure remained motionless, I bent down and reached out. My hand touched what felt like a shoulder, muscled but small. A moment later, the moon reemerged, and I could see that the shoulder belonged to a young woman who'd been beaten badly. Her eyes were closed, her face was dark with bruises and blood, and her thick black hair was a matted tangle. I recoiled in horror, pulling my hand back.

Simultaneously I realized who it was.

"Marceline!" I sank to my knees and groped for her wrist. Her skin was cold and her pulse weak, and as I drew my hand away I felt the stickiness of blood and noticed that her arm lay at an odd angle. "My God, what happened?" I whispered.

She didn't make a sound.

Fearful of hurting her, my hands hovered, not knowing where I might touch. What could I do? Though she was smaller than I, I didn't think I could carry her.

And where could I take her? How would I get her there? My thoughts leaped and scattered uselessly, and I took a deep breath to tamp down my panic. *Think,* I told myself sharply. *Hysteria isn't going to help either of you.*

Could I take her home? No, that was impossible. How could I explain her presence to Matthew and Peggy?

Marceline gave another low groan, as if she were in agonizing pain, both mental and physical. That decided me. I'd take her to Dr. Everett.

I had rested my hand lightly on her back to reassure her of my presence. She moved convulsively as I bent over and spoke in her ear. "Marceline, I'm going to get help."

I raced to Regent Street and raised my arm. Two cabs, occupied, clattered by, and I despaired of finding one that was free at this hour. But at last another appeared and slowed.

"My friend is hurt and needs to go to hospital," I called up to the driver. "She's just at the corner, but I need help fetching her."

He tilted his head back and looked at me suspiciously. "What'd'you mean, she's 'urt? I ain't takin' 'er if'n she's drunk, or just been roughed up by a customer—"

"She's not a prostitute!" I retorted, my mind quick to assemble a story that would bend his sympathies toward us. "It's her brute of a husband that's to blame, when he drinks up every bit of money she earns taking in washing! I'll give you an extra two shillings for the fare." Still he seemed undecided. "Please. If she stays out all night, she'll be dead by morning."

He grunted and began to climb down from his box. "Where is she?"

I pointed. "At the corner, just there. On the ground. But be careful—her arm may be broken."

His eyes narrowed, and I thought I saw a glimmer of curiosity, or perhaps disgust at the thought of a man who would do such a thing. "You stay 'ere with my 'orse."

I nodded and caught the reins he tossed me. The mare took not the slightest notice, and I stared at the entrance to the alley until my eyes burned.

Finally, he emerged, carrying Marceline, and together we put her inside the cab.

"Which 'ospital?" he asked.

"Charing Cross, please, in Agar Street, off the Strand."

We rolled forward, with me cradling Marceline close, trying to absorb the jolts of the ride. But as we drew up to the tall iron gates of the hospital, I realized my own predicament.

I knew there would be a guard to receive her, for as Dr. Everett often said, disease pays no heed to regular hours. But if I took Marceline inside, I'd have to answer questions, and I wouldn't be able to keep up my disguise around people who knew me. I had been here too many times to help the doctor with his books and play the piano for patients.

The cab halted, and I dismounted on the right side and remained in the shadows, close to the wheel.

"I don't want to be seen," I said to the cabdriver. "Can you tell the guard that you found her?"

He snorted and muttered something under his breath but went silent as I handed him the fare plus the extra I'd promised.

"The bell is just there." I pointed to the metal box and hurried away to the far side of the street. From the shadows between two buildings, I observed the guard, Mr. Oliven, emerge from the guardhouse. He and the driver exchanged a few words, and Marceline was shifted out of the cab and into his arms. ▶

Read on

She was so limp and motionless that she might have been dead.
A hard lump filled my throat as I watched him carrying her across
the lit courtyard to the front door, and I remembered the night I'd
met her.

It was my first performance at the Octavian. I'd only had a few
minutes before the show to leaf through the music Mr. Williams had
given me, and I hadn't noticed that two pages were missing from the
final number. When we reached that part of the song, I'd fumbled
and improvised, but it was clear to anyone watching that I'd made
a mess of it. I'd barely closed the piano lid and gathered my things
when Mr. Williams burst into the alcove red-faced and shouting.
When I finally managed to get a word in edgewise to explain that
the pages had been missing, he'd motioned violently toward the piano
bench. "You fool! Why didn't you look in there? If you do anything
like this again, you're finished!"

He'd stormed off, leaving me shaking. Finally, I opened the bench,
and through my tears I saw the two missing pages.

Why on earth hadn't they been in the portfolio where they belonged?

From the direction of the stage came footsteps and then, "Don't
take it to heart. He's always bawling at someone." The voice was
feminine and musical, with a slight accent.

I looked up, blinking the tears back.

The young woman from the trapeze act stood at the threshold of
the alcove. While she had been flying through the air, she looked lithe
and powerful; up close she was petite and very pretty. Her long black
hair was still coiled in braids around her head; her expression was
sympathetic, and her eyes were dark and sparkling.

My attempt to recover my poise failed, and her lips parted in
surprise. "Why—you're a woman!"

I swallowed hard and nodded, too wretched to even attempt the lie.

"Don't worry." She came close enough that she could murmur.
"I won't give you away. It's hard enough for us. If I could masquerade
as a man, I would. But we get paid more if I'm in this." She glanced
down at her pale pink costume, which, in contrast to Sebastian's
severe black one, left her legs and arms bare and was embroidered
with sparkling threads.

"And I get paid more if I'm in this," I said, gesturing to my
masculine garb.

She laughed.

I nodded toward the curtains through which Mr. Williams had vanished. "Does he really always shout like that?"

"Every night that I've been here," she said airily. "I remember once I was late to the stage. He all but had a *fit,* I tell you! He looked like a rabid dog, with spit flying out of his mouth. And the horrid names he called me." Her delicate eyebrows rose. "I thought Sebastian was going to hit him."

A rueful laugh escaped me. "Well, I can't hit him. I need the money."

"So do we," she said cheerfully. "So does everyone, I dare say. But he'll forget it by tomorrow."

"I hope so."

She gave a crooked smile that revealed small white teeth. "My name's Marceline. What's yours?"

"Nell. It's short for Elinor."

She tipped her head toward me, her eyes thoughtful. "Well, Nell, I'll see you tomorrow. And really, don't worry about old Williams." With a graceful little wave, she turned away and went to stage left where her brother was waiting, coat in hand.

I'd felt so grateful to her. I might not even have had the courage to return the following night if it hadn't been for her kindness.

As the hospital door closed behind my friend, I blinked back the tears pricking at the corners of my eyes. What vile person had beaten her and dumped her in that rotten little street? And where was Sebastian? Had something similar befallen him? Did he have any idea what had happened?

I waited until a light appeared in the room used for admitting new patients. I imagined the night nurse settling Marceline in a bed; then, feeling relieved that she was safe for this night at least, I started for home. ᴄ⌢